-THE-
-CHOSEN-ONES-

WORLDQUAKE
2

SCARLETT THOMAS

CANONGATE

Publishing in Great Britain in 2018 by Canongate Books Ltd,
14 High Street, Edinburgh EH1 1TE

canongate.co.uk

1

British Library Cataloguing-in-Publication Data
A catalogue record for this book is available on
request from the British Library

ISBN 978 1 78211 930 2

Typeset in Horley Old Style MT by Palimpsest Book
Production Ltd, Grangemouth, Stirlingshire

Printed and bound in Great Britain by Clays Ltd, St Ives plc.

For Mum & Couze, with love.

And in memory of David Miller.

'The "child" is all that is abandoned and exposed and at the same time divinely powerful; the insignificant, dubious beginning, and the triumphal end.'

C.G. Jung

'Ther saugh I pleye jugelours, Magiciens, and tregetours, And Phitonesses, charmeresses, Olde wicches, sorceresses.'

Geoffrey Chaucer

'Each mortal thing does one thing and the same:
Deals out that being indoors each one dwells;
Selves – goes itself; myself it speaks and spells,
Crying Whát I do is me: for that I came.'

Gerard Manley Hopkins

1

Orwell Bookend was not a very happy man. At this moment, with a small bat peering at him with its peculiar upside-down eyes, he wasn't sure if he'd ever been happy. Perhaps he had been happy once, a long time ago, when his first wife Aurelia had still been around. Before his daughter Effie had got so out-of-control. And before he had climbed into this dusty attic without changing out of his work suit.

Where was that blasted child? Probably out dabbling in 'magic' somewhere with her deluded friends – that fat, bespectacled boy, and the girl who seemed to wear nightdresses all the time. Well, Effie would certainly be in trouble when she got home. She must have been up here in the attic, Orwell concluded, and taken the book already. *The Chosen Ones* by Laurel Wilde was nowhere to be found. Which was the main thing currently making him extremely unhappy.

Orwell Bookend's unhappiness had started, like much unhappiness, when the prospect of happiness had been dangled in front of him and then cruelly snatched away. This had happened approximately 45 minutes earlier. He had been listening to the radio in the car on his way home from the university when a competition had been announced.

Orwell Bookend loved competitions. He didn't admit this to most people, but they even made him happy. Well, until he lost. Every Friday he carefully filled in the prize cryptic crossword from the *Old Town Gazette* and sent it off to a PO Box address in the Borders. The cost of the stamps over the years had far exceeded the value of the prize, which was a fifteen-pound book token, but Orwell would not rest until he had that book token, which he planned to have framed and put up in his office.

The second thing that made Orwell Bookend happy was acquiring money, even though he wasn't very good at it (as demonstrated by the business with the book token). If he could only find the book – the hardback first-edition of *The Chosen Ones* that Aurelia had bought for Effie all those years ago – then he would have the chance to enter a competition *and* make money. That was what it had said on the radio. Anyone lucky enough to own an original copy of *The Chosen Ones* was to take it to the Town Hall on Friday, where they would be given fifty pounds in cash and a chance to win unlimited free electricity for life. And anyone with a paperback edition of the book could swap it for a tenner.

Fifty pounds had become rather a lot of money since the worldquake had happened five years before. After the worldquake, the economy, like many other complex systems, had become tired and sulky and had started to misbehave. It certainly no longer had any interest in following a lot of silly mathematical rules. Today fifty pounds was definitely worth having, although who knew about tomorrow?

But unlimited free electricity for life! Now that really was a prize worth winning. After all, no one, no matter how rich, had access to unlimited electricity, not since the worldquake. Well, no one, of course, apart from Albion Freake, the man who happened to own all the electricity in the world. For some reason his company, Albion Freake Inc., was giving away this huge prize, and putting up all the cash too. All Orwell Bookend had to do was find the book. Of course, it wasn't really his book. It was Effie's. But that didn't bother Orwell Bookend in the slightest.

Mr Green's head looked like a boiled potato. Not a nice, normal boiled potato that had been rinsed and peeled before cooking, but an old, dry potato with leathery skin that had been left in the ground too long and, despite having been boiled, still had strange clumps of hair sprouting from it. To Maximilian Underwood these clumps looked like roots that had bravely ventured into the light and then promptly died.

Mr Green was in the middle of an educational story – the worst kind of story, in Maximilian's opinion – in which a poor little impoverished child has been given a pair of battered old running shoes by a mysterious hunchbacked crone in a food bank.

'The old lady whispers to the child that the shoes are magic,' said Mr Green, in a voice that was sort of soft and wet and greasy,

3

like margarine. Maximilian knew exactly what was going to happen in the story. *Everyone*, surely, knew what would happen in the story. The next day the child puts on the shoes and wins a race with the fastest time ever recorded. Then she gets discovered by a famous sports coach, who implores her to wear better running shoes. Of course, she refuses to wear anything but her tattered-looking 'magic' shoes. Eventually, the inevitable happens. The girl's rival steals the shoes and hides them. The girl is forced to compete in normal shoes. And of course she still wins. Moral: it was never about the shoes. The end.

'Now,' said Mr Green, once he had finished telling the story. 'Some points to ponder.'

He walked over to a blackboard-on-wheels that lived in a cupboard for the rest of the week and only came out on a Monday night for these classes, which were supposed to be for Neophytes – newly epiphanised people, mainly children – to learn the basics of magic. This was Maximilian's first class. He had hoped for bubbling cauldrons at the very least, and ideally things flying around the room and catching fire. But no. It was all very boring.

On the blackboard was a list of things that were forbidden for Neophytes, which had been the subject of most of the class so far.

1. Neophytes must NEVER do magic without supervision of an Adept (or higher).
2. Neophytes are FORBIDDEN from owning a boon without the express permission of the Guild of Craftspeople (which can be revoked at ANY time).

3. ANY NEOPHYTE WHO BRINGS A BOON TO CLASS WILL HAVE IT CONFISCATED.
4. NEOPHYTES ARE FORBIDDEN FROM DISCUSSING MAGIC OUTSIDE OF THIS CLASSROOM.
5. ANY NEOPHYTE WHO TRAVELS, OR ATTEMPTS TO TRAVEL, TO THE OTHERWORLD WILL BE VERY SEVERELY PENALISED.
6. NEOPHYTES ARE FORBIDDEN FROM EXCHANGING ANY BOONS, MAPS, SPELLS, INFORMATION OR KNOWLEDGE OF ANY KIND RELATING TO MAGIC OR THE OTHERWORLD.
7. NEOPHYTES MUST NEVER MENTION THE OTHERWORLD AT ANY TIME TO ANY PERSON.
8. NEOPHYTES MUST ONLY SPEAK ENGLISH AND NEVER ANY OTHERWORLD LANGUAGES. SPEAKING OTHERWORLD LANGUAGES IN THE REALWORLD CARRIES A VERY SEVERE PENALTY.

It was even worse than normal school. And it was colder, too. Mr Green's weekly class was held in a very dusty old church hall with a wooden floor and huge enamelled white radiators that made constant creaking and groaning sounds but never emitted any heat. Each radiator had a china teacup underneath it to catch the drips. There was an old fluorescent light that flickered dimly during the short periods the electricity was on. But the room was mainly lit with candle-lamps.

Maximilian looked at the list again. It just so happened that he had already done most of the forbidden things on it, and he didn't care one little bit.

His friend Effie Truelove had pretty much done all of them, too. She'd certainly been to the Otherworld. Maximilian felt faintly proud that he himself had done some things that weren't even on the list, like attempting to travel to the Underworld and reading someone else's mind.

Still, it was lucky that Lexy Bottle had warned Maximilian and Effie not to bring their boons to class. Apparently, if Mr Green took your boons away you never saw them again. Maximilian's boons – the Spectacles of Knowledge, and the Athame of Stealth – were at this moment hidden safely under his bed at home. He'd used a minor cloaking spell to hide the athame from his mother, in case she randomly decided, as she sometimes did, to tidy his bedroom. His mother knew he had epiphanised and was a scholar, of course, but he hadn't yet owned up to the fact that he was also a mage. He wasn't sure his mother would like that.

Outside the classroom a barn owl hooted and a gentle frost started to spread itself quietly in hollows and on the high moors. Deep in the black sky a meteor fizzed and then died. It was getting late. All the candles in the room seemed to flicker and dance as one. At this moment all Maximilian wanted was his bedtime snack – three coffee creams and a glass of goat's milk – and then a lovely, long, peaceful . . .

Lexy nudged Maximilian. 'Wake up,' she hissed.

On Lexy's other side, Effie Truelove was dropping off too. What was wrong with them both? This class was the very most exciting thing Lexy Bottle had ever experienced. Lexy was going to learn how to be a great healer. She was going to find someone to take her on as an Apprentice, and then she was going to be . . .

'First of all,' said Mr Green, 'I want you to think about how magic works in the story. I want you to identify *where* the magic is in the story. Or even if there *is* magic in the story. Then I want you to list *all* the instances where possible exchanges of M-currency are happening at *each* relevant point of the story.'

Lexy had already turned the page in her new notebook and written the date and the tasks with her new ink pen. She was sure she already knew all the answers. But before the children could get started, the church bell struck nine, which meant it was time for everyone to go home. So soon! Lexy could happily have spent all night soaking up Mr Green's wisdom.

'You can complete the task for homework,' said Mr Green, 'to be handed in at the beginning of the class next Monday at seven o'clock. Thank you, everyone. *Don't* stampede out of the door! Oh, and Euphemia Truelove? A *word*, please.'

2

Euphemia Sixten Bookend Truelove, known as Effie, was regretting ever coming to this class. No one had been forced to come, after all. It was optional. A bit like going to school when you didn't have to. And what kind of idiot did that? Effie's friend Wolf Reed, with whom she'd been playing tennis for most of the afternoon, had gone on to rugby practice instead, and her other good friend Raven Wilde had gone home straight after school to feed her horse. So why had Effie come?

For one simple reason. Because Lexy had told her it was the only way she could go up the magic grades and become a wizard and live in the Otherworld forever.

Effie loved the Otherworld. If only she could find some way of living there all the time, she'd be happy. She had to get better at magic first, though, which was another reason for taking this class. According to Lexy, Mr Green was the very best magical teacher in the whole country. He was a genius, even if he sometimes came across as a little slow and boring. Lexy knew all about Mr Green because he had so far been on three dates with her aunt Octavia.

Mr Green now had his back to Effie. He was wiping the blackboard with jerky little movements. His long list of forbidden things was dissolving into particles of chalk and falling to the floor, where Effie definitely thought it belonged. She sighed. How long was she going to have to stand here waiting to find out what she'd done? She knew she had done something. Mr Green had that air about him.

'Put it on the desk,' he said finally, turning around and scowling.

'Sorry?' said Effie.

'Sorry, *sir*.'

Effie sighed again. 'Sorry, *sir*.'

'Put the ring on the desk, please.'

Oh no. Effie gulped silently.

'What ring, sir?'

'The ring you have hidden in the lining of your cape. The Ring of the True Hero, I believe. A forbidden boon. Hand it over.'

Effie gulped again. How did he know she had it? Lexy had told her not to bring any boons to this class – never mind that hers were unregistered and so were especially risky – and so yesterday Effie had hidden them all in her special box at home. All except for the Ring of the True Hero, which Effie had been wearing for tennis practice earlier.

Effie never wore the ring in actual matches, just in training. The first time she'd put it on it had almost killed her. But as long as she ate and drank enough to restore her energy, it made her strong and agile and all sorts of other things she couldn't quite describe. And it made her feel more connected to the Otherworld. And . . .

'I'm not going to wait all night,' said Mr Green.

He was wearing a brown lounge suit, with flecks of green and orange now being picked out by the moonlight that shone through the window. His shirt was a peculiar shade of yellow. He glanced at his watch and then looked hard at Effie in the way the most horrible teachers tend to just before they haul you out of assembly and make you cry for something you didn't even do.

'Why exactly do you want my ring anyway?' asked Effie.

'I beg your pardon?'

'Why do you want my ring?'

'It is a boon, and you have brought it to my class. Therefore I must confiscate it.'

'But—'

'There's no need to argue. Do as you're told, please.'

'What will you do with it?'

'I will give it to the Guild. If it were a registered boon, I'd be able simply to give it back to you next Monday. But an unregistered boon . . .' He shook his head. 'You'll have to write to the Guild and get an application form to register the item and, I believe, fill in another form to request an application to get it back. And—'

'No,' said Effie, surprising herself.

Mr Green's eyes narrowed. 'What did you say?'

'No,' she repeated. 'I'm not going to give it to you. I'm sorry. I just can't.'

'I do have ways of making you,' said Mr Green, taking a step towards Effie. 'But of course it won't come to that. Hand it over.'

Effie took the ring from where she'd hidden it in the lining of her bottle-green school cape. The ring was silver, with a dark red stone held in place by a number of tiny silver dragons. Her beloved grandfather Griffin had given it to her just before he died. There was no way Effie was handing it over to anybody. She put it on her left thumb, where it fitted best. A feeling of confidence and power rippled through her.

'Stop messing around and give it to me,' said Mr Green, taking another step forward and holding out his hand. 'Now.'

Outside the high windows of the church hall an owl hooted. This owl had been watching what was going on and hadn't liked the look of it. Its call was picked up by a friendly rabbit in a nearby garden, who passed the message on to a dormouse, who passed it to a bat, who told it to another owl who happened to be flying towards the moors. Soon all the animals in the area knew that Euphemia Truelove was in trouble. Perhaps someone would hear the distress call and respond; perhaps they would not. The Cosmic Web was a bit random like that.

Raven and her horse Echo crunched through the frost on the moors. The moon shone down on them, making Raven's black, wavy hair look as if it was streaked with silver. Raven was a true witch and could therefore talk to animals. Ever since she'd epiphanised she had been able to have quite long conversations with Echo. Before, they had communicated only through their feelings. Echo 'just knew' when Raven wanted him to break into a canter, and Raven 'just knew' when Echo was feeling annoyed. But now Raven spoke fluent Caballo (the ancient language of horses) and everything was different.

Every day after supper Raven and Echo went out onto the moors, even though it now got dark so early. Much of the time they had to rely on Echo's night-vision to get them home, but tonight the moon was waning gibbous (which meant it was just past full) and Raven could see quite clearly. Everything looked pale and magical when it was bathed in moonlight. And anything touched by moonlight felt happy and peaceful. Everyone knows that you get vitamin D from sunlight. But not very many people know that there is a special nutrient in moonlight that helps living things develop magical powers and cleanses them of any impurities.

The moorland around Raven and Echo was quite bare. No trees, no streams; not even any old fence-posts, as there were on some parts of the moor. The only modern-looking thing for miles was a pair of steel doors that someone had recently built into a mound near some old crofts.

Echo walked carefully through the barest parts of moorland, because there were bogs and rabbit holes that were difficult to see in the moonlight. Every so often a small meteor streaked across the vast night sky. There was something odd about these meteors, although Echo wasn't sure what it was. Anyway, soon they would be on an ancient path, with its comforting imprints of bygone horses and their riders.

And then, after passing the ruined crofts, Raven was hoping to see the shimmering mystery again. For the last hour, she had been trying to explain to Echo in Caballo what she thought it was. This was almost impossible because not only was the shimmering mystery very difficult to describe, there were no words in Caballo for 'shimmering' or 'mystery'. The closest Raven could get was 'bog in the moonlight', which was something deep and mysterious with a hint of unpredictability and danger. But Echo just snorted and asked why on earth they were looking for bogs in the moonlight. He didn't like bogs; in fact, he went out of his way to avoid them. Bogs were dangerous. You could sink into them and never come out.

'Not a bog, exactly,' said Raven with her mind. Caballo was an unspoken language. 'Maybe like a very high jump.'

Echo didn't much like very high jumps either, and said so.

'But not an *actual* high jump,' Raven tried to say. 'Just something that makes you feel like you're approaching one. Or I suppose like the way I feel about approaching one. Or maybe the way you feel just before you do a *vamos*.'

Echo hardly ever ran away with Raven. But it did very occasionally happen that he would see a vast expanse of beautiful empty moorland in front of him and want to *vamos* through it. And so he would go, not thinking, galloping hard and fast. The way Raven felt about this was a bit like the way Echo felt about very high jumps. And each allowed the other their little indulgence from time to time. He let her jump, and she let him

13

vamos. He never threw her. That was the main thing. And she always gave him such a nice mixture of oats and alfalfa at the end of the day. She even remembered to buy him Polo mints, which were his favourite thing in the whole world. They understood each other.

It had been after a *vamos* episode the previous Saturday that Raven had first seen the shimmering mystery. It had been as if the moorland in front of them was different in some way. Sort of greener, wilder, more vivid, more magical. The more Raven had asked Echo to walk towards it, the further away it had seemed. That day it had taken almost four hours to get back to the folly – a sort of pretend castle where Raven lived with her mother.

Laurel Wilde hadn't even noticed that her daughter had been missing, of course. She had been too busy drinking expensive sparkling wine and talking about the latest money-making scheme invented by her glamorous publisher, Skylurian Midzhar.

'The first billion-dollar book in the world,' Skylurian had said to Laurel Wilde over tea that Saturday afternoon. 'Imagine.'

Raven had been eating her sandwiches and cake quickly so that she could go out on Echo, and had pretended not to be listening. Skylurian and Raven ignored one another most of the time anyway. Laurel Wilde wrote about witches (and warlocks) who went to a magical school, but she didn't believe they really existed. She was half right because there really was no such thing as a warlock. But Laurel Wilde would have been very surprised to learn that both her daughter and her publisher were powerful witches, and, what's more, that they had recently been on different sides in the same battle. Skylurian had never actually done anything bad to Raven, though. Indeed, she still occasionally tried to befriend her. It was all rather creepy.

'Imagine, darling,' Skylurian had gone on. 'And a whole 7 percent of it will be yours.'

'I thought we agreed on 7.5 percent,' Laurel Wilde had said. 'Whatever,' breathed Skylurian dismissively. 'It hardly matters. After all, what's 0.5 percent of one billion?'

It was actually five million, but no one did the sum.

'We will be rich beyond our wildest dreams, darling. And all because you were so clever and wrote such a beautiful book.'

Raven had never completely understood why her mother's first book, *The Chosen Ones*, had done so well. It had sold over ten million copies worldwide, and been made into a film and a board-game. It was about magic of course, but not the real magic that Raven did. In the normal world, the one Raven lived in, anyone could awaken their magical powers if they tried hard enough (or if, as in Raven's case, someone had given them a precious boon from the Otherworld). But in Laurel Wilde's books only a few people were magical.

The Chosen Ones, as they were called, were all born with a strange rash behind their left knee. If you'd been born with the rash, you had almost unlimited supernatural powers. If not, well, bad luck. You were one of the 'Unchosen': unpopular, ugly, often fat, and doomed to a life of having spells cast on you by the Chosen Ones, who were not just beautiful and powerful but quite smug, too.

In the real world, Raven's world, magical power was limited.

In Laurel Wilde's books, anyone born with the rash behind their knee could do pretty much anything they wanted with simply a flick of their thin, white wrist (they were all white). Despite all the magical power at their disposal, the Chosen Ones actually spent much of their time having midnight feasts and worrying about their lost homework. If any of the Unchosen bothered them, they got turned into frogs.

The Chosen Ones was set a very long time ago when people wore frilly bonnets, went on steam trains to boarding school and spent their summer holidays being locked in the cabins of ships or kidnapped by gypsies. Raven had given up halfway through the first one, but most children had read all six in the series.

'And you're sure Albion Freake will buy it?' Laurel had asked Skylurian that previous Saturday afternoon over tea.

'Of course, darling. I have his word. If we can create a limited-edition single volume of *The Chosen Ones*, bound in calf leather with real gold leaf on the page edges, he will give us a billion pounds for it.'

'But every other copy of the book in the world will have to be destroyed first?' Laurel Wilde had looked a bit sad at the thought of that.

'As already discussed, that is indeed what we mean by "limited-edition single volume".'

'But . . .'

'Everyone's read it, darling. Who needs to keep a copy of a book they've already read? And for 7 percent of a billion pounds . . .'

'Or 7.5,' said Laurel.

'With 7 percent, you'll be rich, darling, and that's all that really matters.'

Echo snorted. His breath froze into tiny crystals in the mid-November air. Raven put all thoughts of her mother's books out of her mind. Out here on the moor she felt free of all those unimportant worldly things. Out here she felt closer to nature. Closer to her true spirit. And closer to something she didn't recognise or understand, but was definitely there.

Echo snorted again. 'Is that it?' he asked Raven, nodding to the left. 'Your bog in the moonlight?'

And sure enough, up ahead, slightly to the left, there was the shimmering mystery.

'Give me the ring,' said Mr Green again.

'No,' said Effie.

Feelings of courage, strength and daring were rippling through her. This always happened when she was wearing the ring, and now even sometimes when she wasn't. She could feel power in her shoulders, down her back, through all the muscles of her legs. Effie was only eleven years old, but she would always fight for what she thought was right and true.

'You are going to regret this, young lady,' said Mr Green, who began to turn a shade of purple that looked quite wrong set against his brown suit and yellow shirt.

Effie took one step towards the door, but Mr Green took a step in the same direction, blocking her.

'Don't you dare defy me! I have never—'

'Please let me pass,' said Effie.

'Give me the ring first.'

'I thought you said you could make me give it to you,' said Effie. 'You obviously can't. Now please would you get out of my way?'

'I have never heard such utter rudeness,' said Mr Green. 'Unless you give me that ring right now, you are expelled from this class. Do you hear me? Expelled.'

'Fine,' said Effie. 'Expel me. I don't care. I don't think you know anything worth learning anyway.'

'You impudent little . . . I have *never*, in all my years of teaching this class – which I do for free, mind you, out of the goodness of my heart – heard such rudeness from a child. You, young lady, will be hearing more about this from the Guild of Craftspeople. Threatening a teacher. It won't do. Never in all my years . . .'

'But I didn't threaten you. I—'

'You are expelled. Didn't you hear me? Now get out.'

3

The Old Town was quiet and cold. The frost was now calmly working its way around rooftops and the tops of chimneys. The sundial in the small walled-garden of the Apothecary Museum was entirely draped in silver. The cobblestones were slippery under Effie's feet as she walked down the hill towards the Writer's Monument, which now looked as if it was wearing a white bed-cap. Into the black of the sky came the brief flicker of another small meteor. An owl hooted again, sending into the Cosmic Web news of the frost and the meteor and many other things besides.

Effie wondered what the Guild of Craftspeople would do to her. She remembered that they had once forbidden her grandfather from practising magic for five years. Five years! If that happened to Effie, she didn't know what she'd do. She'd only recently epiphanised and found out she was a true hero. She didn't want to lose her powers so soon afterwards. That would just be too unfair.

Not that she had ever done any real magic, of course. It came so easily to her friends Maximilian and Raven. But Effie's skills seemed more annoyingly practical. She had once defeated a dragon, but had not used a single scrap of magic in so doing. Had being expelled meant she'd lost the chance to learn magic forever? Her grandfather had begun to teach her something called 'Magical Thinking'. Effie knew she needed to progress from that. But how? Perhaps she could ask her cousins in the Otherworld the next time she visited. Or her great uncle Cosmo. She certainly would never be able to go back to Mr Green's classes.

Most people have to go through a portal if they want to visit the Otherworld. Then they have to travel from wherever the portal delivers them to their intended destination. But Effie had a magical calling card – her most precious boon – that transported her directly outside the ornate gates of Truelove House, in the extremely remote and highly secretive Otherworld village of Dragon's Green, where her cousins Clothilde and Rollo lived with the wizard Cosmo and looked after the Great Library that was housed there.

At least that was what the calling card was supposed to do. But for the first few days that Effie'd had it, she hadn't been able to get it to work at all. Just taking it out did precisely nothing. Effie had tried again and again. She had gone to all the portals she knew – including the Funtime Arcade and Mrs Bottle's Bun Shop – and tried taking out the card in each one, but that hadn't worked: she'd just ended up making the acquaintance of a lot of extremely shady people who wanted to offer her unbelievable sums of money for it. She'd tried sitting in her bedroom in darkness and silence and reading out the address on the front in a very solemn voice. Nothing.

Despairing, she'd eventually asked the card what it wanted of her.

To her surprise, it had replied.

It's almost impossible to relate completely in any written language what the card actually said about what you do with a portable portal – they are, in fact, so rare that there are barely more than five left in each of the known worlds – but gradually Effie got the knack.

First, you have to find a natural, magical place where you definitely cannot be seen (behind the hedge on the village green near the old Black Pig pub had proved to be a good spot). Then you have to clear your mind. This is not easy. Then, looking only at the card, you have to sort of knock on its door (which sounds a bit odd, but is the closest way of describing how it feels) and wait for a reply. Keeping your mind completely clear – which is hard to do for more than a couple of seconds, but Effie practised a lot – you then have to wait while the card sort of magically frisks you.

After all, not just anyone can go to Dragon's Green. Indeed, one of Rollo's jobs in Truelove House was finding new ways to keep people out. Once Effie was cleared for entry, and while still keeping her mind blank, she had learned to sort of melt downwards – a bit like going underwater – and thus move from one dimension into the next. She always came out in a sort of grey mist just outside the gates to Truelove House. The guards, who now knew her well, then unlocked the gate and let her through.

So Effie had developed rather a pleasant habit. Each morning on the way to school she took out her calling card and popped off behind the hedge to spend a couple of happy days in the Otherworld. Time passed a lot more quickly in the Otherworld, a quirk that meant Effie's two days there amounted to only about 45 minutes in the Realworld. When her time was up, Effie would hurry away to the portal by the old willow tree on the Keepers' Plains (her calling card only brought her *to* the Otherworld – she had to go back to the Realworld through a normal portal like any other person) and emerge in her school field five minutes before registration. It had taken a bit of practice to get the timing of this right, which had led to several detentions and a rather stern letter home.

But those first few times Effie had been to the Otherworld had been the very best days of her life so far. Effie's beautiful cousin Clothilde had made her two silk jumpsuits – one in silver and one in a very dark blue – because everyone in the Otherworld wore loose, flowing clothes. It was always midsummer in the Otherworld – or so it seemed to Effie. The days were bright and warm enough to swim outdoors, but the nights were cool enough for an open fire. The complex time differences between worlds meant that Effie never knew precisely when she was going to arrive at Truelove House, but she usually got there in time for supper, which her cousins often ate by the fire in the large drawing room. After that, each day would begin with breakfast in bed, brought by a cheerful woman called Bertie. Effie usually had a large, soft, homemade croissant, porridge with cream and honey, and a whole pot of strong tea. Then she was free to do whatever she wanted, as long as she stayed in the house and grounds.

Some children might have taken advantage of the time difference and used the stolen time in the Otherworld to catch up on their homework. But Effie preferred to lie on the lawn reading Otherworld books, eating Otherworld cakes and dreaming of Otherworld adventures. Lunch each day was a picnic by the stream at the bottom of the garden, with dragonflies of every possible colour skimming the clear water. Clothilde occasionally took some time off in the afternoon to swim in the pool with Effie, or to walk with her in the nearby woods. But usually Rollo would come out and find Clothilde and take her back to the Great Library, where something important and secret seemed to be going on.

Effie wasn't allowed in the Great Library until she had the mark of the Keeper. Even though she'd passed the test that meant she could have the mark, she couldn't actually get it until Pelham Longfellow came back from the island (which was the Otherworld word for the Realworld). When Pelham Longfellow returned, he was going to take Effie to Froghole to get her mark and to do some shopping. Effie was also due to have a special consultation to determine her 'kharakter, art and shade', whatever that meant. Well, she knew what kharakter was: that was her main ability as a true hero. But the rest was a mystery.

From snatches of conversation Effie had picked up, it seemed Pelham Longfellow was very busy trying to uncover a big conspiracy brewing in Paris, or maybe London. Effie had meant to ask if she could help him in some way, but she hadn't seen him for ages. She longed to be of some help in the great fight against the Diberi. But even though she had killed the powerful Diberi mage who had attacked her grandfather, no one seemed to want her to do anything else.

Sometimes Effie went up to the very top of one of the towers in Truelove House to see the wizard Cosmo, who had said she could use his small personal library whenever she wanted. It was here that Effie found books to read on the lawn: adventures of true heroes from long ago, strategy guides for fighting demons and monsters, or tales of the Great Split. Cosmo had talked vaguely of things he might teach Effie when he had time. 'Another language,' he'd said recently. 'Map reading. Meditation. Depending on your art and shade, of course. But not until after the *Sterran Guandré* has passed.' Effie had heard the words *Sterran Guandré* a few times recently. She had been planning to ask Clothilde what they meant.

But the last time Effie had visited she had accidentally overheard a conversation between Clothilde and Rollo that she had instantly known was about her. Perhaps she shouldn't have stayed to listen – eavesdroppers never hear good about themselves, after all – but she had.

'Her place is not here,' Rollo had said. 'Why do you keep encouraging her? Especially now that we hear of this new conspiracy on the island, and with the *Sterran Guandré* so close. Griffin is no longer there to watch what's happening around the northern portals. She should be doing something. And she can't be of use on the island if she squanders all her energy here giggling on the lawn with you.'

'She's a child,' said Clothilde, sighing sadly. 'She should not have to bear all this responsibility. And we already know the conspiracy is around the southern portals. She can do nothing about that.'

'For some reason the universe has chosen to give her this "responsibility",' Rollo had said. 'We should be training her to be useful. Although I don't know how exactly a true hero is supposed to be of use to us – why couldn't we have had an interpreter, an explorer, or another engineer?'

'But . . .'

'And the girl needs more lifeforce, not less. Being here just drains her. I think perhaps we should tell her about . . .'

'We can't.'

Before anyone could say anything else, Effie had heard footsteps – probably Bertie's – and ran. She hurried upstairs to her beautiful room with the now familiar smell of old sun-warmed wood and fresh linen, and changed from her silk jumpsuit into her school uniform. She would not come back again until she had proved herself somehow, she had decided. She would find out about this 'conspiracy' in the Realworld and return to Truelove House only when she had something useful to contribute.

As Effie had walked down the stairs that morning, she'd thought of all the hours she'd spent with Clothilde on the lawn, laughing at Clothilde's gentle stories of village life, listening to her talking about growing up in Truelove House with Pelham Longfellow often popping over from his parents' cottage on the other side of the village. Whenever Clothilde talked about

Pelham Longfellow she blushed, and then looked a little bit sad. But while Effie had been relaxing, the Diberi had been out there plotting something and she hadn't even known. Effie felt ashamed somehow, and very alone. She left through the conservatory without saying goodbye.

The next morning, instead of visiting the Otherworld on her way to school, she called her friends together for a meeting in their secret hideout in the basement of their school. The hideout was called Griffin's Library because it held all the rare hardback last editions of books that Effie's grandfather Griffin Truelove had left for her, and that Effie and her friends had rescued. It had once been an old caretaker's cupboard but was the size of a small room.

Effie explained to her friends that it was very important for them each to use their own special skill to find out everything they could about the conspiracy. Maximilian said he'd use his scholarly skills to find out what *Sterran Guandré* meant. Raven said she'd keep an eye on Skylurian Midzhar, who definitely had connections with the Diberi. Lexy said she'd try to make contact with Miss Dora Wright, the children's former teacher who had disappeared earlier in the term and who Effie believed knew something important. Effie and Wolf upped their tennis training sessions to make sure they were strong fighters for whatever happened next.

But Effie didn't just want to be a strong fighter. She wanted to increase her magical energy so she could spend more time in the Otherworld. And she'd worked out that one way of doing that was to train hard in the Realworld while wearing the Ring of the True Hero, which somehow seemed to convert her expended energy into lifeforce – or M-currency. When Effie had enough lifeforce, and enough information, and perhaps even some magic skills, she would go back to Rollo and Clothilde and show them how strong and useful she was. But not until then.

Now, just over a week later, waiting for the bus home in the frosty moonlight, having been expelled from her first magic class, Effie wondered whether she should go back to the Otherworld sooner than she'd planned. She suddenly longed to ask Clothilde for advice about Mr Green and the Guild of Craftspeople. Effie couldn't shake the feeling that she'd made a terrible mistake that would have to be put right. Her grandfather had certainly seemed to abide by the Guild's rules. If Effie could just sit down and properly talk to someone who understood . . .

It was almost ten o' clock when Effie opened the door to the small terraced house she shared with her father, step-mother and baby sister. The place was in darkness. Had they all gone to bed? Effie was sure that this was the night that Cait taught a late seminar at the university. Had her father gone to pick her up? But no, his car had been parked on the street. Perhaps he was just 'saving electricity' again. Effie hung her school cape on a peg and went into the kitchen to make a cup of chamomile tea before bed. Lexy had told her always to have chamomile tea at bedtime. It was a natural tonic, apparently, and helped you to sleep.

'Not so fast,' came a voice from the upstairs landing.

'Sorry?' said Effie.

'Don't pretend you didn't hear me,' said Orwell Bookend. He

walked down the stairs holding a candle-lamp. He always tried to save electricity whenever he could. 'I want some answers, young lady. First of all, where is the book?'

'What book?'

Orwell snorted. 'What book? *The Chosen Ones*, of course. What have you done with it?'

'The first Laurel Wilde book? I don't know. I last read it when I was about six. And then you confiscated it. Why do you want it anyway? It's for seven-to-nine year olds.'

'You don't have it?'

'No. I just told you. You confiscated it.'

'Why did I do that?'

'Because you didn't want me reading about magic. It was ages ago. When Mum was still here.'

'And where did I put it?'

Effie shrugged. 'How am I supposed to know?'

'I don't like your attitude at all, madam. It's exactly like your teacher said. I've just had Mr Green on the phone, Euphemia, and I'm not very happy with you.'

'But . . .'

'I've had enough of this. Go to your room at once. We can talk about your punishment in the morning.'

'But I just want to make a cup of . . .'

'GO,' hissed Orwell Bookend. He liked shouting, but didn't do it so much when baby Luna was asleep. He had become rather an expert in finding ways to shout quietly.

Effie knew it was better not to argue, so she let herself into the ground-floor room she shared with her baby sister. Effie decided that once her father and step-mother were asleep, she would get her calling card, climb out of the window, go to the village green and take a much-needed trip to Truelove House. Just the thought of it – the warm garden, Clothilde's kind face – made her feel better.

She lit a candle and walked over to her bookshelves to get the box where she'd carefully hidden her calling card, along with her other precious boons and everything else that was very special to her, including another calling card that Effie could use to get hold of Pelham Longfellow in an emergency, a jar of damson jam from her grandfather's kitchen, a candlestick, some candles and a mysterious notebook written in Rosian . . .

It wasn't there. It was gone.

The box wasn't anywhere on the shelves. It wasn't under the bed, or under baby Luna's cot or . . . Effie soon became frantic looking for the box that contained her most treasured possessions. She never would have taken off her gold necklace if it hadn't been for Mr Green's class and what Lexy had said about him confiscating boons. And what about Wolf's sword? Effie was on the verge of tears when she got up from the dusty floor for the third time, after checking yet again under her bed. She hadn't realised that the door had silently opened until she turned and saw her father standing there with a half-smile on his face.

'Looking for something?' he said.

'Yes,' she said. 'My . . .' But she didn't finish her sentence because she realised that her father had her special box in his hands.

'Your little box of delights?' said Orwell.

'Thank you,' said Effie. 'Where did you find it?'

Her father laughed. 'You think you're getting this back? Ha! I was going to say that you could have it back when you found the missing copy of *The Chosen Ones*, but now I'm not so sure. The stuff in here is worth something, isn't it? Where was it your grandfather used to go? Oh yes. The Funtime Arcade. What? You think I didn't know all his haunts? Yes, I think I could go there and find someone to buy all this from me. I'd get a lot more than fifty pounds for it all, I'm sure.'

'Those things are mine,' said Effie.

She remembered the moment – only a few weeks ago – when Pelham Longfellow had told her that the only way anyone would get the gold necklace from her would be if they killed her first. So why on earth had she taken it off like some sort of idiot and just put it in a box?

'Mr Green suggested that I search your room for any suspicious objects. I hear you've been getting involved with this Guild, which you know I don't approve of. Mr Green said anything suspicious should be handed over to him, but I'm not sure I trust him, so you're safe for now. I think I'm going to just hang on to this until you decide to behave yourself. And finding me that copy of *The Chosen Ones* will be the first step in getting back in my good books.'

'If I get it for you, will you give me my box back?'

Orwell narrowed his eyes. 'So you do know where it is?'

'No! I told you, I haven't seen it for years.'

'I don't believe you.'

'But it's the truth!'

'Find it, and then we'll talk.'

Orwell slammed the door, silently.

Echo stepped towards the thing-without-name. Raven was right, there was something deep and strange about it. Echo usually felt certain about something, completely sure if it would bring danger or pleasure. But this, he didn't know. He took another step without looking properly at the ground. A skylark flew out of her nest and hovered above the moor. Her call began quite crossly, but then developed into the usual stream of news from the Cosmic Web. And one item on the list was of particular interest.

'Did you hear that?' Echo said to Raven.

'Yes,' said Raven, looking troubled.

'The long-haired hero-child with the ring — that is your friend?'

'Yes,' said Raven sadly.

'She is in deep danger, this friend.'

'Yes. Oh dear, Echo. What shall we do?'

'We can find this sparkling bog again tomorrow. For now we will go and help this friend. Let us *vamos*.'

Raven and Echo cantered home while a brace of meteors leapt unthinkingly through the black sky. As soon as she could, Raven sat down at her desk and wrote a letter to the Luminiferous Ether. She just hoped it wasn't too late.

4

It was not quite dawn when Maximilian let himself into the old caretaker's cupboard in the basement of the Tusitala School for the Gifted, Troubled and Strange. The sun was barely a pink whisper in the sky, but Maximilian wanted plenty of time to go through all the books in Griffin's Library until he found the one he most wanted. The one that he had started but not finished; the one he'd been trying to find for almost a month now: *Beneath the Great Forest*.

He imagined another item for Mr Green's list: *Neophytes are FORBIDDEN from trying to access the Underworld*. But Maximilian didn't care about anyone's rules. He desperately wanted to get back to the dark, mysterious underground world that he had almost accessed through *Beneath the Great Forest*. He so very much wanted to know its secrets. Secrets that he patently was not going to learn from Mr Green on a Monday night.

So he searched for the book.

And, of course, he also searched for information on the *Sterran Guandré,* just as he had promised his friends. Since most of Griffin Truelove's library was fiction, it was not usually the place to go for facts. But Maximilian thought that if only he could get back to the Underworld there would be libraries there that would answer every question he had about life. He didn't know how he knew this, he just did. Of course, the dim web provided information too. But it was not like the old days of the internet. The dim web could not be searched. And lately the Guild was all over it, taking down any interesting pages that told anyone anything about magic.

Maximilian sighed. He knew he wasn't the only person in the city looking for a lost book. Indeed, all over the world, people were trying to find their long-abandoned copy of *The Chosen Ones* so they could get their reward. It had got all the locals particularly excited. Albion Freake was actually coming here, to the city, to give away the grand prize. The Tusitala school was even closing for the day in honour of the event. The city had been chosen because this was where Laurel Wilde lived.

But Maximilian didn't care about stupid children's books. He only cared about *Beneath the Great Forest.* Where was it? He remembered it had been a hardback bound in cloth. Or had it been leather? He was almost certain it had been blue. When he got to the 499th book for the second time, reading titles as well as looking at the colour of the binding, he sighed. It wasn't here. There were all sorts of interesting volumes on the shelves, but not the one he wanted.

Maximilian ran his hand over the spines of a line of hardbacks.

They felt so smooth, so inviting. Almost at random, he pulled out a book called *The Initiation* and idly started flicking through its pages. It was a medium-sized hardback bound in dark maroon leather. The colour, Maximilian thought, of blood. Inside was mostly dense text, broken with the odd line drawing. In one image a boy was sitting cross-legged on a patterned rug; in another the same boy was wielding something that looked like an athame, a small dagger used by mages. The boy looked oddly familiar.

Getting up before dawn had made Maximilian feel exhilarated. But now his lack of sleep was beginning to catch up with him. Maybe he just needed a cup of coffee? Most children didn't like coffee, but Maximilian was not in the least bit like most children. He had his own special cafetière and a bag of extra-strong coffee beans over by the kettle next to the sink. He put a nice big handful of beans through his coffee grinder, then sat on one of the old paint-spattered chairs to have a proper look at this book while the kettle boiled. But he was just so sleepy.

He woke a few moments later to a tap-tapping on the door. It was the elderly headmaster of the school.

'I thought I might find you here,' said the headmaster. 'There's a man outside with a helicopter who says he has come for you. I do hope you have a note from your mother.'

'I . . .' said Maximilian, rubbing his eyes. His short sleep had left him feeling refreshed, but rather dozy. A helicopter? A note from his mother? What on earth was the headmaster talking about?

The headmaster was smiling his crinkly, off-centre smile.

'Go, boy, before I change my mind,' he said.

'But I don't have a note . . .'

'I was *joking*, child. But not about the helicopter. Go.'

With an hour to go before the start of school, Effie was walking from the bus stop at the bottom of the Old Town up the quiet cobbled street towards Leonard Levar's locked and shuttered Antiquarian Bookshop. A tiny faint light came from deep inside the bookshop, but Effie barely noticed it. There was a gentle pink mist that was very beautiful, but it meant there would be another heavy frost later. Beyond the mist, the troposphere, the Luminiferous Ether, and much else besides, impatient meteors danced around, waiting for it to be their turn to sparkle through the sky. But Effie's mind was on other things.

Where would she find a copy of *The Chosen Ones*? Nowhere, it seemed. Neither of the main city bookshops had yet opened, but each had signs on the door saying that they were completely sold out of Laurel Wilde books. On the way from the bus stop Effie had seen a poster offering a hundred pounds for a single paperback. Then, crudely pasted on top of posters for a Beethoven concert featuring the *Pathétique* and *Les Adieux*, and a talk at the Astronomical Society about the upcoming Wandering Star meteor shower, there was a handbill offering two hundred pounds for a hardback copy of *The Chosen Ones*.

Why did everyone want a copy of Laurel Wilde's first book all of a sudden? It was a mystery. But Effie knew that even if she could find a copy of the book, she could not afford it at those prices. Her purse contained £5.50, which was all the money she had in the world.

Or, at least, all the money she had in *this* world.

Effie pulled her bottle-green school cape around her as she walked on through the misty, silent morning. She had no idea whether copies of children's books from this world would even exist in the Otherworld. Why would they? But she had a feeling that if one did, it might be for sale at the big bookstall in the Edgelands Market on the other side of the Funtime Arcade. So that's where she was going. She had plenty of M-currency after all.

The Funtime Arcade was down a small cobbled alleyway in the Old Town. Most people would look at it and see only a run-down old arcade, locked and bolted at this time of the morning, with a small, sad-looking heap of black rubbish sacks outside waiting for collection. But as Effie approached, a familiar neon sign flickered into life. The words FUNTIME ARCADE now flashed in pink letters, and a new sign appeared underneath that said 'Mainlanders and travellers please go through the back door.' Effie already knew the way.

Effie had to be scanned before she could enter. The large man with the machine looked as if he'd had a hard night. A thin cigarette dangled, unlit, from his lips. His eyes were pink and his skin had a pale greenish tone. A large cup of coffee steamed softly on the small table beside him. Effie could hear a helicopter landing somewhere not too far away, and the man winced slightly at the deep throbbing sound.

'Most of it's shut at this time, you know,' he said, and then waved her through into the main bar area.

The last time Effie had been here it had been full of magical-looking people in flowing robes and amazing outfits. But now it was almost empty. The place was a connected jumble of interlinked rooms forming a bar, a café and an arcade. In places, plants were growing through cracks in the walls and the ceiling. Beyond the arcade was the queue to go through to the Otherworld, and all the currency booths where you could change one sort of money for another. Effie looked at her watch, attempting the calculation Maximilian had taught her for telling time in the Otherworld. It was no good. She had no idea what time of day it was. It didn't help that the Funtime Arcade, like all portals, was in a time zone between the Realworld and the Otherworld.

But Effie didn't have to look at her watch to know that it must be late. The lone barman yawned as he polished glasses with a tea-towel. A young Otherworlder had fallen asleep at one of the tables; empty glasses were scattered on some of the others. The only light in the place came from a small number of flickering candle-lamps, some of them almost completely burnt away.

'Breakfast doesn't start for another two hours,' said the barman without looking up.

'Thanks,' Effie said. 'But I've already had breakfast, so don't worry.'

He looked up. 'An islander. Well. Not many from your side been in lately. Greetings and blessings. I suppose I can make you a hot chocolate, if you like.'

'Greetings and blessings returned,' said Effie, remembering

37

the right way to address people in the Otherworld. 'It's all right, thanks, I'm going straight through.'

'To the mainland?'

'That's right.'

'At this time?' the barman said. 'Good heavens. Are you very suicidal or just a little bit?'

'Sorry?'

'You do know what's out there at this time of night?'

'Er, the market?'

'Not for another couple of hours. Only monsters out there now.'

'Monsters?'

'You have *been* to the mainland before, haven't you?'

'Yes, of course,' said Effie. 'But not at night. Maybe I'll wait.'

'Are you sure you don't want that hot chocolate?'

Effie hesitated. She looked around her. Over to her right was a comfortable-looking booth upholstered with red velvet, with a candle-lamp only half burned out. Effie could see a book on the table. It was a large green hardback that reminded her slightly of a special book she had once owned. She wondered what it was.

'OK,' Effie said to the barman. 'I'd love a hot chocolate. Thanks.'

'Marshmallows?'

'Yes, please?'

'Rum?'

'No, thanks.'

The barman expertly frothed some very white-looking milk.

Then he whisked up a spoonful of cocoa from a large red tin and two spoonfuls of honey from a clear jar. When the drink was made, he arranged a small pile of yellow cakes on a pink plate and dusted them lightly with silvery white icing sugar. He put the mug and plate on the counter but didn't wait to be paid. No one paid for anything in the Otherworld. Well, not directly. Effie thanked the barman and went over to the booth.

She sat down and put her school satchel on the seat next to her. What was this book? She picked it up. *The Repertory of Kharakter, Art & Shade*, it said on the front, in a faded gold copperplate. The volume had clearly been well-loved by someone. The pages were soft and worn and the gold ribbon used to keep one's place had frayed away almost to nothing. Had someone left it behind by accident? There was no name in the front. Effie flicked through a few pages. 'When the soul departs from heaven (if we may be permitted to use such outmoded terms) it has bestowed upon it two gifts,' read one line. 'The hedgewitch healer is that stalwart of village life to whom we go for love potions, nasturtium seeds and blankets that help infants to sleep,' read another.

Effie flicked further through the book. There were a few interesting-looking illustrations and charts, including a circular diagram of 'The Shades', with the words *Philosopher*, *Aesthete*, *Artisan*, *Protector*, *Galloglass* and *Shaper* written around its edge.

Then there was another, larger circular diagram of possible *kharakters*, including ones familiar to Effie like mage, witch, scholar, warrior and healer. Hero was right at the top, between trickster and mage. Wizard was in a little circle of its own, right in the middle. There were also plenty of *kharakters* Effie had never heard of, among them interpreter, explorer and bard. She thought Maximillian would quite like to see something like this, although Effie herself felt oddly drawn to it.

'Ah, there's my book,' came a familiar voice from behind her. 'I thought I must have left it here.'

'Festus?' said Effie. She didn't know many people who came here, but Festus Grimm had helped her once before. When she turned, she found it was indeed him, standing tall in a red-lined cloak and turquoise feathered-hat.

'Greetings and blessings, young traveller,' said Festus.

'Greetings and blessings returned,' said Effie.

'And where are you off to at this time of night?'

'I'm waiting for the market to open.'

'Likewise. It never gets any easier to judge the time difference, in case you were wondering. Mind if I join you? I could do with another coffee.'

5

Raven usually had breakfast by herself because her mother liked sleeping in. Their latest house guest, Skylurian Midzhar – who appeared to have more or less moved in – also liked her sleep. But this morning everyone was up. Laurel Wilde was cooking bacon and eggs in her dressing gown, while Skylurian crossed off items on a large stack of papers.

'Only three hundred copies to go,' she said, nodding. 'Good.'

Laurel Wilde frowned. 'Seems like a lot.'

'From ten million, darling? Hardly.'

'And you're' – Laurel gulped – 'actually pulping them?'

Skylurian smiled. 'But of course. My colleague owns a facility that takes care of such things, out in the Borders. The books are being sent there as they are discovered. We are documenting it all for Albion Freake so that he can be quite sure of owning the only copy of *The Chosen Ones* in the world. We're going to have the last ten copies ready for his inspection on Friday. Then we'll burn them during the ceremony.'

'What about my computer file?'

'Your what-what?' said Skylurian.

'My file of the book. I wrote it before the worldquake.'

Since the worldquake most novelists had gone back to typewriters because they were not so affected by greyouts.

'Oh, I hadn't thought of that. Well remembered, darling. We'd better burn that in the garden later. Maybe put it on a diskette, or whatever new-fangled technology one has nowadays.'

Skylurian and Raven's eyes met for a moment. Each knew what the other was thinking. Raven was wondering why Skylurian would want to burn all these books when everyone knew that true witches only ever burned something if they wanted its contents to come true. And Skylurian was thinking that the sooner some dreadful accident befell this nosy child, the better. When she smiled, it was certainly not with her eyes, and barely with her mouth.

'Or maybe we'll just pour a fizzy drink on it,' she said.

But Raven had something much more important on her mind. After breakfast, she put on her school uniform and read through her spell. It was important to get these things completely right. In fact, this was more of a prayer than a spell, although the two things are very similar. Raven knew – without needing to attend Mr Green's classes – that while it was always possible to bend the universe to your will, it was rarely advisable to do so. *Do not dabble*, Raven often told herself. *Good does not come to dabblers*. Someone had said that once, but Raven couldn't think who. Perhaps her English teacher, Mrs Beathag Hide.

But Effie was in trouble. This message had been carried

through the dawn chorus and into the cold pink morning. Euphemia Truelove, said one of the rumours going around, was going to die on Friday.

'Come on,' said the young man, as he hurried Maximilian towards the helicopter that had landed among a group of alpacas in one of the school fields.

The alpacas – sort of like large sheep with long necks – were always annoyed, but this latest intrusion was beyond the pale. The large whirring machine was bad enough, but who or what was this bizarre alien creature? Maximilian was wondering roughly the same thing. The young man was wearing a silk-lined leopard-skin tunic over a pair of yellow tights and an orange silk shirt. On his head was an orange hat with a massive tassel hanging from it. He wore soft flat boots in a kind of cream leather. Maximilian had never seen anyone like him before.

The other thing bothering the alpacas was the otherworldly boy-child currently running as fast as he could through their field, brandishing a dangerous-looking dagger and muttering something about being free at last. But he was soon gone, and they quickly forgot him.

'I am Lorenz,' said the young man in the leopard-skin tunic to Maximilian, ducking under the helicopter blades. 'I have come to take you to Meister Lupoldus. I trust you are already acquainted with your uncle? Please.' Lorenz held open the door of the helicopter, and Maximilian climbed in.

Maximilian was rather looking forward to riding in a helicopter, but the next thing he knew he was waking up to the swish-slosh sound of oars moving through water. Lorenz seemed to be giving directions to an oarsman. He was speaking a foreign language which Maximilian thought he did not understand. But then his brain seemed to retune and he found he knew what the men were saying. Not that anything they said helped him to understand how a large shiny helicopter had turned into a small wooden rowing boat. Perhaps he'd dropped off again. Perhaps a whole day had passed, or even two. Maximilian felt very hungry and thirsty. And his *uncle*? Would this be on his mother's side? No. She only had one sister. Maximilian had never met his father. Could he have sent for him now, via this uncle?

A sort of thrill went through Maximilian that was deeper than anything he'd ever felt. He wasn't at all sleepy now. The small boat was on a river – or maybe it was a canal – going through some kind of city. It seemed to be early in the evening; the sun had set and soft lights flickered in small windows. Maximilian could see stone archways, ornate domes and thin Gothic spires. The smaller streets seemed to be cobbled, but the larger squares and avenues were paved with marble. The boat turned off the main canal into a smaller waterway, under a stone bridge.

'Almost there,' said Lorenz, in the strange language.

Maximilian didn't know quite what to say back.

'Are we going to my uncle's house?' he asked.

'Yes,' said Lorenz. 'You must call him Meister and do whatever he asks of you. He's looking for a new Apprentice. That's why you have been brought here. I leave the day after tomorrow.'

Maximilian wanted to ask about his father, and whether he was in any way involved with this plan. But just then Lorenz leapt off the boat and helped the oarsman to secure it to the bank. Then he offered Maximilian a hand.

'The Meister is a difficult man,' said Lorenz. 'But not impossible.'

'What does he do?'

Lorenz laughed. Perhaps Maximilian had not put this so well in this new language.

'Do? Ha! What *doesn't* he do? Now, hush and follow me. If we're lucky, he will already have left for the opera and you won't meet him until morning. Ah, at last. Here is Franz. He will help with your luggage.'

Maximilian hadn't thought he had any luggage, but the oarsman and Franz between them lifted out of the boat a green trunk with gold trim. Was this Maximilian's? Where on earth had it come from? Had his uncle sent it for him? But why send luggage to be brought back to the place it had come from? Perhaps his mother had packed it for him. Yes, that would make sense. She was always doing things like that.

Franz was very thin and dressed all in black. Maximilian thought he must be some kind of servant. He was much stronger than he looked. On his own, he hefted the trunk onto his back and walked with it through a set of wrought-iron gates into a garden courtyard. The garden smelled strongly of jasmine and other evening flowers that Maximilian could not name. Moths flapped sleepily around candle-lamps in the warm evening air. Where on earth was he?

Maximilian followed Franz and Lorenz up a winding stone path through the garden until they came to a door. Inside was a floor of black-and-white stone tiles and a steep staircase. The walls were painted a deep blood-red and more candle-lamps threw dancing shadows onto them. Franz walked past the stairs to a very old-looking wrought-iron lift. He placed Maximilian's trunk in the lift and began winding with a large metal lever. It looked like hard work.

'Will the boy be taking supper here?' Franz asked Lorenz.

Then the entrance hall was suddenly enveloped in a heady scent of patchouli, vanilla and musk. A man had entered, rather in the way a leading actor might stride onto the stage. He swirled his black cape about him. This, Maximilian supposed, must be Meister Lupoldus. His uncle.

'NO,' bellowed Meister Lupoldus. 'He will dine with ME.'

On hearing his master's voice, Lorenz's posture changed. He seemed to shrink a foot and began visibly to quiver.

'Yes, Meister,' he said, bowing.

'But not in those ridiculous garments! Dress the boy and then BRING him to me.'

Maximilian was hurried up the stairs and along a corridor which stretched far ahead. Franz brought the trunk in and then left. Lorenz opened it and started flinging clothes around the room. A servant then picked them up and placed them neatly on the four-poster bed. Maximilian had never seen clothes like this before. There were silk tunics in odd colours, like dusky pink and pond green, a selection of curious hats, a pair of boots not unlike the ones Lorenz was wearing, two pairs of thin, pointed soft leather slippers and – disturbingly – several pairs of what looked like tights.

Soon Lorenz had assembled an outfit he thought would please the Meister. Maximilian was then washed by another servant – which took rather a long time – and given a set of complicated undergarments. After this came the dreaded tights. Then a kind of corset, which Lorenz tied tight at the back. Then a sky-blue silk shirt with billowing sleeves, followed by a darker blue tunic with a thin gold belt. Lorenz chose a pair of turquoise slippers and a yellow felt hat.

Maximilian felt quite stupid. But, if he was completely honest (and no one was here to see him, after all), the feel of the silk was pleasant. Maximilian had read somewhere that robes of silk were the best thing in which to do magic, because one's aura is free. Or something like that. Not that these were robes, exactly. But anyway, his outfit was not in the least out of place here, wherever here was. Even Franz's simple all-black outfit involved a tunic and a pair of tights.

Someone knocked on the door, and Lorenz left the room. Maximilian looked out of the window and saw, beyond the courtyard garden and the canal bridge, a large palace with green domes and stained-glass windows. Lights flickered inside, and Maximilian saw the outlines of men and women holding champagne glasses. When Lorenzo came back, he handed Maximilian a small but heavy package. Maximilian unwrapped the rose-coloured tissue paper and found a gold athame with a gold chain attached to its handle. Lorenz fastened this to Maximilian's belt.

'Is my uncle a mage?' Maximilian asked Lorenz.

Lorenz laughed. 'You don't know? He's not just any mage, he's a great one. Perhaps the greatest. You will learn much from him. Now, we must go.'

Dear Luminiferous Ether,

I hope you are very well and have enjoyed the passing of Martinmas. I am writing to you on behalf of a dear friend, whose life I believe to be in great danger. But I shouldn't put that, in case it makes it happen. I am writing to you because I am choosing to bring safety and courage to my friend Euphemia Truelove. I believe you will help me by granting my wish that Euphemia be kept safe and well for the foreseeable future.

Yours, as ever, in the spirit of Love and of Life,
Raven Wilde (Miss)

The Luminiferous Ether always enjoyed the letters it received from Raven Wilde. As ever it was touched to have been chosen as the Otherworld recipient of her witch's prayer.

But this new request was going to be very difficult to grant. The Luminiferous Ether looked at all the spells flowing through it and – yes – oh dear – there it was. The future event that would bring death upon one of Raven Wilde's friends before the week was out. It had been willed by one much more powerful than Raven. What could be done about it? Not much. Not much at all. And of course there was the other thing. The prophecy. And the small matter of the universe being saved. The Luminiferous Ether tried to shuffle things around a little and . . . *Well*, that was interesting. So it all would rest on one particular decision. That was better than nothing. And the decision was due to be made any time now.

6

'Creative writing,' said Mrs Beathag Hide.
She said the words in exactly the way one might say 'seeping wound' or 'headless mouse', or perhaps whisper news of a terrible accident. Almost as if she couldn't believe she had uttered something so distasteful, she repeated the words one more time.

'CREATIVE WRITING.'

No one in the class, the top set for English in the first form of the Tusitala School for the Gifted, Troubled and Strange, said anything. What could they say? Everyone knew that creative writing was a great treat. But the way Mrs Beathag Hide had said it made it sound like a terrible punishment. So they waited, silently, to see what would happen next.

There were two empty seats in the room. Effie and Maximilian were both absent. Wolf, Raven and Lexy had already all looked at one another and shrugged. None of them knew where their friends had gone. Raven hoped Effie was all right. She gulped again when she thought of what she'd heard through the Cosmic Web. Of course, the only good thing about knowing that someone is going to die on Friday is that you know they are pretty much invincible until then. Unless you have tried to change it, of course. Could Raven's spell have gone so wrong that it had actually hastened things? She shuddered. This was the problem, of course, with dabbling.

'I have been informed,' said Mrs Beathag Hide, 'that this class wishes to begin creative writing.'

The class froze. Of course. After the annual inspection a couple of weeks earlier they'd had to talk to a man in a beige suit about what they liked and didn't like in Mrs Beathag Hide's classes. Obviously they'd all said everything was fine, that they had no complaints and Mrs Beathag Hide was very kind to them. They weren't stupid. But the man had pressed them each to name something that they would like to do more of. And then he had fed back the results to Mrs Beathag Hide.

To Mrs Beathag Hide's immense disappointment, no one had said they wanted to spend more time rendering Greek tragedy in papier-mâché. No one mentioned wanting to read more Shakespeare or Chaucer. One person – not naming any names, of course – asked if the class could read *Ulysses*, which was an extremely difficult book by James Joyce. Every single other child in the class, when asked what they would like to do more of, chose creative writing.

Way back in the mists of time, before Mrs Beathag Hide had taken over the class, their old teacher Miss Dora Wright had given the children their first task of the school year. They'd had to write a story about their summer holiday that was not true, but that they wished *had* been true. Most of the children, inspired, no doubt, by Laurel Wilde books, wrote about being kidnapped by gypsies or smugglers and travelling to dark caves in rowing boats and finding piles of treasure. It was the most fun thing they had ever done at school. For some poor children, it was the most fun thing they had ever done in their lives.

Mrs Beathag Hide rarely got the children to do anything that involved their imaginations, which she felt enjoyed quite enough expression anyway. The class sighed inwardly as it remembered Miss Dora Wright's soft, round face and her gentle, kind encouragement.

'I expect you all think it's extremely EASY,' said Mrs Beathag Hide. 'After all, everyone knows how to tell a story or write a poem, don't they? DON'T THEY?'

The class didn't know whether it was supposed to reply and so, as usual, remained silent.

'Well, soon we will find out,' Mrs Beathag Hide said mysteriously, 'exactly how easy it is. Take out your pencils and your rough-work books.'

A thin shiver of excitement streaked briefly through the chilly classroom. The children did as they were told.

'Well,' said Mrs Beathag Hide. 'What are you waiting for? Write!'

The children all looked down at their rough-work books. The recycled paper was made from pulped novels, magazines, newspapers and packaging. All this paper had once been covered with words. Now it was blank, and certainly seemed to want to remain that way. What on earth did Mrs Beathag Hide want them to write? If Maximilian had been here, perhaps he would have been able to help. He would have asked Mrs Beathag Hide for more precise instructions, and then probably been put in the corner as usual with the dunce's cap on. The one that smelled of mould and dead mice.

'DIFFICULT, isn't it?' boomed Mrs Beathag Hide, after mass writers' block had settled on the room and made everyone wish they were dead, or at least somewhere else. 'Well, luck has shone on you, for some unknown reason. Perhaps all the good, talented, deserving children were already inundated with luck. Or maybe they were just busy. Who knows? Prepare yourselves, children. Tomorrow afternoon we will be having an AUTHOR VISIT. Terrence Deer-Hart will be coming to tell us all about how he gets his ideas and . . .'

From the usually silent class had broken out an excited murmur. Terrence Deer-Hart? Really? But he was a millionaire! A celebrity! He was Laurel Wilde's main rival in the bestseller lists every month. His novels were far more distressing, complex and violent than Laurel Wilde's, though, and one of his books for older children had over a hundred swear-words in it. His last novel had been banned from schools in at least four countries. Most children were not allowed to read his books at all.

'SILENCE!' said Mrs Beathag Hide. 'We have been asked to prepare for the AUTHOR VISIT with some CREATIVE WRITING. For some reason, luck has shone on your pathetic unimportant lives twice in one week. You have been asked to . . .' Here she glanced down at her notes. 'To write a story about "travelling to other worlds". How dull. Still, this task has come from the AUTHOR himself so you will no doubt find it exciting. Mr Deer-Hart will be reading your stories tomorrow before class. You will hand your rough-work books to me in the staff room before your first period tomorrow.'

Festus Grimm sipped from a huge mug of steaming coffee.

'Not long now,' he said to Effie, after scrutinising his watch. He chuckled. 'Once I popped back to the island for half an hour to get a copy of the *Gazette* and a Cornish pasty and then missed the window altogether. Had to wait another twenty-four hours. Or whatever the exact equivalent is here. Still, if you've got a good book with you . . .' He patted the green leather of *The Repertory of Kharakter, Art & Shade*.

'What's it about?' asked Effie.

'Ha!' said Festus. 'Life. Personality. Everything. However much I think I know about myself, I always come back to this, the absolute classic on the subject of the self and personal development – not that everyone sees it that way, of course. Have you had your consultation?'

Effie shook her head. 'Not yet.'

'I suppose you're still a bit young. But it's good for travellers to know their art and shade as early as possible, I think. Helps you develop. Shows you a few special skills you were not aware you had. Of course, Otherworld children sometimes have their consultations before they're even ten. How old are you?'

'Eleven.'

'Hmm. Well, you're probably ready. I'd get a good consultant, though. Not one of the fortune tellers in the market.'

Effie remembered that Pelham Longfellow had promised to take her for a consultation in Froghole. But, of course, for that to happen, Effie would have to get back to Truelove House. And to do that, she'd have to get her box back from her father with her precious calling card in it. And to do that, she'd have to find a copy of *The Chosen Ones*. How complicated life was.

'What exactly is an art?' asked Effie. 'And what's a shade?'

'How long have you got?' said Festus, with a kind smile. 'You should have come here a couple of hours earlier. We could have whiled away the evening indulging in amateur *kharakter* analysis and plotting our precise arts and shades.' He chuckled. 'Your art is simply your secondary ability. Everyone has one.'

'What's yours?'

'Ah. The thousand kruble question. My *kharakter* is true healer. Do you still say "true" before your *kharakter*? It goes in and out of fashion. I've always been a healer in some form or other, although as I usually heal with words rather than potions I wondered for a time if I was a witch, or even a mage. In the end, I had an Otherworld consultation that finally confirmed me as a true healer. But my art? For a long time I thought I was a guide. I was head of a whole team of psychologists in a hospital on the island. I'd travelled between worlds as a young man but eventually decided to give it up – with quite a lot of encouragement from the Guild. People used to believe that it was dangerous to do as we do and travel regularly between the worlds, so I stopped.

But I was never happy as a manager. I liked actually healing people. But, more than that, I itched to travel again. When I travelled, I always collected rare books, knowledge and so on. For a while I wondered if I was a scholar. But in the end I realised I was an explorer – of places and of knowledge.'

'So you can be wrong about your abilities?'

'Oh yes. A lot of people get them quite wrong. It's easier on the mainland, where they take it all a lot more seriously. Schools there are all about discovering and nurturing your true abilities. If someone fails at something, everyone is happy for them because they have found something to cross off their list. For example, if a boy is awful at sport everyone congratulates him on not being a warrior and he is simply given an extra music or chemistry class to see if he is in fact a composer or an alchemist.'

'How many *kharakters* are there?'

'Twenty,' said Festus. 'Well, if you include wizard, which not everyone does. Otherwise, nineteen. Of course the really interesting thing is the combination of *kharakter* and art. That's what makes people unique.'

'What combination do you think I am?'

Festus smiled kindly. 'You wear the Ring of the True Hero, and you're a plucky little thing. I heard about how you defeated Leonard Levar. It's rare to be a hero, but that surely is your *kharakter*. As for your art . . . That's more difficult. You can sometimes buy do-it-yourself kits in the market, but they're not that accurate. You need someone who can read a test properly. But at a guess . . . Maybe you're an explorer like me?'

'Does your art give you magical abilities, like your *kharakter*?'

'Of course. And you can use all the boons, too. The best thing I ever did was to discover I was an explorer. Once the universe knows you know . . . It's hard to explain, but I suddenly found an explorer's boon – a compass – and my life completely changed.'

Festus took out of his pocket a small, silver globe that looked like a huge ball-bearing, except that it had a silver hinge and a little latch.

'It's an antique,' he said, proudly. 'Here. Have a look.'

Effie picked it up, but it would not open. It started to grow hot, and heavy. She put it down just as her fingers began to burn. The boon clearly did not want her to touch it.

'Seems like I'm not an explorer after all,' she said.

'Oh well, one to cross off the list,' Festus said cheerfully. 'But you can still look.' He opened the silver casing and showed Effie what was inside. There was a needle, like an ordinary compass. But instead of north, south, east and west, the compass points said 'danger', 'knowledge', 'pleasure' and 'charity'.

'From the nineteenth century,' Festus said. 'It guides me on my adventures.'

'It's beautiful,' said Effie, a little sad that her art was not also explorer and that she could not have a compass like this one.

'Thank you.'

'So what's your shade?' asked Effie.

Suddenly, in the distance, a cock crowed, and a faint pink light started to drift into the room. Day was breaking somewhere in the universe, somewhere nearby.

'Aha,' said Festus, standing up. 'Time to go. We'll talk about shades next time perhaps. Happy travels, young hero.'

As Festus walked off quickly towards the door to the Otherworld, Effie suddenly wanted to go after him and tell him all about how she had been expelled from her magic class and ask him what to do about it. But it was too late; he was gone. She drained her hot chocolate and went to be scanned.

At lunchtime Wolf, Lexy and Raven met up in Griffin's Library to talk about Maximilian and Effie and where they might be.

'Do you think they're together?' asked Lexy.

'I hope so,' said Wolf. 'And I hope they come back soon. I need Effie for tennis this afternoon. None of the guys can hit the ball as hard as she can. And we did say we'd work on getting our strength up.'

Wolf was trying to sound cheerful, but secretly he felt his insides twisting up. He didn't like it when people went missing. Like his sister, for example. Wolf wasn't that bothered about his parents, who'd both abandoned him when he was very small. But he had never understood why his mother had taken his baby sister when she'd gone, leaving Wolf alone with his cruel uncle. Wolf longed to see his sister again. Her name was Natasha, but that was all he could really remember.

'I'm really scared,' said Raven.

'Why?' said Lexy. 'I'm sure they're all right. They've probably gone to get some information on the *Sterran Guandré*. I heard my aunt Octavia talking about it this morning, by the way. Apparently it's the Otherworld name for the Wandering Star

Meteor Shower that's happening on Friday. I just wish they'd told us before going off like this, especially now I actually know something. She said it happens every six years. Or six point one or something.'

'Do you think they're in the Otherworld?' asked Wolf. He'd never told the others, but he felt he would give anything to go to there himself. Even as he said the word he got a little pang somewhere near his heart.

'Maximilian can't go, though, can he?' said Lexy. 'I mean, he doesn't have his mark or anything.'

'He did go to the Underworld,' said Raven. 'Well, nearly.'

'That's different,' said Lexy, although she didn't really know anything about the Underworld at all.

'Maybe they're not even together,' said Raven. 'Maybe . . .'

'What's wrong?' Wolf asked her. His friend's eyes were suddenly full of tears. He'd never known Raven to cry about anything.

'It's Effie,' said Raven. 'I probably shouldn't say anything, but . . .' She told them about how she'd been out on Echo when she heard the news from the Cosmic Web about Effie being in trouble. 'Then,' she said, 'the next morning they were all saying that . . .' She gulped, and a single tear started to work its way down her face.

'What?' said Wolf.

'They were all saying that Effie is going to *die*,' said Raven. 'On Friday.'

'Oh my God,' said Lexy.

'That can't be true,' said Wolf. 'We can stop it. Nothing's set in stone. That's what you always say. That's what your spells are for, right?'

'That's right,' said Lexy. 'We can stop whatever is going to happen. You can do something, surely?'

'I've tried my best,' said Raven. 'But I don't know. I'll keep trying but . . . I've never heard of anything like this before.'

'We've got to find Effie,' said Wolf. 'And Max. They'll know what to do.'

'We can't tell Effie,' said Raven, shaking her head. 'I wasn't even supposed to tell you.'

'Why can't we tell Effie?' asked Wolf. 'I'd want to know if I was going to die.'

'You just *can't*,' said Raven. 'It's a basic rule. Don't you remember the story Mrs Beathag Hide told us about that servant meeting with Death in the marketplace?'

'Which one?' said Wolf. He often drifted off during Mrs Beathag Hide's stories.

'I remember,' said Lexy. 'The one where the servant goes to the marketplace in . . . Baghdad? And meets Death there.'

The three children cast their minds back to the dark and stormy late summer afternoon when Mrs Beathag Hide had told them about various different fictional meetings with Death.

In this particular story, when the servant sees Death in the marketplace, Death raises his scythe and so the servant flees. The servant then borrows his master's horse and rides to Samarra, where he goes into hiding. Later, the master goes to the marketplace and finds Death still there. He asks him why he frightened his servant. Death says that he didn't mean to, but he was surprised to see the servant in Baghdad when he had an appointment with him later in Samarra.

Many of the children had experienced nightmares after this particular English class.

'But what does it mean?' said Wolf.

'Well, if the servant hadn't been scared and run away . . . I don't know,' said Raven. 'It's hard to explain. But no one should know the date of their own death. It's a rule.'

'Whose rule?'

She shook her head. 'I don't know. It's just a universal rule. You always try to escape your fate but end up running straight into it.'

'Did the Cosmic Web say *how* she was going to die?' Lexy asked.

'No.' Raven sighed. 'I really shouldn't have told you,' she said. 'We can't let Effie know anything's wrong in case we just push her further into her fate. You've all got to promise to act normal around her.'

'We promise,' said Lexy. 'And we mustn't panic. We can fix this. There's loads of time until Friday. Raven, you need to keep listening into the Cosmic Web and find out what else it knows. Neither of us can hear it, so we need to focus on other stuff. I'll make some potions. A medicine bundle. Wolf will . . . Wolf?'

Wolf was looking quite distracted.

'Won't they have been gone a long time by now?' said Wolf.

'Who?'

'Effie and Max.'

'What do you mean?' asked Raven.

'Didn't Max once tell us about time differences between the worlds? And didn't Effie say that two days in the Otherworld was like 45 minutes here? They've been gone for the whole morning so far. If they are in the Otherworld, what are they doing that would take five days?'

'Maybe Effie knows she's in danger and so she's hiding in the Otherworld?' suggested Raven

'But she can't stay there until Friday!' said Lexy. 'Her dad will have reported her missing by then. And besides, no one stays in the Otherworld for that long. I don't think people from the Realworld even can.' Lexy worked in a portal, and so knew about things like this.

'So where is she?'

'And where's Maximilian?'

7

When Maximilian was dressed, he was taken to be presented to his uncle.

'GOOD,' boomed Meister Lupoldus. 'Now we shall go and dine. Franz? Bring the carriage immediately.'

Most people found Meister Lupoldus insufferably loud, vain, ambitious and cruel. He trailed great wafts of scent behind him – patchouli, vanilla and real musk, which comes from the scent glands of dead stags – as well as the tang of cigars, strong coffee and the very darkest magic. Hanging from his belt was an athame with a diamond-studded handle. Maximilian found him fascinating.

The carriage was painted gold and lined with red velvet. Meister Lupoldus got in first. Then Franz helped Maximilian in. The seats in the carriage were softer than anything Maximilian had ever experienced. They were much more comfortable than even his mother's best sofa at home.

Maximilian breathed in the evening scents. The jasmine, the

perfumes, the salty, oily smells coming from the canal. It was still warm. Church bells rang all over the city. Too soon, the carriage stopped and Franz was offering Maximilian help to descend to the cobbled street. Here, things smelled less pleasant. Spilt alcohol, horse urine and decomposing fish mingled unhappily in Maximilian's nostrils.

'Let us DINE,' said Meister Lupoldus.

Maximilian had not seen the small door in the wall. He followed his uncle into a dense garden and along a path until they reached a large, domed gazebo. Inside, everyone was exquisitely dressed. The women all wore dark dresses and diamond jewellery. The men all had complex jewelled belts and colourful tunics. Lupoldus and Maximilian were led to a table in the corner that was raised on a small dais. Maximilian instantly realised that this was the best table in the room.

'As you can see,' said Lupoldus, 'we can easily observe all the other diners in the room from here if we so wish. Or we can ask to be screened off if they become SHRILL or DULL.'

Maximilian said nothing.

'WELL?' said his uncle.

'It's very nice,' said Maximilian.

'NICE?'

'It seems refined and elegant,' Maximilian said, adding at the last moment, 'Meister.'

A waiter dressed in long white robes brought pale ceramic dishes full of rose petals and warm water. Maximilian was about to tuck into this strange-looking broth with a spoon until he saw that his uncle was dipping his hands in it. So he did the same.

The waiter then brought small black velvety towels for Maximilian and his uncle to dry their hands. The next thing that came was a huge bottle of champagne.

The meal that followed must have cost a fortune. First, Maximilian and his uncle were brought large plates with a dozen oysters on each one. Maximilian copied his uncle, who would pick up an oyster, put a few drops from a bottle of red liquid onto it, then tip the contents of the shell into his mouth. The oysters were cold, slimy, fishy and somehow the most delicious thing Maximilian had ever tasted. He could easily have eaten a dozen more.

Next came a bright yellow soup. After that the waiter brought small bowls of crushed pink ice that tasted of herbs and fruit. Then, with a great deal of ceremony, the main course arrived. It was a whole boar's head, complete with eyes and teeth, and surrounded with cherries, almonds and raisins. A jug of thick black sauce was presented along with it.

After the boar there was another herb sorbet, then a plate of thick, oozing cheeses with black, sticky bread. They reminded Maximilian of the most interesting meal he had ever eaten, which had taken place a long way from here. But perhaps *this* was now becoming the most interesting meal he had ever eaten. It was certainly the nicest by far. After the cheese came small, quivering custard tarts that tasted faintly of vanilla, cinnamon and nutmeg.

Meister Lupoldus ate slowly, as if he were considering each mouthful carefully before swallowing it.

'So, you are to be my new Apprentice,' he said, after he had finished his last custard tart and removed the enormous linen napkin that he had tucked into his frilly collar.

'Yes, Meister,' said Maximilian.

'You desire to be a great mage?'

'Yes, Meister.'

Meister Lupoldus nodded seriously. He nodded some more. Maximilian waited. His uncle seemed to be on the verge of saying something extraordinarily important. But then it became clear that he had fallen asleep. Maximilian wondered what to do. Waking his uncle would be the same as admitting he knew he was asleep. Maximilian had a feeling that the Meister would not want to be caught napping.

Maximilian considered flicking water at his uncle. Just as he was about to do so he found the waiter was looking at him sternly. Then his uncle woke up anyway.

'Where was I?' he said.

'You were telling me how to become a great mage like you, Meister,' said Maximilian.

'Was I? Ah, yes. What skills do you have?'

Maximilian considered this.

'I think I can read minds,' he said.

'You can do WHAT?'

'Read minds. And sort of change them.'

'At your level? IMPOSSIBLE. What else?'

Maximilian thought there was little point in telling his uncle what he could do if his uncle was simply going to tell him what he'd said was impossible. But he couldn't think of anything else to do, so he carried on.

'I almost went to the Underworld,' he ventured.

'ABSURD.'

'I'm quite good at reading and research.'

'That's BETTER.'

'I don't mind doing difficult things.'

'EXCELLENT. And have you yet been initiated into the way of the magus?'

Maximilian shook his head. 'I don't think so.'

'Good. We will initiate you soon, if I find you pleasing. If I do not find you pleasing, you will be executed. Now we must go.'

Maximillian followed his uncle back through the garden in something of a daze.

Outside, Franz was doing a handstand.

Maximilian wondered whether his uncle was going to shout at his servant, but so far he had not said anything at all mean to Franz. Franz looked at Maximilian and Meister Lupoldus from his inverted position and then slowly lowered his legs to the ground and stood up.

'Your carriage awaits, sir,' he said.

'We will walk for a while,' said Meister Lupoldus. 'I desire to touch the poor.'

Maximilian was still trying to process the news that he might be executed. Surely he'd find some way of avoiding it. Perhaps he could run away? What sort of uncle would execute his nephew anyway? Surely not the sort of uncle who was now walking through the thin, dimly lit streets gently touching the arms and legs of any people he encountered. There were scrawny young children in rags, and women who wouldn't have looked out of place in a workhouse Christmas pantomime. There were also a lot of thin, muscular men who obviously worked all day long and now looked very tired. The Meister touched them all as he passed. As he did so, he looked curiously peaceful.

'What's he doing?' Maximilian asked Franz.

'He is draining them,' said Franz, matter-of-factly.

'Draining them?'

'He is taking their energy. He needs it for his magic, and for his digestion, which has been troubling him lately.'

'But—'

'I agree it is not a nice thing to do, if that's what you were going to point out.'

'But why choose these people? Some of them look as if they don't have very much energy in the first place.'

'Because they don't complain. Their lifeforce is purer than the rich. And also because he likes it when they die.'

'*What?*'

'He gains great pleasure from killing the weak. It's easier when they don't have much lifeforce. He likes doing it to animals as well, because they are also easy. Well, most of them. Once he drained a strong, fully grown man and it took all night. But that was not for his energy, rather to punish him.'

For the first time in Maximilian's life, he felt quite afraid.

'We're almost there,' said Franz. 'Don't let him see you talking to me.'

'Why not?'

But suddenly the thin cobbled street ended and Franz led the way into a large marbled square. All the buildings around the square were extremely impressive, but one loomed over all the others. OPERA HOUSE, said its ornate golden sign. Franz stood aside so that the Meister could make an entrance. After dinner he had seemed sleepy and dulled, but now he appeared magnificent. His eyes were bright and his skin gleamed. He was brimming with the pure lifeforce of the poor he had touched. It was a terrible and awesome sight.

Maximilian followed his uncle and Franz up red carpeted stairs. Everything around him was luxurious and beautiful. The ceilings were painted with images from heaven and the walls were decked with silk, gold brocade and exquisite paintings. There were marble pillars and vast chandeliers. But that was just the entrance hall and the staircase.

The inside of the opera house was like nothing Maximillian had ever seen. Everything was gold and covered with angels. There was a central seating area, just like in a normal theatre – not that Maximilian had ever been to the theatre, but he'd seen pictures. Around this area were the opera boxes: velvet lined private cubicles from which the most important patrons could watch the performance without any disturbance. Each one was held up with gold pillars which were decorated with carvings of naked cherubs and what must have been ancient gods and goddesses.

Meister Lupoldus took his seat in what must have been the best box in the place and gestured for Maximilian to sit next to him. Franz sat just beyond the Meister. The orchestra began warming up and, even though they were not yet playing any actual music, the notes sounded deep and pure. Franz developed a quite dreamy look. Meister Lupoldus looked extremely satisfied with himself.

Then the opera began. Maximilian had never really listened to opera before. Sometimes screechy sounds came out of the radio at home, but his mother immediately switched them off. Once a neighbour had joined the local operatic society and Maximilian had sometimes heard the painful but occasionally stirring sounds of her nightly practice. His mother said the noise was like a cat being strangled. Many of the other neighbours agreed with her, and they all clubbed together to ban the poor woman from practising within earshot of any other human beings.

But this was entirely different. This particular opera was mainly performed by women. They sang without microphones, and their pure voices filled the large theatre. Occasionally a man sang too, and his voice was exactly the voice Maximilian would like to have had for singing in the shower, not that he took many showers. But he sounded brave, interesting and complex – just how Maximilian would like to be.

The opera seemed to be about a love triangle that led to faked suicide and madness. Maximilian wondered if Mrs Beathag Hide was familiar with the story. She would probably like it. Franz seemed to be enjoying the performance as well. Every so often he closed his eyes and seemed to go somewhere else. He didn't seem to be sleeping, though. He seemed, rather, to be in a kind of deep meditation.

Maximilian realised he was having both the best and worst evening of his life. The meal had been superb, and now he was hearing these divinely interesting sounds. But it was, of course, all in the company of a vampiric psychopath who probably meant to kill him. Perhaps this would also be the *last* evening of Maximilian's life.

For the moment, however, Meister Lupoldus was fast asleep. Every so often he emitted a gentle snore. Maximilian didn't want to think about his possible execution, so he let himself become entranced by the opera. Of course, most children hate opera because it is complicated and boring and you have to sit still for a long time. But we have already established that Maximilian was not like other children. And surely even the most philistine child would agree that opera is slightly better than being executed.

Twenty minutes later, it was all over.

Meister Lupoldus was awake and clapping and calling, 'BRAVO!'

Franz looked rather dazed.

'Now we will attend the GATHERING,' said Meister Lupoldus.

Terrence Deer-Hart was an extremely attractive man. Or so his many fans told him in the letters they sent. The fans often sprayed their missives with perfume, and to each of them he sent back a mass-produced photograph of himself with his autograph scrawled on it by an assistant. His grown-up fans loved his abundant hair. But the last children he had met had said they thought his hair was 'funny'. *Funny*. Young people were so cruel. He sighed as he ran the heated comb through his thick curls again.

He would have to remember not to swear this time. To use the word 'flipping' when he meant something much worse. And also not to smoke in the classroom. But really, it was just so flipping tiresome spending time with children. They were small, yes, but quite terrifying. The way they looked at you with their beady little eyes and then asked you questions about things. How much is a pint of milk? How the flip was Terrence supposed to know?

Mind you, it hadn't been children asking him that. No. He remembered now. He'd been on the radio talking about his latest book and someone had phoned in from the Borders and suggested he was out of touch!!! Just because he had one – ONE – child playing with a set of wooden skittles and another one wearing a knitted pullover, they had called him old-fashioned!!! No one accused Laurel Wilde of being old-fashioned, with her flipping steam trains and picnic blankets and sandwiches wrapped in flipping greaseproof paper!!!

Terrence Deer-Hart only ever brought out his heated comb on very special occasions. He would not bother with it tomorrow for the children. But today he was meeting the very most important person in his life: his publisher, Skylurian Midzhar. And he was going to convince her to put a stop to these silly school visits and finally allow him to write a book for adults, one in which he could use as many swear-words as he flipping well liked.

And perhaps this would also be the day when he told her his true feelings towards her. Surely it wouldn't come as a surprise? And especially after all the kind things she had said recently about his hair, his skin, and of course his writing. He loved her. Yes, he thought to himself. He loved Skylurian Midzhar. But would she love him back?

8

There was no queue for the Otherworld. The last time Effie had come here it had been very crowded, and she'd had to wait for a long time before she was allowed through. But today there was no one around. Not even Festus. He must have gone through already. He'd certainly appeared to be in quite a hurry.

A woman in a floral dress was waiting with a scanning device. She was different from the woman who'd been on duty the last time Effie had come here.

'Right,' said the woman, scanning her. 'M-currency is 1,003. One boon, a Ring of Strength, coming in at around a hundred pieces of dragon's gold or twenty-thousand M-currency. Next!'

'Wait,' said Effie. 'Are you sure? I should have a lot more M-currency, and my ring isn't . . .'

'NEXT!'

A man at a desk had been writing down figures with his quill pen.

'You're not supposed to argue,' he said.

'But . . .'

'She's new,' he whispered. 'Now scram.'

'NEXT!'

Effie hurried down the corridor and soon emerged in the Edgelands Market. The goblins who ran most of the first few stalls looked sleepy and a little bewildered. The sun was still in the process of coming up and everything looked pink and frail. The meteors had been dancing all night, more in the Otherworld sky than elsewhere, but were now becoming still. One lone meteor commenced its final fizzle into oblivion, then nothing.

The goblins left Effie completely alone. Effie hardly noticed them. She was worrying about what the woman on the door had said when she'd scanned her. She must have got it wrong because she was new. She hadn't correctly identified Effie's Ring of the True Hero after all. But 1,003 M-currency? That was absurd. Especially as Effie had been saving it up deliberately. She hadn't been checking it very often, but the last time she'd been to Mrs Bottle's Bun Shop for a cup of hot chocolate Lexy's aunt Octavia had told her she had had something like forty thousand. It must have been a mistake.

Effie headed straight for the bookstall that had been here last time, walking past stalls both familiar and new to her. Deeper into the Otherworld no one used money for anything. But here all currencies were accepted, and most people traded in krubles or dragon's gold. You could buy or sell magical, Otherworld objects alongside Realworld items that were rare in the Otherworld. Effie walked past the usual stalls selling enchanted weapons, silk clothing and feathered hats, but was then amused to come across a stall she had never seen before that sold denim clothing and old mobile phones that people mainly used as torches.

The book stall was not where it had been last time Effie had been here, so she walked deeper into the market. She soon noticed a stall that offered something called *KHARAKTER KONSULTATIONS*. An unhappy-looking woman sat filing her nails and watching an old Realworld soap opera on a grainy black-and-white TV. Effie remembered Festus's warning not to get a consultation here in the market. He needn't have bothered to warn her. Effie would not have had a consultation with this woman for anything.

Next to the stall was the entrance to one of the indoor bazaars. Its opening had been constructed from vast swathes of purple velvet cloth. Inside was the usual jumble of interconnected tents made from expensive silks and linens, with thick Oriental carpets for their floors. Some of the spaces were tiny, some were as big as normal shops. Effie soon realised that this particular sequence of outlets had a theme. One tiny chamber contained only a single silver-coloured box. 'Composer?' enquired the shopkeeper, as Effie peered in. 'You can keep your great work in here. Only four hundred pieces of dragon's gold.'

The next chamber was larger, and was full of maps, charts, candle-lamps and thick-looking hardbacks. Effie stepped inside to see if any of the books might be *The Chosen Ones*, but these were all books for adults. There was a large section on travel, but also a section on psychology, as well as a number of thick, complex-looking novels.

'Explorer?' said the clerk hopefully.

Effie passed a shop for alchemists containing cauldrons, Bunsen burners and bags of strange yellow rocks; the 'Hedgewitch Emporium', which was a vast colourful mess of different fabrics, wool, packets of dried flowers, tea-bags and books about the moon. She had not come across anything for her own *kharakter* yet. Did heroes not need shops? She wondered what one would sell.

She knew she should turn back and look for the bookshop, but everything here was fascinating to Effie. She told herself she would just go a bit further and then turn back. The large covered market narrowed and became a dark series of twists and turns through corridors lined with the purple velvet fabric. It grew quite dark for a time, and so Effie didn't notice the young man coming towards her at some speed.

'Sorry!' he said, as he careered into her.

He seemed to have come out of a chamber on the left made of yellow silks, with soft, warm lighting glowing from within.

'That's OK,' said Effie.

The young man had dropped something. It was a certificate. Effie bent down to pick it up while the young man caught his breath. She couldn't help noticing some of what it said as she handed it back. ALCHEMIST HEALER, it said on the top. There were several numbers, including one that looked more important than the others because it was written in gold. It said *6.10*.

'My parents are going to be so happy,' he said. 'And when I go back with this!' He beamed. 'They always wanted me to be a healer. I was worried that I was a mage, or worse, a galloglass mage. Galloglasses have to go and live on the island, obviously, and I was so scared I was just going to die even if I could get through. But now I can go home! Being an alchemist is nothing to be ashamed of. I can create remedies for wounded adventurers. I'm so happy!'

Effie had understood less than half of this. But he somehow reminded her of older children at her school who had just got their exam results. Although she'd never seen anyone as happy as this with just an A* in some academic subject. This young man was acting as if he'd won a very valuable prize. As if someone had just told him what his life really meant. Which, Effie realised, someone just had.

'Did you just have a consultation?' she asked him.

'Oh, yes,' he said. 'With Doctor Foulscrape'

'Doctor Foulscrape?'

'She's the very best there is,' said the young man. 'At least in this area. Most of them around here are charlatans, of course. But she works here because she genuinely wants to help runaways like me. She's very good. Incredibly understanding.'

'Where did you run away from?' Effie asked.

'Where does anyone run away from?' he said, smiling ruefully. 'Home. My village. Boring everyday life. You must have done the same, surely, if you're here. I mean, why else does anyone else come to the Edgelands? Unless . . .' He peered at her more closely. 'Heavens. Are you from the actual island?'

'Yes,' said Effie. 'But I'm a traveller. I go between the worlds.'

'Don't you run out of lifeforce really quickly when you're here?'

'No,' said Effie. 'I don't think so.'

'Wow,' he said. 'And is it all true? Is the island really dangerous and dark and full of murderers?'

'Not really,' said Effie. 'Not where I live. Anyway, you have monsters, don't you?'

'Yes, but everyone knows how to deal with monsters.'

The young man rolled up his certificate.

'I must start for home,' he said. 'If I leave now, I might get there by nightfall. I'm going to start building my laboratory straight away. My remedies are going to be known throughout the land!'

He hurried away, leaving Effie looking at the warm light spilling out of the chamber on her left. She walked towards the opening in the fabric that worked as a doorway. There, embroidered in yellowy-gold thread was the name DOCTOR FOULSCRAPE. It didn't sound like a very auspicious name for a doctor. But the young man had recommended her so very highly. She seemed to have completely changed his life.

Effie knew she should turn back now, find a copy of *The Chosen Ones* – if there was one anywhere in the market – and then take it to her father immediately. She had to get her box back and then go to Dragon's Green and see her cousins. As well as that, she had to find out about the *Sterran Guandré* and see if she could discover anything about what the Diberi were planning. She hadn't seen Raven since yesterday afternoon. Perhaps she'd found something out by now.

And Maximilian would have done some useful research, she was sure. He was so reliable like that. He was focused and intelligent, not hot-headed and impulsive like Effie could be.

She wondered what Maximilian would have done if Mr Green had tried to confiscate one of his boons. But he wouldn't have taken it to class in the first place. He was much too careful for that. It could never happen.

Effie sighed when she remembered how much trouble she was in with the Guild of Craftspeople. And how horrible her father had been. She had probably missed another class at school now too, what with all that waiting around in the Funtime Arcade, which would probably mean another letter home. Effie found she didn't much want to hurry back. And if she just stayed here a little longer, perhaps she could get a quick consultation. She so desperately wanted to know what her secondary ability – her *art* – was. And maybe even to buy something nice that went along with it. Something like the silver box for composers, or Festus's compass.

Before she knew what she was doing, Effie had entered the warmly lit chamber. Inside, all was muted white and cream, with flickering candles in yellow glass holders. There was a reception desk with a thick diary and a candle-lamp on it, but no receptionist. The chamber smelled strongly of lavender, with some other scent that Effie couldn't quite place. There were several framed certificates hanging precariously from the fabric that functioned as the right-hand wall. Each one carried the name 'URSULA FOULSCRAPE' and then a different qualification. One was for 'divination', another was for 'scrying', whatever that was. Another certificate looked exactly like the one the young man had been carrying, except that at the top it had the words 'INTERPRETER HEDGEWITCH'. In the middle of this were the numbers 5.50.

Suddenly, a large woman entered the small chamber through a curtained opening behind the reception desk. She was wearing a white coat and carrying a clipboard. She had the largest diamond earrings Effie had ever seen, which looked quite odd with her sensible haircut and clumpy black shoes.

'Are you Daniella Bounty?' she asked Effie.

'No, sorry,' said Effie.

'She hasn't turned up for her appointment,' said the woman crossly. She shook her head and tutted. 'Three YEARS is the current waiting time for a consultation with Madame, I mean DOCTOR Foulscrape. Of course we charge double for missed appointments. Dear oh dear. Anyway, who are you and what do you want?'

'I'm Euphemia Truelove,' said Effie. 'I wanted to find out about having a consultation. But if the wait is really three years . . .'

The woman looked at her watch.

'Well,' she said. 'You might just be in luck. If Miss Bounty doesn't turn up in the next few minutes, I daresay you can take her appointment. Very fortunate you'd be, though. We've had people waiting out there offering clients huge sums of money to take their slots, so desperate they've been. And after that profile of Madame, I mean DOCTOR Foulscrape in *The Liminal* recently . . . Here you go.' The woman gave Effie the clipboard. 'You can fill that in while you're waiting. If Miss Bounty does turn up, we can always put it on file for you for three years' time.'

'What is it?' asked Effie.

'The basic test. Have you done one before?'

Effie shook her head.

'You read each statement and tick box 1, 2, 3, 4 or 5, depending on how strongly you agree with what it says. I'm Nurse Shallowgrave. Let me know if you need anything else. If I don't hear from you, I'll be back in ten minutes to collect the test.'

Shallowgrave? That was even worse than Foulscrape. Effie suddenly had a terrible feeling about this. The test in front of her looked like a bad photocopy and smelled slightly of fried onions. There was something wrong in this chamber too, although Effie couldn't work out what it was. Underneath the comforting lighting and lavender was . . . She wasn't quite sure. Anyway, it was too late now. She could hardly just leave. And besides, if Effie didn't do this now, she'd have to wait three whole years. Effie remembered how happy the young man had been with his consultation. And all those people who paid extra. And she was very lucky that this Daniella Bounty had not shown up. Fate obviously wanted her to do this.

Effie started filling in the test. It was actually quite interesting and she became so absorbed in answering the questions that her worries soon faded. Some of the statements were definite 5s. For example 'I find it easy to learn other languages' and 'I am more fearless than my friends'. Others were definite 1s, for example 'I make a lot of diagrams' and 'I am an excellent cook'. Soon Effie found herself longing to know what all this meant. She finished the test and waited.

A few more minutes passed and then Nurse Shallowgrave strode back into the small chamber. The smell of fried onions intensified. Her large diamond earrings glittered. She took the test from Effie and disappeared back beyond the curtain. More minutes passed. Then Nurse Shallowgrave emerged again and gestured to Effie that she should follow her.

There was a thin dark passageway and then a black velvet curtain. Nurse Shallowgrave held the curtain aside and showed Effie into the small, dark chamber.

'Eugenie Halfhound,' she announced. Then she left.

'Actually, it's Euphemia True—'

'Sit,' came a silky, smooth voice. 'Make yourself comfortable.'

Effie sat on the only chair, which was wooden, and very, very hard. The chamber was far too hot and the only light came from a single flickering candle-lamp on Doctor Foulscrape's desk. The desk was quite untidy. There were matchboxes, notebooks, bottles of ink, tissues, sweet-wrappers and huge piles of paperwork. In the corner of the chamber was a large cauldron. Various crystals hung from the low fabric ceiling by thin pieces of thread. The small amount of light from the candle-lamp danced slowly around the gloomy chamber, changing from red to yellow to green to blue, depending on what crystal it had last travelled through.

'Well,' said Doctor Foulscrape. 'Greetings and blessings.'

Her voice was like thick honey. Very sweet and dense, and with a slight European accent that Effie couldn't place. She was wearing a crumpled black linen jacket and a white silk shirt. Her hair was dyed bright pink. She looked both very old and very young, and extremely wise. Effie immediately wanted to tell her all her secrets. How odd. She didn't usually trust people so immediately.

'Greetings and blessings returned,' said Effie.

'Well,' said Doctor Foulscrape. 'Well, well.'

'Do you have my results?' asked Effie.

'I do.' Doctor Foulscrape pressed her fingers together. 'But I wonder. What do you think you are? Do you already have some idea?'

'Yes,' said Effie. 'I know my *kharakter* already. I know I'm a true hero. But—'

'A *true hero*? Whoever gave you that idea?'

'Oh, um . . .'

'You haven't been speaking to one of those ghastly fortune tellers out there, have you? They'll tell you you're a wizard already and then charge you hundreds of krubles. A true hero. My my.' She laughed and shook her head. 'I haven't heard that one for a very long time. A true hero – if it even existed – would be a positively AWFUL thing to be. All that traipsing around after monsters and dragons and great criminal masterminds!' She laughed again. 'Most people who come in here long to be alchemists, healers or guides. I have the occasional would-be hedgewitch or engineer. Do you know what people are worst at, Eugenie?'

'It's actually—'

'I'll tell you. At *knowing* themselves. People are EXTRAORDINARILY bad at it. Which is why we use the test. The test is never wrong. But of course the test needs something vitally important in order to function. Which is . . .?' Doctor Foulscrape raised her eyebrows. 'I'll tell you. It needs an interpreter. Not just anyone can read this test you know. And do you know how long I've been doing this? I'll tell you. Forty years. Impressive, no? And I am simply NEVER wrong about anyone. So . . . let's see.'

Doctor Foulscrape started shuffling papers on her desk. Surely, Effie thought, if Doctor Foulscrape had just been looking at her test it should be near the top of her pile? While the doctor scrabbled around on her desk, a very old and decrepit-looking cat jumped up from the ground, scattering pieces of paper everywhere. They couldn't be pages from Effie's test, could they? But the pieces of paper didn't look like a test. They looked like some kind of warning or penalty notice, similar to the parking tickets Cait sometimes brought home.

Once a few more pieces of paper had been moved around it became clear that Doctor Foulscrape had found the thing she'd been looking for. It was a bright yellow bowl full of slimy brown cat-food. This was what Effie had been able to smell underneath the lavender.

Doctor Foulscrape stroked the cat as it ate, and it began to purr loudly. She started again on the paperwork. Her red glasses were perched in an uncomfortable-looking position on her nose.

'Halfhound, Halfhound . . .'

'It's Truelove,' said Effie exasperatedly. 'My name is Euphemia Truelove.'

'Oh, why ever didn't you say? Here we are. Oh, yes. An interesting case. What did you say you thought you were? A true hero? Nope. You're a warrior. I could have told you that anyway because of your ring.'

'But my ring is . . .'

'A Ring of Strength. Did you really think it was the Ring of the True Hero?' She laughed again. 'Oh, *bless*. You thought you were going around the Edgelands Market wearing something the goblins would have off your finger in seconds if they saw it? Something worth hundreds of pieces of dragon's gold? Whoever told you this was a true hero's ring needs their head examined.'

Effie started to feel angry.

'The person who told me about my ring was very wise,' she said, remembering her beloved grandfather. Although . . . had he ever actually named the ring? Now that Effie came to think of it, the person who'd told her about her ring had not been a person at all, but a dragon.

'This anger you show,' said Doctor Foulscrape, 'is entirely characteristic of a warrior. You'll want to be careful you don't let it get you into trouble. Now, do you want to know the rest of your result?'

'Yes,' said Effie. 'Sorry. Is it my art and shade next?'

'Just your art. We do the shade together afterwards.'

'OK.'

'And the art comes after payment, of course.'

'Payment?' Effie suddenly realised that she hadn't asked anything about payment before. Of course she'd meant to, but it had all been so distracting with Nurse Shallowgrave looking for Daniella Bounty and then giving Effie her appointment. But of course she'd have to pay. This was the Edgelands after all. Things were not free here.

'How much is it?' said Effie.

'Do you want to pay in dragon's gold or M-currency?'

'M-currency,' said Effie.

'Then it'll be twenty thousand.'

'Twenty thousand!' said Effie. 'But . . .'

Doctor Foulscrape took out a scanning device.

'I see you've only got a thousand or so on you. That's fine. I'm feeling kind today. I'll take the ring instead.'

'My ring? No. I'll . . .'

Doctor Foulscrape's face twisted into a cruel smile.

'You'll what?'

'I'll . . .'

'Nurse Shallowgrave will prevent you from running away, if that's what you were thinking.'

'No! I just meant I'll find some other way of paying you. Let me come back tomorrow. I can have more M-currency by then.'

'Sorry, Eugenie, but that's not how it works.'

A cold chill seemed to go through the room.

'I am NOT called Eugenie. And what's more, I am not a warrior. In fact, I don't actually care what the rest of your analysis is, as it's so likely to be wrong. I'm not paying you anything.'

Effie stood up and turned towards the exit.

'Oh, yes you are,' said Doctor Foulscrape. 'Nurse?'

Nurse Shallowgrave came into the chamber holding a large syringe. Behind her was the young man Effie had run into outside. He didn't seem to have left for home yet. He was now dressed in a black silk cape with black studded boots, and was carrying a gleaming dagger.

'Ah, Curt,' said Doctor Foulscrape. 'I wondered where you'd gone.'

'Curt,' said Effie. 'You have to help me.'

'Help you?' he laughed cruelly. 'What, help you *die*?'

'But . . .' said Effie. 'I thought . . .'

All at once she realised her horrible mistake. When Curt had bumped into her before, he'd just been acting a part. A part cleverly intended to make her desire whatever Doctor Foulscrape had to offer. She was sure that there was no such person as Daniella Bounty either. It had just been another ploy to make her agree to the consultation without asking any questions.

'You're con-artists,' said Effie.

'And you're about to die,' said Nurse Shallowgrave. 'Now hand over the ring and I promise I'll make it quick.'

'You are never having my ring,' said Effie. 'I'll—' She touched her neck where her Sword of Light should have been. Of course, there was nothing there, just skin.

'You'll what?' said Doctor Foulscrape. 'With no weapon and only 1003 M-currency? Good luck. It will certainly be interesting to see what you think of to attack us. Maybe you've got friends here, but I think not. All your friends are elsewhere.'

Suddenly, Curt slumped to the floor.

'No, they're not,' said a familiar voice. 'Effie, duck.'

Effie did as she was told. As soon as she'd done so, an arrow pierced Doctor Foulscrape's chest. Then another arrow struck Nurse Shallowgrave. Effie, now shaking, turned slowly and stood to face her rescuer.

'Festus?' she said.

Festus put away his bow. He didn't seem very happy.

'What did I tell you about these fortune tellers?'

'I didn't realise. I thought . . .'

'You have to be a lot more careful if you're going to come here,' he said. 'It's not a game, you know. These people probably wouldn't have killed you in the end. They just wanted your ring. But there are much worse villains out here. And, of course, I had to shoot them as soon as they threatened you, which is actually a great pity. We could have learned a lot from questioning them. Now they'll be reborn somewhere and go completely unpunished.'

He sounded very cross indeed.

'I'm really so sorry,' said Effie.

'We're going to have to start again with this whole operation now.'

'What operation?'

'Oh child, you have an awful lot to learn. You have no idea of what goes on here, do you?' He sighed. 'Can you keep a secret? What did you put on your test? I assume they at least gave you the real test. Did they have that as a statement? *I am good at keeping secrets?*'

'Yes,' said Effie, nodding. 'I think I put a 4.'

'Only true mages get a 5 on that one,' said Festus. 'But you'd better keep *this* secret.' Festus looked around, and then dropped his voice to a whisper. 'I'm an undercover agent investigating a large conspiracy in this marketplace. These vile galloglasses were just the tip of the iceberg. Later on I'm going to arrange the arrest of the new woman on the gate. I expect she fed this lot knowledge about what you had on you, so they knew to target you. It's a good job you didn't have anything apart from the ring this time.'

Effie bit her lip. She had never felt more sorry about anything in her life. She had no idea how she would make this up to Festus.

'I'm sorry,' she said again.

Festus shook his head. 'For some reason the black market price of magical rings has tripled in the last few weeks. There's talk of some prophecy. I'd make sure no one suspicious sees you wearing that for a while.'

He didn't say anything else. He went over to Curt and pulled the arrow out of his neck. There was surprisingly little blood. Effie remembered his certificate, how proud he had seemed of it. But of course it had been a forgery. Effie doubted he was either a healer or an alchemist.

Festus retrieved the rest of his arrows and began to clean them.

'What's a galloglass?' asked Effie.

'Someone who acts only for their own profit. Galloglasses are expelled from the Otherworld and have to live in the Realworld. When I find them here, they are often trying to get to the island anyway. They've heard its streets are paved with gold. I take them to the Guild and then they rehome them somewhere on the island. And sometimes punish them, or offer them healing, depending on what they've done.'

'I thought the Guild didn't like people moving between the mainland and the island,' said Effie.

'They don't like the *wrong* people and creatures moving between worlds, that's true,' said Festus. 'There was an agreement, not long after the Great Split. The Otherworld has to keep its monsters in check, and never let them anywhere near the island, but in return the Realworld has to agree to take all galloglasses.'

Festus had finished cleaning his arrows and now turned his attention to all the papers on Doctor Foulscrape's desk. He was leafing through them and putting them into different piles.

'So, you're not really an explorer?' said Effie.

'What makes you say that?'

'Well, if you're really an undercover agent . . .?'

'What do you think undercover agents do? They *explore*. It's not just about exotic holidays and complicated books, you know. I work with someone who is a hunter healer, and another person who's a healer scholar. We decided that one good way of healing the weak is by eliminating those who prey on them. But I've told you too much already. You should go home now. With the *Sterran Guandré* coming . . .'

Effie was surprised to hear the term again.

'What exactly is the *Sterran Guandré*?' she asked immediately.

'Never you mind,' said Festus.

'Please,' Effie said. 'I have to find out. It might be really important.'

'You bet it's important,' said Festus.

'Festus, please?'

'All right. It's a big meteor shower, peaking at the end of this week. It happens between the worlds. I recommend you stay in on Friday with a good book, because on the night of the *Sterran Guandré* things don't do what they are supposed to. The fabric between the worlds becomes very thin and, well, with all the galloglasses trying to go one way, and monsters drifting randomly the other way, into your world . . . But I've said too much. There will be measures in place this time. It won't be like last time. It can't be. Anyway, just be careful, child.'

'Thank you,' said Effie. 'And thank you for rescuing me.'

'Just try to learn from the experience,' said Festus, with a long, deep sigh.

9

When Effie left the Funtime Arcade, the feeble late autumn sun had reached its low peak in the pale blue sky. Being in the Otherworld always did strange things to Effie's watch, but before long she heard one of the Old Town clocks strike twelve. So it was midday. Effie reset her watch and hurried to school.

She had a strange, almost sick feeling in her stomach. She knew she'd be in trouble when she got there. *And* when she got home. And she was still in big trouble with the Guild. Her cousins in Dragon's Green would no doubt be wondering where she was, and they'd probably be cross with her now as well. And she'd just been so stupid that she'd almost been killed. And so now Festus was angry with her too. Effie sighed. She was just a big disappointment to everybody.

She arrived at Griffin's Library just before it was time to go to double PE. Lexy took one look at her and immediately put the kettle on for a cup of sweet tea.

'At last,' said Wolf. 'Where have you been?'

'What happened to you?' said Raven.

'And where's Maximilian?' said Lexy, giving Effie a bright green tonic and three chocolate shortbread biscuits to keep her going until her tea was ready.

Effie suddenly realised she was too ashamed to tell her friends about how stupid she'd been. Instead of telling them about how she'd been expelled from Mr Green's class and then been deceived by con-artists, she simply said she'd been looking for a copy of *The Chosen Ones* for her father. She didn't mention that if she didn't find a copy she had no chance of getting back all her precious boons – including Wolf's Sword of Orphennyus. Failing to hide the box properly was yet another stupid thing she'd done.

'Well, that's easy,' said Raven. 'We've got loads of copies of the book lying around at home waiting to go to the pulpers. I'm sure they won't miss one. Come for tea after school?'

'Thank you,' said Effie. The horrible feeling in her stomach was still there, but it felt slightly better suddenly, because Effie realised she could always rely on her friends. Only . . . would they even still want to be her friends if they knew how easily she could be conned? The sick feeling intensified again.

'Is Maximilian not with you?' asked Raven.

'No,' Effie said. 'Is he not here?'

Lexy shook her head. 'He seems to have disappeared.'

The golden carriage clattered over cobblestones and through the thin back-streets of the city. The moon was high in the sky and Maximilian could see the shadows of people getting out of the way of the carriage. He could see silhouettes of figures in windows. There was a man in a night-cap holding a candle. A woman sitting on the edge of a bed rolling a stocking down her leg. All over the city people were preparing to go to bed.

'The night is yet YOUNG,' said Meister Lupoldus, and then promptly fell asleep.

The horse-drawn carriage jittered along. Maximilian realised that they were now travelling uphill. Before long the city smells faded and Maximilian sensed that they were now travelling through some sort of countryside. He could hear crickets chirruping, and there was also the occasional hoot of an owl. The air freshened and Maximilian now smelled earth and long grass. Something howled in the distance.

It was completely dark, except for the moonlight.

Suddenly, the carriage stopped.

'Who goes there?' said Franz.

The carriage shook. Maximilian could hear Franz say something to calm the horses. Then the carriage wobbled again slightly as Franz got down from his driver's seat. There was a gunshot, followed by a short period of silence, and then laughter. Meister Lupoldus woke up. Another gunshot followed, and then more laughter.

'Meister?' called Franz. 'You might want to have a look at this.'

Maximilian followed his uncle out of the carriage. There was a bedraggled-looking masked highwayman peering down the barrel of his own gun. He seemed rather bewildered.

Now he pointed the gun at Meister Lupoldus. Meister Lupoldus completely ignored this and looked instead at Franz.

'We appear to be in luck,' he said.

'Indeed, Meister,' said Franz.

'Your money or your life!' said the highwayman.

Franz and Meister Lupoldus continued to ignore him. The highwayman grabbed Maximilian and put the gun to his head.

'Your money or the child's life!'

Maximilian felt properly afraid for the second time that night. Were his uncle and Franz not going to try to help him at all? He could feel the cold metal of the gun digging into his head, just above his right ear. Was this actually how he was going to die? Before he'd even found out anything about his father, or done any really impressive magic? But then Maximilian remembered. He knew how to make people do things. If his uncle and Franz were not going to try and save him, he was just going to have to save himself.

The highwayman didn't realise this, of course – he had no idea of the huge mistake he had just made in holding up this particular carriage – but the fact that he was touching Maximilian made it a lot easier for Maximilian to reach into his mind and have a good rummage around. Before long, Maximilian had this man's whole life story. He also knew that there was a box full of jewels buried not far from where they were standing. He was able to whisper his commands straight into the man's brain. The highwayman did not understand why, but he now released Maximilian and calmly put the gun on the ground.

Franz seemed to be showing Meister Lupoldus two bullets, which he was holding in the palm of his hand.

'GOOD,' Meister Lupoldus was saying. 'You are progressing well. FASTER than Lorenz. Tell me, when are we to execute him?'

'Lorenz has actually left, Meister.'

Maximilian cleared his throat. 'Ahem,' he said. 'Um . . .'

'It appears that your nephew has saved himself,' said Franz.

'BRAVO,' said Meister Lupoldus. 'But . . .' He looked quite troubled for a moment. 'HOW did the boy do this?'

The highwayman was now sitting cross-legged on the ground, drawing a map to show how to get to his buried treasure. His tongue was poking out of his lips slightly. He hummed lightly to himself.

'And WHAT is this?'

'I—' began Maximilian.

'*I* did this, Meister,' said Franz, quickly. 'The thief is simply showing us where his treasure is to be found. No doubt you would have devised a superior way to find out this information.'

'No doubt,' said Meister Lupoldus. 'TORTURE would have been much quicker. Still, you have done your best.'

'But I . . .' began Maximilian. Then he shut up as soon as he saw the expression on Franz's face.

Half an hour later, Maximillian and Franz were carrying a small treasure chest to the carriage, in which Meister Lupoldus was having another short nap. The highwayman was also asleep, having fallen down next to the hole he had dug and from which the treasure had been taken.

Each time Maximilian had tried to ask Franz what was going on, Franz had put a finger to his lips and shaken his head. Maximilian eventually understood what must be happening. If Meister Lupoldus were awake, he would be demanding the execution of the highwayman. Maximilian disliked killing, and he sensed that Franz felt the same way. His uncle, though, seemed to thrive on it. Which was another reason not to upset him.

Maximilian climbed silently into the carriage and resumed his position next to his uncle. Franz quietly took up his position in the driver's seat and urged the horses to trot on. After five minutes or so, Meister Lupoldus woke with a start.

'Who are you?' he demanded of Maximilian.

'Your nephew, Meister.'

'Of course. I remember. But . . . Wait. What about the EXECUTION?'

'What execution, Uncle?'

'The hapless highwayman who decided it was an excellent idea to rob a carriage containing a great mage, of course. Franz?'

Franz did not respond. Perhaps he couldn't hear.

'WELL?'

'You did execute him, Meister,' said Maximilian. 'It was so quickly and expertly done that perhaps you have forgotten.'

'Did I? Perhaps I did. Yes. Very good. ONWARDS!'

Maximilian sensed that Franz was smiling in the driver's seat, although of course he could not know for sure.

The carriage jangled on. After ten more minutes or so the

road became smoother. Then the carriage stopped for a few moments and Franz said something in a hushed voice. Maximilian heard gates clunk behind them, as the carriage continued on. Maximilian looked back through the glass window as the carriage turned to the left and saw an impressive gatehouse. A few short minutes later the carriage pulled up outside the entrance to a vast castle. They had arrived.

Effie changed for PE in silence. Raven and Lexy were chattering about something, but she could hardly hear them. Her head felt full of pressure. But she knew what she had to do. She had to make amends for everything she had done wrong. At least if she had a copy of *The Chosen Ones* her father would have to give her box back. Then Effie would be able to go to the Otherworld and tell Clothilde everything. She would know how to help, Effie was sure of it. The thought of Clothilde made Effie want to cry. But she tried not to cry, ever.

When Effie was changed, she slipped on her ring and walked to the tennis centre. She had to cover the ring with a piece of micro-pore tape so that the teachers didn't tell her off for wearing it, but that was fine, and no one even asked her about it now. She was going to do her best to generate as much M-currency as possible today. She couldn't believe it had gone so low.

She was almost sure that she knew how the Ring of the True Hero worked. She'd tested it, hadn't she? All she had to do was play tennis for as long as possible and then replace the physical energy she'd expended with snacks and energy drinks. As long as she kept the ring on, the energy she'd used playing tennis would magically have turned to lifeforce.

Effie was the best tennis player in the Lower School, even without the ring on. She hadn't been that sporty before she'd epiphanised, but now all that had changed. Wolf could beat everyone else in the Lower School, but now Effie always beat him. The first time she had beaten him without the ring on, he'd seemed rather put out. But he soon got over that. Wolf was a true warrior and a natural sportsman and always respected those with greater skill than his own. Some people like spending time with people weaker than themselves, to make themselves look better. Wolf was the opposite. He was proud of his friend, and loved training with her whenever he could.

Today they were playing mixed doubles. Effie and Wolf were currently the Under 13 mixed doubles champions of the whole area, and so they were never allowed to play together in lessons. Sometimes Mr Peters, the head of PE, made them play left-handed (both Effie and Wolf were right-handed, although Lexy, Raven and Maximilian were all left-handed). Today, Effie played right-handed and didn't care about going easy on the weaker children, nor about giving her partner a chance to hit some shots too. She still felt ashamed and sad, and so she took it out on the tennis ball, and her opponents.

'Wow,' said Wolf during one of the changeovers. 'You're on fire! Take it easy on the rest of us.'

Usually Wolf would have carried on joking around with Effie, but today he sounded more concerned than impressed. He also offered her some of his sports drink and at one point also insisted she sit down on his chair. He was almost acting as if she were ill. It was very strange.

After PE all members of the Lower School tennis teams were asked to stay behind. Coach Bruce strode into the tennis centre looking serious. Coach Bruce was not known for caring about much other than the Under 13 rugby team, the Lower School tennis team, drug testing and sports nutrition. No one at the Tusitala School for the Gifted, Troubled and Strange knew that Coach Bruce also had a Harley-Davidson motorbike, was very fond of his aunt Margaret and regularly went with his men's group to Quirin Forest to take part in bonding activities that involved a lot of drumming, crying and semi-permanent tattoos made from crushed berries.

'Right,' he said. 'As you know, we have been unbeaten for the last six weeks. If we remain unbeaten at the end of the season we will jump a division and go straight into the Northern Associated Schools Tennis Youth League Premier Division. And what does this mean?'

'Great glory?' said one of the boys.

'What else?'

'Cool new team kit?'

'What else?'

'New rackets!'

'What else?'

Everyone grew silent. It was true that the elderly headmaster of the school had promised them new kit and rackets if they made it to the Premier Division. What else was there? Well, apart from great glory of course, but they'd already said that.

'My promotion,' said Coach Bruce, eventually, 'to Head of PE. Not just that, but also my acceptance onto the master's course in sports psychology at the Old Town University. *My* glory, for a change. Do you think I spend my life wallowing in your pee for fun?'

No one enjoyed the image that this produced. Had Coach Bruce gone slightly off his rocker? He didn't normally talk like this. And surely all he did with their pee was to take it to Dr Cloudburst in the chemistry lab for it to be tested for illegal substances.

'It seems that for both my promotion AND my acceptance onto the course, I have to demonstrate "Leadership beyond what would normally be expected of a Level 3 coach". And how do you think I am going to demonstrate that? I am going to lead you to great glory.'

Everyone thought it appropriate to clap at this point, so they did. Coach Bruce looked pleased for a moment. But then his face darkened into a frown. The clapping stopped.

'So what,' he said, 'do you think might stand in our way? What is the one thing that could potentially ruin your chances of winning the division unbeaten and, by association, my only chances of happiness and success?'

It slowly began to dawn on everyone what he was talking about. Of course. Blessed Bartolo's. The most notorious school in the whole of the North. The school they were due to play in the league fixture tomorrow. Blessed Bartolo pupils all had cruel eyes, never smiled and were supposed to be clever, but everyone knew there was something evil about them. Their school uniform was entirely black. The girls wore sophisticated shift dresses or wool trousers with smoking jackets. The boys wore full three-piece suits with black silk bow ties. All the pupils took compulsory classes in fencing, stockbroking, dressage and advanced music composition. The entrance exam for the school took four days. It was extremely secretive, but everyone knew that the children who failed it were never quite the same afterwards.

And Blessed Bartolo's never, ever lost at anything.

'Well?' said Coach Bruce.

A murmur developed.

'Well?'

'Blessed Bartolo's,' someone managed to say, in a sort of whisper, the same kind of whisper you might use to say the name of the worst thing in your religion or the biggest baddie in the scariest book you have ever read.

'Exactly. And how are we going to beat them?'

'Cheat?' suggested someone.

'We will call it *strategy*,' said Coach Bruce. 'We don't cheat here. We employ strategy. There are books on the subject. *Trusted Tennis Tactics*. *Winning Ugly*. That sort of thing.'

Coach Bruce went to the tennis cupboard, a vast dark space full of fluorescent yellow ball fluff and miniature orange traffic cones, and emerged with a whiteboard on wheels. From deep within his tracksuit he took several whiteboard markers in different colours. None of the children quite followed him as he drew various diagrams explaining things like the value of the deep lob and why you should never serve first.

'Why is Blessed Bartolo's in Division 3 anyway?' someone whispered. It was quite a good question.

'Isn't it like their *fifth* team, though?' someone else whispered back.

It was true. All the other Blessed Bartolo teams were in the Premier Division. In fact, the Northern Associated Schools Tennis Youth League Premier Division (unfortunately but accurately known as the NASTY LPD) was only made up of Blessed Bartolo teams, which meant that all NASTY league home and away fixtures currently took place in their purpose-built sports centre, which was in a massive black dome on the end of a rocky peninsular that jutted somewhat dangerously into the harbour.

Someone with an older sibling – these are always the most well-informed members of any school – suddenly remembered something.

'Wasn't there that thing last year? Didn't one of the Blessed Bartolo's teams actually kill someone?'

'No, he didn't die. But he was in a coma for two weeks.'

'What happened exactly?'

'No one knows. But it was in a NASTY league tennis match. Anyway, their penalty was going down two divisions. It must have been the fifth team.'

'And now *we* have to play them?'

Coach Bruce was still wrapped up in his diagrams. He was also planning to go to Dr Cloudburst later and get some caffeine powder to put in the children's sports drinks. What else could he do? Dress Euphemia Truelove up as a boy and have her play with Wolf in the boy's doubles? No. Someone would find out. But she could certainly wear that ring she always insisted on taking off for matches. That would give her a psychological advantage, surely? Not that she was likely to lose anything anyway. No one had *ever* beaten Effie Truelove in a league tennis match.

10

Meister Lupoldus was unusually quiet. He allowed his cloak to be taken by a servant without even a murmur. He seemed to be silently enjoying his surroundings, which were the most overwhelming Maximilian had ever encountered. The entrance hall on its own made the opera house look like a garden shed.

Its polished wooden floor stretched away into the distance like an exercise in perspective. Opulent velvet chairs sat vacant on either side of the long passageway. The ornate chandeliers produced a steady light that was brighter than any Maximilian had ever seen. The walls of the passageway were impressively hung with huge oil paintings of men on horseback and women in very long dresses.

Soon a man in a bright red tunic appeared in the distance.

'Greetings, Meister,' he said. 'The princess is very keen to meet you, and the other learned men. She is longing to see what you can achieve. Most of the other members of the gathering

have already arrived. However, you will be require
a reading before you are permitted to enter.'

Lupoldus nodded.

'A reading?' said Franz, looking worried.

'A triple reading of herbs, cards and sticks,' confirmed the guide.

'I trust my master's nephew will be permitted to attend, along with me?' said Franz.

'Indeed, it is required. Please follow me.'

Maximilian was intrigued. He followed the guide, Franz and his uncle down the long passageway and into a cloistered garden surrounded by Grecian columns, with white marble statues silvery in the moonlight. He could hear music. Maximilian thought it might be coming from the statues. One of them, a woman in flowing robes, was carrying a small stringed instrument. On the other side of the cloisters was a statue of a man in similar robes standing by a harp.

Maximilian's soft leather-soled boots made no sound as he followed the other men out of the cloisters and into another long hallway with a black-and-white tiled floor and more paintings, chairs and polished wooden tables and cabinets. Around a corner and into another passageway and then through a large, black wooden door and up a compact spiral staircase. The guide knocked on the door and waited for the occupant's reply. Then he gestured for the Meister, Franz and Maximillian to enter.

'Oh,' said Lupoldus, once the door had been closed behind them. He sounded surprised. 'It's you, Elspeth.'

The room was of medium size and smelled of the smoke you

.ght get if you were to burn all the oldest and most interesting things you owned. There were no paintings on any of the walls, which were painted a deep midnight blue. In the centre of the room was a large mauve velvet chair, and on this sat a slight elderly woman with long grey hair and sparkling, jewel-like azure eyes.

'Approach, please,' said Elspeth.

'I did not know that you had joined the court,' said Lupoldus, walking towards the mauve chair.

'My skills are of great interest to the princess,' said Elspeth.

'As are MINE,' said Lupoldus. 'The princess desires to attract great mages to the castle – which is the reason for her holding our gathering here this evening. But why would she be interested in a common tea-leaf reader? A backstreet scryer?'

'You yourself have been interested enough in my arts to come to me for consultations in the past, Meister.'

'And you confirmed me as a great mage. What is left to say?'

'The princess wishes all mages to be scrutinised before the gathering. She has heard a prophecy that there is one among you who does not hold the true power of the magus, who is in fact using diabolical means to gain magical energy.'

'Prophecies are not necessarily TRUE,' said Meister Lupoldus.

'Perhaps you would like to inform the princess of that?'

Meister Lupoldus said nothing.

'Now, kneel before me,' said Elspeth.

Lupoldus adopted an expression of extreme distaste, but did what she asked. Elspeth began crumbling leaves, buds and dried flowers into a small copper bowl on the table in front of her. She then lit a small taper and set fire to the contents of the bowl. The room filled with a smoky perfume. Elspeth then cut a lock of the Meister's hair and added it to the bowl. She shook out the burnt mixture onto a piece of white parchment on a small table beside her.

'Interesting,' she murmured.

She then took a pack of cards from a drawer in the table in front of her. She shuffled these and started placing them on the table, as if she were setting up a very complex game of patience. Maximilian tried to step forwards to see what the cards were like, but Franz yanked him backwards and elbowed him in the ribs.

'The hanged-man,' said Elspeth. 'Well.'

And so the reading continued. The cards were examined and then put away. Then Elspeth closed her eyes for several minutes before throwing a set of sticks onto the table. She leant down to examine their precise patterns.

'Fascinating,' she murmured. She then clicked her fingers and a small boy came into the room. He was younger even than Maximilian. He scurried over to the bookshelves and, after climbing a small ladder, selected a volume bound in cream leather with what appeared to be Chinese characters on its spine. He took this to Elspeth and then exited the room. Elspeth browsed the book for several minutes.

'An imposter, hmm?' said Elspeth, seemingly to the sticks.

'Get ON with it, woman,' said Meister Lupoldus. 'I desire some drinking, merriment and debauchery before the serious business of the evening commences.'

'Silence,' said Elspeth.

Lupoldus rolled his eyes and then stared at the ceiling while Elspeth concluded her reading.

'This room contains two great mages and an imposter,' declared Elspeth, her blue eyes flashing around the room.

'And the imposter is YOU, witch?' said Lupoldus, laughing.

Maximilian thought his uncle was not doing a very good job of getting this woman to do what he must surely have wanted – to declare him a great mage as quickly as possible so that they could be on their way to this gathering, whatever that was. For the first time, Maximilian realised that his uncle really was quite stupid.

Franz had his eyes closed and seemed to be concentrating very hard on something.

Meister Lupoldus sighed extravagantly.

'You have identified TWO great mages because my servant here has been showing the signs. I have been DEVELOPING him. The imposter you sense is not an imposter at all. He is merely a boy that I will be taking as my Apprentice. He is, of course, not yet a great mage but aspires to be one day. I thought that you were only reading me. I am the one who has been invited, after all.'

'It is often impossible to remove the interference in the room. As I'm sure you realise.'

'I don't go in for SCRYING myself. Your art seems both laborious and amateur. Its results are imprecise and insignificant.'

'That is not what the princess believes.'

'Then the princess is an IDIOT.'

An incredible silence came over the room. Maximilian half

expected the princess herself to emerge from a dark corner of the room and say, 'Oh, I am, am I?' and then execute his ridiculous uncle. But this was not what happened.

'Lock them up,' said Elspeth. 'The princess will complete the testing process herself, and then the imposter will be dealt with.'

Maximilian was taken with his uncle and Franz to the dungeons. This involved a long, dizzying walk down a very deep stone spiral staircase. Franz kept miming something at Maximilian, but Maximilian couldn't work out what he was trying to say. He seemed to be pointing to himself, and then to the Meister, and then to Maximilian. He also kept tapping his head. If only Maximilian could talk to him somehow. But they were being escorted down the stairs by two very burly guards who had made it clear that the prisoners should remain silent.

If only . . . Maximilian suddenly remembered again that he could read minds. This usually seemed like quite an impolite thing to do, like reading someone's diary, or listening in on a phone call. He wouldn't normally have dreamed of trying to do it to Franz. But perhaps that was what Franz was trying to tell him. So he concentrated. It was more difficult when walking, particularly when walking round and round and down and down. But Maximilian gave it a go.

'At last,' said Franz back to him, silently, as their minds connected.

The guards then took Maximilian in one direction and Franz in another. They were not going to be imprisoned together. But somehow, by concentrating very hard, Maximilian managed to keep the connection going until he had been securely manacled in his dungeon. 'Manacled' means handcuffed, although the guards didn't stop at Maximilian's hands. They secured his legs as well with large iron rings, and clamped something around his middle that was like a strange metal doughnut.

'Are we talking telepathically?' said Maximilian to Franz, with his mind. Although the word 'telepathically' was not invented until the late nineteenth century (1882, to be precise) the idea has existed since the beginning of time. When two minds meet and talk, words are not necessary, only concepts. So Franz quite understood what Maximilian was saying.

'Yes,' replied Franz. 'We have to hurry.'

'Where are you?'

'I am in the next dungeon along from yours. Lupoldus is on the other side of me.'

'What should I do?'

'First you must take what I have. I have opened as much as possible to you. Hurry. Once you have the knowledge we will rescue your uncle and escape.'

Maximilian suddenly understood that while he was inside Franz's mind he had access to all Franz's knowledge and memories. Well, at least the ones that Franz had 'opened' to him. Maximilian realised that Franz was giving him a great gift. He filed away for now this idea that it was possible to open and close parts of your mind, and continued, as quickly as he could, deeper into Franz's memories. He had to be fast. Franz had said so. But everything here was so interesting. He could see, hear and smell things from completely outside his own experience. There, on a wooden table from long ago, was a sticky dark cake that must have been Franz's favourite. There was a girl, his playmate, called Anna. There was hide-and-seek in the forest. Camping trips. Handmade bows and arrows. A larder full of homemade jams, biscuits, spices, preserved fruits and cured meats.

Then came great darkness. Two cloaked men arrived at the cottage on horseback with some kind of official-looking parchment, and then Franz's parents were taken away in a sort of wooden cage, while Franz hid in the attic. Maximilian had trouble finding any more details about what had happened to Franz's parents. This part of the memory was sealed off, although he sensed this was not deliberate. Perhaps it was just too painful.

Franz himself seemed to be directing Maximilian to one particular part of this memory. And indeed, it was easily the most interesting thing Maximilian had ever found in someone's mind. At the moment when the cloaked men had burst into the attic room where he was hiding, Franz had made himself disappear. One moment he was there in the room. The next, he was gone.

Everyone knows that invisibility is a skill that comes most naturally to witches. With practice, they can make themselves blend into the background wherever they are. But a few very skilled mages are able to actually disappear, to fade their bodies into the little dimensional pockets – like the sections in a quilt – that exist between this world and the Underworld.

It takes a special kind of concentration to disappear. Usually only Adept mages would even attempt it. But Franz, twelve years old, terrified and helpless, found that it also could happen to young, inexperienced mages in extreme situations. As with swimming or riding a bike, after you have disappeared once, you find you can always do it. And since Maximilian had experienced Franz's memory, he could now do it too. He knew how to disappear! He felt completely changed, deep inside. Maximilian sensed that Franz understood that this piece of learning was now complete. It was almost as if an invisible box had been ticked.

Maximilian knew he had to hurry, but Franz's mind was so full of exciting stories. Not long after the disappearance of Franz's parents, the cloaked men on horseback came back, this time to visit Anna's house. The third time they came, Franz and Anna were ready for them. Franz constructed an ambush in the forest and created such confusion that the men shot each other at the same time.

Then Franz and Anna stole their horses and rode away into the depths of the countryside, surviving by eating rabbits, wild plums and field mushrooms. Anna was good at gathering herbs and very good at singing. When she sang . . . But many of those memories were locked away. The two teenagers made their way to the city, where they found their way into domestic service together.

Servants in those days (and often today) were kept in terrible conditions and never had days off. But Franz knew how to accomplish things quickly and then move around unseen. Soon he learned to disappear for longer and longer into the strange patchwork quilt between the dimensions and move short distances without being observed. He had read the contents of his master's library by the time he was fourteen and was eager to move to a new position with a better library. Most of all, he wanted to visit the Underworld, the dark and complex land he sensed whenever he disappeared. But he needed knowledge in order to do this.

However much he searched, he could not find what he wanted to know. Three hundred years ago there had been many more mages in the land. But most magical societies had been wiped out by cruel leaders almost two hundred years before, and then after that many mages had simply disappeared.

There was a lot of the history of magic in Franz's head, a sort of timeline from ancient shamans and wise women, through Hermes Trismegistus, the English witches, Paracelsus, Rudolph II, John Dee, the Rosicrucians . . . But Franz steered Maximilian out of these areas of his mind and back into his memories of those first few years he spent in service.

A wealthy visitor to the house had heard Anna sing and became completely obsessed with her. The man was cruel, but Anna did not care. She left to pursue a life on the stage under the management of this man, singing the new operas. This period was another dark, forbidden area of Franz's mind. Maximilian caught brief glimpses of the man with the pointed cane who came to take Anna away, bringing with him furs and exquisite perfumes, and the blind rage Franz felt. The loneliness afterwards . . . Then lots of securely locked memories.

Franz seemed to be deliberately guiding Maximilian through the many corridors and passageways of his mind. He seemed to want him to experience some particular memories of visits to the opera with his new master, Lupoldus, and to a series of concerts given by a new composer with wild hair. Lupoldus liked the opera because it was flashy, but Franz preferred hearing the intense music played by the man with the hair on the pianoforte – quite a new instrument.

Maximilian did not understand why he kept being guided to these memories. With so much of interest in this mind, who wanted to sit through long, boring concerts? Especially now he was learning about his uncle. Maximilian searched Franz's mind for references to his uncle's brother – his father – but there were none. 'Hurry,' said Franz telepathically. 'There is no time for this . . . Concentrate . . . Listen to the music.'

Back went Maximilian to the small drawing room with the piano. The man about to play had extremely hairy hands, and bits of wool sticking out of his ears. On the top of the piano was a glass jar full of a curiously fluorescent yellow liquid, alongside a pile of papers scrawled on with the most terrible handwriting anyone could imagine.

When the playing began it was slow, low, but quite dramatic. Maximilian, his mind now almost completely fused with Franz's, saw, or rather *felt*, in these notes a purple, almost black sky, some rumbles of thunder, a tiny plop of rain – or perhaps an angel's tear – followed by a flash of lightning briefly highlighting some beautiful mystery. Then a little run of secrets, some curious nymphs, and then a sequence of pale rocky steps descending into an underground cave. A pause. One of the pieces of wool fell out of the pianist's ear.

Then – bang! It began. A fast, relentless melody like nothing Maximilian had ever heard. Notes running up and down, here and there, faster, faster, the music becoming wilder and deeper

116

like a great storm in the middle of a tragic love affair (it must have been Franz's memory thinking that bit). Some calm followed. The secrets and the nymphs again. But not for long. Soon the secrets were carried away on rolling waves and there was a sort of big ship and . . .

The sonata continued. The hairy pianist's hands grew wilder, quicker. The remaining piece of wool fell out of his other ear. And then Maximilian suddenly realised that he was alone in Franz's mind. Franz himself had gone. And it wasn't like when he had disappeared before. His whole being had completely departed. He had somehow managed to leave *himself*. It had happened several seconds ago, and he'd left Maximilian behind in his now empty self.

Where had he gone? Maximilian rewound the memory. There Franz was. And there . . . he *wasn't*. Just before Franz's mind departed, Maximilian could feel it sort of becoming one with the music. Until, suddenly. *There*. A higher note. One of the angel's tears. It was as if Franz was running very fast, and had just timed his jump correctly and managed to land his mind on this tiny moment and . . .

Maximilian could feel Franz returning. He had clearly learned something, but he wasn't sure what it was. Well, he sort of knew. It was that running jump. But where had it taken Franz? Why hadn't Maximilian gone there too? 'Very good,' said Franz, inside Maximilian's mind. 'You learn well. Now we will disconnect and meet in your uncle's cell. I will collect the keys on the way.' And suddenly Maximilian's whole connection with Franz disappeared, and the pianist, and his whole world, was gone.

11

It was already getting dark as Effie and Raven walked from the school gates down the hill to the bus stop. A few young, bold meteors leapt impatiently in the sky, burning through the atmosphere almost as fast as the terrible, soon-to-be-forgotten ideas being generated in Orwell Bookend's committee meeting in a dingy basement room in the Old Town University. As usual, Orwell had no real idea where his daughter was.

Normally Effie wouldn't see any Blessed Bartolo children on her way home, because Blessed Bartolo's was in the north of the city and most of its pupils lived in the north-west or the west, which were the areas with most trees, coffee shops and quaint weekend markets. Effie lived in the south, where most children went to the Mrs Joyful School and didn't have enough money even for their bus fare. But there were plenty of Blessed Bartolo children on the bus out to the village where Raven lived.

Effie and Raven sat at the top of the bus near the front. All the Blessed Bartolo children were at the back, looking rich and pleased with themselves in their black uniforms that smelled faintly of scented candles, polished wood and dry-cleaning chemicals. Their pagers beeped regularly. One of the boys was cleaning his fingernails with what looked like a small knife. Another seemed to be holding a ball of fire in his hands. They were odd, unsettling children.

Even adults found Blessed Bartolo pupils a bit creepy. Most adults still claimed in public not to believe in magic, even after the worldquake. In private, many of them feared that if anyone were doing real magic it was probably children like this. Adults avoided all after-school buses, of course, because every after-school bus contained children, and no one in their right mind wanted to be confined in a small space with children. But adults particularly avoided these Blessed Bartolo buses, which, despite being the newest, plushest buses coming out of the Old Town, nevertheless quite often broke down or caught fire. Three bus drivers so far had gone missing from this route. Two of them had been found some time later living wild in Quirin Forest. The third was still unaccounted for.

'Why do they keep saying your name in that weird way?' whispered Raven.

It was true. Every so often one of the black-clad children from the back of the bus said the word *Effie* or *Euphemia* in a strange kind of drawn-out hiss. Effie was trying not to let it bother her.

'I don't know,' said Effie. 'I think it might have something to do with this league tennis match tomorrow.'

'Shall I cast the Shadows?' asked Raven.

This was the first spell that Raven had learned after she had epiphanised. It didn't quite make you invisible, but it did cast a conceptual shadow over you and whoever happened to be with you at the time. It meant you almost disappeared and people around you then generally ignored you.

'You can try, but it doesn't really matter what they say.' Effie twisted the ring on her finger. 'They're just trying to scare us – they can't actually do anything. Maybe you should save your lifeforce.'

The bus wound its way out of the city and down country lanes where maple trees glowed orange and pink in the early evening dusk. Effie wished, not for the first time, that she could do magic. Of course, travelling to another dimension might reasonably be thought of as doing magic, but Effie didn't count that. And there was her amazing strength and power when wearing her ring . . . But she couldn't do proper magic like casting spells or reading people's minds. Perhaps if she found out her art . . . But she'd messed that up once already.

At the next stop more Blessed Bartolo children got on. Three older boys dressed in black velvet capes stomped up the stairs. Two of them sat in the double seat next to Effie and Raven's; the other one sat in front of the first two, his long legs splayed lazily. He had long, shiny dark auburn hair. The other two had black hair. Effie heard Raven sort of gulp. She was in the aisle seat and therefore closest to all of them. One of them carried a massive school bag. Another held a wooden staff. The one with red hair was carrying a transistor radio from which came the dull thudding beats of Borders hip-hop.

'Well, well,' he said. 'Tusitala trash. On *our* bus.'

Effie knew that Raven usually got the earlier bus, which had far fewer Blessed Bartolo children on it than this one. But Coach Bruce was not known for his brevity (why say something in ten words when you could spin it out into a hundred, or a thousand?) and had kept lecturing the tennis team on strategy until way after the bell had rung for the end of school.

The black-haired boy by the window sneered.

'Including, I do believe, the Truelove girl who is going to beat us at tennis tomorrow, according to rumour.' He laughed. 'Although looking at her now, I wouldn't have thought she could beat anyone at anything. No one said how small and weak and pathetic she looks.'

Effie glanced at Raven. The time to cast the Shadows was now, but Effie couldn't seem to catch her friend's eye. Raven seemed frozen. Were the boys . . .? Effie had a horrible feeling they were doing some sort of magic, and Raven was unable to block it. Not for the first time, Effie felt strangely powerless. Of course, with her strength she could easily get up and hit one or all of the boys and make them stop what they were doing. But what use was great strength when you didn't really like using violence as a way of solving things?

'Raven?' said Effie. Her friend did not respond. Effie turned on the boys. 'What have you done to her?'

The boy by the window looked as if he was about to say something. But just then the bus jolted and shuddered and swerved crazily to the right, ending up with its front half in a large hawthorn bush. The boy's school bag ended up under Effie's legs, and his neighbour's odd-looking staff ended up in Raven's lap. Whatever magic had been working on Raven stopped. And just as Effie picked up the staff to give back to the boy, Raven managed to cast the Shadows.

'Where have they gone?' said the red-haired boy.

'And where's my caduceus?' said the one nearest the girls. He pronounced this *cad-juicy-us*.

He must have meant the staff. As Effie held it in her hands she developed a warm sensation similar to the way you might feel sinking into a hot bath at the end of a long day, or lying in a quiet meadow in the sun on a perfect summer's afternoon.

The caduceus was clearly very old. It was made of a dark polished wood and had two snakes winding around it, with a pair of carved wooden wings at the top. Luckily the Shadows meant Effie didn't have to give it back immediately, although that had been her intention. Effie didn't just feel warm and comfortable holding it. She suddenly became aware that she could see, hear and understand much more around her than usual. It wasn't an effect of the Shadows: Effie was sure it was because of the caduceus.

But what did it mean? Effie suddenly had a yearning to learn spells – strange, exotic, unknown spells – and cast them, something she had never desired to do before. Her hearing was different as well. She could now pick up on conversations all over the bus. She understood exactly how it had come to swerve into the bush: two first-year Blessed Bartolo pupils downstairs had been trying out mind control and one of them had got into the bus driver's head and it had all gone horribly wrong.

All at once, Effie understood Blessed Bartolo's. It was a school for mages. Yes, it was full of rich, stylish, cruel, haughty children. All the rumours about it were true. But everything made more sense when you realised that all its pupils were young mages, with their dark power and ambiguous morals. Effie could now feel their complex energy all around her, and she could read it as easily as she would read a book.

'You shouldn't have done that,' one of the first years was saying to the other, downstairs, where they should have been out of Effie's hearing, but, while she held the caduceus, were not.

'But you dared me . . .'

'When the Guild finds out, you'll be banned. What'll your dad say? You'll probably be expelled too.'

'But you *dared* me!'

'No, I didn't. You did it all by yourself. Loser.'

'But . . .'

'I can't believe you *actually* used mind control on someone. They might even put you in prison.'

All at once, the bus managed to reverse out of the bush and Raven's Shadows spell was broken. She must have lost concentration because of the sudden movement.

'Give that back,' said the black-haired Blessed Bartolo boy, glaring at Effie, who realised that everyone could now see her holding onto the caduceus rather tightly.

'Sorry,' she said. 'I meant to . . .'

'Thief,' hissed the other dark-haired boy.

'Don't, Gregory,' said the first boy, as Effie handed him his staff back.

There was then an odd moment. As Effie and the boy both held the staff, something like an electric shock went through Effie and the world seemed very bright all of a sudden. Things seemed to come into an unimaginable kind of focus and then . . . Whatever was happening abruptly stopped once Effie let go of the caduceus.

'Come on, Leander,' said Gregory. 'Let's punish the Tusitala trash.'

'No, let's just go.'

Leander caught Effie's eye. She understood suddenly that she had touched his boon, and it had worked on her. So whatever he was, she was too. But she had no way of asking him what that was, because just then the three boys got up and started walking down the stairs, their black capes swishing behind them. Effie wanted to go after Leander and ask him what his strange wooden staff meant, but it was too late.

'What happened then?' asked Raven.

'I'm not sure,' said Effie.

'Why was he looking at you like that? And what was that stick you were holding?'

'I don't know exactly,' said Effie. 'But I'll tell you about it when we get off.'

'It was definitely a boon,' said Raven, after she had considered everything Effie had told her.

'That's what I thought, too,' said Effie. 'But what does it mean?'

124

The two girls were sitting on Raven's large bed drinking hot chocolate and eating homemade cake. Apparently, Laurel Wilde baked whenever she was stressed. Something particularly upsetting must have happened recently because when the girls had gone into the kitchen they had found a Victoria sponge, an iced fruit cake, a black forest gateau, a large treacle tart, a wholemeal carrot cake and a lot of cupcakes, shortbread and flapjacks.

There had been no one in when the girls arrived. No Laurel. No Skylurian. Just piles and piles of *The Chosen Ones* everywhere, and all the cake. Effie had already taken one of the copies of *The Chosen Ones* and put it in her school bag. Raven had assured her that no one would miss it. Then they'd gone up to Raven's bedroom. It was a cosy space at the top of one of the folly's four square turrets with its own special staircase. It also had a door out onto the folly's battlements, from which you could see the village in one direction and the garden, stables and moors in the other. In Raven's room there was a four-poster bed, an oak desk and lots of cluttered bookshelves.

'It must be your secondary ability,' said Raven now, excitedly. 'Your art. The boon must go with that!'

She reached for another piece of wholemeal carrot cake, which was her favourite, and passed Effie the Victoria sponge, which was hers. Laurel Wilde refused to eat most things that went in cake, because she thought they were unhealthy, and you had to watch out because sometimes she decided to make cakes with potatoes instead of flour, or aubergines instead of butter. The best-looking cakes often tasted the worst and so the girls hadn't had high hopes for the Victoria sponge. Surprisingly, it was actually very nice.

'But I don't want to be a mage,' said Effie, through her slice of cake. 'I'm sure everyone at Blessed Bartolo's is a mage. I sensed it when I was holding the caduceus. But I don't feel anything like a mage. It just seems wrong somehow. I don't know why. It suits Maximilian, but I'm not sure it suits me.'

'Well, the caduceus doesn't sound like a mage's boon to me,' said Raven. 'What exactly did it make you feel, again?'

'Just more connected to everything. I could hear all the conversations around me. I *really* wanted to cast a spell, and . . .'

'Mages don't cast spells.'

'Don't they?'

'Nope.'

'How do you know all this?'

Raven shook her black hair. 'I went to the library. It was because I couldn't go to Mr Green's classes. He gave me a reading list. And then there was this really helpful librarian. He recommended . . . um . . . *The thingy of thingy, thingy and thingy?*'

'*The Repertory of Kharakter, Art & Shade?*'

'That's it! I'll get it from my shelf. I thought I'd look at it because I still don't know my art either. But it was sort of long, and a bit complicated, and I haven't quite got round to finishing it yet. But mage was the first *kharakter* in there, so I did read that. Hang on . . .'

Effie hadn't looked properly at Raven's bookshelves before, except to note just how many books she had. There seemed to be more than ever now. Effie could see many old-looking cloth-bound books with titles like *Casting a Circle* and *Nature Rites*. There were all sorts of almanacs, guides to the moon and the tides, books of herbs, flowers and mushrooms, and, in a little pile, several paper pamphlets tied together with string, all by a woman called Glennie Kindred.

'Wow,' said Effie. 'Where did you get all these new books?'

'My mum's got an account with Rosewater Books in the Old Town,' said Raven. 'I'm allowed to get as many books as I want from there. They can order stuff for you if it's not in stock. And then for the rarer stuff there's the library.'

Raven reached up and pulled down a thick hardback bound in green leather. She handed it to Effie. It was so heavy and solid – except for the delicate gold ribbon that snaked through the pages.

Effie flicked through it. It still fascinated her. She again got something of the feeling she'd had holding the caduceus. It was most odd. She felt warm and sort of comfortable again. Inside were all sorts of words and phrases that intrigued her. In the section on 'The Mage', Effie read, 'The true mage will treat darkness as if it were black velvet, the flank of a complex horse, the depths of the ocean, the ink of the night.' In the section on 'The Healer', there was a beautiful line-drawing of an intricate medicine bundle. Effie longed to carry on reading.

'Can I . . .?' she began. 'I mean, would you mind if . . .?'

'Do you want to borrow it?' Raven said. 'Sure. I've got it out for three weeks since last Tuesday. I can always get it out again. Or try to order one from Rosewater Books. Although apparently it's a very rare book that you have to get second-hand now.'

'Are you sure?' said Effie. 'I promise I won't lose it.'

'I know you won't,' said Raven, smiling. 'And anyway, the man in the library said he'd put a homing spell on all the rare books so that if they do get lost they simply return themselves.'

'Thank you.'

Effie put the book in her bag, on top of the copy of *The Chosen Ones* from downstairs.

'And are you definitely sure your mum won't mind?' Effie asked. 'I mean about me taking one of those copies of *The Chosen Ones*.'

'I doubt she'll even notice. Skylurian might, though. She's funny about those books. But if your dad's taking it to the Town Hall on Friday it'll end up in the same place anyway.'

'Why are there so many copies everywhere?'

'Because of the appeal,' said Raven.

'What appeal?'

Raven smiled and shook her head. 'Have you been living on another planet?

'Sort of. Well, I guess I've been in the Otherworld quite a lot.'

Until Effie had lost her calling card she had been becoming much more interested in the Otherworld than the Realworld. Her time spent in the Realworld had started to feel less and less important, and she had sort of stopped paying close attention to it. She only now realised she didn't even know why her father wanted her copy of *The Chosen Ones*. All she knew was she had to find it so she could get her box back, so she could go back to the Otherworld.

'So you don't even know why your dad wants a copy of the book?'

'He said something about selling it for fifty pounds. But apart from that I don't know.'

'OK, so basically Mum and Skylurian are getting people all over the world to return their copies of *The Chosen Ones* and giving them fifty pounds or whatever the equivalent is in their own currency. Some people have realised how much they want the copies of the book back and are asking for more money. They're basically paying whatever people ask – although don't tell your dad that bit.'

'But why are they doing it at all?'

'Because they're producing a limited-edition single volume copy of the book. Basically making it so there's only one copy left in the entire world.'

'Why would they want to do that?'

'Because there's a very rich man who is prepared to buy the last copy on Earth for a billion pounds. Albion Freake.'

'But . . .'

Whatever Effie was going to say was lost in a sudden urgent flapping and tapping on the window pane. Raven opened the window and a robin hopped in and landed on her hand. Raven soon developed a dreamy look, nodding and smiling, as if she were talking to the robin. Maybe she was. After another nod she gave the robin a little kiss, and then he hopped back onto the windowsill and flew away.

'How peculiar,' said Raven.

'What is it?'

'There's a boy lost on the moor.' Raven gulped. 'And apparently I know him. The Cosmic Web's a bit weak coming from the moor at this time of day, but when the robin heard it was someone connected with me . . .'

'Who is it?' said Effie. 'You don't think it could be . . .?'

'Maximilian!' said both girls together.

'We'll have to go and rescue him,' said Raven. 'Can you ride?'

'Yes,' Effie said immediately, without thinking. She didn't mean to lie. On some level she genuinely thought she *could* ride – so many of the books she'd read in the Otherworld featured heroes on horseback. And anyway, how hard could it be? She hurried after Raven, down one set of stairs and then the creaking spiral staircase that led into the main sitting room of the folly. There was still no sign of Laurel or Skylurian.

Raven threw together some supplies – Polo mints and sugar lumps for the horses; more cake for her and Effie and Maximilian. She wrapped the cake in foil and put it in her rucksack. Effie noticed that she also put in her wonde – the boon that Effie had given her just a few weeks ago when they had both epiphanised. It was a thin stick that had been cut from a particularly mystical hazel tree several centuries before.

Effie followed Raven to the boot room. There were so many old pairs of jodhpur boots, gloves and riding hats in there that it didn't take long for Raven to find everything Effie needed. It helped that Effie was the same shoe size as Laurel Wilde.

'Won't she mind?' Effie said, as Raven passed her a pair of her mother's beautiful but hardly worn brown leather boots.

'She hasn't got time to ride any more,' said Raven. 'She'll just be happy to know that Jet's been out.'

The girls both grabbed comfortable old waxed jackets from

130

the hooks by the door, and a saddle and bridle each (Effie just copied the way Raven held hers), and then went out into the cold evening.

Echo snorted gently into the still early evening air when he heard Raven's footsteps approaching. Poor Jet hadn't been ridden for days and was standing sadly in his stable, not really expecting anything good to happen. He certainly wasn't expecting . . . *Well.* Who was this child now opening his stable door? Jet had half a mind to kick her, but there was something about her that stopped him. She was . . . She was . . .

'Do you know how to tack-up?' asked Raven.

'No,' said Effie. 'But I'm sure I can try.'

Raven laughed. 'Ha ha! You're so funny. It takes years to learn to tack-up properly. And Jet likes it done a certain way anyway.'

Effie watched while Raven expertly put saddles and bridles on both horses. Effie didn't even know the names for half the things Raven was doing. Echo and Jet both stamped and pawed at the ground a couple of times and when one whinnied, the other followed, their hot breath almost freezing in the November air.

When Jet was ready, Raven led him over and held onto his reins.

'Well, on you get,' she said to Effie.

Effie looked at the large pony in front of her. Jet was black and shiny, with a strange glint in his eyes. She suddenly felt afraid. She didn't, in reality, even know how to get on a horse. He was so much bigger than she'd thought, and . . .

'Come on,' said Raven. 'We don't want Maximilian to get even more lost.'

'Sorry,' said Effie.

She approached Jet rather gingerly, but the big pony stood completely still while Effie slipped her foot into the stirrup and mounted him in one swift movement. It was easier than she'd thought. Raven handed Effie the reins.

'I know you've done this before,' said Raven. 'But just in case you've forgotten, you have to put your feet like this, and hold the reins like this, and . . .' She expertly adjusted Effie's legs and hands and changed the length of the stirrups so they were just right. And then, with a lot less fuss, she mounted Echo and trotted off down the narrow path in the direction of the bridleway onto the moor.

Effie didn't know what to do next. How did you get a horse to move? She remembered one riding lesson long ago with her primary school class. Was it that you kicked a horse to make it go, or did you pull the reins? What was it they did in the books? Effie tried a little experimental nudge with her legs and, to her surprise, Jet began walking forwards. It felt very peculiar being this high up, sitting on an animal who was moving underneath you in that odd side-to-side sort of way.

'Come on!' called Raven in front. 'Let's canter!'

Something – perhaps just hearing the word 'canter' – made Jet lurch from his stately walk into a sort of fast trot, with Effie clinging on with her knees and pulling at the reins, trying hard not to fall off.

'I say, old thing,' said a slow, deep voice in Effie's head. It was a refined, old-fashioned voice of a sort you might find in antique books. 'Would you mind not pulling so hard on my bit, please? It rather jars the teeth. There's a good sport.'

Effie immediately relaxed the reins a little. But where was this voice coming from? It couldn't be . . . Was it *Jet* who was speaking to her? But how? Effie wasn't a witch! Surely only witches could talk to animals!

'Sorry,' said Effie, with her mind.

'Thank you,' said Jet.

'But how am I going to stay on?' Effie asked. Now that she wasn't clinging to the reins so hard, it really did feel as if she might fall off at any moment.

'Hold my mane, of course. NOT LIKE THAT, beloved child. *Don't* pull. That's better. Good. Now, are you ready?'

'What for?'

'Oh, I can go a LOT faster than this.'

'Well—'

'Good. Let us *vamos*,' said Jet. 'You'll live, I'm sure. All true heroes know how to ride horses, I believe. It's in the literature.'

12

The bell tinkled as someone opened the door to Mrs Bottle's Bun Shop. It had been a quiet afternoon and Lexy was longing for something interesting to happen. They never got very much custom at Mrs Bottle's Bun Shop anyway and lately the café was being used more as a hang-out for local students than an actual portal. After all, no one knew exactly where the portal went, or how to get back. Among the epiphanised young of the city this made it rather cool. But of course no one cool went anywhere on a Tuesday.

'Hang on,' called Lexy's mother, Hazel, wiping her hands on a tea towel. She walked through to the front of the shop. 'Oh, it's you, Arnold.'

Arnold? But that was Mr Green's first name. Surely he couldn't be here, now, could he? Lexy put down the tonic she was working on – a deep red rosehip syrup – and peeked out of the kitchen. It *was* Mr Green! For some reason Lexy suddenly felt shy. She wanted to say hello, but found she couldn't. What if he didn't remember her? What if he *did*? She felt like she might die if he said anything to her at all.

So she went back into the kitchen and pretended to be working on her tonic. Everyone knows that rosehip syrup needs careful straining. Though Lexy promptly forgot that bit, with the result that her tonic now had lots of semi-poisonous hairs floating in it. Luckily she was just about to drop the whole thing on the floor, so it didn't really matter.

'Octavia's upstairs,' said Hazel to Mr Green, after they had exchanged a few words of small-talk. 'Go straight up. I think she's expecting you.'

Another date! It must be. As predicted, Lexy dropped the whole jar of rosehip syrup on the floor as she tried to get another look at Mr Green as he went through the door that led to Lexy's aunt Octavia's flat. He was dressed almost exactly as he had been the day before, in a brown lounge suit and sensible brown shoes. But, perhaps in honour of his date, today he was wearing a flamboyant turquoise silk shirt that so didn't go with the rest of his ensemble it almost did.

Lexy's aunt Octavia had never had much luck with men. Her first boyfriend had unfortunately turned out to be a vampire demon who had come into the bun shop supposedly looking for a way home to the Otherworld. Demons are, as everyone knows, usually projections of a person's unspoken fears or problems. This vampire represented a fear of commitment in an otherwise quite nice baker from a small Otherworld village. Octavia never got to meet the baker, but she certainly would never forget the demon.

Then there was the good-looking journalist from the *Gazette*, who, it turned out, only wanted to find out about portals and the Otherworld so that he could do an exposé. After that came the artist who was mainly interested in the light in Octavia's flat, and a young oboe player who kept inviting all of his musician friends round for silent discos, and eventually ran off with one of them.

As a result of all this, Octavia Bottle had completely given up men. But then Arnold had come along. Dear, sweet Arnold. Their eyes had met across the long wooden table at the most recent Old Town branch meeting of the Guild of Craftspeople. The subject had been the newly epiphanised children in the area, and what should be done about them. Octavia never had much to say at these meetings, but this time she had been able to describe the way the young Truelove girl, Euphemia, known as Effie, had wandered in that cold afternoon in October, bless her, with her bag of rare boons, not even knowing she'd just epiphanised.

Effie soon got used to the smooth, fast motion of the horse beneath her. She began to feel warm, and she realised this was partly because Jet himself was getting hot. Steam was coming off his sleek black flanks and through his big nostrils. As he gathered pace, Effie began to feel almost weightless, as if she were flying. Jet didn't say very much more to her, just the occasional 'Hold on!' or 'Watch out!' or – just once, when going through a small woodland glade – 'Duck!'

Riding a horse was the most exhilarating thing Effie had ever done. She could see why Raven liked it so much. The air was soft and cold, and every so often the sky lit up with another shooting star. The soundlessness of the moor was like nothing Effie had ever experienced – except perhaps in the Otherworld. The moor felt like the Otherworld in several other ways, too. It had the same calm, dreamy atmosphere of being very far away from everything else.

After about ten more minutes, Raven and Echo slowed. Effie pulled gently on Jet's reins and he slowed to a fast trot, a slow trot and then a walk. It was now quite dark and Effie couldn't see very much. There were shapes that looked a little like houses, although most of them without roofs.

'Where are we?' she called to Raven.

'We're quite near to Maximilian, I think,' Raven called back. 'I just need to find . . . *Aha*.'

In the dark, Effie could see three shapes coming out of one of the roofless houses. They looked like large floating cotton-wool balls, or very low, very small clouds. As they got closer, Effie could see that they were sheep. The fact they were *baaa*ing loudly also helped to identify them. They seemed to be *baaa*ing at Raven. They must have heard something through the Cosmic Web.

'They say your friend is just beyond here, over the river,' Jet translated for Effie.

'They say—' Raven began to tell Effie.

'Don't worry,' said Effie. 'Jet told me.'

'But how . . .?'

Effie shrugged. 'It turns out that true heroes can talk to horses. And ride them, too. Come on, let's go!'

Effie nudged Jet with her heels and he almost immediately broke into a canter, just like horses in old films about the Wild West. This time, Raven was the one following. The girls cantered past the ruined crofts – more roofless houses – to the edge of a river. It was low tide and the horses gratefully drank some water, then walked across.

'This is where I saw it,' Raven said to Effie, as their horses slowly crossed the river. 'Near here. There was a kind of . . . I don't know. Like something shimmering and mysterious in the air. I can't see it now that it's dark.'

'What do you think it was?'

'I don't know. But it's strange that Maximilian is somewhere nearby. I wonder how he got here. I wonder if there's a connection.'

'If he *is* still here.'

'He is. The sheep say he has been walking around in circles for the last two hours. I suppose mages don't really have that many outdoor survival skills.'

Effie couldn't help smiling in the darkness. 'I suppose not.'

'Come on. He must be around here somewhere.'

Before long Effie heard a whinnying, harrumphing sound that wasn't coming from Jet or Echo. They had come to a slope on which there were wild ponies grazing. One of them came up to the girls and started explaining where Maximilian was. Apparently he had tried to read the ponies' minds to find out how to survive in the wilderness. After that he had tried eating grass, been sick, fallen over, cursed all of nature and then cried.

The horses made their way carefully up an ancient track to the top of the hill. And there, shivering and alone, was Maximilian.

'Are you a mirage?' he asked, gloomily.

'Don't be silly. You get mirages in the desert, not on the moor,' said Raven.

'I thought I was going to die. Have you got any food?'

Raven took the cake out of her rucksack and gave it to Maximilian. He devoured it greedily, crumbs flying everywhere, all the while saying incomprehensible things about having been locked in a dungeon and having to escape and rescue his master. At some point he took out a small business card and waved it around, saying, 'What use is this in such a bleak wilderness?' While he was babbling away, Raven gave the horses sugar lumps and Polos.

'Right,' she said to Maximillian. 'Can you ride?'

'Of course not!' he said. 'I think it's become quite clear that I don't really *do* wilderness.'

'Well, we have to work out how to get you back. Do you think you could hold on to one of us while we—'

'Wait,' said Maximilian. 'Actually . . .' He looked at Raven quite intensely. 'Would you mind if I . . .' He stared into her eyes. 'Just there. I won't look at anything private, just the bits about . . . OK. Got it.'

'What did you just do?' said Raven, rubbing her head.

'Learned how to ride,' said Maximilian. 'I've sort of discovered how to take things like that from someone's mind. It's a long story. Thank you. But yes, now I can ride. I don't think I'm going to like it, but I can do it.'

'OK,' said Raven. 'You take Echo. Be kind to him. He doesn't like being kicked or pulled too much. I'll hold him while you get on.'

'What are you going to do?' Effie asked.

Raven smiled shyly. 'Well,' she said. 'There is something I've been meaning to try.'

She reached into her rucksack again and pulled out two thin sticks and what looked like a small dead shrub. She held them together in one hand, waved the other hand over them, and . . .

The pieces fell to the ground.

'Oh no,' she said. 'OK, Raven. Concentrate. Maybe if I try . . .'

She went through she same actions again, with the same result. Echo was pawing the ground and starting to get impatient. He wanted to *vamos*, ideally to where his oats, alfalfa and straw were. It was getting late. And he didn't like this lump on his back either. He smelled of culture and intellectuals. Echo didn't have much patience for such things. Should he try to throw him? Maybe not just yet.

Raven again put the three sticks together in her right hand. This time when she waved her left hand over them there was a little spark. Effie realised she'd seen someone else do something like this recently. The pieces had fused together to form . . .

'A broomstick!' said Effie.

'I wondered when I'd get the chance to try it out,' said Raven. 'It's not very impressive, I know – it was all I could afford, even putting two weeks' allowance together. Apparently it works best if you're in trouble and it feels sorry for you. I wonder . . .'

Raven got on the broomstick and it lifted into the air.

'OK,' she said. 'I already feel a bit sick, but . . . Let's go!'

Both horses heard their witch friend clearly saying *vamos*, albeit in English, and so they cantered away as fast as they could, following the broomstick through the cold evening until they were back in their stables again, each with a big bag of oats and alfalfa.

Maximilian and Effie followed Raven into the folly through the tack-room and the boot room and into the kitchen. And there, in a dark red dress with an apron over the top, was Skylurian Midzhar.

'What time do you call this?' said Skylurian to Raven. 'I've been worried sick. I see you've brought friends home for tea. You could have told me! Still, I'm sure there's enough smoked game pie for everyone. Hello, dear children. I don't believe we've met . . .'

'I think we have,' said Effie under her breath. The last time she had seen Skylurian Midzhar was when Effie had been battling the evil mage who had killed her grandfather. Leonard Levar had called on Skylurian Midzhar for help, and she had appeared, but had not in fact helped. It had been clear that she was a Diberi, though – part of a secret society of Book Eaters who planned to do something terrible to the universe – but on that night all she had done was ask Effie to join them. Effie and her friends knew that Skylurian Midzhar was up to no good, but had not yet had the chance to prove it.

'Where's my mum?' asked Raven.

'Book tour,' said Skylurian breezily. 'A sudden, unexpected, whirlwind book tour.'

'A book tour of where?'

'Oh, um . . .' Skylurian seemed to need to think about this. 'Bavaria, perhaps? Scandinavia? Somewhere with a "v" in it anyway.'

'When's she coming back?'

'Next week, I think. Maybe the week after. Still, I've agreed to babysit you in the meantime. What fun we shall have!'

Effie and Maximilian looked at each other. A chill went through the dark folly. It was the kind of place that could feel cosy one minute and horribly frightening the next. There were lots of stone passageways and strange paintings and things that made creaking sounds in the middle of the night. They couldn't leave their friend alone here with a Diberi. They would have to . . . Maximilian silently sent a message to both Effie and Raven with his mind.

'My friends are staying the night,' said Raven shakily. 'Can you please page their parents to let them know?'

'But of course, darling,' said Skylurian. 'And in that case I'll just whip up a blood-orange soufflé for pudding. And then maybe a jolly game of Hangman in front of the fire?'

'We've got homework,' said Maximilian.

It was true. They did have homework. They were supposed to be writing about travelling to other worlds to hand in to Mrs Beathag Hide first thing tomorrow. But Maximilian and Effie didn't even know that yet. And they had many more urgent things to talk about, like where exactly Maximilian had been.

Lexy crept up the stairs by the light of the moon that came in through a small window. If she was caught she'd just say she'd come up to see if they wanted . . . what? A cup of tea? But Mr Green had been carrying a bottle of wine. Grown-ups didn't drink tea in the evening anyway. They always complained that it made them want to pee all night and kept them awake. Um, maybe a potion? But why would they want a potion? A *love* potion, perhaps? Lexy blushed at her own thoughts. She didn't like to think of Mr Green being in love with her aunt Octavia. Of course, if he was, that meant she'd see more of him. But something about it seemed strange and embarrassing.

From inside the small flat, Lexy could hear the bright clinks of glassware and crockery. It sounded as if someone was laying the table.

'That's right, luvvie,' Octavia was saying. 'You sit yourself down. No, don't bother with that. I can finish laying up. I've invited you for dinner and so you're the guest. Let me give you a nice big glass of this lovely wine you've brought.' There was a dull popping noise, and then a *glugluglug* sound. 'There you are, my sweet. Cheers!' There was a crackle, and then some romantic music began playing quietly.

'Here's to us,' said Mr Green.

Lexy settled in for a long night of eavesdropping.

13

'*A* *helicopter*?' said Raven. 'In the school field? Really?'

'OK,' said Maximilian. 'We're not going to get very far if you say "a *helicopter*" like that every time one appears. Although, to be honest, there aren't any more actual helicopters, but there is a boat and a carriage and a castle and . . .'

'A *castle*?'

'Raven,' said Maximilian. 'I'm warning you. This is going to take all night if you keep interrupting me.'

'All right. Sorry. Go on.'

The three friends had finished their smoked game pie and blood-orange soufflé as quickly as they could and come upstairs to do their homework. Maximilian was going to be sleeping on a camp-bed in the keep because Skylurian had taken over the guest wing. Effie was going to top-and-tail with Raven. But for now they were all sitting on Raven's bed and Maximilian was telling his story.

It took quite a long time to get to the part where Maximilian and Franz were in the dungeon. And then it was quite complicated explaining how Maximilian had gone inside Franz's mind and learned some of the things he knew how to do, including that strange thing with music.

'Who was the man at the piano, do you think?' Raven asked.

'Was it a famous composer?' asked Effie.

'Probably,' said Maximilian. 'I'll do some research when I get home. Anyway, just after that I heard the guards coming and made myself disappear, just as I'd learned in Franz's mind.'

'Can you do it now?' asked Raven.

'No!' said Maximilian. 'I'm not wasting M-currency on a party trick. I'll do it next time we're in danger.'

'Maybe if Skylurian comes to murder you in the night?'

'Yes, if Skylurian comes to murder me in the night I'll call you and you can watch me disappear. Anyway, I became invisible and then slipped through this strange sort of corridor between the worlds until I came to where Franz was being held.'

'Is it the same thing?' Effie mused. 'Disappearing, and becoming invisible?'

'No,' said Maximilian. 'But it doesn't matter for the purposes of my story. Anyway, Franz and I were able to slip off to my uncle's cell but we were too late, because he had gone and—'

Raven gasped.

'What?' said Maximilian.

'Where had he gone?'

'I'm about to tell you that!'

Maximilian's story continued in the same fashion, with Raven interrupting him, and then him telling her off but, Effie thought, also rather enjoying being the centre of attention. Effie had borrowed one of Raven's nightdresses and felt a little like she was about to attend a glitzy party. All Raven's nightdresses were black and shiny and looked like long, expensive gowns. Maximilian was wearing a pair of old pyjamas that Raven said she thought may once have belonged to a poet and were covered in pink flamingos and red wine stains.

Maximilian told the girls about how he and Franz had crept through the castle, completely hidden in the space between the dimensions, until they'd found themselves in a room with two stylishly-dressed young men. Something about the conversation these men were having had made Franz stop and put his fingers to his lips.

'What were they saying?' asked Raven.

'They were spies,' said Maximilian. 'They'd been sent to find corrupt mages and bring them to the castle. The princess was a patron of the city's various magi – which means she was funding their gatherings. There had been this prophecy about a corrupt mage . . .'

'Lupoldus!' said Raven.

'Yes, exactly,' said Maximilian. 'It turned out that a few weeks before Lupoldus had chosen the wrong person to drain. Someone he'd thought was just a random poor person had in fact been a cousin of Elspeth's – the fortune teller from before. Unfortunately, he'd killed her. One of the spies said he thought Elspeth had probably cooked up the prophecy herself to get revenge on Lupoldus on behalf of her cousin. But in any case, no one wanted a corrupt mage around ruining everything. The princess was planning a magical attack on Napoleon's forces, and didn't want a weak link among her army of magi. And it turned out that Lupoldus wasn't even a real mage.'

'What do you think he actually was?' said Effie.

'What do you mean?' said Maximilian.

'Well, his *kharakter*. If he wasn't a mage.'

'We'll get to that,' he said, mysteriously.

'So what happened next?' asked Raven.

Maximilian described how he and Franz had carried on moving completely invisibly through the castle until they had come to the princess's drawing room.

'I wish you could have seen this room,' he said to the girls. 'It was amazing. It was painted a very, very dark sort of maroon colour – almost black. And the walls were covered in symbols and charts. There were globes and crystal balls and the rarest books you could imagine. Incense was burning and it was quite smoky. In the corner of the room there was a pianist playing quietly.'

'Where was Lupoldus?'

'On his knees in front of the princess, begging for his life.'

'Oh my God!' said Raven.

'What was the princess like?' asked Effie.

Maximilian tried his best to describe the imposing young woman he'd found holding a dagger to his uncle's throat, but he found it was impossible to do her justice. She'd been wearing a loose silk dress in midnight blue, over which was thrown a dark grey cloak with a repeating pattern of what Maximilian first thought were jellyfish, but then realised were probably flowers.

The cloak was tied with a silk ribbon around her neck. Her dark curls fell to her shoulders.

As the memories replayed in Maximilian's head, he translated them as best he could for Effie and Raven.

'Napoleon is coming,' the princess was saying, in Maximilian's memory. 'And you have betrayed us all. You told him where he could find the city's mages and their patron, didn't you?'

'I, uh . . .'

Franz stepped forward out of his intra-dimensional hiding place, and became visible again.

'Is this true?' he asked Lupoldus.

'Of course not! Where have you been? I command you to release me from the clutches of this evil—'

'You!' said the princess, when she saw Franz.

'Anna?' said Franz. 'But . . . I thought the princess had come from, from . . . *Paris*.'

'You did not know I had gone to Paris? I tried my best to send word. No matter. Hush and tell me how you know this scoundrel,' said the princess.

'But you . . . How did you . . .?' said Franz.

'Please answer me first,' said the princess. 'We may not have much more time.'

'Lupoldus is my master,' said Franz. 'After you left, I couldn't go on in the place that so reminded me of you, so—'

'And is there any particular reason I should not execute him?' said the princess.

Franz seemed to think very hard. He screwed up his face this way and then that way, tipping it sideways like animals do when they are trying very hard to hear something. It was as if Franz was trying very hard to hear a voice in the ether that might remind him of any of Lupoldus's redeeming features. The voice was clearly not forthcoming. The princess drew back the dagger, ready to plunge it into . . .

As Maximilian described the look of fear in Lupoldus's eyes, Raven gulped.

'I don't like the violent bits,' she said. 'Get it over with.'

'It's all right,' said Maximilian. 'I saved him.'

'You? Why?'

'Because he was my uncle. Or I thought he was.'

'Wasn't he?' said Effie. 'Oh, I see what you mean. He was only your uncle in the story. That's a shame. Well, sort of.'

'What story?' said Raven. 'Anyway, how did you rescue him?'

'I used mind control on the princess. I sort of stimulated the parts of her brain that believed in kindness and goodness and in the end she couldn't bring herself to kill Lupoldus.'

'But wasn't she way too strong for that?' said Effie. 'She sounded much stronger even than Franz. I mean, surely she would have blocked off her mind?'

'I only managed it for a second,' said Maximilian. 'Just long enough for her to put down the dagger and remember how much she loved Franz. While the two of them embraced I grabbed my uncle and took him into the hidden realm. We made a run for it, although he wasn't really used to exertion, and he soon used up the energy he'd taken from the poor. He was sort of heaving and puffing all over the place, and I almost wished I hadn't rescued him, but it was too late.'

'I suppose you probably had to rescue him for the story to work,' mused Effie.

'What are you talking about?' said Raven. 'Why do you keep talking about "the story" like that?'

'Because it is a story,' said Effie.

'What do you mean?' said Raven, looking truly baffled.

'Do you think Maximilian's really been to actual Napoleonic Europe?' said Effie, laughing. 'He's been in a book, silly. He was obviously its Last Reader. Like when I read *Dragon's Green*.'

'How was I supposed to know that?' said Raven. 'And anyway, the helicopter really came this morning – I heard it. And how did Maximilian get to the moors?'

'The book must have thrown him out near a portal. That must have been what you saw on the moors, as well. What did you call it? Shimmering and mysterious? That sounds a lot like a portal to me.'

'I thought portals had to be in coffee shops and stuff?'

'Only the ones the Guild controls,' said Effie. 'The one I use to come back from the Otherworld is just like you describe.'

'Wow,' said Raven. 'So . . .'

'Does no one at all care even the slightest bit about how the story ends?' said Maximilian, huffily.

'Sorry,' said Effie. 'Of course we care.'

'I'm desperate to know!' said Raven. 'Go on, please.'

'After we'd been moving through the hidden realm for a while, my uncle begged me to leave him behind. "You go on, boy," he said to me. "Leave me. My time is up. All the mages will now

150

know that I am an imposter. At best a joke and at worst a traitor. They'll kill me.'"

'Poor Lupoldus,' said Raven.

'Have you forgotten about him draining the weak?' said Effie.

'People can change,' said Raven.

Maximilian cleared his throat dramatically, waited for the girls to shut up and then went on with the end of the story. There was quite a good bit coming up next in which Lupoldus was going to apologise to Maximilian for being such a disappointment.

'I was born a lowly trickster,' Lupoldus was saying, in Maximilian's memory. 'But I longed to be a mage, with a mage's power. Tricksters can use the power of others, so as long as I had a powerful mage in my employ, then . . .'

Just then there had been a loud bang, and the hidden realm had seemed to disappear. Maximilian had tried to slip back into it, but it was no good. He and his uncle were now exposed. They were still in the castle grounds, but outside in a very elaborate garden, with more of the singing statues and several complex mazes and labyrinths. Maximilian and Lupoldus were standing by the entrance to one of the mazes.

Then came the sound of explosions and horses and men's cries.

'Napoleon,' said Lupoldus. 'They were right. I did tip him off.'

'But why?' said Maximilian.

'If all the mages in the city were wiped out, then perhaps I wouldn't have to be ashamed any more.' He shrugged. 'I don't know. Maybe I haven't got a reason. Tricksters don't always have them. We're unpredictable, you see.'

'OK. Well . . .'

'You need to go back to Franz. He'll save you. Leave me here to wander the maze. No one will bother entering a maze to get rid of one man. I'll probably endure. Evil tends to.'

'I don't think you're evil,' said Maximilian. 'Maybe you just had a bad childhood, or . . . Which reminds me. I really wanted to ask you something important. Do you know who my father is? Is he still alive?'

But Lupoldus had already gone. Maximilian couldn't follow him into the maze, not if he truly wanted to save himself. It was too much of a risk. He had to get back to Franz, and the princess. There was another explosion. Maximilian fell to the ground. The maze was now on fire. Would that be the end of Lupoldus? Perhaps not. He'd probably find some way to get out of it. Maximilian coughed. He wasn't sure he could get up. Maybe this was the end. Maybe . . .

'I can't bear it,' said Raven. 'Tell us what happened!'

'I'm trying,' he protested.

Maximilian went on with his story. The next thing he knew he was being helped up by a surprisingly strong child whom he half-recognised. It was the boy who had assisted Elspeth, the fortune teller, before. And suddenly there was Elspeth, too, beckoning Maximilian to follow her.

'Greetings, great mage,' she said to him. 'Come. We must hurry.'

Maximilian followed the fortune teller and the boy down a short flight of stairs. He worried for a moment that he was simply being taken back to the dungeons. But instead they ended up in a secret passage that led back to the room next to the princess's drawing room. Maximilian could hear voices and then a sudden hush. What was happening? There was music coming from somewhere.

Maximilian entered the drawing room and was greeted with an extremely peculiar sight. While explosions raged outside, with Napoleon obviously getting closer, and his army probably entering the castle, a room full of mages stood still, listening to the pianist as he played. Franz noticed Maximilian come into the room and winked at him. Maximilian recognised the melody the pianist was playing. And suddenly he realised what they were all going to do.

Some of the mages were clearly better at it than others. One by one they simply disappeared into the music. It was like a room full of bubbles that had started to burst. Maximilian still didn't quite know how he should do it. He remembered the running jump that Franz had taken, but didn't know how, or when or . . .

Pop, pop, pop, went the mages in the room.

Soon Maximilian, Franz and the princess were the only ones left. Then, after another flurry of notes, the princess disappeared.

'You have to pick the moment that moves you most,' said Franz. 'And then you will be *literally* moved. For example . . .'

A dreamy look came over his face. The pianist started down the steps that Maximilian remembered from before. It was a truly beautiful passage of music and . . .

Suddenly Maximilian was alone. Franz had gone. Maximilian had no idea where he'd gone to, but he knew he had to go there as well.

'You'd better get a move on,' said the pianist. 'And then I can play myself out before the army arrives.'

'But I don't understand,' said Maximilian.

'Feel the music,' said the pianist. 'Let it enter you, and then you will find you can enter it.'

'But . . .'

'You must hurry.'

Maximilian screwed up his face and tried his hardest to feel the music. But it wasn't easy. He realised he was frightened, and his fear made it impossible to concentrate.

'Try to relax,' said the pianist. 'Let the music be the only thing apart from you in the whole world.'

The pianist then closed his eyes and seemed to throw himself into the music with renewed gusto. Maximilian knew that if he didn't hurry the pianist would go too and he would be left here with the approaching army and no hope of escape. Would they kill him immediately or torture him first? But this was no way to relax. This was—

'That's exactly how I felt!' said Raven.

'What? When?' said Effie.

'Just after I'd epiphanised properly. With the spiders. When I had to learn to talk to them.'

'Oh yes, of course . . .'

'Ahem,' said Maximilian. 'If you *don't* mind . . .'

'Sorry. Go on. What happened? Did you do it?'

'What do you think? Of course I did it, or I wouldn't be here now.'

'It's actually very dangerous being a Last Reader,' said Effie.

'So many things can go wrong. You can end up stuck in a book for ever, and—'

'*Anyway . . .*' said Maximilian.

He described again how afraid he was of the approaching army. Would he be shot or bayonetted? Would he bleed a lot? Perhaps they'd leave him alone to bleed to death for days and days and . . .

'Stop it!' said Raven. 'You're only doing that because I interrupted you.'

'Well, don't do it, then.'

'All right, but please, no more blood.'

Back in the story, Maximilian tried to put all the horrible images out of his mind as he listened to the music coming from the piano.

The pianist had reached the stepping stones again. Maximilian took a deep breath, relaxed and sort of mentally stepped onto one of them, and downdowndown they went and also, bizarrely, upupup. And then . . .

Ping. One C minor chord to signal the start of the hurling waves and the great storm and then . . .

And then Maximilian, having abandoned himself completely to the music, was thrown out of the world he was in and through the hidden realm and – BANG – the music came tumbling over and over him in a great torrent and he was falling, falling, falling until . . .

'I found myself on the moors,' he said. 'Back in this world, in complete silence, holding this.' He pulled the slim silver business card from his pocket. On it there was simply one word, printed in turquoise foil. *Pathétique*. There was no further explanation.

'The end,' said Maximilian.

That hadn't been the end, though, not quite. There was the bit that he hadn't told his friends. As he was falling, Maximilian had sensed a sort of fork in an invisible road – if you can fall down a road. In the distance he could see Franz and Anna and the other mages also falling, like a strange dark snowstorm, towards a place he realised he recognised. It was the entrance to the Underworld, the place Maximilian had been trying to get back to ever since his previous experience of (almost) being a Last Reader. There was the little cottage, and the river, and . . .

He couldn't get there. Not this time. He couldn't change to that fork in the road. The book was ejecting him, his part in it complete. But he sensed that if only he could find the piece of music again and listen to it in this world, then perhaps he would be able to jump again, and find himself back on the path to the place he most wanted to visit. A place where – as Maximilian had once been told by the arch-villain Leonard Levar – only dark mages can go.

Maximilian was still a bit worried about what it meant to be a 'dark' mage. Did that mean he was evil? He hoped not. He didn't feel evil. And he had just saved someone's life, after all, even though it was only in a story. But he'd never told his friends about what Leonard Levar had said just in case they never trusted him again afterwards.

The girls were looking at the business card.

'What does it mean?' said Raven.

'It's definitely a boon,' said Effie. 'I got one when I finished my Last Reader experience, along with a lot of M-currency and all the skills I learned on my adventure. It must do something amazing. I wonder what.' She turned it over once in her fingers and then gave it to Raven to look at.

'What does your boon do?' said Raven to Effie, reaching for the card.

'Lets me go to visit the Otherworld whenever I want without using a portal,' said Effie. 'And go directly to the place where my cousins are. It's impossible to get to otherwise.' As she said this she felt a horrible pang. Why had she been so stupid? Effie couldn't believe that she'd actually lost the card, her most precious possession. But she couldn't let her friends see how upset she was.

'I wonder what this one does,' said Raven, stroking the silver card once before giving it back to Maximilian.

'Have you tried the spectacles on it?' said Effie to Maximilian. The Spectacles of Knowledge usually knew about everything.

'I think they're still in Griffin's Library in my school bag,' said Maximilian. 'I won't be able to get them back before tomorrow. That is, unless they went into the book with me.' He frowned. 'But in that case wouldn't they have come out? Can you lose things inside a book? It wouldn't make any sense.'

Effie would normally have a response to this. She was the expert in being a Last Reader after all. But she'd suddenly gone very quiet and closed her eyes. It was almost as if she was meditating.

'Effie?' said Maximilian.

She held up a hand to indicate that she was thinking. Raven and Maximilian looked at each other and shrugged. They waited. And waited.

Then, after several more moments, Effie opened her eyes.

'I know what she's up to,' Effie said. 'I completely understand.'

'What? Who?' said Raven.

'Skylurian Midzhar,' said Effie. 'I know exactly what she's planning.'

14

'Did someone mention my name?' came a mellifluous voice, as it entered the room slightly ahead of its owner. 'Skylurian!' said Raven. 'Um . . . Hello.'

Skylurian's taste in nightdresses was even more extravagant than Raven's. The one she was wearing now was made of real silk, had a ruffled collar that went all the way up her neck, and came with a matching dressing gown bordered with real fur and feathers. The whole ensemble was bright red. Except for the fur and feathers, which were black. On her feet she wore black slippers made from some curiously familiar substance that reminded Raven of something.

Oh yes. It had been in that exhibition Mrs Beathag Hide had taken them to at the Writers' Museum. A tiny pair of black shoes made partly from hair. Raven had learned that one of the Bronte sisters had mended her shoes with the hair of her dead sisters, which she'd found quite poetic, but also a little bit disgusting. Skylurian's slippers looked almost exactly like those Bronte shoes, except the toes were pointed and they had kitten heels, and the hair – if that's what it was – looked a bit fresher.

'What naughty children you are,' she said. 'I expect you're up so late working on your homework, so I will forgive you. Haven't you got an author visit tomorrow? I believe you are going to be talking about travelling to other worlds. I do hope you've done a good job, darlings. I know how much dear Terrence is looking forward to reading your little offerings. He mentioned that he might even use the best one as the basis for his new book, and give the winning child some of his royalties. Anyway, lights off, darlings.'

She swept out of the room.

'You'd better tell us in the morning,' Raven whispered to Effie.

'And we'll have to do this stupid homework on the bus,' said Maximilian.

There was a horrible slurping sound coming from Octavia's flat that Lexy hoped was all to do with eating pudding and nothing to do with – perish the thought – kissing.

She knew she shouldn't still be there. In fact, she was considering leaving. She still hadn't done her homework for Mrs Beathag Hide, for one thing. And she had to finish her rosehip syrup, and also start making a medicine bundle to keep Effie safe. At this rate she was going to be up all night.

And her eavesdropping hadn't even been particularly interesting. Mr Green had complimented Octavia on her cooking, and her choice of wine, and her dress. He had somehow spent a large portion of the evening telling her about a football match he'd listened to on the radio, and another long period talking about all the best car parks in the city. Octavia had asked Mr Green what his favourite colour was, and whether he preferred cats or dogs.

But then, after the slurping, they had started talking about Effie.

'I was very intrigued,' said Mr Green, 'by the story of the Truelove girl you told at the Guild meeting. I wonder whether you might tell it to me again?'

Octavia started telling Mr Green all about the day Effie had come into the shop, having just learned her grandfather had died. She had asked all about magic and epiphanisation and the meaning of all the objects she had inherited and . . .

'You tell the story so well,' interrupted Mr Green. 'One might almost think you were a bard. And remind me, what were these items?'

'Well, the ring, of course, like I said before, and a crystal, and some kind of wonde, I think. She also mentioned a set of Spectacles of Knowledge, and a warrior's sword of some sort, but she'd already given these away to her friends.'

'And what happened to the crystal and the wonde?'

'The wonde went to a young witch from Effie's school,' said Octavia. 'And the crystal, well, she gave that to our Lexy – Alexa. I think you know her from your class? Very keen, she is. Very bright. Going to be a wonderful little healer.'

Lexy began to glow. There is, after all, almost nothing more pleasurable than overhearing oneself being praised. Was this at last the part of the evening when they would talk about Lexy, and her great promise, and her hard work and diligence? Perhaps Mr Green would offer to teach her special advanced classes, maybe even take her on as an Apprentice. Lexy began to fantasise about Mr Green revealing himself to be a true healer, just like Lexy. She imagined long nights with their heads bent together over dried twigs and herbal tea blends, forgetting the time, forgetting—

'And this Truelove child,' said Mr Green. 'Did she seem troublesome to you?'

'What, Effie? Oh no. Ever so kind, she is. I hear she turned out to be a true hero—'

'But that would make her boon the Ring of the True Hero?'

'I suppose so. Yes. She has taken to wearing it. So I suppose—'

'Does she have any idea how rare it is?'

'I don't know,' said Octavia.

'And she wears it all the time, you say?'

'Well, yes. Oh, except for competitive sports. She believes it gives her an unfair advantage. She was talking to our Lexy about it just the other day. But why are you so interested in the ring?'

'I'm not really very interested at all,' said Mr Green, huffily. 'Not in the slightest. Wherever did you get that idea? I enjoyed hearing your story, that's all. It's always heart-warming when a child epiphanises. I simply wanted all the details.' There was the sound of a chair scraping. 'Well, anyway. I must get on.'

'But,' said Octavia hastily, 'wouldn't you like a cup of coffee? I've got some after-dinner mints. And we could play that record again, the one you liked so much . . .'

Suddenly, the voices were right by the door. Lexy scrambled down the stairs as quickly as she could. She only just made it back into the bun shop before the door opened and Mr Green came down the stairs.

'So, *now* will you tell us?' said Raven.

It was not quite eight-thirty in the morning and very cold, dark and mostly quiet in the basement of the school. The only sounds came from the heating system, which kept making pathetic gurgling noises and occasionally managed a great metallic heave. It was all to no avail. The big enamel radiator was still freezing.

Effie, Maximilian, Wolf, Lexy and Raven were shivering together under the same large, woollen, slightly scratchy blanket that someone had helpfully left in Griffin's Library. It was impossible to tell how long it had been there. Like everything else in the school it was likely decades old, possibly centuries. Still, the children were grateful for it. There had been a greyout overnight which had taken out the whole school heating system.

'Yes,' said Effie. 'But surely you can all guess?'

She, Raven and Maximilian had been filling in Lexy and Wolf on what had happened the previous day, including finding Maximilian on the moor, and his whole Last Reader adventure. This had taken quite a long time. Then Effie had said again that she knew exactly what Skylurian was up to.

'Just tell us,' said Wolf.

'Please!' said Raven.

'All right. Well, what do we know about last editions of books?'

'If you read one, you become its Last Reader and actually go into the book and live it,' said Raven.

'And come out with boons and stuff,' said Wolf.

'And lots of M-currency,' said Maximillian. He paused and frowned. 'Oh. *Aha*. I see now.'

'See what?' said Lexy, yawning. She'd only got about an hour's sleep in the end, and had been forced to do her homework by candlelight because the greyout had started pretty much the minute she'd opened her rough work book.

'Skylurian Midzhar is busy right now turning *The Chosen Ones* into a last edition,' said Effie. 'She's destroying every other copy of the book in the entire world – except for this "limited-edition single volume" she's creating for Albion Freake, who must be another Diberi – a Book Eater. Presumably, Albion Freake plans to become the Last Reader of *The Chosen Ones* – by consuming and then destroying the last copy of the book. Someone told me that the more people have read and loved a book, the more power it stores up. There can't be many more powerful books than *The Chosen Ones*. If Albion Freake reads the last edition of it, he'll become so powerful he'll be able to do almost anything.'

'What's Skylurian going to get out of it?' asked Wolf.

'A billion pounds, for a start,' said Raven.

Effie frowned. 'It's a good question. There must be something else. She's already rich.' She shook her head. 'I don't know. There's something I'm not seeing, but I'm not sure what it could be.'

After Effie's experience in the Edgelands market she had made a vow to herself never to take anything else at face value. There was more to this – more to everything – than met the eye. She just had to make sure she always worked out what it was. But she was not going to be duped or fooled ever again. Something about holding the caduceus the day before had made her feel this strongly. She was more determined than ever to know the true meaning of things. She also yearned to see – and hold – the magical staff one more time in order to understand properly why it made her feel this way. She had no idea how she would do this.

'I'm going to find out all I can about Albion Freake,' said Maximilian. 'See what he might be planning to do with all that power.' This, Maximilian thought, would almost certainly need to involve a trip to the Underworld, a place where he sensed all the best secret knowledge was kept. All he had to do was work out how to get there. He probably just needed a pianist, and . . . Maximilian looked at the bookshelves, full of Griffin Truelove's old hardback last editions, and realised he was troubled by something. But he pushed it to the back of his mind for now.

'I'll start working on battle plans for how to stop him,' said Wolf. 'The best thing would be to stop this limited-edition single volume being created at all. But I'll create a back-up plan in case we can't.'

'Great,' said Effie. 'And I'm going to the Otherworld to see what my cousins know, and if Cosmo has any advice. I'll go straight after school. I still think the *Sterran Guandré* has

165

something to do with this, but I'm not sure what. Apparently it peaks on Friday.'

When Effie said the word 'Friday', Raven and Wolf exchanged a worried look. Lexy would have looked concerned too, had she not been almost asleep. Wolf nudged her awake.

'What?' she said, drowsily. 'Where am I?'

'You were just saying what you're going to do to help stop Albion Freake,' said Maximilian.

'Oh yes. I'll make some medicine bundles,' she said, and then fell asleep again. She knew vaguely she had something to tell Effie, but she felt a bit too tired to remember just now. It was so warm and comfortable under this blanket and . . . She could tell Effie later whatever it was. She was sure it had seemed important last night.

'And Raven?' said Effie.

But Raven also had her eyes closed. She seemed to be listening very hard to something.

'Raven? What's happening?'

She opened her eyes. 'It's the Cosmic Web,' she said. 'But . . .'

'What is it? Something about Albion Freake?' said Wolf. 'Or . . .?' He couldn't say *Effie*. He couldn't let her know how frightened he was in case it made it worse somehow. But inside he desperately hoped the Cosmic Web was saying that Effie was now safe, that Raven's spell had worked, that everything was going to be OK on Friday.

'No,' said Raven. 'Something about . . . about my mother. I can hear the mice chattering under the floorboards and they keep

166

saying something about the "red-haired one who writes of fictional magic", which is what they always call her. But I can't work out exactly what they're saying. And now they're chattering about the shooting stars again.'

'Do you think your mum knows about Skylurian's plans?' Effie asked.

Raven looked sad. 'Do you mean do I think my mother is secretly a Diberi?' she said.

'No,' said Effie, touching her friend's arm. 'I didn't mean it like that at all. I only meant—'

'It's all right,' said Raven. 'It's not like I haven't wondered. I mean, all the time she spends with Skylurian Midzhar can't be healthy. And I always thought there was something suspicious about this limited-edition single-volume plan. But then Skylurian *is* Mum's publisher. Mum has to do what she says. And Skylurian keeps going on about all the money they'll make from Albion Freake. My mum stands to get quite a lot. I think she's planning to give some of it to charity . . .'

And use the rest to fund the lavish lifestyle to which she and Raven had been becoming so accustomed. Unlimited accounts at all the best shops in the Old Town, new clothes whenever they both liked, including hand-made silk gowns, antique night-dresses, and the vast cashmere shawls Laurel loved so much. The tasteful dinner parties, staffed by faithful members of the village and attended by the most important publishing people in the whole North. The vintage champagne, the elegant live music, the magical supplies for Raven that would soon become unlimited . . .

167

'She means well,' said Raven. 'But she does love money and nice things. So she does whatever Skylurian tells her. But she's not bad. Not really.'

'I don't think she's bad,' said Effie. 'Not at all.'

'I just wonder where on earth she is,' said Raven.

'We'll find out,' said Wolf. 'Don't worry.'

Effie breathed in more air than she meant to and then found herself sighing out deeply. She'd last seen her own mother on the night of the worldquake five years before. According to Effie's father, Aurelia Truelove had died that night. But Effie still wasn't sure. Her mother had travelled to the Otherworld and then . . .

Whenever Effie tried to ask Cosmo about it he said she would find out when the time was right. Effie knew she had to be patient and strong, but sometimes it was hard. She would give anything for just one more chance to hear her mother say her name or kiss her goodnight. Sometimes Effie dreamed of her mother. These were always sad dreams, because they always ended with the worldquake and Effie waking up to find her mother gone.

Effie remembered her father telling Aurelia off for 'smothering' her daughter. 'Let her grow up,' he'd said. 'Learn to stand on her own two feet.' Effie had only been six at the time. But soon she had no choice but to learn to cope by herself. After Aurelia had gone Effie had felt more alone than anyone in the world. Until, that is, her grandfather had started looking after her. But that had just been on school days. Effie's weekends were long, sad and cold. If she felt hungry, she had to make her own soup. If she felt bored, all she could do was daydream. Effie loved reading, but all the interesting books had always been at her grandfather's place. Effie's father's books were all in different languages and kept on high shelves in his study.

By the time the bell rang for the first period, Effie and her friends had grown completely silent. Effie was still thinking about her mother, Lexy was fast asleep, Raven was listening to the mice, Maximilian was wondering about where he would find a pianist, and Wolf was dreaming of a perfect battle set-up that was sort of based on a wide-wide attack drill from rugby. If it came to it, he would find a way of protecting Effie on Friday. The bell made them all jump and scramble out from under the blanket clutching their rough work books ready to hand in to the staff room on the way to double history.

15

Terrence Deer-Hart was having a flipping good day. He didn't usually find himself enjoying his role of bestselling author; certainly not as much as some might have imagined he would. The life of a bestselling author is actually much flipping harder than most people think. For one thing, you have to write a lot of books. You have to sit there and come up with story after story after story. For some people – natural storytellers and bards in particular – those weirdoes – this would be a dream come true, of course, but not for Terrence.

He simply loathed the sight of the empty page that greeted him every morning. He hated the cold shaft of his expensive fountain pen. He rather felt that, having written so flipping many of them, he now even detested words. Well, except for the ones you weren't allowed to say. He despised the children who read his books only a little less than he despised the children – usually the unpopular goody-goodies – who did not read them, usually because they were "not allowed".

But things had recently taken a strange turn, and so Terrence was feeling something unfamiliar. What was it called? Oh yes. *Love*. And hope. And excitement. So many flipping feelings all at once! And all because of that beautiful, delightful, gorgeous, talented – and, let's face it, also impressively merciless and evil – woman: Skylurian Midzhar. Terrence's one true love and heart's desire.

The thing any author hates more than anything in the world is, as everyone knows, other authors. So imagine Terrence's delight and surprise when his publisher had asked for his help to kidnap his main rival! Flipping Laurel Wilde!

She loved *him* the most. That's what Skylurian had said. She loved *his* books the best! His books were flipping marvellous. What's more, Skylurian had explained to him that she had been systematically destroying Laurel Wilde's books! What sweet words these were for any author to hear. The pulping of the work of your main rival. It was almost enough to make one glad to be alive.

They had gone for a late lunch in a dark and cosy little pub that Skylurian knew, right on the edge of the moor. Poor old Laurel Wilde was tied up in the boot of the car. That would flipping well serve her right for outselling Terrence for all these years!

Terrence and Skylurian ate prawn cocktails by the fireside, gazing into one another's eyes. And that was when she'd told him her whole plan. Flipping heck! He had been, as they say, gobsmacked. It had been a little hard to take in at first, especially while trying not to get Marie Rose sauce down his jumper. But, if he'd heard her correctly, Skylurian – his one true love – wanted him to use his next author visit to infiltrate the world of the children. Like the Pied Piper, she'd said, but better.

'We are heading for a place called Dragon's Green, my sweet,' Skylurian had purred, while picking bits of iceberg lettuce out of Terrence's hair. 'You have to follow the child called Euphemia Truelove. She goes by the name Effie. Do whatever it takes to get the information from her. She is the only one who knows how to get there. Perhaps she has a device to help her? You must discover what it is. We are planning a big invasion, my pickled gherkin. How would you like to be the queen's consort in a brave new universe? How would you care to be the plus-one of doom?'

She had giggled then, and it was a cold, harsh noise, like a stalactite falling in a remote cave and shattering into a million icy pieces.

Terrence had never been called a pickled gherkin before. No one had ever offered him the chance to be the plus-one of doom. What could he say? He had longed to join the Diberi for years, and now here was one of their leaders promising him – quite literally – the world. All he had to do was find out how to get to Dragon's Green. How hard could that be? And then, Skylurian had promised him, he would never have to write another flipping children's book ever again. He would instead, she assured him, be writing the most important book in the entire universe.

Which is not too much for an author to expect, surely?

172

'I do believe,' said Mrs Beathag Hide, sourly, 'that not only are you all here, you are all here ON TIME.'

The children watched her in silence as a half-smile played over her lips and then vanished.

'Perhaps we should have an AUTHOR VISIT every day?' she suggested, sarcastically. 'Though I really wonder what one could ever learn from such a creature.' She sighed. 'Now if it were TOLSTOY or SHAKESPEARE or SOPHOCLES it would be different. Remember, children, that the only good authors in this world are long dead.' She stood up. 'Right. Brace yourselves, then, class. I am about to go and fetch him from the staff room. If even ONE of you moves the tiniest bit while I am away, the author visit will be CANCELLED and whoever causes this disappointment will no doubt be DESPISED for the rest of his or her school days.'

She left the room. The children looked at one another but did not move. They were too frightened. And excited. And nervous. What on earth would a real author look like? They'd barely had a chance to conjure up pictures of tall men in monocles and sleek women who own their own leopards and live in a zoo, when the door opened and . . .

There he was.

He was, well, not as tall as they may have hoped. He seemed to have fallen victim to the craze for turquoise shirts that was currently sweeping the city. His hair was a little too long and his trousers a little too short. Those in the front row noticed that he smelled strongly of aftershave, cigarettes and cocktail onions. Even some of the children in the second row noticed it.

Mrs Beathag Hide sat down behind her desk. Terrence Deer-Hart remained standing. He didn't look particularly comfortable.

'WELL,' said Mrs Beathag Hide, 'I expect you are here to persuade us to buy your books. That, surely, is the purpose of an author visit?'

'Um,' said Terrence Deer-Hart. 'Well, yes, it is always nice if one manages to shift some, uh, units, but that is not in fact the purpose of this morning's visit.'

'To WHAT, then, do we owe the pleasure?'

'I am looking for a collaborator,' said Terrence. 'A child collaborator.'

'And you have passed the necessary BACKGROUND tests?'

'What on earth do you mean? Oh, yes, of course. Of course.'

'We do like to keep the children safe, Mr Dark Heart.'

'Deer-Hart.'

'As you wish. Well?'

'Well what?'

The children were not sure who to admire more, Mrs Beathag Hide, for speaking that way to a world-renowned author, or the author himself for not being at all frightened of her.

Mrs Beathag Hide glanced at her watch.

'Well, on with the visit!'

'Good morning, children,' said Terrence.

'Good morning, Mr Deer-Hart,' they chorused back. Terrence looked quite surprised by this, as if he hadn't known that the first thing all children learn when they go to school is to start chanting at anyone who wishes them a good morning. But then Terrence's previous author visits had been to sad little schools

174

like Mrs Joyful's where the children were so pathetically grateful when anything nice happened to them that they could barely speak.

'I have been reading your work,' said Terrence. He paused to see if they would chant his own words back at him again. They did not. 'It is very good. Very good indeed. But before we declare the winner, perhaps some of you have questions about what it's like to be an author?'

All at once the questions began.

'Have you ever seen an alligator?'

'Have you ever been rescued from a fire?'

'Can you drive?'

'Have you ever met a spy?'

And so on.

'Do none of you have questions about any of my books?' he asked.

'If you'd wanted them to ask questions about your books, you should have told them,' said Mrs Beathag Hide. 'They are a very obedient class, and so did as you wished and asked about being an author. In any case, I expect most of them will not have been allowed to read your books. Which one do you particularly recommend?'

'*Children of Winter* got rather good reviews.'

'And what is it about?'

'Well, there's been a nuclear war and—'

'How GHASTLY,' said Mrs Beathag Hide. 'Have you written any good tragedies?'

'You could try *The Last Child*,' said Terrence. 'It's extremely

175

sad. It's about a boy whose parents die in a horrible accident and—'

'NO!' said Mrs Beathag Hide. 'That is not real tragedy. Tragedy is UPLIFTING.'

'Um, well, then how about *Scarecrow*? It's about a boy who is bullied and then . . .' Terrence and the class waited for Mrs Beathag Hide to declare this "ghastly" as well. She did not. Well, not out loud. Instead she made the kind of face you might make if someone had just dropped a stink bomb at your feet.

Terrence talked for a while about *Scarecrow*, in which the unfortunate boy dresses up as a scarecrow and hides in a field so as to escape being beaten up by the bullies. He ends up befriending the scarecrows, who teach him the value of true friendship. Objectively, it was the most original and moving of all Terrence's books, although it had sold the least amount of copies.

'It sounds exceedingly sentimental and trite,' said Mrs Beathag Hide. 'Still, if you genuinely recommend it as your most uplifting book, we shall all rush out and buy it immediately, won't we class?'

'Yes, Mrs Hide,' chanted the class.

'And now,' said Mrs Beathag Hide. 'ON with the visit. You have some feedback for the children on their CREATIVE WRITING, I believe?'

'Indeed,' said Terrence. 'I was very impressed with the standard.'

The class began to glow, rather as Lexy had done the night before. The glow was slightly warming, which was a good thing,

176

given that the heating was still not working. Surely if Terrence Deer-Hart approved of their creative writing they'd be allowed to do more of it?

'Such imagination!' Terrence went on. 'But now it is time for the announcement of the name of the child I am choosing to be my unique collaborator. The child who submitted the best entry for this competition is . . .'

The class took a deep breath.

'Euphemia Truelove!'

Everyone clapped. Effie was astonished. Her entry had, she knew, been extremely poor. For one thing, she'd written it on the bus from Raven's village that morning. It had been scrawled in her very worst handwriting. She knew she'd made a number of spelling errors, but her dictionary had been at home and so she hadn't checked any of the words. It had also been – quite deliberately, in fact – stupid and unbelievable.

Travelling to other worlds was, of course, something Effie knew a great deal about. But, having learned her lesson in the Edgelands market the previous day, she had deliberately concealed her knowledge. No one was ever going to find out what Effie knew about travelling to the Otherworld – not apart from her very most trusted friends. So how she had won this competition was a complete mystery.

'Euphemia has written a most charming story,' Terrence was saying, 'about a little goat who goes off in a spaceship but leaves his breakfast behind. Such a wonderful command of the language! Such delightful metaphors and similes. And what a great number of glorious adverbs and adjectives!'

'I do not APPROVE of adverbs and adjectives in stories,' said Mrs Beathag Hide. 'They are lazy and banal. I do hope the rest of the class won't get any ideas from this. What exactly does the child win?' she asked Terrence.

'The chance to have her life written about,' he replied. 'I am going to shadow her for the next two days and learn all about her. Then I am going to craft my knowledge into a story that will be the basis for my next novel. And Euphemia will get a percentage of the profits. Yes, indeed, a whole 0.00001 percent! And who knows, she might even be cast to play herself in the film version.'

Everyone in the class felt extremely jealous. Although 0.00001 percent sounded quite small, everyone knew that novelists made so much money that this could easily end up being millions, billions or even trillions of pounds. And Effie would probably get her name in the book somewhere too. But playing herself in the film version of her life? That was too much. And all because she'd written a stupid story about a goat in a spaceship? Suddenly life seemed quite unfair.

The only people who were neither jealous nor disappointed were Effie's friends. As the weak sound of the bell came tinkling from the corridor, and everyone stood up to go to lunch, they all exchanged glances. How on earth were they going to investigate Skylurian Midzhar's activities with one of her authors following their every move? And how were they going to protect Effie?

178

'So,' said Terrence Deer-Hart as they left the classroom. He smiled an empty smile. 'Where do we have lunch, little flower?'

'The canteen's this way,' said Effie.

As she walked down the old, wooden-panelled corridor with Terrence Deer-Hart beside her she became aware of a presence entering her consciousness. It was Maximilian.

'Hello,' he said inside her head. 'Don't worry. I'm not going to look at any of your memories. Although can I just say that they are a complete shambles? When we have a quiet moment, I think I'm going to have to teach you to order your mind properly. Anyway, I wanted to let you know that we can speak like this and Terrence can't hear us. Just think your thoughts – ideally try to think the ones you want me to hear towards the front of your mind, and then I won't have to see – oh *yuck* – things like that!'

'Like what?' said Effie inside her mind.

'Spotted dick and custard! Why on earth are you thinking about spotted dick and custard?'

'I've got to fuel up for my tennis match this afternoon. Anyway, what's wrong with spotted dick and custard?'

'All the dead flies in it!'

'They're raisins. A good source of concentrated—'

'Anyway, look, I just wanted to ask what you think we should do. Shall we pretend not to know you?'

'Yes,' said Effie. 'Good idea. You take charge and help the others work out what to do next. You need to find out everything you can about Albion Freake, don't forget. I'm also worried about what's happened to Laurel Wilde. And what's Skylurian's role in all this?'

'All right,' said Maximilian. 'I'll get digging. You see what you can find out from Terrence. Maybe he knows something about Skylurian that will be useful.'

'I wish I hadn't won this stupid prize,' said Effie.

'I know. But it's only for two days.'

'How am I going to go to the Otherworld now?'

'Maybe at night?' said Maximilian. 'He'll have to leave you on your own to sleep, presumably?'

'Yes,' said Effie. 'I'll go tonight.'

Of course she still had to get her box back from her father. But at least she now had the book he so wanted. Surely he'd give it back to her now?

16

The Tusitala School for the Gifted, Troubled and Strange had one rickety school bus into which you could fit approximately twenty children before you started breaking the law. It was bright yellow, or had been once. Even going through the bus-wash in town, which it did annually, did not remove the decades' worth of slogans that witty pupils had written onto its back with their fingers. 'Clean me.' 'Also available in yellow.' 'No children left in this vehicle overnight.' The brushes just didn't reach that far.

No one ever usually came to watch the NASTY league tennis matches, especially not the away fixtures. But this one sounded like it might get violent, and so the bus had been slowly filling up with the more bloodthirsty members of the school, who were always willing to travel if it meant a chance of seeing someone get badly injured. But just before the bus left, a rumour went around that suggested that all 300 Blessed Bartolo pupils were going to be attending the match, and that their worst violence was usually directed at the visiting teams' supporters. At that point, most of the children on the bus remembered their homework or a sick aunt and there was quite a crush as they scrambled to leave.

So in the end it was just Coach Bruce, the four members of the tennis team and a couple of reserves (the third reserve had run away with the supporters), along with Terrence Deer-Hart, who had remained by Effie's side all day, and of course Lexy, Raven and Maximilian, who were still pretending not to know Effie but were working on strategies to help her and Wolf, or at least keep them safe. They sat together at the back.

The bus therefore seemed quite empty as it wound its way up through the Old Town, past the university, the Library of Folklore, the puppet museum, the piano repair shop, the Esoteric Emporium and all the strange delicatessens and coffee shops around the gated entrance to the Blessed Bartolo School grounds. As the bus bravely spluttered up the cobbled streets, Coach Bruce attempted a team talk. This was hard to follow, but seemed mainly to be about the 'ethical grey areas' surrounding the achievement of great glory.

'Just to be clear,' Coach Bruce said at the end of his talk. 'There will be no drug tests after this match, as Dr Cloudburst is unfortunately ill. Do you hear me, children?' He winked meaningfully. 'NO DRUG TESTS TODAY.'

The children looked baffled, as they always did when Coach Bruce started talking about drugs. After all, not one child in the entire history of the Tusitala School for the Gifted, Troubled and Strange had ever used performance-enhancing drugs. The odd bit of magic? Perhaps. But illegal substances? Definitely not. The concept of the desperate child athlete who would do anything to succeed only really existed in Coach Bruce's imagination, where it had nevertheless taken a strong hold.

After Coach Bruce had finished talking, the children and Terrence Deer-Hart all clapped. This was not because they understood or agreed with anything he had said, but simply in order to make him feel better.

The Blessed Bartolo sports centre was nowhere near the main school building. The rickety old school bus climbed slowly out of the Old Town, wound its way through one of the less pleasant areas of Middle Town and then along a precarious cliff-road before winding back down to the remote car-park at the end of a jetty, where the visiting teams were told to leave their school buses.

Blessed Bartolo pupils and staff travelled to their sports centre through a tunnel that had been used by smugglers for centuries but was now owned by the school. The tunnel was heated and lit, and had a mono-rail system that was extremely efficient and could get all 300 pupils to the sports centre in less than half an hour. The mono-rail carriages were, apparently, lined with fur and ancient tapestries and each one had a mini-fridge filled with drinks and snacks to get the children in the mood for supporting their teams.

The car park at the end of the jetty was unlit, and had been constructed in a way that exposed it to the worst of the north wind and also, at high tide, to the occasional breaking wave. Visiting teams, if they survived the car park (they didn't always, and Blessed Bartolo's always claimed the victory), then had to walk down the narrow stone jetty to reach the visitors' entrance to the vast, black-domed sports centre that loomed out of the sea like the hump of a mythical creature.

The meteors were still and quiet tonight. Instead, a fine mizzle coated the children, Coach Bruce and Terrence Deer-Hart as they shivered their way up the jetty. The stone path seemed to go on forever, stretching into the dark and the cold and the wet. As the waves broke perilously close to the small party, Terrence wondered if he might die out here. If he did, he told himself, at least it would have been in the cause of true love. He tried to warm himself with thoughts of Skylurian Midzhar. He imagined her striding down here in her high heels without the weather or the sea bothering her in the slightest.

When they eventually reached the visitors' entrance to the sports centre, the small party was drenched, freezing and on the verge of hypothermia. How relieved they were to see the grey metal door! Of course, as anyone familiar with away fixtures will be able to predict, they then discovered that the door was locked and there was no one to meet them. Coach Bruce started trying to page someone from the Blessed Bartolo sports staff, but seemed to have the wrong code. Eventually Maximilian got out his spectacles and Wolf helped him pick the lock when Coach Bruce wasn't looking.

'Here, sir,' called Maximilian. 'I think it's open now.'

'Is this definitely the way?' asked Terrence Deer-Hart, peering in.

The door had opened with a creak to reveal a concrete passageway that seemed even colder and darker than the stone jetty. There was the sound of something dripping. Drip, drip, drip. There was an occasional unidentifiable screech. Maximilian had an old phone with a torch function, and Raven illuminated the end of her wonde. The metal door slam-crashed behind them as they made their way towards a metal staircase that led, at length, to the visitors' changing rooms which were, of course, mouldy, damp and unheated. Still, at least they had arrived.

Luckily, Terrence Deer-Hart didn't seem to want to follow Effie into the girls' changing room. Effie was not a bad person, but she had sort of half hoped that he might die, or at least get lost somewhere along the way, or give up on her in the cold car-park. But no, he now assured her that he was going to be in the front row taking notes through the tennis match. He wanted, he said, to know *everything* about her.

He had become extremely tiresome. Effie had expected him to ask her lots of annoying questions about her life, which he had done. But once he'd got bored of that he had begun moaning about his sales figures, his shortness, the fact that his parents never really loved him and his lack of success in what he called 'the romance department'. Still, his 'luck with the ladies', he had said meaningfully to Effie, was possibly about to change. Then he had winked at her in a peculiar way. And all that had just been over lunch.

So Effie was relieved to find herself alone at last in the changing room, putting on her tennis kit. Her team-mate Olivia had changed before getting on the bus, which meant she had frozen on the jetty but at least didn't have to endure this changing room. Effie tried to block out the damp smell by trying to remember the strategies that they had decided on in yesterday's team meeting. The big question in her mind was whether or not to wear the ring. Was it cheating if she did? Or was it 'strategy'? Effie didn't want to be a cheat.

On the other hand, she needed to generate some M-currency. She had no idea where hers had gone, but it was very, very low. If she played tennis wearing the ring, she'd be able to convert the energy she expended into M-currency. If she and her friends were going to have any chance of defeating Albion Freake, she'd need M-currency. And she was planning to go to the Otherworld later, which also used M-currency.

Effie also suspected that the match with Blessed Bartolo's was not going to be straightforward. Coach Bruce had told her to wear the ring for 'psychological reasons'. Still, it didn't feel right. In the end, Effie decided to keep the ring on until the warm-up was over, but not wear it for any competitive points. After the warm-up, it could go in her tennis bag, where she could keep an eye on it.

When Effie walked out of the changing room and into the sports centre, she was immediately taken aback by the amount of noise. The place was completely full. Effie couldn't see any of her friends, or Coach Bruce. Even the sight of Terrence Deer-Hart might have been mildly comforting. Instead, all Effie could see was a mass of black virgin wool, cashmere and silk, and the cruel, angular faces of the Blessed Bartolo student body.

A man strode over to Effie. He looked sort of familiar, although he was wearing the uniform of the Blessed Bartolo's sports faculty. This was a precisely tailored black silk tracksuit with lime green felt trim. This one was completed with a baseball cap with the word UMPIRE on it. He was carrying a plastic tub.

'Well, hand it over,' said the man. He even sounded familiar.

'I'm sorry?' said Effie.

'Don't start all that again,' said the umpire. 'Give me the ring. You can't play with it on. We both know that would be cheating.'

Effie realised that the person under the large black cap was Mr Green. She hadn't known that he taught at Blessed Bartolo's. Was he one of their PE teachers? It seemed unlikely. He wasn't exactly the most athletic man she'd ever seen. How had he become their tennis umpire? But none of that mattered. She was stuck. There was no way she could not hand over her ring if the umpire was asking for it. She couldn't defy him again. If she did, she'd be dropped from the tennis team and probably expelled from school as well.

'Get on with it, girl,' growled Mr Green.

The spectators close to Effie had quietened. They'd realised that a confrontation was going on between their teacher and this small Tusitala girl – the one who was supposed to be such a great tennis player. Blessed Bartolo children loved any kind of confrontation, violent or not. The ones nearest to Effie and Mr Green leaned closer. This wasn't just so they could hear better, but because many of them were tricksters able to draw energy out of troubling situations.

A few rows up sat Leander and his friend Gregory. Gregory was currently topping up his own M-currency by eating small dried pieces of animal heart. His mother had just had a new box sent from Brain & Son's Cured Meat & Pickles in the north-west

187

corner of the Old Town. The dried hearts were extremely expensive, due to their complex (and rather disgusting) production methods. Elsewhere in the tennis centre other Blessed Bartolo children were eating candied snakes' eyes, dragons'-blood cakes and 'lucky' rabbits' ears.

Leander got up and walked down the few steps to where Mr Green and Effie were standing. He seemed to be moving extremely fast, while around him everything had slowed to an almost complete halt. Effie felt light-headed for a moment. It was as if the world in front of her had split into two different time streams.

'I'll look after that, Sir,' Leander said to Mr Green. He glanced at Effie with an expression that was neither friendly nor hostile, but his eyes intensified ever so slightly when they caught hers. Then a sort of invisible fog briefly came down over the three of them. When it lifted, Leander had taken the ring, and Mr Green seemed to have suffered some kind of amnesia.

'What are you standing there for, girl?' he asked Effie. 'Hurry along. Let's get this match underway. You're on Court 1, I believe.'

Effie looked up at Leander. Had he just stolen her ring, or rescued it from Mr Green? He'd used magic – but what sort of magic had it been? But she didn't have time to find out.

'What are you doing?' said Wolf, coming over. 'They've already cheated and won the toss. They're serving.'

'What about the warm-up?' said Effie.

'Apparently we've forfeited the chance for a warm-up because you're late.'

'But I'm not!'

'Officially, you are.'

'By 30 seconds! And that's because . . .'

One of Effie and Wolf's opponents walked over.

'Hello, I'm Tabitha,' she said. 'Don't bother telling me your names. I don't care what they are. I've come to tell you that unless you're ready to begin immediately we're going to claim the first set.'

Tabitha's voice was like fine crystal, but her eyes were as deep and dark as bottomless pits. Her tennis outfit was a 1920s style tennis dress made – like almost everything else here – of black silk. Her black visor had the words TENNIS TEAM spelled out in what appeared to be diamonds. There were clearly no rules against wearing jewellery to play sports at Blessed Bartolo's. Tabitha was wearing several strings of pearls around her neck and a pair of antique diamond drop earrings.

Effie and Wolf hurried into position. The surface of the Blessed Bartolo tennis centre was like nothing Effie had ever played on. It was not hard greeny-grey acrylic like the courts at her school, or concrete, like many of the other schools' outdoor courts. It was shiny, soft and bright green. It looked bizarrely like a luxury carpet that had recently been mown and heavy-rollered. Which, as it happens, was exactly what it was. Some indoor tennis centres did have 'carpet' as a surface. But none had carpet quite like this. Needless to say, it played extremely fast.

The first four serves, from Tabitha's partner Barnaby, were aces. Effie didn't even see the ones headed for her. She and Wolf looked at each other as they changed ends. They had never even

189

lost a game before in all their tennis matches. Normally Wolf served first, because his serve was the strongest part of his game. But his right arm had inexplicably gone numb, so Effie offered to go first instead.

Unfortunately, as soon as she threw the ball up above her head, Effie went temporarily blind. She swung her racket down onto air. The ball dropped at her feet. The Blessed Bartolo children all laughed.

Magic. It had to be. Effie blinked a couple of times. Nothing. She could still see absolutely nothing but darkness. This was ridiculous.

'Time warning,' said Mr Green from his umpire's chair.

'I'm just . . . it's just . . .' said Effie.

Maximilian's voice came into her head.

'What's happened?' he asked, telepathically.

'I'm blind,' said Effie with her mind. 'I can't see anything.'

'Don't let them see you're upset,' said Maximilian. 'Don't panic. OK, I just have to think. Who can blind with their magic? Hang on. I'm going to ask Raven. She's saying she's read a book and . . .' Maximilian's voice left and then returned. 'Right. It's something a mage can do, apparently. But mages don't use spells. They can only use their minds to change things. So that means someone in here is using their mind to convince *your* mind that you can't see. You have to believe more strongly that you can.'

'Time penalty,' said Mr Green. 'Love fifteen.'

Effie tried hard to repel the magic attack happening in her mind. But she didn't know how to go about it, and everything

190

was more difficult without her ring. But she needed to be quick, or . . .

'Love thirty,' said Mr Green. 'Another time penalty and you'll forfeit the game, and then the set. Are you injured, Miss Truelove?'

'I'm fine,' said Effie. Maximilian was right, she shouldn't let anyone see how much this was frightening her. 'Sorry.'

Wolf came over. Effie didn't realise this until his voice was right by her ear.

'What's happening?' he said.

'Some mage has got into my mind and affected my sight. They must have done the same with your arm. We've got to repel them, but I don't know how.'

'Use your M-currency,' said Wolf.

'I don't know how to,' said Effie. 'I don't even know what magic a true hero can do. And I've lost my ring. The only possible thing I can think of is . . .'

'Game forfeited,' said Mr Green.

'What?' said Wolf. 'What can you do?'

'If I had . . . There was this thing. This boy stole my ring, but he has this staff, a caduceus.' Effie searched for Maximilian in her mind. He was there, quietly, observing. 'Go into my memories,' she said to him. 'You'll see what I mean. Find Leander and get his caduceus for me. He's stolen my ring after all, so it's quite fair. Maybe he'll even give me my ring back if we can take something of his.'

'OK,' said Maximilian back. 'I understand. We're on it.'

'How's your arm?' said Effie to Wolf.

'Not great. I'm going to play this game left-handed. Look, I'll get you in position for each point until your sight comes back. We can't let them see that they're upsetting us.'

'I agree,' said Effie. 'We have to act strong, even if we don't feel it.'

Tabitha served to Effie. Of course Effie couldn't see a thing. If she had been able to see she would have realised that the serve was almost unplayable anyway. It was a fast, wide kick serve that hit the dividing curtain before any normal person would have time to hit it. In order to properly receive such a serve you'd have to be standing on the edge of Court 3. And there would have to be no curtains dividing the courts.

Wolf noticed this and so stood right on the edge of the tramlines waiting for the next serve, with his racket in his left hand. Of course now Tabitha blasted her serve down the middle. It was an ace. Hardly anyone ever hit aces against Wolf. Tabitha smirked and moved across to serve at Effie. As if to mock her opponent, Tabitha now played a slow looping serve that bounced in the middle of the box and then plopped down on Effie's head. The spectators roared with delight.

This was becoming intolerable. Wolf and Effie had yet to win a point, and Blessed Bartolo were now three games up. The next two games continued in more or less the same way. Wolf served left-handed, only to find each of his efforts blasted back for a winner. After each point Tabitha and Barnaby high-fived each other in a particularly smug way, while Wolf tried to manoeuvre Effie into the right position. What on earth were they going to do?

17

After they'd lost the first set 0–6 Wolf requested a toilet break, and he and Effie went out into the quiet corridor. Soon, Raven and Lexy found them. Raven took out her wonde and cast the Shadows, and then they found a quiet room off the hallway where they could hide for a few minutes. Apparently Terrence Deer-Hart was on the prowl looking for Effie. Lexy set about rubbing an ointment into Wolf's arm, while Raven chanted a healing spell over Effie.

'Where's Maximilian?' said Wolf.

'He's trying to steal the caduceus from Leander,' said Lexy. 'Apparently he can disappear now, which is quite helpful.'

'Can you see anything yet?' asked Wolf.

'No,' said Effie. She didn't admit to her friends that she was actually becoming quite scared. She knew that they looked to her for leadership and there was no way she was going to let them down. Especially when they were trying so hard to help her.

Soon it was time to go back. There was no sign of Maximilian or the caduceus. Wolf led Effie back to her seat by the umpire's chair and got her water bottle out for her. Not that she needed to replace any fluids. She hadn't had to run at all in the whole of the last set.

On Court 2 the Tusitala School second pair, Olivia and Josh, were also having a hard time. Effie could hear jeering and booing coming from the spectators.

'What's happening?' she asked Wolf.

'I think they might have just won their first point,' he said.

Just then something dropped into Effie's lap. It was the caduceus. Maximilian had got it! And he must have slipped through between the dimensions in order to deliver it. As soon as Effie touched it, her sight was restored. How could that be? She blinked once, twice. Yes, her sight was fine. Effie knew the words to the Shadows well after having heard Raven recite them so often. She had a sense that she could say the spell now and it would work. She muttered it and – yes – to her surprise, she managed to hide the caduceus. What else could she do? She didn't want to cheat exactly, but . . .

Her hearing was enhanced, just as it had been on the bus, and so she could hear what Tabitha was saying to Barnaby on the other side of the umpire's chair.

'Well, I've got no more M-currency either.'

'You must have something in your bag?'

'I've got a chocolate bar.'

'No, you idiot. Something to replace my power. There's no way we'll win otherwise.'

'Are you insane? We didn't drop a point in the last set.'

'Yes, because I had plenty of M-currency.'

'Well, it's chocolate or nothing.'

'I'm sure I had one more dried monkey brain in here somewhere.'

'God, you're disgusting,' said Tabitha. 'I don't know how you can eat that revolting stuff.'

'You eat crushed butterflies for breakfast every morning!'

'That's different.'

'Can't your friends do something?'

'They're selfishly saving their power for their own matches,' said Tabitha. 'What about yours?'

'Same. We'll have to rely on our skill.'

'Great.'

'Time, please,' said Mr Green.

'Right. I'll serve,' said Tabitha to Barnaby in her cut-glass voice. 'I believe I've had the most aces so far.'

'Yes, well, I think all that's about to change,' said Barnaby.

He was right. This time, when Tabitha served to Effie, Effie could actually see the ball. It wasn't quite as wide as Tabitha's previous serves, which had cost a little bit of M-currency each time. Indeed, now that Mr Green could see the lines properly and was no longer under Barnaby's blur curse, he was able to call the serve out. Effie attacked Tabitha's second-serve, blasting the ball down the tramlines behind Barnaby. It was the first point Effie and Wolf had won.

It doesn't take much to turn the momentum of a tennis match. If you can put doubt in the mind of your opponents, then what has been a 6–0 lead can soon turn into one set all. And doubt seemed to come easily to Tabitha. The more points she lost, the more sulky and petulant she became. At one point she got in such a huff about one of Mr Green's line calls that she ignored four of Wolf's serves in a row. When Tabitha and Barnaby lost the set, she yanked her necklaces so hard that they broke, and pearls were scattered everywhere.

Many of these pearls made their way onto Court 2, where Olivia and Josh were currently one set down and losing the second by three games to one. Unfortunately, most of the pearls rolled onto Blessed Bartolo's end of the court. The boy, Edward, slipped on the pearls and fell, breaking his ankle in three different places. Even though his partner begged him to limp on, he could not. Alas, they forfeited their match. Two points to the Tusitala School. Coach Bruce actually shed a tear.

All of which meant that the Tusitala School had done the unthinkable and got ahead. In the NASTY league, each school is awarded a point for every set it wins, plus a point for an overall win. So, with Effie and Wolf just having drawn their match at one set all, the Tusitala School suddenly had three points and Blessed Bartolo had two. If Blessed Bartolo was to draw this fixture, then Tabitha and Barnaby would have to win the championship tie-break that always took the place of the third set. They would have to be the first to reach ten points, clear by two.

Before the tie-break began, Effie sat on her chair holding the caduceus and listening to Tabitha and Barnaby arguing. He was saying that she should let him hit more balls because he was a boy and stronger, and she was telling him that she could beat him any day.

Something strange had been happening to Effie while she was holding the caduceus. The umpire's chair had been manufactured in another country, and had some foreign writing on its leg. Effie could now read this as easily as if it had been her own language. It didn't say anything particularly interesting – it was just some health and safety advice – but the main thing was that Effie could understand it. And Tabitha's tennis bag had been made by a fashionable company on the other side of the world. Effie could now understand that the strange logo was a word meaning 'vanquisher' in an ancient version of this country's language.

'So what's our strategy?' Wolf asked Effie as they stood up to go and play.

'We'll just let them beat themselves,' said Effie. 'They've already started. Look.' She gestured to Wolf to look over at Tabitha and Barnaby, who were still arguing. As they got up to play, Tabitha rather spitefully kicked Barnaby in the shin.

'Oh, Maximilian just brought this, by the way,' said Wolf, giving Effie back her ring. 'Maybe you should wear it?'

'I don't want to cheat like they are,' said Effie. 'Let's try and win the old-fashioned way.'

'All right,' said Wolf. 'But put it somewhere safe. I don't like the atmosphere in here. What if someone tries to steal it back again?'

Effie's tennis skirt, despite being for 10–11 year olds, had a little zipped pocket in which you could put a car key. Effie had always thought this very stupid. Now she realised it was actually quite useful. She put the ring inside and stepped on the court to play. Something was bothering her, even so.

The caduceus. It had felt all right to have it while Leander had her ring. But now Effie had both boons. And she had used Leander's if not to cheat then at least to get an unfair advantage. Of course, this was insignificant compared to what Blessed Bartolo's had been doing. But even so, Effie now asked herself why she had told Maximilian to get the caduceus in the first place. Why hadn't she just asked him to return her ring? It was as if she had felt compelled to touch the caduceus. But why?

Now that the Blessed Bartolo team had run out of M-currency, Effie and Wolf didn't need any further help. By the time the Tusitala team were leading eight points to three, Tabitha was crying so much she could not even see the ball. Effie then aced her, for the tenth time in the match. Tabitha was on her last tennis racket, having smashed all her others, but that didn't stop her now flinging it on the ground and then stamping on it. Effie couldn't believe they had almost done it. One more serve to Barnaby, which he tried to hit back for a winner and failed. 'Out!' called Mr Green. And . . . They had won! Even Terrence Deer-Hart became quite excited and shouted 'Bravo!' several times until Maximilian somehow got him to stop.

When Tabitha and Barnaby came to the net they limply shook hands with Effie and Wolf, but didn't smile.

'We're going to get you for this,' hissed Tabitha. 'You won't know where, or when, or how. But we will never forget. You will suffer so much you'll wish you had never been born.'

Which was not the most sporting thing to say after losing a tennis match, but then Blessed Bartolo pupils had never been the most sporting of opponents.

When Effie got back to the changing room, Leander was waiting in an alcove near the door. He looked a bit like a bat, with his black velvet cape folded around him. He had merged with the dark concrete wall in a way that had made him almost invisible.

'Well,' he said, stepping out. 'I suppose you think I'm going to let you keep it.'

'What?' said Effie. 'Oh, your caduceus. Of course not. Here.' She held it out to him. 'I was going to try to find you to give it back.'

'And after I rescued your ring from Mr Green, too.' Leander snorted. 'Nice way of thanking me, sending your friend to steal my boon.'

'You *rescued* it? Why didn't you give it back to me then? Why did you go off with it?'

'I was looking after it for you. And anyway, I wanted you to see what it felt like.'

'What do you mean?'

'When someone else touches your boon. When they hide it, like you did on the bus.'

'But I didn't! I . . .'

'It's worse when they can use it, like you obviously can.' He shook his head in a confused way. 'But I can't use your ring. I should be able to use any boon, certainly any ring, but not that one. What is it?'

Effie didn't understand what he was asking her for a moment.

'What are you?' asked Leander.

Effie knew that she couldn't tell him. She couldn't let him

know what her ring was. Everyone seemed to want to get their hands on it, and she had no idea why. She wasn't going to help them by identifying it to anyone who happened to ask. And she was determined not to trust just anyone now, not after what had happened in the market. Effie did want to tell Leander who she was and what the ring did, because there was something kind and familiar in his eyes, and she had a feeling he might even be on her side, but she just couldn't. She shook her head.

Leander sighed and held out his hand for the caduceus. Effie pushed it towards him. And then, as he reached out and took hold of it, something peculiar happened. While his hand and Effie's were both on the caduceus, Effie had a momentary feeling of being able to understand anything in the whole world: any book, any language, any person. It was similar to the feeling she'd had on the bus, but stronger, because this time Leander didn't pull the caduceus from her, and she forgot to let go. In fact, the feeling was so strong that she must have blacked out for a moment. When she opened her eyes, Leander, and his caduceus, were gone.

On the way home, Terrence insisted on buying gifts for Effie's family, as he'd decided to invite himself for dinner. He thought the best place to do this was the Esoteric Emporium, so he got the bus driver to drop them off. He promised Effie that once the shopping was done they'd get a taxi back to her house.

Coach Bruce was still weeping softly at the front of the school bus. His strong, heroic team had won! They had beaten Blessed Bartolo's! Of course, winning meant promotion to a division filled exclusively with Blessed Bartolo teams, and so he had doomed his players to many months of being cursed, hexed and subject to forms of voodoo that only the worst children can think of. Still, there was great glory in winning, regardless of the actual consequences.

The Esoteric Emporium was a dusty and dark supermarket that sold almost everything edible or drinkable you can think of that exists in the Realworld and is old or fermented. All old and fermented things have some natural magical power, of course. Unfortunately M-currency dissolves in alcohol, but that didn't seem to be an issue for Terrence.

'Does your father like wine?' asked Terrence. 'I do. I think we'll have a lovely bottle of this vintage champagne, which we'll follow with this delightful Chablis and then perhaps this . . .' He picked up a particularly dusty bottle of red wine. 'Oh yes,' he breathed. 'Thirty years' bottle age. An excellent gift. Does your father like Margaux? Of course he does. Every living being likes a good Margaux. Do you think your father will mind if I sleep on your sofa? It's just that I've recently had quite a problem with my boiler and . . .'

As they walked along the aisle containing jars of sauerkraut, miso, kimchi, kombucha and other kinds of fermented vegetable matter, Terrence carried on talking about problems with his boiler and then drifted into his recent medical history. It struck Effie then that although Terrence seemed to want to find out about her, she knew an awful lot more about him.

They reached the cheese section, and Effie was overwhelmed with the smell. It was as if thousands of boys had all taken their socks off at once and then dangled them in front of her nose.

'And an époisses,' said Terrence, picking up a round cheese in a wooden box. 'And a large slab of Stinking Bishop. A very thoughtful gift, Stinking Bishop, I think everyone would agree about that. I am, you realise, a very generous man.' Terrence's eyes sort of misted over. 'I wonder if Skylurian realises that. Do you think . . .' he began, looking at Effie. 'Do you think that Skylurian is the most beautiful woman in the world? I do.' They walked on. 'Does your father like charcuterie? Ha! Who doesn't like charcuterie? I suppose not the "darker" charcuterie, although dear Skylurian does love a bag of dried sparrows' eyeballs. Maybe just a nice salami and some liver sausage.'

The bill came to over three hundred pounds, which Terrence Deer-Hart handed over in cash.

'Now, where will we find a taxi?' said Terrence, as they left.

It was a good question. Old people always moaned about how difficult everything was now, and would reminisce about the days when you could order a taxi using just your phone. Now, after the worldquake, it was not so easy. You could page one of the taxi companies, or go to one of their offices, but there was often a long wait. Mages could usually summon a taxi fairly easily, though, and witches could send out a call via the Cosmic Web. Although, of course, most witches had portable broomsticks and so had limited use for taxis.

'What are you?' said Effie to Terrence, as they walked down the hill to where he thought a taxi office might be.

'What do you mean, what am I? I'm a famous author,' he said. 'And a Capricorn, and um . . .'

'No. What's your *kharakter*?'

'Ah. Composer, of course.' He tossed his long curls. 'Skylurian analysed me. She thought perhaps I was a bard, like Laurel Wilde – all that classical, archetypal storytelling and so forth – but no; it turns out I'm a *much* more important writer than that. Apparently some writers can be engineers – they are the ones who spend all their time making little models and diagrams of their locations and doing vulgar things like "world-building". No, I'm a composer.'

'What do composers do?'

'They *compose*, little flower, they compose. They create the new, the ground-breaking, the innovative. They are the true avant-garde. Do you know what the avant-garde is?'

Effie shook her head.

'I do,' said Terrence. 'It's . . . Well, it's when very important artworks are . . . Well, the artworks are very new and original and sometimes French and . . . It's extremely interesting, anyway.'

'So what have you composed?' Effie asked.

'My books, of course! Apparently it's quite rare for a composer to create books. Although when they do, according to Skylurian, they are the greatest and most important books in the world. Some composers make music, or art, or . . .' He visibly struggled for a moment to think of something else. 'Other things.'

'Can you do magic?' asked Effie.

'Of course I can! Yes. Well, more accurately, no. Not currently.

203

Not *yet*. Although I am to begin learning very soon. Dear Skylurian says I am also a mage, the most magical and powerful of all the *kharakters*. I must say, it's an interesting world, once you've epiphanised.'

'When did you?' said Effie. 'Epiphanise, I mean.'

'I think it was last Tuesday,' said Terrence. 'It certainly opens your eyes, I can tell you.'

'And how do you know Skylurian Midzhar?'

'She's my publisher, little flower. My gorgeous publisher.'

'And do you know someone called Albion Freake? He might be a friend of Skylurian's.'

Terrence frowned. Albion Freake. The name sounded vaguely familiar. Ought he to be jealous? Was this another author? Or a love rival! He wasn't sure which was worse.

'A *friend*, you say?'

'Or maybe a business associate?'

'No, little flower. I've never heard of him. I'm sure he's utterly insignificant. Probably just some pathetic nobody.'

'I think he might be a famous billionaire,' said Effie.

There was a long pause.

'Money, little flower, is not everything.'

But Terrence felt troubled as they continued down the cobbled street to the taxi rank. He'd never heard of any famous people because he was only really concerned with his own fame. Just the idea of another famous person upset him greatly.

When Terrence imagined this Albion Freake – stupid flipping name, that – he saw him as a vast cliff-face of a man, fair and rugged and strong. But after some minutes of using the advanced visualisation techniques that his therapist had taught him, he was able to reduce this Freake to a tiny, timid librarian with dandruff. Terrence clearly had no idea how dangerous librarians can be, but that is a story for another time. For now, he felt better.

He had unfortunately forgotten that he was supposed to be finding out about Effie's life. But it is always so pleasant to talk about oneself, after all, and the girl was certainly good at asking questions. Terrence had never acquired the useful social skill of asking questions back, and so had not asked Effie when she had epiphanised, or how, indeed, she travelled to other worlds. It was only once they were in the taxi that he remembered his flipping mission at all. Would Skylurian be angry with him? But there was still time. He would wine and dine the family and then . . . What? He would wait and see.

18

'What on earth is that revolting smell?' said Orwell Bookend, without looking up from his prize crossword.

He was sitting in his favourite armchair with a small fire burning in the grate and a candle-lamp flickering on the table beside him. Baby Luna was in her playpen reading – which actually meant chewing – an old board-book about a witch and her cat that she'd brought home from nursery. All should have been well. However, there were at least two major things missing from Orwell Bookend's life. He felt a faint longing for something, but couldn't quite put his finger on what it was . . .

'Hi Dad,' said Effie. 'We've brought dinner.'

That was it. Dinner! That was what he had been longing for. Had his daughter actually done something useful for a change? But what was the other thing . . .

'Who are you?' said Orwell, looking up at Terrence suspiciously. He had recently decided that his family was going to be ordinary. More like the common man and less like, well, themselves. This did not look like an ordinary visitor. His turquoise shirt was, frankly, ridiculous. No one in this part of town wore a fur gilet. And that hair. And, of course, the smell. Which wasn't actually that bad, now that Orwell realised it might be dinner.

'He's a famous author, Dad. Terrence Deer-Hart.'

'Never heard of him.'

'Well, he's bought you some very expensive wine. And some liver sausage. And some cheese and . . .'

'Liver sausage, eh? Why ever didn't you say?'

'Perhaps I should not bother your father with my thirty-year-old bottle of Margaux,' said Terrence, huffily. 'He seems rather busy. Perhaps I should go and find someone who has heard of me with whom to share my Stinking Bishop.'

'Wait. *Margaux*, you say?' said Orwell. 'I'll go and get the best glasses. Of course I've heard of you,' he said smoothly to Terrence, with a slightly reptilian smile. 'I was joking. My daughter will attest to my wonderful sense of humour. Euphemia? Some help in the kitchen, please. The extremely famous Mr Deer-Stalker will not mind watching the baby for a few moments, I'm sure.'

'Deer-*Hart*,' said Terrence.

'He's still joking,' said Effie. 'Aren't you, Dad?'

'What? Yes. Of course.'

Effie followed her father into the kitchen, carrying a candle-lamp. Orwell unlocked a wooden cabinet and took out two crystal wine glasses and began to dust one of them off with a tea towel. He gave the other one to Effie with a second tea-towel.

'Well?' said Orwell. 'What's he doing here?'

'I won a competition at school,' said Effie.

'What, you won your very own author? What was the second prize? Two authors?'

'Very funny, Dad. He's going to write about me. About my life. Anyway, never mind him. I've got something for you,' Effie said. 'The book you wanted. *The Chosen Ones.*'

Orwell Bookend narrowed his eyes.

'Where did you get it? It said on the news that copies are now virtually impossible to find. And they have become extraordinarily expensive.'

'Well, you said you wanted it and so I . . .'

'Did you get it from *him*? Deer-Stalker?'

Effie sighed. 'Dad, if you want the wine he's brought you, should probably try and get his name right.'

'All right. Point taken. But *Deer-Hart*? What sort of a name is that? He sounds like something from *The Magic Roundabout*. Or the war scenes in Tolstoy when they're all hallucinating from exhaustion.' Orwell started fake-swooning. 'Alas, dear heart, I have lost all the cannonballs . . .'

'Dad, what *are* you talking about?'

Orwell sighed. 'No one ever gets my jokes. Well, where did he find it?'

'What?'

'The wine. It certainly looked expensive.'

'The Esoteric Emporium.'

'What on earth were you doing at the Esoteric Emporium? It's on the other side of town.'

'On my way home from a tennis match. We won, by the way.'

'Oh, congratulations,' Orwell said, insincerely. 'I'm sure your sports teacher is terribly pleased. And your little tennis chums. Just don't forget that sport withers the mind. Anyway, all this is trivial. You say you have my book.'

'Yes. But we made a deal, remember.'

'A deal?'

'Yes. You were going to give me back my box.'

'Your box?' Orwell feigned ignorance. 'Alas, dear heart I . . .'

'*Dad!*'

'Oh, all right. But . . .' Orwell made a face as if something was troubling him. 'Are you sure there's nothing dangerous in that box? I don't want you dabbling any more than necessary in so-called magic and getting yourself in trouble. Don't forget what happened to your grandfather. And your mother, for that matter.'

As if Effie was likely to forget. Although of course she still didn't understand exactly what had happened to either of them. Effie knew that her grandfather had been attacked by a powerful Diberi. He had died in this world but had possibly been resurrected in a far-off location in the Otherworld. Effie didn't know for sure, and there was no one who could really tell her, except for Cosmo Truelove, and she'd need to get back to the Otherworld to talk to him.

As for Effie's mother, Orwell had first said she was dead, then said she'd run off with another man – which, he'd declared, was as good as being dead anyway – then he said she was dead after all. It had happened on the night of the worldquake. Aurelia had read Effie her bedtime story – a chapter from one of the Laurel

Wilde books, which she had loved so much she always ignored Orwell's attempts to confiscate or ban them – dimmed the lights and kissed her goodnight. Effie had noticed her mother putting on a silk cape and slipping a book into her large brown handbag that looked a bit like a briefcase.

Then she had put her finger to her lips and climbed out of Effie's bedroom window. It hadn't been the first time Aurelia had secretly left the house using Effie's window. But something had felt different on that night. Effie'd had no idea that she would never see her mother again, of course; but there had been a strange atmosphere left in the room, like the memory of a bad dream.

The next day, while Orwell stormed around the house shouting and phoning people, Effie had found something under her bed. It was a slim, brown hardback book with gold lettering. It was written in a language she didn't know and had pictures of strange creatures she had never seen before. She had taken it to her father and asked him what it was. He'd grabbed it from her angrily and sent her back to her room. Effie had always had a feeling the book had had something to do with her mother's disappearance, but she didn't know what. And she had never seen it again after that, even though she had asked and asked.

'Well?' said Orwell now.

'There's nothing dangerous in the box,' said Effie. 'I promise.'

Of course Orwell didn't believe her.

Effie and Orwell stared at each other with the same dark, jewel-like eyes. And suddenly, in the moment that followed, both had complete understanding of the other. They didn't need to speak. Effie knew that if she asked for the box, Orwell would demand the book first. He knew that if he asked for the book, she would demand the box first. Each of them suddenly admired the other's stubbornness. Orwell also found he admired his daughter's determination and resourcefulness. Everything they most despised about each other turned, briefly, to a reason for love. In that short moment, both father and daughter felt that although they would continue to fight against one another, each would fiercely protect the other from any outsider who threatened them.

Wordlessly, Orwell went upstairs to get the box.

Maximilian was tucking into his third coffee cream while he searched the archive of *The Liminal* for information about Albion Freake. It wasn't going that well. Maximilian had got no matches for the words Albion and Freake at all. He was only allowed another half an hour of electricity, and so he had to get on with it. There must be something. All magical people usually showed up in *The Liminal* at least once. Now he was going through matches for Skylurian and Midzhar and hoping to find a connection that way. But so far there was nothing. Skylurian Midzhar had done well to keep herself off *The Liminal*'s radar. In fact, there were only three results for her name.

The first was in connection with a business venture with Leonard Levar, whose name had once appeared all over *The Liminal*. Another was simply a brief mention of Skylurian in connection with Laurel Wilde, about whom *The Liminal*'s chief arts correspondent had written a rather sniffy piece outlining all the major ways that her novels had brought magic into disrepute. The third was a short gossip piece about a young and attractive male Otherworld witch called Pelham Longfellow who occasionally appeared in *The Liminal* and had attended a cocktail party with Skylurian back in September.

In the olden days of the internet, searching for information had been easy. But technology was so slow these days. On the dim web, which was a crudely cobbled together amalgam of what was left of the dark web and the original worldwide web, there was no longer any such thing as a 'search engine' or a 'website'. There were simply the Bulletin Boards Systems, crudely pixelated, that you needed advanced computer skills even to see. It was like 1992 all over again. And it was, literally, dim, a bit like everything else in this world now. Computer screens didn't have very powerful lights behind them, and they were usually in rooms lit by candle-lamps.

The archive of *The Liminal* was searchable, in theory, but relied on a tired old algorithm which was further hampered by a good deal of human error. Then there were all the spells and curses and hexes and so forth that people had used to prevent them being found. Cloaking spells were simple, after all.

Tired and disappointed, Maximilian gave up. Instead, he got out his new boon. At least, he thought it was a boon. It must be a boon. It was what he'd been given on exiting the book *The Initiation*. He stroked the silver card gently as candle-light danced over it.. *Pathétique*. What did it mean? The word wasn't entirely unfamiliar to him. He had seen it somewhere recently, but where? However hard he tried to search his newly ordered mind, he couldn't find it. He'd tried the Spectacles of Knowledge on it, but they knew nothing at all about it.

Or maybe they did, and they just weren't telling him. The Spectacles of Knowledge had been in a bit of a huff with Maximilian ever since he had discovered that his true *kharakter* was mage, rather than scholar, which had been downgraded to his art. The spectacles seemed to think that Maximilian should spend just as much time honing his scholarly skills as he did reading people's minds and running around trying to find the Underworld. They certainly were not going to help him with that. It was too dangerous, and involved far too much action for the spectacles' liking. They had been designed to work best with studious, careful people who don't move around very much, not intrepid boys set on visiting the dark side. Also, boons did not much like being used on other boons. It was just one of those things, like two wrong ends of a magnet not liking to touch.

All the ways Maximilian usually found out information were not working. He was going to have to try something else. But what? And then there was the other thing that kept bothering him. *The Initiation.* Should he destroy it, or leave it alone? Destroying it would make him a Book Eater, and, given that he was also a dark mage, if he was going to do that he may as well just say goodbye to all his friends now and go and join the Diberi. But what if he didn't destroy it? What if someone else read it? Would he lose his knowledge and his boon? But surely if someone else was going to read the book, Maximilian couldn't have been its Last Reader. It was all very confusing.

The door slammed and a cold wind briefly felt its way around the hallway of Effie's house. Cait was home.

'I've brought chips,' she called. Then: 'What's that smell?'

This was the second thing that Orwell Bookend had been longing for. The return of his wife. He'd completely forgotten that she'd gone out for chips. But how glorious that she had! What an unexpectedly nice evening this was turning out to be. Orwell, Terrence, Effie and Cait soon found themselves enjoying an impromptu feast. Someone had found a baguette in the back of the freezer and put it in the oven. Another glass had been dusted for Cait. The grown-ups all drank wine and Effie had a cup of chamomile tea while they ate hot chips with gooey, smelly cheese, some bright pink sauerkraut made from red cabbage, and rather a lot of tiny silver cocktail onions. The grown-ups had liver sausage too, which Effie didn't like.

The warm feelings that Effie and her father had shared in the kitchen had lingered, and Cait had started wondering what was wrong with them both. Normally they could not be in a room together for more than two minutes without some kind of world war starting. Instead, the two of them ended up working together on Orwell's crossword – something they had not done for a very long time, and certainly not while Cait had been living with them.

While they were doing that, Cait talked to Terrence.

Cait could not believe that one of her favourite authors was actually in their house. She had long been a fan of Terrence Deer-Hart's work. She'd first discovered him when she had been a PhD student suffering from stress and someone had suggested reading children's fiction to cheer herself up. Terrence's books were, of course, not the cheeriest in the world. They contained no magic, no travel to other lands, no mythical creatures and no exciting action scenes. Instead, there were a lot of swear-words and miserable children. But for some reason Cait had found that reading about miserable children made her feel a lot better. She now told Terrence all about how his books had changed her life.

This, along with a lot of cocktail onions and an extra-large helping of Stinking Bishop, had cheered Terrence up no end. At last, someone who had actually read his books! Someone who appreciated him! The only problem was that the gloomy husband suddenly looked up from his crossword and seemed intent on quizzing her about it.

'You've really read his books?'

'Yes, I just said.'

'But they're for children!'

'Lots of adults read children's fiction.'

'Doesn't it stunt your mind?'

'Orwell!'

'Mind you, anything's better than those romances you were reading last month. Can you believe,' said Orwell to Terrence, 'that an intelligent woman like this, *Dr* Ransom-Bookend no less, went through a phase of reading anything sellotaped to a plastic tub?'

'I did them for the competitions!' Cait said.

It was something of a new fad, introduced by Matchstick Press. The thin romance novels were given away free with tubs of diet milkshake powder. If you finished one of the books and returned it to the Matchstick Press with your name and address filled out on the form on the inside back cover, you could win something, unfortunately usually another book with a picture of a nurse swooning in the arms of a doctor, or a woman in a short skirt tied to a tree. But there was the occasional big cash prize too, and the odd holiday.

Terrence didn't like to admit that he himself had written several of those romances when he had been at a low ebb early in his career. Skylurian had paid him quite a lot of money to go and sit with a bunch of other writers in an old factory in Walthamstow where a man with a megaphone shouted at them to go faster. There was a prize each day for the person who had written the most words. Terrence had got a funny feeling when he was there that he was about to be taken prisoner – imagine! – and not be paid any money at all. Then one of his books had got into the bestseller chart and dear Skylurian had come to rescue him in a taxi.

Terrence asked Cait to tell him the thing she had liked most about each of his novels. Each time she came up with something, Terrence poured her another glass of the dark, syrupy Tokaj desert wine. Meanwhile, Effie and her father finished the prize crossword. Effie felt somehow sharper than usual. Ever since the tennis match she'd just felt as if she somehow *understood* more things. And of course there'd been that business with the umpire's chair and Tabitha's sports bag. Effie had been able to read a language she didn't even know.

Which had rather made her think.

Soon after finishing the crossword she excused herself, saying she had to get to bed because it was a school night. She took baby Luna with her and settled her into her cot before getting into bed with the important things she had acquired that day.

Terrence Deer-Hart had been given a pile of blankets and told that he was welcome to make himself at home on the sofa – but only once the adults had drunk at least another couple of glasses of wine each and made a good start on the époisses. So Effie was safe for a while in her room.

She had her box back. That was the main thing. It felt heavier, somehow: more solid. Inside were all her precious things. Her half of a walkie-talkie radio set for talking to Lexy, her grandfather's notebook, her precious calling cards, Wolf's sword and her gold necklace with the Sword of Light on it. Effie put her necklace back on and promised herself she would never take it off again. She'd needed it in the Edgelands market and hadn't had it. Pelham Longfellow had given her something that her grandfather had left for her to protect herself – and she hadn't even been able to use it. Never again.

Now Effie had one more special thing, although of course she had only borrowed it. *The Repertory of Kharakter, Art & Shade*. Effie knew she couldn't risk going to the Otherworld as long as her father and Cait were awake, so she started browsing in the big green hardback, looking for something in particular. She needed to know what *kharakter* had a caduceus as its boon.

19

Maximilian ate his supper much more quickly than usual. And he ate less of it too. He'd recently become a bit sick of being the fat kid. Maximilian wanted to be much more like the elegant men he'd met in the Underworld. More like Franz. And something about that dinner he'd had in *The Initiation* with Lupoldus had in some peculiar way cured him of his love of food. He'd never eat anything in this world as delicious as that, so why even bother to try?

'Are you absolutely sure you don't want another helping?' his mother Odile asked. 'It's steak and kidney pudding. Your favourite.'

'Can I not have salad occasionally?' asked Maximilian.

'Salad? You're a growing boy!'

'But . . .'

'I don't want you turning into one of those vegetarians like Mr Hammer across the road,' said Odile. 'Have you seen how weak and pale and pathetic he looks? He can barely carry all those newspapers he has delivered. You need meat at your age. Protein.'

As Odile carried on talking about the merits of protein, Maximilian began to develop an idea.

After his pudding of fruit pie and custard – he left the pie and the custard and only ate the fruit – Maximilian told his mother he was popping out for a while.

'You're always out these days. Where are you going this time?'

'Just to visit one of the neighbours. I want to find out about . . . Oh, never mind. Just something to do with school.'

Maximilian didn't need to lie to his mother about his magical activities, but he still wasn't sure she was ready to find out he was a mage. She knew enough about magic that if he seemed to have developed a sudden interest in classical music she would definitely be suspicious.

Maximilian let himself out of the bungalow and surveyed the other houses in the small close. What was the name of the opera singer? Mrs Magpie? Mrs Blackbird? Mrs . . . As Maximilian walked along trying to come up with his neighbour's name, the Cosmic Web went from slight to moderate panic. No one ever usually walked in this close at night. What was going on? Was the world about to end?

'Hello, Mrs Starling,' said Maximilian when the neighbour opened the door. She looked down at him with kindly green eyes.

'Hello, young Max,' said Mrs Starling. 'What can I do for you?'

Her house smelled strongly of roses and other pink things.

'I want to talk to you about music,' said Maximilian. 'You're an opera singer, aren't you?'

'Oh, strictly amateur,' said Mrs Starling. 'But I did sing at the Conrad Theatre with my little group last Christmas. What do you want to know? My Arthur's a whizz on the piano, if that's any good.'

'Actually, that might be very good,' said Maximilian. 'Yes.'

'Who's that, Elaine?' came a deep voice from what must have been the living room.

'It's Maximilian from four doors down, love,' said Elaine Starling. 'Odile's youngest. He wants to know something about music.'

'Ah, well, he has certainly come to the right place! Show him in, show him in.'

Maximilian entered the rose-scented hallway. Almost everything in the bungalow was pink. What wasn't pink was gold. The wallpaper was pink with gold pears on it. The hallway curtain was gold with a silky pink tie-back. There was a crystal chandelier that didn't look quite right in a bungalow, but didn't look completely wrong either. The pale carpet was very deep and very soft, and exactly the colour of low cloud at sunrise.

Maximilian followed Mrs Starling into the front room, which smelled of scented candles and paper. Two walls were covered with framed prints of musicians and the other two were lined with what seemed like hundreds of books and music scores, some of which had fallen on the floor and not been picked up. Mr Starling was sitting on the sofa reading a book called *Improve your Piano Technique in just 40 days*. On the spine was the familiar logo of a matchstick propping open an eye that meant the book was published by the Matchstick Press.

220

'Oh, Arthur. You're always reading these complicated books nowadays,' said Mrs Starling. 'What about just playing?'

'I have to completely relearn everything I know,' he said, slightly sadly. 'I have no time for playing. Playing is for beginners. That's what it says here.' He went back to his reading, instantly absorbed in it.

'I don't know what's got into him lately,' Mrs Starling said to Maximilian. 'Would you like a cup of cocoa? The electric's still on.'

'No, thank you,' said Maximilian. 'I just wanted to ask you something. Does this word mean anything to you?'

Maximilian got out a piece of paper onto which he'd written the word *Pathétique*. He didn't want to risk showing anyone his actual boon. He passed the piece of paper to Mrs Starling. She shook her head and handed it to Mr Starling. She had to prod him to get his attention away from the book.

'What's all this?' he said, taking the paper note. 'Have you taken to communicating with me like this, Elaine? And in French, too!'

'No,' she said. 'The boy brought it. He wants to know what it is.'

'It's a French word, of course, meaning "pathetic".'

'I guessed that,' said Maximilian. 'But musically, what is it?'

'Aha,' said Mr Starling. 'Well, it's either a symphony by Tchaikovsky or a piano sonata by Beethoven. They're both up on the wall, there.' Mr Starling pointed at one of the walls that was covered in framed images of musicians. 'That's Tchaikovsky, with the white beard. The one with the wild hair and messy piano is Beethoven.'

Maximilian recognised him instantly. The artist had not quite made the hands hairy enough, and had left the bits of wool out of his ears, but . . .

'Beethoven,' said Maximilian.

'Good choice,' said Mr Starling. 'Beautiful, beautiful.' But then he didn't say anything else. His eyes drifted back to his book, almost as if they had been enchanted into doing so.

'When did Beethoven write it?' Maximilian asked.

Mr Starling looked up again and seemed to shake off the enchantment of his book. He put the bookmark back in it, closed it and put it on the table at a slight angle. Mrs Starling immediately straightened it, but Mr Starling didn't appear to notice.

'Eighteen something, I expect. Early eighteen-something. I'll get down the *Musical Encyclopaedia*.' Arthur Starling got up from the sofa and pulled a large, well-loved book from one of the sagging shelves. He flicked to the B section and muttered to himself for a while.

'Almost right,' he said. 'Seventeen ninety-eight. Beethoven was twenty-seven. He was already beginning to go quite deaf. Did you know Beethoven went deaf? Tragic, tragic. It's his eighth sonata. It's . . .'

'Can you play it?' Maximilian asked.

'*Play* it?' Mr Starling said, as if Maximilian had asked him to eat next door's cat, or go outside in his underwear. 'Play it?' he repeated. 'Of course I can't play it.'

'Why not?' asked Maximilian.

'It's far too difficult, that's why not. Play it, indeed.' He shook his head. 'Now, if I had a record . . . But I don't think I've got it any more. I think I lent it to—'

'I actually want to hear it played live,' said Maximilian, sensing correctly that his technique wouldn't work on a recording. 'Would you happen to know anyone who *can* play it?'

'Isn't it on in town?' said Mrs Starling, picking up a printed programme and running her finger down one of its pages. 'Yes, here it is. Well, young Max, if you want to hear the sonata, you're in luck. Tomorrow night, in the Oddfellows Hall. Arthur'll take you, won't you, Arthur? We get free tickets because of our musical connections, you see,' added Mrs Starling.

'But—' began Arthur and Maximilian together.

'And I won't hear any arguments,' Mrs Starling said.

Effie could hear laughter coming from the front room. Would the adults never go to bed? Now that she had her precious calling card back, she was desperate to go to the Otherworld and see her cousins and Cosmo. Still, it wasn't as if she was bored waiting. *The Repertory of Kharakter, Art & Shade* was one of the most interesting books she had ever read. It contained two different tests to find out your *kharakter* and your art, as well as charts, diagrams and lengthy descriptions and discussion of each *kharakter* type.

The longer test was the same one Effie had already taken in the Edgelands market. It gave her an odd, sad feeling when she looked at it. But she was determined not to let those Edgelands crooks ruin her discovery of her art, and the pleasant experience of looking through this wonderful book, so she mentally removed the association from her memory. From now on, this book would only make her think of Festus, and Raven, and the Otherworld. Was this what Maximilian had referred to as ordering one's mind? It felt quite cleansing.

Effie wanted to find out about the caduceus, but it wasn't that easy. The book had no index. Well, not exactly. There was an index of the symptoms one might use to find one's *kharakter* or art. Some of them were quite straightforward, like 'Dreams of flying'. But others were quite outlandish. 'Desires to eat frogs' was one. 'Compelled to dance wildly upon dreaming of the colour red' was another. Each of these was followed by a letter or combination of letters that Effie quickly learned were abbreviations for the *kharakters*. Witch was signified by the letter 'w', and 'warrior' was 'wa', for example.

It seemed that the only way of finding out which boons went with which *kharakter* was to flick through them all one by one. Effie soon found herself memorising the attributes of the major *kharakters*. There was the witch, who loves luxury and beauty and believes the whole universe is profoundly connected; the hunter, who refuses to stop seeking; the explorer, who also seeks, but focuses on the journey rather than the object of the journey. Effie learned about the druid, who is the most connected to nature of all the *kharakters*, and the cleric, who is good at praying and meditation.

Then she found it. *Caduceus*. It was listed as one of the boons used by the interpreter. As soon as Effie saw the entry for interpreter a sort of thrill went through her. Yes, this was her. Every word, almost!

The interpreter is the *kharakter* who is most skilled at reading and can, if they choose, speak many languages. Interpreters can see what is often called the 'hidden' meaning in things, and can usually crack codes and solve puzzles. Interpreters are often great sportsmen and women, favouring those games that rely on interpretation and hand–eye coordination. Interpreters excel at any ball game. They make particularly good tennis players. They can also make excellent natural scientists and historians. Carl Linnaeus, that great botanist of yore, must surely have been a composer interpreter, one who creates something entirely new through the reading of something already in existence.

Their patron is the Roman God Mercury, and the Greek God Hermes, the great travelling communicator. Interpreters often carry the caduceus, as Hermes did. They are themselves mercurial, and can get angry more easily than other *kharakters*. On the other hand, theirs can also be an extremely conciliatory nature, as they understand a great many things.

The entry went on, listing abilities and boons. There were lots of both. As an interpreter Effie could use any magical dictionary, atlas or field guide. She could use objects of divination, like tarot cards or runes. She could even cast some spells! Effie felt happy for the first time in days. Warm feelings flowed through her. So she was a true hero and an interpreter too. Her grandfather must have known that. Almost the first thing he'd taught her had been how to solve puzzles. And then there were the languages, Rosian and Old Bastard English, both spoken in the Otherworld, that had come so easily to Effie. As she looked at the page in front of her it felt as if a whole world of possibility was opening up.

She was just about to flick to the entry for hero to find out what other new skills she could develop when a welcome sound drifted through from the front room. The adults had been quiet for a while now, and Effie had heard the slow creak-creak-click that meant her father and Cait were going up to bed. Now she could hear something that could only be the sound of Terrence Deer-Hart snoring. It was a heavy baritone rumble: very loud, and very prolonged. Would it wake baby Luna? Effie wondered if there was a spell that she could use to muffle it. There probably was, somewhere. She'd have to find a book, and practice, and . . .

Never mind that now. She had to go to the Otherworld while she could. And she was taking no chances with any of her precious things ever again. She put *The Repertory of Kharakter, Art & Shade* into her box and carried it with her as she silently climbed out of the window, just as her mother had done five years before. In the dark sky Effie saw a meteor bursting like a tiny silver fruit, and it reminded her of something, she just wasn't sure exactly what.

Maximilian had a theory. It was such a good theory that the scholar part of him immediately began fantasising about writing a book about it. What would he call his first great work? *The Network of People*. No. *The Knowledge of Crowds*. No. Something snappier. Anyway, the theory, briefly, was this. In these days of unreliable technology, one had to find information in new places. Maximilian had realised that one of these places was the insides of the minds of old people. For Maximilian, an 'old person' was anyone over the age of about 26.

Even the mage part of Maximilian was interested in this theory. It meant the chance to read minds and possibly steal information from them! But Maximilian politely told the mage part of himself to keep quiet as he left the Starlings' house and walked through the cold, dark close, further distressing the Cosmic Web.

What did Maximilian want now? Why was he still wandering around in the dark? He wanted facts. Facts about Albion Freake. And he had decided that the best way of getting these facts was to find an adult who read a lot of newspapers and go and quiz them What was the name of that small man who read three newspapers from cover to cover every day and then made a big show of recycling them every Thursday? Oh yes. Mr Hammer. The vegetarian.

The only problem with Maximilian's theory was that information from humans came with a lot of other stuff you didn't want: pink wafers with fluff on them, for example, like the ones Mrs Starling had insisted on giving him before sending him out into the night. And in order to extract from Mr

Hammer's brain all the things he knew about Albion Freake, it turned out that Maximilian had to eat a large bowl of quinoa and then admire Mr Hammer's wormery. He had to follow him through his echoey house, which did smell pleasantly of wood, spices and herbs, and admire his barometer, his dream-catcher and his half-finished knitted blanket that he had apparently been working on for the last three years.

Still, Mr Hammer certainly had a good brain for facts and figures. From him, Maximilian learned that Albion Freake was the second richest man in the world. Everyone knew that Albion Freake controlled all the electricity on Earth. But no one knew in great detail (nor, thought Maximilian, would want to) about his involvement in the worldwide trade in palm oil (a subject, it turned out, close to Mr Hammer's heart), factory-farmed pigs and a particularly lethal kind of hand grenade.

None of which was that unusual for your average entrepreneur these days. Of course, what Maximilian really wanted to know was . . . In fact, he was quite tempted to . . . He let his mind drift into Mr Hammer's like a bad pickpocket, whistling innocently, unlikely to be noticed, until—

Mr Hammer blocked him. Interesting.

'Well,' said Mr Hammer, staring at Maximillian with his small, raisin-like eyes. 'I see the quinoa has worked.'

'What?' said Maximilian.

'Young mage, you have a lot to learn.'

'How do you know that I'm a—'

'Particularly about entering the minds of hedgewitches. My advice to you? Don't try it. But particularly not after they have

228

obviously, and in full view of you, eaten a bowl of anything earthy or grounding, and especially not if you have eaten some too. Quinoa is an anti-magic agent. You must know that. Same goes for buckwheat, amaranth, parsnips, horseradish and garlic. Of course if you want to enhance magical flow you might use nutmeg, saffron, lime, ginger, cacao or— '

Maximilian's eyes had grown wide. 'You're actually a—'

Mr Hammer gave Maximilian a stern look.

'Why are you really here?'

Maximilian sighed. 'I do want to know about Albion Freake,' he said. 'But I mainly want to know if he is a Diberi.'

Mr Hammer winced when Maximilian said the word 'Diberi'.

'No, he is not a Diberi,' he said. 'What made you think he was?'

'How can you be sure?'

'The Diberi are all publishers, writers, librarians. There was an exposé last year sometime in *The Liminal*. Or maybe it was on the wireless. What was it called? 'When Good Intellectuals Go Bad'. That's right. All a bit sensational for my liking, but factually accurate, nonetheless. The Diberi are all mages and scholars, with the odd well-read trickster thrown in. They are highly educated. Very, very intellectual, the lot of them. But Albion Freake has never read a book in his life. Here, look at this.'

Mr Hammer went to his recycling pile and pulled out a shiny supplement from the weekend before. In it was an interview with Freake, who was running for some minor political office in the United States, where he was from. Freake was, he said in his interview, proudly standing up for the 'little guy' who, like him, had grown up unable to afford books or education or other such luxuries. That was why, he said, he was investing in the most expensive book in the world. As a gesture to all those people who had yet to make it in the way he had. As an inspiration to them. You could come from nothing, make your fortune, and then, Freake said, buy the most 'expensive goddamned book on the darn planet'.

Maximilian read on. The journalist asked Albion Freake whether he was going to read the book after he'd bought it. Freake had laughed, according to the report, and then put his hand on the journalist's knee (something she hadn't much appreciated). 'Honey,' he had said, 'have you ever invested in anything in your pretty little life? Did you ever collect stamps? Did you ever *use* one of those stamps to mail something? Of course you didn't, sugar. My bet is that my billion-dollar book will be worth five times that in five years. But not if I tamper with the merchandise. Of course I'm not going to read it.'

Then the journalist had asked him if he *could* read.

'I pay people to read and write for me, sugar. Why would I need to bother?'

All of which was extremely interesting.

'Can I borrow this?' Maximilian asked Mr Hammer.

'Of course,' said his neighbour. 'And do give my regards to your mother. Tell her I'll have a new batch of her elderberry syrup done soon, now that winter's properly setting in.'

20

Terrence Deer-Hart woke up feeling compelled to start dancing. He'd been dreaming of the colour red and then . . . Where in flip was he? He could smell many familiar things: cocktail onions, cigarettes, salami, old socks, wine. But all of those just made up the natural smell of Terrence and didn't give him any clue at all as to where he was. Terrence had a bit of a headache because he was dehydrated from all the wine he had drunk. Where was the kitchen? Whose flipping house was this . . .?

He was in this unfamiliar place for a reason. What was it?

The flipping child. Of *course*. He was supposed to be following her to some 'other realm' or something. What was it that the lovely Skylurian had said? Terrence couldn't completely remember. Oh dear. She wasn't going to be very flipping happy if Terrence came back to her with nothing. A few hours ago, the only important thing in the world had been Terrence's dinner. But now that he had eaten, slept it off and stopped dancing

(Terrence had been doing a half-hearted Charleston the whole time he had been thinking these thoughts so far, but as it was not a pretty sight we have refrained from dwelling on it), Terrence's imagination had returned once more to love.

Love equalled Skylurian. But Skylurian had told him not to come back until he had this information about this 'other realm' that the girl supposedly visited. And Terrence had forgotten to even ask her. Would she have told him? Unlikely. She was devious, like the gloomy father. But the step-mother, what was she called? Cait. She was a sensible person. She was a nice person. A discerning reader. And . . . Flipping heck. Terrence's thoughts had drifted away from his mission yet *again*.

The night had grown rather chilly. Terrence pulled on his trousers and his fur gilet and ran his hands through his tangled hair. His hair was troubling him. He'd need to be reunited with his heated comb before he could see Skylurian again. But his mind was drifting yet again. He needed to find the girl. Where would she be?

He crept along the corridor to a door to a room that looked like it might contain a child. There was a colourful sign on it saying 'Private – keep out!' that Effie had made when she'd been about eight, and of which no one had ever taken the blindest bit of notice. There was also something hanging from the doorknob; some sort of effigy of a pink pig? It looked like something a baby might like. Of course! Terrence had forgotten about the flipping baby. What would he do if it woke up? And what was he going to say if he was discovered going into Effie's room? Terrence was quite sure that it was improper to go creeping through children's bedroom doors in the middle of the night.

Then there was a noise. The creak of a window opening and closing. Terrence found the front door and peered out. There, dimly visible through the weak street lighting and the cold mist, was the faint outline of a girl in a cape disappearing around the corner at the end of the road. It was Effie, probably sneaking off to this other realm. Well, good. He would follow her, discover how to get there and then be at Skylurian's place in time for breakfast.

Effie walked quickly, but Terrence soon caught up with her, leaving just enough space so she wouldn't know she was being followed. He felt he was rather talented at this. Perhaps he might look into becoming a private detective in his spare time? But . . . Hang on. Where was she now? Aha. Yes, taking a short cut across an old village green. Terrence quickened his pace and was just in time to see his quarry disappear behind a hedge and then . . . She was gone. *Really* gone this time. He searched everywhere. Yes. One minute she'd been behind the hedge, and the next: *poof*. Gone. Like a flipping magic trick.

What had he actually seen her do? He searched his tired, weak and still a little inebriated memory. She'd been holding something, hadn't she? And looking at it intently. Some sort of antique credit card? No. It hadn't been made from plastic. But it was a similar shape. It was a card made from, well, card. Paper. Flipping heck.

Well. At least the main thing was settled. The girl obviously used the little card to get to the hidden realm. How easy this mission had been! So what if the girl had not given away all her

233

secrets in her silly Creative Writing assignment? All you have to do is follow a child for long enough and eventually all will be revealed. Terrence hurried away to try and find a taxi to take him to his one true love, carrying the precious information she had sent him to get.

Effie had missed the Otherworld so much. As soon as she arrived at the gates of Truelove House she felt contentment and peace, deep in her soul. It helped, of course, that she'd gone from a cold November night to a mild summer's day. As she walked up the driveway of the large, higgledy-piggledy mansion, with its many turrets and domes, she could smell the warm honeysuckle hedge and hear the buzzing of happy bees that were all jumbled up in its yellow flowers. She could faintly hear one of the gardeners whistling, and there was birdsong all around.

But as Effie approached the house she became worried. Would her cousins be angry with her for staying away for so long? Or maybe they hadn't missed her at all. After all, there had been that conversation she had overheard, when Rollo had said she wasn't being very useful. Perhaps Rollo was glad that Clothilde was no longer being distracted by Effie when she should be helping with the Great Library.

But anyway, Effie was determined that she would be useful now. She would walk in and apologise and explain everything and tell them what she knew about Skylurian Midzhar and Albion Freake. Effie was completely sure that the Diberi were planning to create a powerful last edition of *The Chosen Ones* that would give this man Freake unlimited powers. Surely that was useful information? And she could also now tell Rollo that she was an interpreter, not just a true hero. She could help with books, and translations and . . .

She entered the house via the conservatory doors, which were always open during the day. There were no signs of anyone, not even Bertie. Where were they all? Effie walked from the conservatory into the large entrance hall, with the grand sweep of the staircase curving up to the first-floor gallery.

'Hello?' she called, but there was no reply.

She was still carrying her box. It felt much safer keeping it here in the Otherworld than it did leaving it in her bedroom at home. Should she go and put it upstairs, and get changed into one of her jumpsuits and go and sit in the sunshine waiting for her cousins to arrive? No. There would be no more sitting in the sun, lounging about being useless. But what could she do that was useful?

Effie had never seen the Great Library. She knew where it was, of course. She'd seen Rollo disappear through the large panelled door behind the grand staircase often enough. If only Pelham Longfellow had taken Effie to get her mark of the Keeper she'd be allowed in there too. It was quite unfair really. She'd passed her test. And if only they'd let her into the Great Library she could be useful, helping with whatever it was they did in there all the time.

While Effie had been thinking, she had been approaching the large panelled doors to the library. And almost without realising what she was doing, she found herself opening one of them. Just a crack. Just to have a look. Effie was surprised when the wooden door swung easily open – much more than just a crack – almost as if it wanted her to come in. Well, Effie could hardly be blamed for trespassing in the library when the door opened so readily, could she? If they didn't want her in here, maybe they should have locked it. With her heart already heavy with guilt, she took one step, and then two steps, into the forbidden library.

It was much smaller than Effie had expected, but then she had always pictured something quite vast. This was more what you might imagine a country house library to look like. There were several rows of dark bookshelves and a wooden ladder on wheels you could use if you wanted to reach a book from one of the higher shelves. By the window on the right there was a wooden table with two leather armchairs on either side of it. Against one wall was an ancient-looking wooden card index file, with drawers labelled things like *Shelf List: Books F12-F25*. On another wall was a large painting of a rural landscape.

There was a gallery above the main library area, with more shelves running around it. Effie could also see a spiral staircase leading from the gallery to somewhere. Maybe this library was a bit bigger than she'd thought when she'd first opened the doors.

Effie took another step into the library. And then another. She went to the table and put her box down.

'Don't move any further,' said a quiet but serious voice.

'Cosmo?'

He was standing on the balcony of the gallery above, with his hands held up before him as if he was holding a large invisible ball. Cosmo looked a lot like Effie's grandfather Griffin, but was unmistakably dressed like a wizard, in long blue silk robes. He had a soft pointed hat that was very old and worn. Effie was used to him patting her hand kindly, with his long white beard full of biscuit crumbs or harbouring lost bits of cake, not looming over her with his hands like that, and his eyes full of . . . Effie almost couldn't bear to look at him. His expression was a mixture of disappointment and fear.

'Do not take another step,' said Cosmo.

'But . . .'

'Your life is in danger. Do not move. Do not think of anything other than where you are right at this moment. Hold it in your mind. If you can't hold it in your mind we might lose you. Concentrate hard.'

Effie began to feel very afraid. What had she done?

'You can see something,' said Cosmo. 'Tell me what you see. Spare no detail.'

'I can only see the library,' said Effie.

'Yes. Describe it to me.'

'But . . .'

'I am not seeing what you are seeing, child. Describe it to me. Now.'

If Effie had not been so afraid, she would have felt rather silly describing to Cosmo a scene he surely could see perfectly well for himself. What did he mean by saying he couldn't see what she was seeing? Effie described the bookshelves and the chairs and the table and everything else around her.

'Not bad,' said Cosmo, as if she'd simply made up what she'd said. 'What colour are the books?'

'All different colours. Blue, red, gold, brown. A lot of brown.'

'What colour are the walls?'

'Pale yellow, with a sort of faint mint green stripe.'

'Excellent. Is there carpet?'

Here Effie hesitated. She looked down at the floor. It was polished floorboards of course, wasn't it? In that moment of hesitation something very strange happened. When Effie looked at the floor to check what it was made of, there was nothing there. Effie suddenly felt that she was falling through the entire universe. For a second when she looked down there was black nothingness with, she thought, the odd star. But the sky should surely be above her, not below her and . . .

'Concentrate, girl,' said Cosmo. 'IS THERE CARPET?'

'No. No,' said Effie. 'It's floorboards. Shiny and dark.'

This time when Effie looked down, that was what she saw.

'Good. And where am I?' asked Cosmo.

'You're on a sort of balcony.' Effie realised she didn't have words for half the things she wanted to describe. 'With wooden sort of railing things stopping you from falling down to this level.'

'Good. Now, tell me where the stairs are to get down to your level from here.'

The stairs. The stairs. But there were no stairs. Obviously that couldn't be right. Of course there must be stairs.

'If you can't see any stairs, we might have a big problem,' said Cosmo. 'Blink. Look away. Don't lose the impression of the place. Keep it all in your mind just so, but try to create some stairs. Don't ask me what that means, or think about it too much. Just do it.'

Effie tried to follow his instructions. She had to 'create' some stairs, even though she didn't understand in the slightest what this might mean. But somehow her mind just didn't believe there were any stairs coming down from the gallery, and so she couldn't create any.

'Well?' said Cosmo. 'Where are they?'

'There are only stairs going up,' said Effie. 'A spiral staircase in the far left hand corner.'

'And where do they go?'

'I don't know.'

'YOU DO KNOW!' boomed Cosmo. His voice had become more and more serious and terrifying. Cosmo was the least shouty person Effie had ever met, and suddenly he was acting like this. Why?

'They lead to a door to the gallery in the house,' said Effie. 'There's a separate entrance to the Great Library from up there. Between my room and the stairs up to your study.'

'Good. Hold all this in your mind, child, just for a little while longer. I will come down and help you. Do not move in the meantime. Just keep thinking about the stairs that lead back into the house.'

The next few moments felt like a lifetime. But soon enough Effie heard the faint squeak of a door behind her. Cosmo had successfully come through the house and then entered the door behind Effie. She heard his light footsteps and then the comforting feeling of his soft old hand in hers.

'You are safe as long as you hold my hand,' he said. 'So don't let go. Tell me. How did you get in here?'

'Through the door,' said Effie.

'That's impossible,' said Cosmo.

'It's true. I'm sorry. I—'

'No. It can't happen. You must have got in some other way. There must have been a breach and . . .'

'I came through the main door. Really. I know I shouldn't have. I'm so sorry. I . . .' Effie's voice caught in her throat. She had no idea what was happening, but she knew that she had made a big mistake. Perhaps even bigger than she could contemplate.

'Don't get upset, child. It's still important that you concentrate. But you have to understand that it's impossible that you came through that door. You have to be initiated first. It's quite a long learning process. The door will only let you in if it knows you are ready, and that you have completed the process. Or . . .? But no. No. That would truly be impossible.'

'Or what? What would be impossible?'

'Did you by any chance have something with you when you came in here?'

'Yes. My box. I put it on the table, just there.'

'What's in the box?'

'All my most precious things. I brought it here because my father confiscated it before and . . .' Effie was still too ashamed to tell anyone that she'd lost all her most precious boons, including the calling card that transported her to the Otherworld. 'I just wanted to keep it with me. There are people in the Realworld I don't trust, and . . .'

240

'Are there any books in the box?'

'No. Wait. Yes. My grandfather's notebook. It was some sort of translation he was doing just before he was attacked. And actually also a book I borrowed from my friend. *The Repertory of Kharakter, Art & Shade.*'

'I know it well. Nothing else?'

Effie shook her head. 'Nothing.'

'Can I look?'

'Of course. It's on the table. Just here.'

'The table by the window,' said Cosmo, repeating Effie's description from earlier.

'Yes?'

'Have you looked out of this window?'

'No. Why?'

'I need you to decide what is out of the window before we both look at it. Don't think about it too hard. Don't let your mind worry about what should or should not be out there. Space works differently in here than it does in other parts of the house. But it's very, very important that we don't look out of the window and find nothing there. If we do, I fear we may lose our connection and then I won't be able to save you.'

'*Save* me?'

'Yes.' Cosmo's voice was still grave. 'I need to work out why the library wanted you here, and then help you to leave. The library might not let you out without my help.'

Effie gulped. 'OK,' she said. 'I know what's outside the window. It's an apple orchard with a path running through the middle of it.'

'Good. Do you believe in it 100 percent?'

'Yes.'

'All right. Now let us examine this box.'

Cosmo kept hold of Effie's hand with one of his. With the other, he went through the box. When he picked up Effie's grandfather's notebook, a smaller volume fell out. It had got caught up in the bigger book's pages. Cosmo reached down to the floor to pick it up and . . . It was . . . It looked like . . . But no. It couldn't be. A thin brown book with gold lettering.

'Where did you get this?' said Cosmo.

'I don't know,' said Effie. 'I had no idea it was in there, honestly.'

It was her mother's book. The one she'd found under her bed on the night of the worldquake. The slim hardback volume that Effie thought her mother might have left behind by accident, or maybe even wanted Effie to look after. The amount of times Effie had kicked herself for taking it straight to her father, when she should have hidden it from him.

But now . . .? How on earth had it ended up in her box? Had her father put it there for her to find? But why? Was it to thank her for giving him that copy of *The Chosen Ones*? Was it some kind of reward? It would make a sort of sense. After all, Orwell never did anything for Effie unless she did something for him first. If ever she wanted money for a school trip, she'd have to do a certain number of chores, for example. Sometimes she wondered how he kept all the invisible tallies going in his mind.

'The book was my mother's,' explained Effie. 'But I didn't

know it was in my box. I think my father might have put it there, but I don't know why.'

'Well, it certainly explains why the library wanted you in here,' said Cosmo.

'Does it?'

'Oh yes. This is a most important book. Did you try to read it?'

Effie shook her head. 'When I first saw it I looked at it, but it was impossible. I haven't seen it for years,' she said. 'My father hid it from me. Maybe I'd be able to read it now. I'm good at languages and stuff. But the last time I saw it I was only six.'

'The last time you saw it was on the night of the worldquake?'

'Yes! How did you know?'

'Because this was the book your mother was supposed to be bringing back to us that night. It had been stolen from our library, probably by a Diberi spy who found his way into Truelove House somehow. Your mother was very brave, Effie. She led the mission to get the book back. But when she turned up here during that fateful *Sterran Guandré*, she . . .'

'What?' said Effie.

This talk about her mother was distracting Effie from thinking about the library, and it was starting to show. The landscape painting at the end of the room had changed three times in the last two minutes. And a storm was beginning to develop over the orchard outside the window. These were not good signs.

'We shouldn't talk about this now,' said Cosmo. 'You must help me to return the book and then I'll help you get back into the main house. I'll explain everything then.'

243

'All right,' said Effie. 'What do I have to do?'

'Is there some sort of directory in the library?'

'Yes,' said Effie. 'It's over there. It's a big wooden sort of chest with little drawers in it. A card index.'

'Good. Excellent. Well, that should make your task easier. It's a very promising sign if your library comes to you in good order. Now I want you to look on the edge of the book and see if there's a number there.'

Effie looked. There was. F34. It seemed momentarily strange to her that such an important library should only have one letter and two numbers in its classification system. Then she wondered how she suddenly knew enough about libraries that she had even noticed. Then she began to feel a bit sick. It was a deep nausea that seemed to grow out of the ground beneath her feet somehow. It was beginning to squeeze her insides. She stopped thinking about the classification system and the feeling subsided, but did not disappear completely.

'What is the number?'

Effie told Cosmo. Then together they walked over to the wooden filing cabinet and found the drawer F25-F38. With a shaking hand, Effie took the F34 card out of the filing system, and put it in the book, just as they did at her local library. Then, with Cosmo still holding her hand, she worked out how the shelves were arranged. There was G, and there was H. So F must be . . . Yes. She found the right shelf and the F22 books, the F23 books, the F24 books – of which there seemed to be a great many – and then there was a gap, slightly tight, for her mother's book. Effie pushed it into position, and the library seemed to sigh with gratitude.

But Effie still felt rather sick. In fact, she barely had a chance to notice the other books on the shelf, all of which were in strange languages except for one, which looked more ordinary, and sort of familiar for some reason, when the nausea crept over her again and her legs started to give way underneath her.

'You've been here too long,' said Cosmo. 'We must leave now.'

'I don't feel that well,' admitted Effie. 'But I'm sure I'll be all right.'

'You will need all your strength now, child. Keep hold of my hand. And brace yourself.'

21

Getting to the library door was one of the hardest things Effie had ever done. Each step was painful to her. And she had no energy left. It was a curious feeling, as if her whole soul wanted to just give up. What happens when your whole soul gives up? Surely you just die on the spot? Effie didn't even have the strength to be afraid. But somehow they got to the end of the library, and Cosmo opened the door. And . . .

Weakness. Blackness. Faintly falling, falling faintly . . .

The next thing Effie knew, she was in bed in her room in Truelove House and Cosmo was speaking sternly to someone, although Effie couldn't see who it was. The room smelled comfortingly familiar: old wood and clean linen. But Effie had a horrible feeling – as if she'd left the iron on, or a door unlocked, and something awful was going to happen.

'Well,' Cosmo was saying. 'The child has managed to accomplish what you all failed to do at the last *Sterran Guandré*. But she has used up all her power and won't last long here now.

She is hanging by a mere thread of lifeforce. She has had so little time to learn. And now I fear we are going to lose her.'

Effie couldn't open her eyes. Cosmo was still talking about her. She wasn't in trouble for going into the library, it seemed. In fact, Cosmo had given the impression that he was very pleased that she'd brought the book, the one he said the Diberi had stolen all those years ago. But still, Effie knew she shouldn't have gone in to the Great Library on her own like that, in secret. She should have given the book to someone else. From what Cosmo was saying, what she'd done had taken away almost all her lifeforce. Her M-currency. Her magical power.

But maybe that didn't even matter any more. Was she going to die? It certainly looked like it. Effie had never felt so ill in her life. Perhaps it was worth it, if she had done something truly useful. But it would be much nicer to stay alive. Effie did so desperately want to see more of the Otherworld, and help more with the fight against the Diberi, and be a true hero and an interpreter and maybe even ride Jet again and . . .

'You'll have to take her to London,' said Cosmo. 'To Dr Black. He is there now, I understand?'

'But that's against everything we believe in,' began a voice Effie recognised. Rollo. 'Everything we stand for. We can't . . .'

'Let me be clear,' said Cosmo's voice again. It was mild, but also very stern. 'The problems began with *you*. With both of you. Aurelia was married already, for goodness' sake. But you still had to squabble over her like a pair of schoolboys, and break Clothilde's heart in the process. And you, Rollo. Don't think you're any better because you were not engaged to someone else

247

at the time. What you did was stupid and dangerous, and we are still dealing with the consequences now.'

'This quarrel is draining us all,' said another voice. It was Pelham Longfellow. 'I wish I could say I understood your point of view and offer you blessings, Rollo, but at this moment I cannot. I wrestle with myself, as we all do. But I too find it hard to forgive your actions on that night. We all lost Aurelia. And my father died as well, because . . .'

'Your father's death was an accident,' said Rollo. 'And we all feel very sorry for you, of course. But I think it's become clear you have found ways to derive considerable comfort from your life on the island,' said Rollo. 'And just for the record, I had *no* feelings for Aurelia. I simply wanted to spare my sister pain. She did not have the choices you have.'

Effie was having trouble following this argument. It seemed to be about her mother. It sounded as if everyone had been in love with her, which was a nice thing to hear, except that it didn't sound as if it had ended very well. And would her mother really have got involved with two different men at the same time, while also being married to a third? Effie remembered her mother as kind and good and uncomplicated. It all sounded wrong. What on earth had happened? But the more she thought about it, the weaker she felt.

'She's fading,' said Cosmo. 'So you have a choice, which I am going to make for you. Take her to Dr Black, Pelham. We will face the consequences later.'

'Are we simply to face *consequences* forever?' said Rollo.

'Yes,' said Cosmo. 'If we have to.'

When Laurel Wilde woke up, it was cold and dark. Where was she? And where was Skylurian? One minute they had been friends, and the next minute her publisher had insisted that Laurel Wilde drink a cup of odd-tasting tea, which must have been drugged, and had then tied her up and put her in the back of her car!

What on earth had Laurel done to deserve this? Was it because she hadn't approved that dreadful book cover? Or was it because she kept complaining about the limited-edition single-volume plan for *The Chosen Ones*? Although most of her complaining had happened in her head, really. Laurel, as usual, hadn't actually made that much fuss at all.

Perhaps it was because of the 7.5 percent. Or seven. Or whatever it was. Laurel Wilde wasn't good with numbers. She was good with words. Where was her typewriter? Her notebook? Her best pen? Was it evening now? Laurel longed for her glass of wine, her music, a pomegranate, her cashmere shawl. Instead, she was lying on something scratchy that smelled of barnyards. Hay. Was it too much to hope that she had been simply put in one of the spare stables? Laurel's hands were still tied behind her back, but as she struggled to her feet she realised that she was in fact a very long way away from anywhere. Through a small window, Laurel could see stars, and lots of them. Oh! And a meteor with an odd pinkish tail. Then another. But there were no lights from any houses at all.

What did she have with her? She couldn't see anything. But she could smell mints and leather and her perfume. She hadn't put any perfume on before her kidnap. She knew that. Which meant that her handbag must be here somewhere. She must have somehow managed to grab it before the drugs properly kicked in.

Laurel scrabbled around in the hay. Having her handbag was a very good thing. Being a novelist meant she always anticipated the worst. It was her job to always think of dramatic things involving kidnaps and falling down mine-shafts and so on. This meant Laurel was always prepared for things. And – yes – there it was. Her handbag that contained a Satsuma, a luxury energy bar, three small cans of soda water, a penknife, an old phone and a compact mirror. All the things she would need to stay alive, and, she hoped, effect her escape.

Effie found she could not open her eyes even if she tried. She felt sleepy and comfortable, and as if she was about to go on a long journey to somewhere very remote and very mysterious.

'She is not going to survive here much longer. You must take her back to the island now,' said Cosmo.

'I can't get her to the portal,' said Pelham. 'She's not even awake. You'll have to use magic.'

'Yes,' said Cosmo distractedly. 'I can try something, I suppose. But I don't know exactly how to accomplish sending you both to the island directly from here. It is possible, but I fear it might take longer than we have.'

'But then what am I to do?' said Pelham.

'There is something we could try,' said Rollo. 'But it might be too dangerous. I don't know.'

'What is it?' said Pelham, his tone to Rollo still rather cold.

'It's a device I made . . . To send intruders back to the island. I came up with it when we were arming ourselves against the Diberi before the last *Sterran Guandré*. It simulates a mainland death in the sense that it sends you back to the island, but it doesn't de-age you and you are not reborn. I think it also keeps your lifeforce intact, although obviously I was trying to make a version that wipes it out. For that reason I thought it a failure. But it might be just what we need now.'

'Where does it send you?'

'Somewhere on the island.'

Pelham snorted. 'What, like the middle of the Pacific? The top of Mount Everest?'

'No. That was another problem with the design. You have to give it coordinates. I chose a few remote places to test it out. Or, at any rate, places that seemed remote to me. I could send you both to one of them. Then you'd have to find your way back to London, if you are set on seeing this Dr Black. I think it might be your only hope of getting the girl to the island quickly. Of course if she runs out of lifeforce completely while she's here she may well end up in the Pacific, or worse, and alone. And never able to return.'

'I think you'd better do it,' said Cosmo. 'Thank you, Rollo. At least once the poor child is back on the island she'll be able to restore her physical health. But her lifeforce is almost gone. You must hurry.'

Lifeforce and physical health. Lifeforce and physical health. The

251

words started repeating in Effie's mind like a strange poem. Lifeforce was magical power. Otherworld power. Known in the Realworld as M-currency. And Effie realised that all hers was now gone.

There was the sound of the door opening, and Rollo's fast footsteps going along the gallery outside. Then the door opened again. There were a few strange noises, and the sound of something being put together in a hurry.

'All right,' said Pelham. 'I'm ready when you are.'

'Do you have enough Realworld currency?' asked Cosmo.

'You mean money? Oh yes; I've got plenty of that.'

Effie could smell Pelham Longfellow's subtle patchouli and vanilla aftershave, and the warm cinnamon scent of his skin as he sat her up in bed and held her frail body to his. He was going to rescue her, to carry her somewhere. To . . .

The next thing Effie knew, she was opening her eyes somewhere bright and very warm. Was she still in the Otherworld after all? She seemed to be wrapped in a blanket on a sun-lounger on the porch of a small hut somewhere. There was a mountain in front of her in the distance, and, before that, some sort of lagoon. She felt warm and comfortable physically. But she found she also felt deeply sad, and somewhat empty. It was as if she had been turned inside out; her soul was no longer hidden safely deep inside her but instead now formed the outer layer of her existence, like it had been stretched over her skin. Effie wanted to tell someone that this was wrong; that her soul should not be on the outside of her like this. She felt frightened, which was unusual, because as a true hero she was usually so brave.

Pelham Longfellow was pacing up and down in front of the hut, tapping something into his pager. A woman approached him.

'Your car will be here in two hours, sir,' she said. 'It will take you around an hour to get to Cape Town airport. Your flight leaves at ten o' clock p.m. and gets to London tomorrow morning.'

'Thank you so much,' said Pelham. 'You've been extremely kind.'

He turned around and saw that Effie was awake.

'Well,' he said. 'Hello, young hero. You've had a bit of an adventure, I hear.'

'I don't feel like a hero,' said Effie. 'Where are we?'

'Oh, South Africa,' said Pelham cheerfully. 'Overshot a tiny bit. We'll fly back to London this evening. I've booked economy on the basis that I can cast a couple of spells to upgrade us to first class. More economical than paying for actual first class, although I do that too sometimes when the lifeforce is low.' He stopped abruptly and then sighed. 'As yours now is, of course. How do you feel, you poor child?'

Effie shrugged. 'I don't know,' she said. 'A bit tired. But OK, I think. It's just . . .'

'What?'

'I don't know how to describe it. It's a feeling I've never had before.' Effie didn't know how to begin explaining the sensation of her soul being on the outside. It wouldn't sound right if she tried to say it. Also, she had a feeling it might make it worse if she did. 'I feel sort of sad. And as if I've lost something, inside. Does that sound stupid?'

Pelham shook his head. 'No. You're experiencing what it feels like to have no lifeforce,' he said. 'Some people call it the Yearning. I've had it only once, a very long time ago. It's one of the worst feelings in the whole world. I'd much rather break a limb – or several – than ever go through the Yearning again. But we'll have you fixed up soon. You just need to hang on. It takes a little while to top your lifeforce back up, but you'll get there.'

'What if I can't hang on?'

'There's no choice. You have to.'

'I sort of feel like I'm about to fall off a cliff, even though there isn't a cliff here,' said Effie.

'I know,' said Pelham. 'It's a dreadful feeling. But it doesn't last forever, and it can't hurt you. The sooner you realise that, the sooner your lifeforce will come back.'

'But I'm frightened. What if I become less and less like myself? What if I forget my friends, and the Otherworld and—'

'You won't. The Yearning somehow manages to find the thing you're most afraid of, and then makes you worry about it all the time. I knew a very kind vicar once who had the Yearning. He became terribly afraid that he might start calling people names in the street. He would begin to wish someone a good day, and then something in his head would suggest adding "you ugly old cow" or "you pathetic idiot". He never actually said those things, he just became very scared he would. The Yearning always makes you think of things that are the complete opposite of what you would actually do. But no one *ever* does the thing that they fear. Not ever. You can't let the Yearning take you over. The worst thing is to start believing in it.'

'If you believe in it, then does it come true?'

'No. It just feels terrible. And if you start doing the things it wants you to – for example, when the vicar decided not to go out in case he really *did* call people names – then it completely takes over your life.'

'Is there nothing I can do until we get to London?'

'The main thing is to be yourself and ignore these feelings. You could also try to meditate. That'll probably give you a bit of lifeforce. And I'll go and see what they've got in the kitchens. Maybe something pickled would help. When the Yearning comes, you must just accept it and try not to worry about it. Relax as much as you can. Resisting the feelings will just deplete your lifeforce even further.'

'What will happen if it depletes further?' asked Effie.

'You just feel bad for longer.' Pelham smiled kindly. 'The only danger of the Yearning in the Realworld is entering a cycle where you become so afraid all the time that you drain your own lifeforce as quick as it is being topped up. Then it can take a long time to get better.'

'Can I die?'

'No,' said Pelham. 'Not from the Yearning, not in this world. Lots of people in the Realworld are in this state all the time, not recognising what it is, because they have no concept of lifeforce, and they don't know that islanders need magical energy too. But it's only on the mainland that you can die from lack of lifeforce. All that can happen here is that you feel worse.'

'I can't imagine feeling any worse,' said Effie gloomily. She twisted the ring on her finger. Should she take it off? It had almost killed her that first time she wore it. But of course then it had drained her physical energy, not her magical lifeforce. As far as Effie knew, her ring still helped her generate M-currency. Although it hadn't done a very good job of it lately.

'Well, don't try, because if there's one thing that is guaranteed to make you feel worse, it's thinking about it. Try to be cheerful. And meditate.'

'How exactly do you meditate?'

'You must already know how.'

Effie shook her head.

'But what about when you use the calling card to get to Truelove House. You have to be in a meditative state for that to work, surely?'

'You mean when I clear my mind and breathe deeply?'

'Exactly. Do that.'

'Is that all meditating is?'

'Yes. That's all it is. In fact, you don't even have to breathe deeply. You just try to clear your mind, and then fail – everyone fails, because it's almost impossible. But you just become slowly more aware of yourself. And sometimes you find you can switch off your thoughts for a few moments, and that's when you heal.'

'I think I know what you mean.'

'Excellent. I'll leave you to it. I'm off to the kitchens.'

'Pelham?'

'What?'

'Please don't leave me on my own. I don't know what I'll do. I don't think I can bear it.'

Pelham signed. 'I *am* going to leave you on your own, and

you are going to meditate. It will bring you some peace, I'm sure of it.'

'But . . .'

'You must never give in to fear,' said Pelham. 'Fear strips your lifeforce faster than anything else.'

'But . . .'

'Have faith in yourself.'

Pelham Longfellow walked off across the grass towards a wooden walkway leading through small, old-looking trees to a large veranda with a door. Effie felt terrified. It was so unlike her to feel this way. Then that thought terrified her too. How could she have become so unlike herself in just a few short hours? But, following Pelham's instructions, she accepted the feeling. For a few seconds it got a lot worse, so much so she thought she wouldn't be able to bear it. Then it went away. When it came again, she did the same thing. Again, the feeling got worse, and then better. This time it was worse for a shorter time, and better for a longer time. It was like waves breaking on a ragged shore, again and again, with the tide slowly going out.

Effie began trying to meditate. She was soon joined by a bird with a crest on its head that looked like a Mohican from the olden days. Then another bird came. It was small, with a pointed beak, and its tiny body was a mixture of green, blue, red and yellow patches. The sight of the bird made Effie smile. It was the most beautiful thing she had ever seen. Had the Yearning made her think that too? How strange. Having her soul on the outside made everything different, it seemed.

There was a small slice of cake on a plate next to her. Pelham must have brought it for her before. She was feeling a little bit hungry, but so, too, presumably, were these birds. Effie held out a few crumbs on her hand, and then the brightly coloured bird actually came and took them! Effie smiled again, and added a few more crumbs. She threw a larger bit of cake to the other bird on the grass. It ate it rather comically, with its Mohican bobbing up and down. The smaller bird was now eating out of Effie's palm. Very slowly, Effie's lifeforce started to increase, tiny bit by tiny bit.

Once the cake was all gone, Effie closed her eyes and began to meditate. It wasn't easy at first. She kept thinking about the Great Library. She couldn't help trying to work out what had happened to her there, and what it was.

She *had* to try to meditate. She closed her eyes, but all she could see were the panelled doors of the Great Library and then the yellow walls with the precise mint green stripes, and the rows and rows of books, and . . .

The one thing she was sure of was that Cosmo had been in the library with her, but that for some reason he hadn't been able to see it. She'd needed to tell him where everything was, and even how to get out. It had been as if he were blind. Perhaps he had seen the library differently? But what sort of place was it that two people could see it completely differently? And why was it so dangerous? Effie was sure that her experience in the Great Library had completely drained what had remained of her lifeforce, but why?

Effie managed to clear her mind for two, maybe three, seconds. It was calming, restorative. But then she opened her eyes with a start. She was in the Realworld again, wasn't she? In South Africa, thousands of miles from home, and running on Realworld time. She didn't even know what day it was. Which meant that everyone back home would be looking for her, and worrying and . . . When she got back, her father would probably never let her out of the house again.

The journey to the airport should have been exciting. There were mountains and baboons and views of the blue glistening sea in the distance. But all Effie could think of were the dangerous and sad things everywhere and how much trouble she'd be in when she got home.

As promised, Pelham cast an upgrade spell at the airport that gave them both first-class tickets, which meant a comfortable wait in a lounge surrounded by free sandwiches and fruit, and then their own little suite on the plane, with their own beds, dressing gowns and soft cotton pyjamas. Effie wished she could enjoy it. She'd never flown before, and had always wanted to. And in such luxury! But in the end she slept through the whole flight, dreaming of strange libraries and sets of stairs that kept going up forever with no obvious way down.

When the plane landed at Heathrow, Effie barely noticed the private golden jet that was taxiing in to the gate next to theirs, with the words ALBION FREAKE INC on the side of it. And she completely missed the man himself, with his shock of bright red hair and silver lamé pinstriped suit, as he made his way through the airport and into a waiting gold limousine.

22

'Darlings,' breathed Skylurian Midzhar over breakfast on Thursday. 'I do declare that we have almost reached our target. There are only twelve more copies of *The Chosen Ones* to come in and then we have done it. Albion will be so happy when he arrives later today.'

Terrence Deer-Hart looked rather put out.

'Albion Freake's arriving today?'

'Yes, my sweet.'

'And he's a . . . *friend*, you say?'

'A business associate. I told you about the limited-edition single volume we are creating for him, didn't I?'

'Yes, you did.' Terrence chewed his lower lip. He almost looked as if he were about to start crying. 'You told me all about how Laurel Wilde, as your *favourite* and most *bestselling* author ever, had been chosen for this extreme honour and . . .' Terrence had gone quite red and suddenly seemed to have forgotten to breathe. He spluttered, blanched, and reached for a glass of water.

'Have you heard anything from my mother?' said Raven.

'No, darling, sorry. She's outside pager contact just now.'

'Do you even know what country she's in?'

'Perhaps Bolivia? One does so easily lose track of authors on tour. I'm sure she's doing jolly well.'

'Why am *I* not on a book tour?' said Terrence.

'Because you are here with me, my sweet.'

'But why does Laurel Wilde get to go on tour and . . .' Terrence remembered that of course Laurel Wilde was not on a book tour at all, but had been kidnapped and imprisoned in an old croft on the moor. But, frankly, even the very *idea* of another author being on a book tour while he, Terrence, had not even been allowed to write his first serious adult novel was just too much to bear.

Skylurian and Raven exchanged a look. This man was extremely stupid. Raven knew Skylurian was up to something, and Skylurian knew that Raven knew she was up to something. But all this man cared about were his sales figures and his hair. For a moment Skylurian forgot why he was even here. Oh yes. He'd been sent to find out information about how the Truelove girl travelled between worlds. And at least he had been useful in that respect. He'd told her all she needed to know. The sooner she could smite this silly, pathetic man, the better. Although perhaps she would just toy with him a little while longer. As well as being stupid he was, she had to admit, rather attractive.

'She can't stay here for three days!' said Pelham Longfellow to Dr Black. 'Is there nothing you can do that's any quicker?'

Effie was sitting in a comfortable leather chair in the office of Dr Black in Soho, London. She'd met Dr Black once before, on the day he had performed the surgery that had been supposed to send her grandfather Griffin to the Otherworld after he had died in the Realworld. Effie had never been to London before. It was all so interesting, but her tired mind couldn't take much of it in. Outside the window women walked down the thin, cobbled street wearing skin-tight leather leggings with ballet leotards and faux fur coats, or slogan T-shirts from the previous century with fleece-lined denim jackets.

Many of the buildings were semi-ruins now, of course, and had been even before the worldquake, but most of them had flowers growing out of their crumbling walls and spilling from home-made window boxes – even in November. Effie watched a cat through the window opposite that seemed also to be watching her.

'I'm sorry,' said Dr Black. 'Her lifeforce really is down to nothing. I need to put her on a drip and try to get it back up as fast as I can, but in reality that is going to take at least three days.'

'Her father will have called the police by then. And maybe the Northern Guild. He has some old connections there, I believe.'

'The Northern Guild is problematic, I agree.'

'Indeed. So . . .?'

'Can we not simply tell the father she's here? That would be the best course of action.'

'No,' said Pelham. 'He's not a supporter of our cause. He

absolutely can't know that this has happened. I'm regressing his memories until we get back, but, as you know, that kind of magic is extremely costly, and I can't keep it up for more than another day. Is there anything you can send her away with? Anti-yearning tablets, maybe?'

'We don't suppress symptoms here,' said Dr Black. 'Probably the only thing we won't do.' He smiled the smile of a man who knows that what he does is not approved of by most people, and that those people are all wrong.

'I realise that. But can't you put whatever was going to be in the drip into tablet form? Or cast it as a spell?'

'I am no witch, Longfellow. And anyway, I thought you understood what we do here? I thought you – and your kind – even disapproved of it?'

'Yes, well, we do usually. But we can't leave a child in this state. And she has helped us all with her recent actions. She returned the missing book. We have to repay her somehow.'

'You do realise that what you've asked for is the top treatment requested by the Diberi in their Swiss clinic?'

'We can live with that in this case.'

'Anyway, it's immaterial if you won't leave her here. We simply can't complete the treatment.'

Pelham Longfellow sighed. 'Is there really nothing else? I may not have mentioned that money is no object.'

'I spoke to the directors earlier today. They don't want money.'

'You say that as if they want something that is not money.'

'Yes,' said Dr Black, slowly.

'Well? What is it?'

'They want you to leave London. Turn a blind eye to the factory in Walthamstow.'

'But—' began Pelham.

'They know how much you want Skylurian Midzhar, and how long you've been working on her operations here. But she's small fry, compared to the bigger Diberi.' Dr Black looked troubled by something. 'What she's done in Walthamstow . . . I can't exactly say I approved of it at first, but what I can say is that it works. No one has to suffer the Yearning any more. Yes, yes, I know all the objections you're going to make. But whatever else she has done, Skylurian Midzhar, the corrupt and dreadful Diberi, has actually produced something that genuinely increases the goodness of the world.'

'It's a short cut. It goes against everything—'

'But you came here for a short cut, did you not?'

'Yes. Because the circumstances are—'

'Everyone believes their own circumstances deserve special treatment, Longfellow. And that is what we can now offer. Special treatment for everyone.'

'But—'

Dr Black opened a drawer in his large desk. 'Perhaps you've been wondering what these look like? I know you've been making enquiries. Here.' He held out a small glass box, in which there were three clear capsules containing a dark gold, slightly shimmering substance. 'You can have these. But only on condition that you leave London. Let's say for a year? You could go to Europe, chase the bigger Diberi. We have no problems with that – in that, we're on the same side.'

Pelham Longfellow took the box from Dr Black.

'And they work, do they?'

'Oh yes.'

'They're not like the old-fashioned anti-Yearning treatments?'

'Not at all. They replace lifeforce directly, in a usable form.'

'And how is that different from just force-feeding the child owl's eyeballs or guinea-pig hearts?'

'You know full well that those methods give tiny amounts of currency to those whose *kharakter* and art take them to the darker areas. This child is pure light. She's a traveller. Her spirit is partly Otherworld. Quite a lot of it, judging by the tests I did. That's why this is affecting her so strongly. Anyway, those methods won't work on her. They'd simply make her worse.'

'So what's in these?' asked Longfellow.

'Concentrated . . .' Dr Black's eyes moved slowly from Pelham Longfellow's to his desk top.

'Concentrated . . .?'

Dr Black sighed angrily. 'You already know what they are, Longfellow. It's up to you whether you want to take them and give them to the girl or not.'

'And how many thousands of krubles do they cost?'

'As I said before, you will agree to leave London, and let the factory remain open. Stop investigating Skylurian Midzhar. If you can agree to that, the medication is free. Think of it as being part of a trial.'

'You're not giving me any choice, are you?'

'Sorry,' said Dr Black. 'No.'

Pelham Longfellow was quiet as the black cab wound its way through Bloomsbury, with its overgrown parks and gardens, and its strange basements with puppet shows and fortune-tellers, towards the train station. Effie was thinking hard about everything she'd heard in Dr Black's office. She was feeling a little better after being given an injection and a treatment with oils and flower petals rubbed into her skin, but she was still deeply troubled by everything. Why had Pelham Longfellow agreed to leave London? *To save my life*, thought Effie. And then she felt ashamed. She'd got something dreadfully wrong at some point, she just wasn't sure what.

'Pelham?' she said.

'Hmm?' he replied, distracted by something he was typing into his pager.

'I know what Skylurian Midzhar is up to.'

'Well, it doesn't matter now, even if you do.'

'But Pelham?'

'You must rest child. You've got a long train journey ahead.'

'But . . .'

'I've just agreed not to investigate Skylurian Midzhar any more. Which is perhaps a good thing, given that no one knows where exactly she is.'

'I do,' said Effie.

Pelham looked up. 'How?'

'She's at my friend's house, staying with her mother. I went to the Otherworld to tell Clothilde and Rollo and Cosmo everything I knew, but I didn't get the chance. I think she's planning something big. I mean, I think I know what she's planning. It involves Albion Freake and . . .'

'Albion Freake? The American businessman?'

'That's right.'

'Go on.'

As quickly as she could, Effie explained to Pelham Longfellow everything she knew about the limited-edition single volume.

'I think he's a Book Eater,' said Effie. 'He's going to make himself the Last Reader of *The Chosen Ones* and then destroy it and—'

'But a book that popular would give them enough power to launch a serious attack on Dragon's Green,' said Pelham.

'That's what I thought,' said Effie. 'I have to help stop them . . . I have to . . .'

'You have to *rest*.'

'But I didn't promise that *I* wouldn't investigate Skylurian Midzhar. Only you did. And no one said anything about Albion Freake. I could . . .' Effie suddenly felt a little faint again, and weak. She closed her hands into fists to try to will back some power. She was used to feeling strong. This was not like her at all. But she couldn't give up. She would never give up.

'You have to take these tablets, one a day for three days, it says here, and REST.'

'But I think what Skylurian has planned is going to coincide with the *Sterran Guandré*. I don't know why, or how. But . . .'

'Yes, that would make sense.' Pelham sighed and looked more anxious than Effie had ever seen him before.

'Why?'

'It's too complicated to explain. And we're here.'

The taxi pulled up outside St Pancras Station. All trains to the north and south of the country now went from St Pancras. Trains to the east and west went from Paddington. All the other old railway stations had been left as beautiful ruins, destined to become luxury cocktail bars or bird sanctuaries. Euston was now a massive butterfly house. But St Pancras had finally been restored to its Victorian glory, with its beautiful ridge-and-furrow roof, and its vast booking office.

Pelham paid the driver and helped Effie out onto the pavement. 'Can you walk?' he asked.

'Yes, I think so,' said Effie. 'I don't think my physical energy has been affected that much.'

St Pancras Station smelled of coffee, and was full of the dry squawking sounds of the bright green parakeets that filled London. The parakeets spent their days swooping in and out of large buildings in small flocks, calling to one another, adding to the complex and significant part of the Cosmic Web that covered the whole of the city.

Next to the vendor selling the *Evening Standard* (which was now back in print) was a gentleman in a dark hat selling printed copies of *The Liminal*. He was chatting to one of the many witch journalists who roamed large buildings and nature reserves getting leads from the Cosmic Web to pass on to the *The Liminal*'s editor. This young witch was wearing a black lace skirt over several petticoats, with a black cashmere jumper and a velvet cape. The velvet cape made Effie think about Leander for a moment. She wanted to see him again, to talk to him about being an interpreter. But the feeling soon left her. Like so much else, it seemed too difficult, and remote, and strange.

Effie followed Pelham into the huge booking office, wishing she could feel more excited about what she was seeing, hearing and smelling. Instead, she felt jumpy, as if what was going on around her was so big, loud and overwhelming that it had stopped being real at all. Effie had never been to the cinema – it was too expensive these days for most people – but she wondered if this was what it was like.

'One child, please,' said Pelham, after naming the city where Effie lived. 'Super First Class.'

The clerk printed out the yellow paper ticket with the letters SFC in gold foil and handed it to Pelham. Effie expected him to then ask for an adult ticket, but he did not.

'Right, come on,' he said. 'Platform One, I believe.'

Effie hurried to keep up with his long-legged stride. They were at Platform One before she had the chance to say anything.

'Professor Quinn will meet you when you arrive,' said Pelham. 'I don't think you've been introduced yet? In the meantime, you've got your own compartment with a bed. There's a chef on board. I suggest you eat something wholesome and then sleep. Take one of the tablets first. Take the second one at bedtime tonight, and the last one when you wake up in the morning.'

'But—'

'And I'll come and see you in a day or so.'

'But what about Skylurian Midzhar?'

'We can't do anything about her now. But Albion Freake might be a different matter. I'm going to look into him, work out what he has planned. It adds a new dimension to this whole thing. You've done a lot for the Otherworld in the last few days, Effie. You've played your part in helping to protect Dragon's Green. We thank you. But you must rest and get your strength back up now.'

The guard blew his whistle. 'All aboard!' he shouted.

Pelham was one of those adults whom you would never describe as 'cuddly'. He was too bony and angular, for one thing. For another, he was always in a rush to go somewhere or send a message to someone. But now he did pull Effie into an awkward, somewhat elbowy embrace. Effie breathed in his comforting Otherworld smell as if for the last time.

'Please don't leave me,' she said.

'You'll be fine, child,' he said. 'Although I think you might need this.' He opened his leather bag and took out of it Effie's precious box. 'Some reading for the train, I think. And also of course, my card, which I can sense in there somewhere. Don't forget, you can call me at any time.'

'Can I call you now?' said Effie.

Pelham smiled. 'You are a strong force, Euphemia. You don't need babysitting. I think you'll like your compartment. I got you the very best one, although of course nowadays they're all so nice. The guard will get you anything you need. Have a comfortable trip.'

The guard blew his whistle again and gave Effie a rather meaningful look.

'Thank you for saving me,' said Effie to Pelham.

The look he gave her back was full of love, but also seemed

to say to her, *You're not saved yet, poor child.* Then he was gone, and Effie was being hurried onto the train by the guard who seemed simultaneously to be tutting and shaking his head and punching a hole in Effie's ticket, and then slamming the heavy metal door behind her and showing her to her compartment.

Pelham had been right. Effie's compartment was like nothing she'd ever seen. It was a bit like the plane all over again, except that everything here was much bigger. On three sides its walls were panelled with dark polished wood. The fourth side was entirely taken up with windows out of which the occupant could watch the scenery rolling by in complete comfort and privacy.

If only Effie could have enjoyed it more. She slipped off her boots and lay down on the large bed to read the menu for afternoon tea. She yawned. Pelham had told her to eat something to get her strength up. Remembering some of the advertisements she'd seen in the Esoteric Emporium, Effie ordered a plate of mixed pickles with some sourdough bread, and a box of six hand-made violet creams. But she was so tired that she had fallen asleep before it even arrived, and before she had remembered to take the golden tablet.

271

23

Wolf was being followed. He was sure of it. He had not seen the person who was following him since he'd left school, but he was aware of them. The odd click of a footstep; the sound of someone breathing. He had not turned around, of course. If you are being followed, you may as well let the person doing it think you don't know. Then you still have the element of surprise on your side. You let your enemy believe they are more powerful than they are, which makes them complacent.

Wolf knew all about strategy, because for the last month he had been reading every book he could find on the subject. Wolf had never thought of himself as a particularly bookish person before – despite somehow getting into the top set for English – but he found he just loved learning about this subject. Books on Napoleon were his favourite. But he would read anything about military strategy, strategy in sports, even strange old-fashioned guides on leadership and decision-making. It helped that Wolf had managed to acquire his own bookshop, of course. But, as he reminded himself yet again, it wasn't really. his. He would have to give it back. But to whom?

Effie would know. But she hadn't been at school today, again. Luckily they'd had a supply teacher for maths who'd forgotten even to bring the register. And Coach Bruce never remembered his and always just said everyone had been present, including the more 'troubled' children who always bunked off and no one wanted in their classes anyway. Wolf sighed. He had to tell Effie his secret as soon as possible. He knew he had to. He wouldn't feel right until he did. And he'd decided that today would be the day. And then . . . she'd disappeared *again*. Where was she? If he didn't tell her soon, it would be as if he had been deliberately keeping it all to himself.

But wasn't that what he had done? After all, he'd had almost a month to tell her, and he hadn't. But then she had never asked. No one had. No one had asked what had happened to Leonard Levar's Antiquarian Bookshop, to which Wolf now possessed the only set of keys. Looking after the shop meant he'd had a chance to read all those books, and learn things that would help him and his friends fight the Diberi. He'd even found out quite a bit more about who the Diberi were and what they wanted. Wolf had never opened the shop. He'd never taken any money. Well, except just a tiny bit from the till for food and essentials. And he'd given the shop a good clean in return.

And of course he'd used the old desktop computer in the office – with its dusty old dial-up modem – to get the address of the Missing Persons Office in London. He'd written to them about

Natasha. His sister. So far there had been no response, but he wasn't going to give up.

The footsteps click-clicked behind him. Who on earth could it be? No one from his school ever came this way. There wasn't much in the way of housing on this side of the Old Town. There was the university, with its big old library, and the hospital. And then . . .

The Old Rectory. Where Effie's grandfather Griffin had lived.

This was Wolf's other secret. Something else he really needed Effie to know about before anyone else did. Surely she would understand that he needed somewhere safe to bring Natasha when he did find her. She'd be about nine by now. If she was even still alive.

Anyway, he couldn't be seen here by anyone. So instead of entering through the small gate, as he'd done every day after school for the last few weeks, he walked on. Oddly, the footsteps seemed to stop. Wolf heard the sound of the small gate's latch being lifted, and the familiar squeak as it opened onto the front garden. If the person following him had gone through the gate, then their back would now be to him. It was safe for him to look. He turned and there was . . . Lexy!

What was she doing here? Had she found him out? Wolf considered hiding for a bit longer, but then reminded himself that Lexy was one of his closest friends. But in that case, why had she been following him? Wolf watched as Lexy looked under the flowerpot for a spare key and, finding none, started trying to look for a way into the Old Rectory. What was she up to?

Wolf watched as Lexy crept around the side of the large

red-brick house and then disappeared. There was an open window just before the back door. It was too small for anyone but a child to get in. But Lexy was a child. Had she gone in through the window? The flat below Griffin Truelove's had not been occupied for quite a while, and Wolf had rather stupidly never even thought about securing it. But he now realised that if anyone got into the ground floor flat they could easily enter the shared hallway and go up the stairs and . . .

But why would Lexy want to do any of that?

Wolf went round the front of the house and let himself in with his key. It wasn't strictly his key, of course. Wolf had wondered whether someone would come and throw him out of what had been Griffin's old flat, but they had not. And then he had found a lot of legal papers in Leonard Levar's shop that showed that Levar had bought this flat from Griffin Truelove, using a complicated alias. Leonard Levar had existed purely in the world of nefarious magical people and all his property, now that he had finally been killed, seemed to belong to no one.

And Wolf had needed somewhere to live after walking out on the uncle who used to beat him for fun, and who made him work after school for no pay. The uncle who sent Wolf out every night to buy his large cod and chips, but who'd fed his nephew on the scraps of soggy batter and burnt chips he left. Wolf had been treated worse than a neglected pet. So here he was. He'd told himself it was just temporary. Just until he found Natasha and sorted himself out a bit.

So far, he was doing fine.

And now here was Lexy. Why?

Soon the front door of the downstairs flat clicked softly and began to open. Wolf crossed his arms and waited. Lexy crept out, her hands full of postcards that she dropped immediately on seeing Wolf. She gasped, and pressed her hand to her chest and looked as if she was about to pass out from fear.

'Oh my God, *Wolf*!' she said. 'What are you doing here?'

'I could ask you the same thing,' said Wolf. 'Why were you following me?'

'Following *you*? But you're following me!'

'What? Don't be stupid. You must have seen me walking in front of you as we came out of school.'

'Not without my glasses,' said Lexy. 'Stuff in the distance is just a blur to me. My eyesight only works well close up. Which is handy, given what I do.'

'I've never seen you in glasses.'

'Yep. And you never will,' said Lexy, firmly.

'But—'

'Anyway, what are you doing here?' said Lexy.

'I live here. I know, I know. It's a long story. I've basically been here since we killed Leonard Levar. What are *you* doing here?'

'Looking for information on Miss Dora Wright, of course. Like we agreed? You were going to be working out strategies, and Maximilian was going to be finding out about Albion Freake and . . .'

'Oh yes. Of course. I'd completely forgotten that this is where Miss Wright used to live. It makes sense now. What have you got there?'

Lexy was picking up the pieces of card from the floor where she'd dropped them. Wolf leant down to help her.

'Postcards, sent about a month ago, all postmarked London,' said Lexy. 'Look. They're either blank, or written in a language I've never seen before. There's something else that's odd about them. For one thing, they are clearly *from* Miss Wright. Who sends postcards to themselves? I'm going to take them to Effie and see what she makes of them. If she's come back from wherever she went, that is.'

'Yeah. I need to have a chat with Effie as well,' said Wolf. 'I'll come with you.'

Just then a crackle came from Lexy's school bag. It was the sound of someone beginning to make contact through a walkie-talkie. It had to be Effie. It was, but she didn't sound quite herself.

'At last,' said Wolf. 'She's all right. Let's go.'

Professor Quinn was still persuading Orwell Bookend – via an ancient blend of hypnosis and dark magic – that his daughter had not disappeared last night at all but had in fact been at home in bed with a fever the whole time. Orwell Bookend was naturally resistant to magic. Luckily, though, he was not at all resistant to the charms of Professor Quinn. It helped that she was on the promotions committee at the university this year. Orwell would do pretty much anything – including change his entire belief system – if it meant a chance of promotion. So he had the kettle on for a second cup of tea and was considering opening the best packet of biscuits in the house.

Effie had been surprised when she had been met off the train by this large, beautiful woman with shiny hair that seemed to take in every possible colour all at once. She was wearing bright red lipstick and a long, dark-green silk dress with high-heeled ankle boots. Her nails were painted a deep plum colour. Effie had liked her immediately, but had been confused.

'I thought . . .' she had begun, in the taxi home.

'What?' said Professor Quinn.

'I thought you were a man. I thought you taught at my school.'

'My husband is a man who teaches at your school, if that's any help. He's also called Professor Quinn, although I've been a professor for longer. I was told to keep an eye on you a while ago, but I've just been finishing my latest book and . . . Well, anyway. I'm here now. We'll pop you home, and . . .'

There was a slightly awkward pause. Professor Quinn had stopped speaking, but carried on looking at Effie intently.

'Oh,' said Effie, suddenly, shaking her head. 'You can do that?'

'What? Oh. You know when someone's in your mind. Useful. In that case I'm sorry to be rude. I should have asked first. Normally I'd ask you to tell me what happened, but I can see that you're worn out, poor child.'

'So you're a mage?'

'Yes. A mage explorer, which makes life rather interesting. Have you heard of the Department for Subterranean Geography at the university? I'm currently its Director of Research. We do very well in terms of large and complex grants.' She raised an eyebrow. 'Your father will know me.'

And so he had.

While Professor Quinn continued to charm her father, Effie was lying in bed. Maximilian, who had recently come in the window, was pacing her room, waiting for their other friends to arrive. Maximilian hadn't even really needed to come in the window. Effie's father was still being nice to her and was therefore in the mood to welcome any friends who happened to drop by. This is, of course, what can happen when magic is allowed to enter the mind of a resistant.

Orwell was also in a good mood because tomorrow he was to go to the Town Hall to hand over his copy of *The Chosen Ones* and receive his fifty pounds and the chance to win free electricity for life. Albion Freake was actually going to be there in person, drawing the winning entry. It had to be Orwell. He just felt lucky, suddenly.

The owners of the last ten copies in the world of *The Chosen Ones* were all being brought to the Town Hall for the ceremony and were to be given some extra honour, which was to remain a secret, but which was rumoured to be more money. Orwell Bookend had been sent a badge with the word SUPERFAN on it, which he was supposed to wear tomorrow. The badge looked stupid, but if it meant more money he would wear it. If it meant more money, he would wear anything.

Soon Lexy and Wolf arrived and knocked at the front door. Orwell greeted them with a slightly reptilian smile and offered them each a biscuit.

'Take a plate of them into my daughter,' he said. 'She's not been well, you know.'

'Where's Raven?' asked Effie when everyone was assembled.

'We couldn't get through to her,' said Lexy. 'I hope she's OK.'

As quickly as she could, Effie explained what had happened to her. When she talked about the Yearning everyone went very still and very quiet, as if she was telling a ghost story.

'How do you feel now?' said Wolf.

'The same,' said Effie. 'It's horrible. I wouldn't wish it on anyone.' She shivered, and reached for her glass of water, which she didn't even want. But she felt she had to do something to break the mood and stop her friends staring at her in that strange way.

'And where are these golden tablets?' asked Lexy.

'Here,' said Effie, taking them out of her box. She passed the plastic container to Lexy.

'But there are still three of them,' said Wolf. 'You were supposed to have taken one by now.'

Lexy was looking at the tablets and frowning.

'What do you think?' Effie asked her.

'I don't know,' said Lexy.

'Something's not right about them,' said Effie. 'If Skylurian Midzhar is behind their production, I don't want to take them.'

'But Dr Black told you to,' said Wolf. 'If they're going to make you better . . .' He shook his head. 'Don't be stupid, Effie. You don't know everything. If it's medicine, you ought to take it.'

Effie thought for a moment about what Wolf had said. Maybe

he was right, but something still felt wrong about the tablets. She sighed.

'I don't know,' she said. 'I just keep thinking about the sacrifice Pelham Longfellow had to make in return for them. They're, I don't know, *tainted* in some way. It's like what we learned about tragedy. It's like . . .' Because Effie was an interpreter, she was more able than normal people to take things from stories and relate them to life. Being a true hero helped as well, because true heroes always find themselves wrapped up in story-like situations. But she was tired, and the Yearning was bad, and so the thought fizzled out.

'I think you're right,' said Maximilian, looking at his watch. 'There's something wrong with those tablets. We just don't know what it is yet. And there might be another way.'

He looked at Effie and when their eyes met she knew he understood everything she was thinking, and not because he was reading her mind. Their friendship had always been like that, especially just recently, since Maximilian had gone inside a book like Effie had. Even though they were so different, Effie and Maximilian knew they would always understand each other.

'What other way?' said Effie.

'I can't describe it until I've done it. Just give me this evening,' he said. 'I think I might be able to do something to help. Let me try.'

'But—' said Wolf.

'There's a piano concert,' said Maximilian meaningfully.

Effie nodded. 'Thank you,' she said. 'But be careful.'

'I'll come and knock on your window later,' said Maximilian.

'And I'm going to take one of these tablets to Aunt Octavia,' said Lexy. 'If she doesn't know what they are, then I think I might try Dr Cloudburst.'

'Dr Cloudburst?' said Wolf. 'But . . .'

'If he can test for dodgy substances in our pee, then he should be able to test for them in these tablets.'

'That's a great idea. Thank you,' said Effie, squeezing her friend's arm. 'Although I'm not sure he'll find anything. I think it's even more sinister than that.' A single tear slipped down her face. 'Oh, this is so stupid,' she said. 'I don't even know what's wrong with me.'

'We'll help you,' said Wolf, putting his hand on her shoulder. 'That's what friends do. And we'll do it your way. Don't worry.'

Soon, Effie's friends went to get on with their investigations. Maximilian was going to the piano concert to see if he could use it to get to the Underworld at last. Lexy and Wolf were going to try to find out more about the golden tablets.

Effie was left alone with the pile of postcards that Lexy had brought her. Each one had a sort of historical image on the front. There was a factory, a boat, some books. Lexy had also left Effie as many tonics as she could carry, along with a medicine bundle that she said she had been working on this week 'just in case'.

You can't die in this world, not from the Yearning, Effie reminded herself. *You can't die; you can just feel worse.* For a moment Effie imagined what it would be like to feel worse. She could cry and cry. She could feel as sad as it was possible to feel. She could sit in her bedroom and think the worst thoughts it was possible to think. But still, despite all that, she would survive. She knew she would. The thought gave her strength. The Yearning could not really hurt her. It was just her spirit asking for lifeforce. There was no need to be afraid. As Effie thought these things, her lifeforce slowly increased, although she could not yet quite feel it.

Effie unwrapped Lexy's medicine bundle. Inside were two different green stones, and two sprigs of dried herbs. One sprig was made of leaves and the other was made of flowers that looked a bit like daisies. There was also a small triangle of incense and a tea-light candle made of yellow beeswax. Effie went to the kitchen and made an infusion of the herbs by steeping them in boiling water. Then she went back to her room and took out the candle-holder she'd got from her grandfather's place but had not yet used. It was silver, with a pattern of dragons, and several red stones. Effie put the candle in the holder and lit it. She lit the incense. She sent a request out to the universe, that not just she but all sufferers of the Yearning be helped. She sat down on the rug on the floor to meditate, holding onto both green stones. After about fifteen minutes of that, she did feel a little better. She got back on her bed and picked up the postcards again that Lexy had brought, and started to examine them, one by one. She was still sure that there was something funny about them.

24

It was taking Raven Wilde longer and longer each evening to bless the creatures around the folly. They all seemed to have something wrong with them. As Raven blessed the robin, she sensed that he'd been suffering from a severe bird-migraine all day. The blackbirds all had IBS, which in the avian world means Irritable Beak Syndrome. The grey squirrels had come out in eczema around their hind paws. The tarantulas were moulting. It was quite peculiar. Even Echo and Jet were moaning and groaning about something that had been happening. But for some reason they wouldn't say exactly what it was.

While Raven was changing the water in the bird-bath – which seemed to have gone completely green and unhealthy-looking just in the course of one day – she noticed an odd light shining in the sky. It was peculiar. It reminded her of something . . .

'Darling,' came Skylurian's mellifluous voice. 'You'll get cold out here. Come in. Terrence is making you a butternut squash curry. It's your favourite, I believe? And then I've lined up a whole evening of entertainment for you both. I sent Terrence to the video shop and he brought back some real delights. *The Craft. Lolly Willowes.* That sort of thing.'

'I'm not allowed to watch videos on a school night.'

Skylurian sighed and then fake-smiled.

'Yes, well, you *are* allowed on this night. Meanwhile, I'm going to bathe, dress and then go and dine with Albion Freake in his suite at the Regency Hotel in the city.'

'Actually, I was thinking of going back into the city myself to see my friends,' said Raven. 'You don't mind, do you?'

'I'd really rather you didn't leave the folly, my sweet,' said Skylurian. 'Although . . . Actually, you've given me an idea. Yes, of course. If you really do want to come into the city, then I think it would be much better if you came with me. You're quite an attractive little accessory, after all. You own an evening gown, do you not? Yes. It will be better to keep you with me, I think, than imprison you here ready for tomorrow.'

'Imprison me?'

'Just a figure of speech, darling. More or less.'

'Well, in that case, I think I'm just going to go and see my friends as I planned. I hope you don't mind. But thanks for the offer of dinner.'

Raven turned to go back into the folly. The light flashed in the sky again. Was it a meteor? But it was too low for that, surely? And it went off and on in a sort of pattern.

'Oh dear. It seems, then, that I'm just going to have to properly take you prisoner,' said Skylurian pleasantly. 'And therefore keep a much closer eye on you. You will bathe, dress and be ready to leave to accompany me to dinner with Albion Freake at seven o'clock precisely. Do you understand?'

Raven narrowed her eyes. She was not going to be bossed around by this ridiculous woman. She was not the boldest of twelve-year-old girls, but she had never liked being told what to do. And as for those lights shining in the darkness . . . Yes, she could understand it now. It was Morse Code. *Dot, dot, dot; dash, dash dash; dot, dot, dot. S . . .O . . .S.* Her mother had used it in one of her books a couple of years before, and Raven had helped her research how you used a mirror and a torch to beam your help message into the sky. Laurel Wilde was somewhere on the moors, and she needed Raven to rescue her.

Suddenly the robin, who had been perched on a branch enjoying his evening blessing from his witch friend, let out a pitiful squawk and flapped his wings as if something underneath them was hot or painful. What was happening? Raven looked at Skylurian, who had one manicured finger raised and pointing directly at the robin. At once Raven understood why all the animals and birds were so unhappy.

'What are you doing to him? Stop it!' said Raven.

'Why do you bless all these animals?' said Skylurian. 'It's so very twee. It means I have to go around smiting them all just to balance things out. It's exhausting.'

'And what have you done to my mother? She's not on a book tour at all! You lied. She's on the moor somewhere, and she's in trouble.'

'And so are you, darling,' breathed Skylurian. 'I wouldn't bother trying to resist. As of now, you do exactly as I tell you.

I can't kill you, not quite yet, but I can make your ridiculous pets suffer. I can destroy all three of your pathetic tarantulas with one single smite. Do you want that? No, I thought not. So you'd better get inside, now, and dress in a manner suitable to come with me to meet Albion Freake. Of course, I'm going to kill him tomorrow. But tonight we will dine as if he is the most important customer we have ever had.'

'And what about my mother?' said Raven.

'If you do exactly what you're told I might spare her, and all your stupid animals. But if not?' Skylurian slowly drew her long finger across her throat. 'It's your choice, darling.'

Maximilian had never been to a classical music concert before. Indeed, he'd never been to any kind of concert before, unless you counted the opera he'd attended with Lupoldus and Franz. He was therefore almost glad he had Mr Starling with him, although it was a bit unnerving that Mr Starling had kept trying to read his piano book on the bus, even though it was obviously giving him motion sickness. He was quite green by the time they arrived in the Old Town, and totally viridescent by the time they got off outside the Oddfellows Hall.

Maximilian was the youngest person in the hall by about 150 years. Or so it felt. However, all the old people around him were strangely glamorous. Maximilian was fascinated by the different silk bow-ties the men were wearing, and the gowns in different shades of wine and olive, some obviously decades old, that the women had on. There was one woman who was a little younger than the rest, and she looked familiar, although Maximillian couldn't place her. She was wearing a green silk gown and plum nail varnish. Just before the pianist came in and sat down, the woman winked at Maximilian.

The pianist was a young, thin woman with a severe fringe and a ring through her nose. She was wearing a black evening gown. Maximilian's mouth felt dry. Was he going to be able to do this? He knew it was his only chance of getting back to the Underworld.

The pianist began. The piece of music now sounded quite familiar. Yes; Maximilian knew what note was coming next, and when the long pause was going to come, and the stepping stones, and . . .

Then the woman in the green silk gown disappeared.

Interesting. Maximilian blinked and made himself go back to concentrating on the music. An angel's tear. More stepping stones and . . . He let his mind leap into the music.

And then he was in too. He was falling, falling. The sensation was like going down a very long slide in a theme park that had closed many years ago. Soon Maximilian could see the gatekeepers' cottage that he had visited when he'd read *Beneath the Great Forest*, but he didn't stop there this time. He saw the river pass below him. Then he entered a thick mist which turned into a drizzle as he landed gently in a clearing in a forest.

It was a crossroads of sorts. There were four paths, each stretching off in a different direction into the dense, dark forest. Each path had its own sign. UNIVERSITY OF THE UNDERWORLD, said one. The others were in a language

Maximilian could not understand. He reached for his Spectacles of Knowledge, but they were not in his pocket where they had been. It seemed they didn't want to come to the Underworld with him. Which was a shame, because they would have been extremely useful at this moment.

So he was here, in the Underworld, at last, a place he'd so desperately longed to get to. Why was it so confusing? Of the four paths, which was he supposed to take? And what would he do when he wanted to go back? There was no obvious way of returning to the concert in the Realworld.

Underneath his feet were damp autumn leaves. He could not see the sky beyond the great canopy of trees. Maximilian didn't often feel scared. He was more likely simply to feel interested in whatever was happening to him. But it was so silent and still that when he heard a twig cracking behind him he jumped.

'Hello,' said a female voice.

Maximilian turned around. It was the woman from the concert. The one in the long green dress. She was now carrying a brown leather briefcase.

'You seem a little lost,' she said.

'Do I?' said Maximilian.

'Yes.' She smiled. 'You keep looking at the signs but not actually going anywhere. Who are you? I saw you in the concert.'

'Maximilian Underwood.'

'I'm Professor Quinn,' she said. 'Are you supposed to be here?'

'What do you mean?'

'Are you a mage?'

'Yes.'

'So perhaps you're an Apprentice off for your first day at university?'

'I'm not quite an Apprentice yet,' said Maximilian.

'You're a *Neophyte*?'

He nodded.

'And you've come here by yourself?'

'Is that wrong?'

'Well, it's certainly quite brave. But people don't usually come here by accident. I don't particularly recommend getting lost in this forest. It has a tendency to disappear and leave you in a void. You don't want that, I promise you. Although some people bizarrely do. There was that group of hippy demons who—'

'Why are you here?' interrupted Maximilian.

'Me? I'm off to give a lecture at the university. Most people are here for the university, of course. But can I point you in some other direction?'

'Where do the other paths go?'

'Can't you read the signs?'

He shook his head. 'No.'

'Then they're closed to you. You'll probably need to graduate from the university first. Maybe you should come with me and enrol?'

'How long will it take?'

'To enrol? A couple of hours. And to graduate? Maybe four years or so.'

'Oh dear,' said Maximilian. 'I've actually got to find something to help my friend and then get back as quickly as I can.'

'Aha! You DO know why you're here. To help your friend.'

'Do you think I could use the university library *without* enrolling?'

Maximilian still thought that what he most needed was a nice thick book called something like *The Yearning: Symptoms and Cures*. There he might find a good Underworld remedy, which he could write down and take back for Lexy and—

'But why on earth would you want to do that? Surely you're simply looking for the wishing well?'

In this situation Effie or Wolf would no doubt just say 'Yes' in that confident way that heroes and warriors do and wait to be led to the next part of their adventure. But Maximilian was different.

'What wishing well?' he said.

Professor Quinn sighed. 'Do you really know nothing about the Underworld at all?'

Maximillian shook his head. 'But I'm trying my best to learn.'

'Are you sure you don't want to just come to the university with me? Otherwise I'm going to be late. And at least at the university there are lots of apertures to get back and . . . Please tell me you know how to get back?'

Maximilian shook his head again.

'Good grief. So let me get this straight. You've somehow learned how to travel to the Underworld, but not how to get back, and, without any fear at all, you've come straight here because it is important to you to help your friend?'

'Yes.'

Professor Quinn smiled. 'I wish my friends were more like you,' she said. 'I don't know whether you're admirable or just stupid. But in any case you'd better come with me. I'll take you as far as the wishing well. I can go into the university the back way, I suppose.'

Maximilian followed Professor Quinn downhill along a winding path, past trees with thick dark trunks and ancient-looking bark. Soon they reached a bank covered with plants with shiny green leaves and purple flowers. There were also several bushes with blue berries on them.

'Don't eat the berries,' said Professor Quinn cheerfully. 'Unless you want to spend the rest of your life in hell, that is.'

'OK,' said Maximilian.

'Don't touch the leaves either.'

'Are there monsters in the forest?'

'Probably. There *are* a lot of monsters down here, although they usually stick to the cities. But they won't bother you. It's much safer here than the Otherworld, despite what everyone says.'

Maximilian realised he knew hardly anything about where he was. But in the very core of his soul he felt he belonged here.

'Oh, there's one now,' said Professor Quinn.

Maximilian saw a dark shape flash past and then disappear into the undergrowth. He shuddered, but Professor Quinn simply carried on walking.

Soon they came to another clearing. There was a small white cottage with blue window-frames and a blue door, and a little blue fence around its simple cottage garden. Smoke was curling from its stout white chimney. All at once Maximilian recalled every fairy tale he'd ever read, and the experience gave him a powerful sensation that was equal parts fascination and fear. You could go into a cottage like that and be boiled alive for your bones, or eaten by a wolf, or turned into sweets to be fed to other children, or enslaved to a cruel master, or any number of other awful things.

But it also felt comfortable, like coming home. In a cottage like that you could live happily ever after, telling stories by the fire, roasting marshmallows, dreaming of . . .

'Don't look at the cottage for too long,' said Professor Quinn. 'It's quite a powerful one. Come on. We need to go to the wood shed.'

Maximilian followed Professor Quinn around the back of the cottage. The sky seemed to dim and become more purple than before, although Maximilian didn't think it was yet night-time here. Maybe this was what counted as 'dusk'. Or maybe it was about to rain again.

In the back garden was a shed, and in the shed was a man with a neat grey beard and round glasses. He was wearing a three-piece suit with a polka-dot tie and a silver watch chain. He was sitting at a wooden desk, and appeared to be correcting a long and complicated manuscript with a very short pencil stub. Pages were stacked up everywhere. The paper was yellow, and the ink was green. Each page seemed to have hundreds of corrections and lots of illegible notes, all in pencil. On the shed wall was a cross-stitch sampler that read 'There are no mistakes'.

'*Guten Abend*, doctor,' said Professor Quinn.

The man didn't respond, so she said it again, a bit louder.

Eventually he looked up. '*Servus*,' he said, nodding formally. 'Yew must place ze drimz in ze box and zen yew may proceed.'

Professor Quinn took a purse out of her briefcase and from it withdrew a piece of paper that had been folded several times. She dropped it in a cardboard box just inside the shed. Apart from the box, the man and his manuscript, everything else in the shed was draped in thin white cobwebs.

'I take it you haven't brought any dreams?' Professor Quinn said to Maximilian.

'Dreams?' Maximilian said, baffled.

'You can try telling him one. He might accept it.'

'Plizz put ze drimz in ze box,' said the man again.

'I don't have any,' said Maximilian.

The man looked at him sternly over the round rims of his glasses. 'Yew haff no drimz?'

'I do have dreams, of course, but—'

'Plizz tell me vun of zese drimz.'

'Really?' said Maximilian. 'Well, OK. My last dream was about being late for school. My mother usually takes me in her car, but in my dream I had to get a bus. The bus was yellow and very old and kept breaking down. It kept going uphill for a long time. Then when I eventually got to school I realised I'd forgotten to get dressed and my teacher made me wear a dunce's hat and sit in the corner in the nude while everyone laughed at me.'

'Yew are naked and yew are late!' The man with the beard chuckled. 'Ziss iz a VERY good drim. Ze nakidness shows zat you are vulnerable but also pure. Ze bus going uphill iz yore STRUGGLE threw life, because yew hav chozen yore own path.

294

Ziss, also, leads to much laughter from uzzers. Here iz your change.' He scrabbled in the cardboard box and handed Maximilian two folded pieces of paper. 'Now you may enter ze garden and take ze vater, ze *dip*vater from ze vishing vell. Az mush as yew like. Will yew need a vial?'

'Yes,' said Professor Quinn, quickly. 'He will. Thank you.'

'Tek,' said the doctor, nodding to another cardboard box. 'It vill cost yew vun more drim.'

Professor Quinn took one of the pieces of paper from Maximilian's hand and dropped it in the first cardboard box. Then she leant down and pulled something out of the second box. She blew the dust and cobwebs off it and handed it to Maximilian. 'Here,' she said. 'Oh. It's a nice one.'

Maximilian took it. It was a beautiful little silver bottle on a chain.

'But—'

'Come on,' she said. 'Or I really am going to be late.'

The doctor went back to correcting his manuscript with the stubby pencil, complaining to no one in particular that he wished someone he liked would give him a pen so his unconscious wouldn't make him lose it.

Maximilian followed Professor Quinn down the garden path until it bent around to the right. In the near distance he could see the dark outlines of buildings that probably belonged to the university. The evening sky now seemed full of strange neon shadows, puffs of steam, and the voices of the young. Some of the voices seemed particularly close, and Maximilian realised they were coming from inside the garden.

'I wish we could use deepwater to top up our own M-currency,' a girl was saying.

A boy's voice replied. 'Yeah, but that's not the point, is it?'

'I don't even know anyone who can use it.'

'Me neither. But we'll pass the test. That's the main thing.'

Then the wishing well came into view. It was round, and made of pale butter-yellow bricks. The two university students seemed now to be leaving the well by a path that headed towards the university, each holding a silver vial of their own.

'You'll want to take some deepwater back for your friend,' said Professor Quinn to Maximilian. 'I assume it's the Truelove girl?'

'Yes,' said Maximilian. 'How did you know?'

Professor Quinn didn't answer. Instead she showed Maximilian how to draw up the water from the well in a little wooden bucket on a rope. She filled a vial of her own and put it in her briefcase. When Maximilian's vial was full he put it around his neck. The deepwater was completely clear with a very slight blueness about it.

'This will cure Effie, won't it?' he said.

Professor Quinn nodded.

'But the problem is how you get back,' she said. 'Perhaps . . .' She frowned and appeared to be thinking hard. Maximilian looked at her, and before he knew it, he felt his mind drifting into, or rather being pulled into, a very complicated, dark, extraordinary place, where . . .

He seemed to black out for a second, or maybe longer.

'There,' she said. 'I've passed on all I can. If you were a student you'd need to be expelled now, because I've essentially given you your whole first year through illegal means. But I too have been asked to look out for the young Truelove girl, and so this is my contribution.'

'But—'

'Good luck,' said Professor Quinn, and, without looking back, she continued down the path towards the university.

25

Effie sat on her bed and started to examine the postcards that Lexy had brought from Miss Dora Wright's apartment. There were exactly ten of them. Most of them did not have any text beyond the address, but one had a full paragraph. It was written in Rosian, which Effie could now read as easily as English. Effie had had no idea that her teacher had known anything about the Otherworld, or its languages. But Effie had known so little about anything back then.

> Dear G,
> I am sending this to myself as we agreed. I am inside, but I expect I will never come back. It is as we feared. I can't say more. You must fight!
> With love and friendship,
> Dora Wright

What did this mean? Effie cast her mind back to the beginning of the school year. They'd had almost a month of English classes with Miss Dora Wright and then she'd simply left. The official story was that she'd won a short story competition and part of the prize had been a publishing contract. Most of the children thought it completely reasonable that their nice, round-faced teacher would dump them unceremoniously for the chance to make trillions of pounds as an author. So most people had ignored the rumour that she'd actually been kidnapped by dark forces.

Not for the first time, Effie deeply missed her grandfather. He'd obviously known quite a lot about where Dora Wright had gone. He must have been the 'G' to whom she had written. Why hadn't he told Effie? Because at the time she was an eleven-year-old who didn't know anything about magic, or the Diberi. Effie sighed as she remembered those days. Why hadn't Griffin started preparing Effie sooner? He'd been in trouble with the Guild, Effie remembered, who had prevented him from doing magic for five years. But then suddenly he had taught her Rosian and Old Bastard English, and he'd got the Ring of the True Hero and . . . But Effie had only got the ring because he'd died.

Not died. He was alive in the Otherworld. Effie was sure of that. And when she could get back to the Otherworld, and once she was strong enough, she was going to find him. Effie sighed again, and flicked through the postcards. She started to wonder . . . What if *both* stories about Dora Wright's disappearance had been true? What if she had won a competition and then been kidnapped because of it?

Effie realised that the message Dora was trying to convey with the postcards wasn't in the text at all. It was in the images. One was a postcard of a factory from history with smoke pouring out of its chimneys. Another had an image of a ship docking in Liverpool a very long time ago. Another had a scene from Plato's Allegory of the Cave. Several postcards had images of antique books on them. One of the books was *Oliver Twist* by Charles Dickens. Another was *Gone with the Wind*.

If you put them together it was almost as if someone was trying to say that they were captive – a slave even – in a factory that had something to do with books.

And then Effie noticed something else.

They had all been sent from Walthamstow, the place where Skylurian Midzhar had her factory.

The Tusitala School for the Gifted, Troubled and Strange had a small boarding house for its sixth-formers. The boarding house, which was said to have been condemned at some point in the last century, and was definitely haunted, had, for reasons unknown, originally been built to resemble Dublin Castle's old clock tower. It was a red-brick and bath-stone oblong with a classical balcony, a little cloister and, of course, a massive clock looming out of its roof. The clock had a turquoise dome plonked on top of it like an amusing hat.

Dr Cloudburst was one of the three staff who lived-in, and his little study-bedroom was right at the top of the clock tower. When he'd first become a housemaster, he'd cheerfully taken his turn in dealing with all the nightmares, midnight feasts, apple-pie beds, wanderings, fights, floods, kidnap attempts, intruders, bullying, bloodshed and murders that happen after dark in any boarding school. But did he get any thanks? Of course not. The sixth-formers just thought he was a weirdo loser with no life – otherwise why on earth would he want to spend his entire existence looking after *them*?

Lexy and Wolf found him in his ground-floor chemistry lab, marking student assignments by the light of a small lamp. Next to him was an empty coffee cup and a plate with a few crumbs on it. All around him were test-tubes filled with fluid in every possible shade of yellow, from buttercup to sunshine to custard. So much pee in one place was rather alarming, and Wolf and Lexy both tried not to look.

'Children,' said Dr Cloudburst. 'I do hope you haven't come to try tampering with Coach Bruce's samples.'

'No,' said Lexy. 'We need your help.'

Effie had given them one of the golden tablets and kept two safely hidden. They'd taken the tablet first to Lexy's Aunt Octavia in Mrs Bottle's Bun Shop, but Octavia hadn't been able to find anything out about it at all. She'd simply shaken her head and said she'd never seen anything like it.

Wolf now held out the tablet to Dr Cloudburst.

'We want you to do some tests on this,' he said.

'Oh you do, do you?'

Dr Cloudburst had become increasingly less cheerful with every year of service as a housemaster and was now verging on bitter.

'It's very important,' said Lexy.

'Oh it is, is it?' He sighed. At least these were nice children from the Lower School. They never tormented or abused him the way the sixth-formers did. And the girl was good at chemistry. 'Well, give it here, then.'

As soon as Dr Cloudburst looked properly at the tablet, his whole manner changed. He seemed fascinated by it, and a little in awe.

'Now, you children aren't planning to use this in any sporting fixture, are you?' he said. 'Because Coach Bruce would take a very dim view of that . . . Although I must say, it would probably do wonders for the tennis team in particular, and . . .'

As he was talking, Dr Cloudburst was preparing his microscope. He held the tablet in a large pair of tweezers and then positioned it under the lens, turning it this way and that, making a range of different *hmm*ing sounds as he did so.

'Hmm,' he said again. 'And where did you get this?'

'We can't say,' said Wolf. 'What do you think it is?'

'What do *you* think it is?' asked Dr Cloudburst.

'We think it's some kind of liquid lifeforce,' said Lexy. 'But we don't know where it came from, or whether there's something sort of wrong with it. We just need to find out everything we can about it. It's important, but we can't say why exactly.'

'Well, you're right. It is liquid lifeforce,' said Dr Cloudburst. 'Which is rare enough to begin with. But this is the most potent example I've ever seen. I can't tell you anything about its origins, except that I'm picking up traces of two strange substances mixed in with the lifeforce.'

'What are they?' said Wolf.

'Paper,' said Dr Cloudburst. 'And sodium chloride.'

'Salt?' said Lexy.

'Yes. Exactly the sort you get in human blood, sweat and tears,' said Dr Cloudburst. 'Someone's gone to quite a lot of trouble to make these.'

'Are they safe?' asked Wolf.

Dr Cloudburst shrugged. 'Is anything safe?' he asked, philosophically.

'Would you take one of them?' said Lexy.

'Not if you paid me,' said Dr Cloudburst. 'They've got sadness in them. Not what you'd want mixed up with your lifeforce, I don't think.'

In the north of the city, in the Regency Hotel, Raven Wilde was wondering if she could escape. At the moment it didn't look very likely. She and Skylurian had just been shown into the Presidential Suite, which had its own small, private restaurant in which they were shortly due to dine with Albion Freake. There were armed guards on every door. But even if Raven could get away, what would Skylurian then do to her mother? Raven would have to get to her first.

Skylurian was wearing what looked like a dress, but on closer inspection turned out to be a leopard-print leotard with a see-through black chiffon layer over it, which had been pulled together with a gold chain-link belt. On top of this she wore a vast chiffon garment with so many ostrich feathers on its edges that it was hard to tell if it was a cape or actually the largest feather boa in the world. She wore a black velvet choker with an enormous dark green jewel quivering at her throat, and carried an absurdly glamorous parasol made of ostrich feathers that matched her cape. On her feet she wore pointed black sling-back kitten heels tied around her ankles with large velvet ribbons.

'Vintage Dior, darling,' she'd said to Raven in the taxi when she'd caught her looking at them. 'From long, long ago. Do as you're told and I'll give them to you as a gift. You could do with better shoes.'

Raven was wearing black jodhpur boots, which didn't quite go with her second-best best evening gown: floor-length black silk with wizard sleeves. Her mother had bought the gown for her eleventh birthday just over a year ago, and it still fitted.

Usually Raven enjoyed getting dressed up for her mother's dinner parties and soirées. She hadn't much enjoyed getting dressed this evening, of course, although the occasion was much more important than any dinner or soirée she'd ever attended before. She would have to convince Skylurian Midzhar that she meant to go along with whatever she said, while all the time looking for some way to escape, or send a message to her friends. The boots were in case she did manage to get out. And she thought they didn't look bad, exactly. What was that thing from history again? Grunge? If anyone asked, she'd say it was that.

The hotel suite was very elegant, but Albion Freake, sadly, was not. He was enormously fat, with several massive boils on his red face. He was still wearing a shiny suit, today in gold. As he stood to welcome his guests Raven wondered if he was actually made of wax. His skin seemed to glow all over, but not in the way promised by all of Laurel Wilde's moisturisers. It was as if he was sweating, but without there being any actual sweat. When he extended his hand to shake Raven's, it was just like the time she'd touched a toad in the garden. She'd also expected that to be wet and slimy but had found it dry, and sort of uncanny.

'Ladies,' he boomed, showering both Skylurian and Raven with spittle. 'I am most honoured to make your acquaintance! Michel, bring them cocktails at once! They will drink Black Manhattans like the rest of us, although perhaps a non-alcohol version for the little lady.' He winked at Raven.

'Actually, sir, the Black Manhattan *only* has alcohol in it,' said Michel, who seemed to be the bar.man. As well as having its own private restaurant, the Presidential Suite seemed to have its own bar.

'I'm fine with water,' said Raven. 'Thank you.'

'Oh, piffle,' said Skylurian. 'The girl is so quaint. She'll have a Virgin Mary with all the trimmings.'

The barman started making the drinks. Skylurian's came in a cocktail glass and was black with a dark red cherry on the top. Raven's was an alarmingly bright red with a stick of celery in it. She tried it and found that it was tomato juice with a lot of different spicy things in it. That was all right. Raven liked spicy things.

Albion Freake was not alone. As well as the many hotel staff that bustled around refilling drinks and handing out canapés, the room contained seven other people. Raven noticed that there was only one woman, and she was extremely beautiful. She must

305

be Freake's wife or girlfriend. She was wearing a pale rose gown with the lower part of the skirt made from pink feathers and white fur. Two great plumes of pink feathers erupted from the top of her chest as if she was in fact a real bird. She was sitting stiffly on a red chair.

The men looked like thinner, more anxious versions of Albion Freake. One of them had a large black case that he didn't seem to want to let out of his sight. The atmosphere in the room was difficult to read, although Raven had always been good with an atmosphere. The beautiful woman in the pale rose gown caught Raven's eye and then looked away, as if . . . What was it . . .? What was it . . .? Raven began to sense the feeling in the room.

It was mistrust. It was fear. Raven and Skylurian looked at one another. Yes, they could both feel it. These Americans were wondering whether or not to murder them. And whether to do it now, or later.

As soon as Skylurian and Raven had been seated on the immaculate cream suede sofa in the slightly too-warm reception area of the suite, Skylurian opened her large leopard-skin clutch bag and drew out of it the limited-edition single volume edition of *The Chosen Ones*, bound in calf leather and edged in real gold.

'I expect you've been dying to see this, darling,' Skylurian said to Albion Freake. 'To touch it. To own it. Well, wait no more. It is yours.'

She passed the book to him. Raven noticed her hand tremble ever so slightly.

'I thought maybe you were coming to tell me it could not be done,' Freake said, stroking the cream cover of the book. He looked around at his lackeys suspiciously. 'Everyone usually lets me down. But you've really nailed this, honey. My very own private luxury book. I will see you are rewarded.'

'I think we agreed on a billion,' said Skylurian.

'A billion dollars,' said Albion, nodding. 'Cheap at half the price! HAHA! Joking. OK, Mike, transfer a billion dollars to the lady's account, please.'

'Ahem,' said Skylurian.

'What is it, sweetheart?'

'It was actually a billion *pounds*.'

'Pounds, dollars, who cares? Pay the broad.'

The man with the black case put it on the table and opened it up to reveal a very old-looking black Bakelite telephone with a silver dial. He plugged it into some kind of modem and some sort of mini-computer and then into the wall. He began to dial a very long number with quite a lot of 9s in it. Everyone watched, mesmerised, as the dial made its slow way back each time, making a long, lazy buzzing sound. Effie knew all about dial-up modems, of course. Maximilian had one to get on the dim web. But she'd never seen one you actually had to physically dial yourself.

The beautiful woman caught Raven's eye again, but, again, looked away. What was she trying to say? Raven already knew she was in danger. If Albion Freake didn't get her, then Skylurian would.

'Of course,' said Albion Freake to Skylurian Midzhar, as the man dialled the numbers, 'you will be able to give me evidence of the destruction of every other copy of this . . . this . . . What's the damn thing called again? *The Chosen Ones*.'

'Of course, darling,' said Skylurian. 'But I've planned something far better than that. Tomorrow, as arranged, you will come to the Town Hall to draw the prize we agreed. You are going to give some lucky person free electricity for life, if you remember.'

'Wait, lady. I never said I was actually going to *do* that.'

'Don't worry, it's just for show. The winner will of course be dealt with and won't trouble you any more.' Skylurian smiled, but looked ever so slightly as if she might throw up at any moment.

Raven felt oddly tired. Whenever she was near Skylurian she felt lacking in energy and fatigued. For a while Raven had thought this was simply because they didn't get on. But the feeling was getting worse, and worse and . . .

It's because she's a trickster, and she's draining you, said a voice in Raven's head. *You need to escape from her.*

What? Where was the voice coming from? It had to be a mage, if it could get inside her mind. It had a female voice. Female and American . . . Raven realised it was Albion Freake's young wife. It had to be. She was the only other woman in the room, apart from Skylurian.

I think you might need to escape too, Raven said back with her mind, but she didn't know if the woman had picked it up or not.

'Tomorrow we will be taking possession of the last remaining ten copies of *The Chosen Ones*, owned by its most passionate fans,' said Skylurian, 'and then we're going to take the Superfans, and the books, to the moors and burn them.'

'The fans too?' said Albion Freake, laughing.

'No, of course not,' lied Skylurian.

'I've never seen one of your British moors,' said Albion Freake. 'I think I might own one, but I've never been to it. I think we're planning to make it into a golf course.'

'Well, tomorrow, you shall see one in its untouched pagan glory,' said Skylurian, gaily. 'There will be a meteor shower as well, which we will see particularly well from the moor. We will also have the author with us, and she will take a central role in the sacrifice – I mean, *ceremony*. We will go to the moors and burn the last books by the light of the first evening stars and then we will conduct the official handing-over ceremony while meteors crash and burn above us. Of course, in the meantime you must look after the limited-edition single volume. It is yours after all. But do bring it along tomorrow so that we can take some pictures for your scrapbook.'

Everyone in the room relaxed slightly. The book was, of course, worthless until those last ten copies were destroyed. Since their destruction could not take place without Skylurian Midzhar, she would probably be allowed to live for another day. But Albion Freake had never, ever done any kind of business deal in which the other person had survived.

'And then after this we'll move on every other book in the world, eh, sugar?' Freake was addressing the beautiful woman in the pale rose dress.

'But—' she began.

'Don't argue with me, Frankincense, honey,' said Freake. 'You know I don't like it when we argue. Be happy for me? Is that too much to ask? I've just acquired the first book in our ultimate

309

private, luxury library. Soon there will be no books in the world except the ones I own. Can you not even pretend to be happy about that?'

Raven couldn't quite believe what she was hearing. Had Effie actually been wrong? Was Albion Freake not a Book Eater after all? Or maybe it was just a lot worse than they'd thought. Could it be that he planned to create this library of last editions and then give himself ultimate power by eating all the books at once? Raven took a particularly spicy mouthful of Virgin Mary and then tried to pretend she wasn't spluttering and choking. She could feel her face going redder and redder. Skylurian kicked her with her pointed Dior shoe.

'Ow,' said Raven.

'There some sort of problem, little lady?' asked Albion Freake, turning his waxy gaze on her.

'No. Sorry,' said Raven. 'Sounds, um, really great.'

'What does?'

'Your library,' said Raven.

'See,' Freake said to Frankincense. 'The little girl understands better than you do.'

26

The Cosmic Web was in full flow that Thursday night. It told of the young, kind witch, Raven Wilde, currently prisoner of the great trickster Skylurian Midzhar, and now locked in her bedroom at the top of the folly, being guarded by the long-haired author who smelled of cheese. It told of her mother, the red-haired one who writes of fictional magic, sending messages from the moor, and Raven sending long replies with a mirror and a candle from her bedroom window.

Elsewhere there were two black-clad children cooking up a revenge plot, and their teacher reading an old leather-bound book on the movements of the heavens, and frowning.

There was much else besides, including the young mage, Maximilian Underwood, lately arrived from the Underworld with a vial of the most precious deepwater, which he was now taking to give to his friend Euphemia Truelove.

The prophecy, that Euphemia was due to die today – for midnight had now passed, and it was already Friday – was beginning to fade. But the Cosmic Web was heavy with such prophecies this dark, moonless night. It felt strongly that many people were going to die before the clock next struck midnight. Of course, it couldn't do anything about such deaths. All it could do was talk of them, anticipate them and then record them for posterity.

Maximilian Underwood, recently the young star of many of the Cosmic Web's stories, had arrived back at the piano recital just as Raven Wilde and Skylurian Midzhar had sat down for dinner in the private restaurant in Albion Freake's hotel suite. The Cosmic Web didn't understand exactly how Maximilian had made it back to the Realworld, although it did note the precise location of Maximilian's re-emergence: the Modernism shelf in Leonard Levar's Antiquarian Bookshop. It was as if there was some sort of portal there, a portal the Cosmic Web did not understand.

The bookshop had been locked, but luckily Maximilian found he could open the door from the inside. Interestingly, the shop seemed recently to have been occupied. There was an empty sports drink bottle on the counter, and an orange peel. But Maximilian hadn't had time to think about that. He'd hurried back to the piano recital and found that only a few minutes had passed since he'd left. The pianist had just begun the third movement of the *Pathétique*.

Maximilian took his seat again next to Mr Starling.

'Needed the loo, did you, boy?' his neighbour asked.

'Yes, sorry,' whispered Maximilian.

'Shhh!' said an old lady behind him.

Maximilian touched the silver vial hanging around his neck.

Soon he'd be able to go and help his friend. The only real problem he faced was accidentally popping off back to the Underworld during the third movement of the second sonata in the recital, *Les Adieux*, which was quite the most beautiful piece of music he had ever heard. Now that he had the technique, it was hard not to let it happen. But he managed to remain in the Realworld. After he had said goodnight to Mr Starling, he hurried to Effie's house and knocked on her window.

And the Cosmic Web saw, and the Cosmic Web recorded, and the Cosmic Web broadcast everything that happened. It spread the word of the joyful news that Effie Truelove, potential saviour of all, recently restored to health by her own fearlessness and the bravery of her friend, might not die this coming night after all. But Raven Wilde? The Cosmic Web suddenly couldn't be certain if she would survive this moon or not.

Such is the mysterious way of the world.

Effie woke on Friday morning feeling completely different. The water Maximilian had given her the night before had healed her completely. The Yearning was gone. So many sensations rolled over her that she had trouble keeping up with them. She felt happy, that was the main thing. So happy. But she also felt strong. Not just physically strong, but as if nothing could harm her, not even prison, torture or death. Whatever happened to her she would still be Effie. And if she died, she'd at least have been (probably) trying to save the world. All her fear was gone.

Everything felt beautiful and magnificent to Effie. The air smelled sweet. Her breakfast – one stale piece of toast with Marmite, a small bowl of yogurt and a cup of tea – was the most delicious meal she had ever eaten. She wanted lots of people around her so that she could share some of this feeling, but she also wanted to go off and hide, alone, so no one would think she was odd, because she could not stop grinning. It was such a very real sensation of joy that Effie was sure it was visibly surrounding her in great silver and gold waves, and anyone who came close to her couldn't help but be part of it. And she wanted to share it so very much. Despite its power, the feeling was also oddly calm and gentle. It felt as if it could never, ever run out.

She was completely better, thanks to Maximilian, her very best friend in the world. She now had so much lifeforce that she wouldn't run out for a very long time. She'd be able to go back to the Otherworld and see her cousins and Cosmo. But most importantly she'd be able to lead her friends in their fight against the Diberi. She wondered what Wolf and Lexy had been able to find out last night. And she also wondered what had happened to Raven. She felt that all would be resolved today.

'Well, I don't know what's made you all so cheerful,' said Cait over breakfast.

It was clear that Orwell had also been blessed with a feeling of unusual well-being this morning. Why? Well, today he was going to make a lot of money, simply from taking a silly children's book to the Town Hall! And then next week he was probably going to get promoted. That's what Professor Quinn had said. And it was almost the weekend. His new friend Terrence Deer-

Hart had promised to bring more wine and cheese. Life was looking up. Everyone was happy. Even Baby Luna gurgled away contentedly in her high chair and threw spoonfuls of yogurt at the wall without anyone stopping her.

The only member of the family who didn't seem happy was Cait. After the night of cheese (as she had come to think of it) she was back on another diet, which meant only drinking milkshakes called *Shake Your Stuff* throughout the day. She was also reading another one of the awful paperbacks that came free with the giant tubs of powder. This one had an image on the front of a woman tied to a railway line. It was as if she didn't really want to read it, but also couldn't stop herself.

Which made Effie sort of wonder. What was it about those books? Whenever Cait was near one, she couldn't help picking it up. But Cait was a post-doctoral fellow at the university. She was highly intelligent. OK, there'd been that period when she'd read a lot of children's books, but at least they'd been good books. And most of the time she read medieval manuscripts. So why was she so drawn to these silly, cheap-looking novels?

When Cait and the others had gone up to the bathroom, Effie had a proper look at the thin volume. It was published by the Matchstick Press, like all of them.

And printed in Walthamstow.

As Effie opened it and started reading the first page, she felt a strange urge to carry on, as if the book was enchanted. Effie suddenly realised that the book *was* enchanted. Like all Matchstick Press books, it had been slightly cursed in such a way as to become compelling and addictive as soon as it was opened. But Effie was too strong for the enchantment to take hold, and she threw the book down on the table in disgust. She was becoming more and more sure about what had been going on in Walthamstow. But what she didn't understand was exactly how everything fitted together.

Skylurian Midzhar needed to be stopped, that was certain. But stopped from doing what? And what was Albion Freake's part in it all? There was no school today because of the event in the Town Hall, so Effie would have to wait until then to see her friends and try to put it all together. There was something she was missing, still. But what was it?

The atmosphere around the Town Hall was tense, but full of excitement. Television camera-operators and journalists jostled for position around the pale neo-classical columns by the entrance. No one wanted to miss the story of the winner of the greatest competition there'd been for years. Free electricity for life! And with the elusive Albion Freake awarding the prize himself. The winner would probably cry, and every person in possession of a camera wanted a good close-up of the tears.

Orwell Bookend had to park quite a long way away, under the Butterwalk near the Esoteric Emporium. But he didn't care. Nothing was going to ruin his day. Not even having to wear this stupid badge that said SUPERFAN on it. Orwell Bookend told himself it would be worth it if he were to be awarded the top prize. Everyone spent at least two-thirds of their salary on electricity nowadays, but even then it was necessary to have mostly cold baths, and only ever to use one bar of your three bar heater. Unlimited free electricity was simply unimaginable. And with Orwell's upcoming promotion as well . . . He could play records! Switch the lights on! Watch television again! Life would be sweet once more.

And even if he didn't win the electricity, he was still going to be given a thousand pounds. Yes, that was to be the reward for the last ten Superfans to give up their beloved copies of *The Chosen Ones*. Orwell thought that he might even buy his daughter something nice. After all, it had been her book. Maybe a new school cape to replace the tatty one she'd got from the second-hand basket. And as well as a thousand pounds, he and his family were going to be given a free lunch at a gala before the presentations this afternoon.

Effie was lost in her own thoughts in the back of the car next to Baby Luna. She was wearing her favourite outfit, the one she had worn when she'd defeated a dragon during her first journey to Truelove House. Jeans, a T-shirt with a star on it, studded ankle boots and a fitted blazer that made her look at least two years older than she was. She also wore her favourite leather shoulder bag, which Pelham Longfellow had got for her in the Otherworld.

Effie had packed her bag carefully. She had Wolf's sword in its benign form as an old letter opener. She had her precious calling card that she was never going to let out of her sight again. She had a new medicine bundle that Lexy had made for her, and the magical damson jam her grandfather always used for restoring

317

strength. Effie was wearing her Sword of Light, of course, and her Ring of the True Hero. She had a feeling that something was going to happen today, and she wanted to be ready for it. Stay in, Festus had told her. It was this night that the fabric between worlds was going to be at its thinnest and . . .

What was Skylurian Midzhar planning? And what was Albion Freake's role in it? Were they both intending to storm the Otherworld? But how? How did Albion Freake owning a very powerful last edition of *The Chosen Ones* help Skylurian Midzhar? Effie had a feeling that soon everything was going to be revealed, and she wanted to be ready.

The Town Hall was packed with people. Orwell, Cait and baby Luna went off to attend several photo calls and Effie, who'd talked her way out of the photos, promised to meet them inside for the gala lunch. There were going to be five courses, and each Superfan's family was to share a table with their very own local 'celebrity' and an authority on some interesting matter. Mrs Beathag Hide was going to delight one table with her thoughts on Greek Tragedy, and at another, Doctor Cloudburst was going to be talking about bacteria.

Effie soon found Wolf and Lexy, and they told her about what they'd discovered from Dr Cloudburst.

'Thank you,' said Effie. 'I'm so glad I didn't take those tablets.'

'You seem much better now anyway,' said Wolf.

'Maximilian brought me something. Some water from the Underworld. And yes, I am completely better now.'

'Well, you should still be careful today,' said Wolf. He had no idea, of course, that the prophecy had changed.

'Where *is* Maximilian?' said Lexy. 'He was here a moment ago.'

Unfortunately, Maximilian had popped off into the Underworld by accident. It was becoming a bit of a problem. One minute he'd been looking at the one decent painting in the Town Hall – a strange little cubist thing from very long ago that hung in the mayor's office – and the next minute he was back at the crossroads. Still, at least it had given him a chance to get some more deepwater, just in case.

'Oh, there you are,' said Effie.

'Sorry,' said Maximilian. 'What did I miss?'

Lexy and Wolf repeated their story about going to Dr Cloudburst. Then Effie explained her suspicions about the factory in Walthamstow.

'It all makes sense,' she said. 'These golden tablets are made from the lifeforce created from the last editions; the books are mass produced in a factory and then pulped, except for one single book, which is kept. I think that Miss Dora Wright – and no doubt countless more writers – have been taken prisoner and forced to churn out books that are then enchanted to make people want to read them. The ingenious bit is the competitions. My step-mother Cait does them all the time. Along with thousands of other people, she reads one of these books – therefore giving it power – and then sends it back to Walthamstow in the hope of winning something. But in reality the books that have been read and returned are destroyed until a last edition is created. I think these tablets are somehow made from energy extracted from melted-down last editions. You don't even have to go to the trouble of reading a last edition: all the lifeforce you would have gained by doing so is here in a convenient little pill.'

'Oh my God, you're right!' said Lexy.

'Dr Cloudburst could see traces of paper in them, which makes sense given what they're made from. And the blood, sweat and tears – those are the traces of how the tablets were produced,' said Effie.

'It's evil,' said Wolf, angrily.

'What, making lifeforce from last editions?' said Lexy. 'It's certainly very clever. I mean, it's the ultimate tonic, really. That's what they've managed to create. Being a Last Reader in a pill.'

'Yes, but doing it this way? It's just wrong. Mass production, in a factory?' Wolf said. 'That's not how it's supposed to work. Isn't it supposed to be a special thing that happens by accident when you read a last edition?'

'Yes, well. The Diberi certainly do like abusing the natural magic of books for their own ends,' said Maximilian.

'But why?' said Effie. 'I mean, why now? And what has it got to do with the *Sterran Guandré*?'

'And where on earth is Raven?' said Lexy.

27

'So what would you like to do next?' asked Terrence Deer-Hart.

He had completed the first of his tasks that morning with little fuss. The yellow school bus had been handed over to him cheerfully by Coach Bruce, who had even replaced the Tusitala School logo with the word SUPERFANS on each side as arranged. Later on, Terrence was to drive the bus of Superfans to the moor for the final ceremony.

But for now he was stuck with the sad little witch Raven Wilde, and he was supposed to be showing her a good time.

'I would like to be taken to my mother,' said Raven.

'Your mother is on a book tour, little flower.'

'We both know she's not.'

'Look, I'm supposed to be making you happy. What makes you happy?'

'Seeing my mother.'

Terrence sighed. 'What about an ice cream?'

'In this freezing cold?'

'All right. Well . . . a trip to the zoo!'

'I despise seeing animals in cages.'

Terrence sighed. He very much hoped that when he joined Skylurian as the plus-one of doom – or whatever charming way she had put it – that there would be no flipping children involved. For now, he'd been told not to let this girl out of his sight. And apparently, the happier he made her, the more powerful Skylurian was going to be.

Before she was allowed through to the ballroom for the gala lunch, for which she was already very late, Effie had to go through a bag check. Unfortunately, Blessed Bartolo pupils had been brought in to do the 'security' and staff the cloakroom. They were being overseen by Mr Green. Among them were Tabitha and Barnaby.

Effie really hoped that she was going to be able to take her bag to the nondescript boy she'd never seen before on the table to the left. But he seemed to develop a sudden tummy-ache, so she ended up having to show all her most precious things to Tabitha.

'Look at this, Barnaby,' said Tabitha, in her cut-glass voice. 'Unregistered boons. Oh – and an extremely magical calling card. You wouldn't want to lose that, *Euphemia*, would you?'

'Just give me my things back,' said Effie, sighing.

'Well, I'd be very careful, if I were you,' said Tabitha, plonking all Effie's precious things roughly back in her bag. 'Next!'

Effie headed straight for the door to grand ballroom, still there from the days when the Town Hall had also functioned as the city's assembly rooms.

'Not so fast,' came a voice Effie recognised. Oh no. Mr Green.

'I'm late to meet my father,' said Effie. 'He's one of the Superfans and . . .'

'You will come with me,' said Mr Green, grasping Effie's arm firmly. 'Now. I believe you are carrying a number of unregistered boons. I shall need to do a thorough investigation. In here, please.'

He pushed Effie into the mayor's office, currently unoccupied, as the mayor was on the big stage in the ballroom getting ready to reveal the winner of the grand prize.

'Right,' said Mr Green, shutting the door behind him and turning a big brass key in the lock. 'I am going to ask you for the last time. Hand it over. I don't care about your other boons for now. Keep them. I'll report them to the Guild and they can decide what to do with them. And you. But I need your ring *now*, girl.'

'Why do you keep trying to take my ring?' Effie asked.

Mr Green sighed. 'I hear that you think you are fighting the Diberi,' he said. 'With your little chums. Which is all very sweet and honourable, but you have no idea – I repeat, *no idea* – what you are up against. I need to requisition that ring immediately.'

'Requisition?' said Effie. Her dictionary was at home as usual. She had no idea what the word meant. But her answer was the same anyway. 'No.'

'But we're on the same side, you dense child.'

323

'Well, then—'

'I don't have time to explain, but I need your ring. I am confiscating it, for your own good, and the good of the universe. Don't you understand? You must have heard the prophecy. Everyone else has.'

'What prophecy?'

'The one that says that it is someone wearing the Ring of the True Hero that will save the universe from destruction on the night of the *Sterran Guandré*,' came a familiar voice.

It was Leander. He had sort of melted out of the rather ugly painting on the mayor's wall.

'Oh for heaven's sakes, Quinn,' said Mr Green. 'I've told you sixth-formers to STOP doing that.'

'And I've told you to leave her alone.'

'I am acting on orders from the Guild of Craftspeople,' said Mr Green. 'They are requisitioning this ring.'

'I'm not giving it to you,' said Effie.

'Then, young lady, you will be responsible for the ultimate destruction of our universe. Worth a bit more than a detention, I'd say.' He started rolling up his sleeves. 'I can see I'm going to have to fight you for it. And probably kill you. But what's one child's life when held up against the fate of the universe?'

'Oh, please,' said Leander. 'For one thing, any universe that requires the sacrifice of even one child to survive is not worth saving. You know that. But for another thing, you – forgive me, Sir – *utter moron*, don't you think that given that it is Effie who wears this ring, that it might be SHE who is going to save the universe from destruction? Has it not occurred to you that by keeping her here and trying to take her ring that YOU might be the person responsible for all our deaths? Worth a bit more than a detention, I agree.'

Effie quietly brought her hand to the gold necklace at her throat and touched the miniature sword that hung there. 'Truelove,' she whispered. The sword seemed to form in her hand out of the brightest and most beautiful glimmers of light in the room.

'I repeat, you're not taking my ring,' said Effie.

Mr Green looked at her, and the large Sword of Light in her hands. He went quiet. Stepped back. Rolled down his sleeves. Sighed.

'You can put your little sword away,' he said. 'But you'll be hearing more about this, you stubborn girl. If, that is, we survive this night at all. And you,' he began saying to Leander. 'If your mother wasn't who she is . . .'

'Oh,' said Leander. 'But she is. Come on, Effie.'

Leander took Effie by the hand and led her from the room. The sword fizzled back into light now that Effie no longer needed it.

'Right,' Leander said, once they reached the grand foyer of the Town Hall. 'Where next?'

'What do you mean?'

'The prophecy. You're due to save the universe today, although up until now no one has told you that, in case it disrupts the prophecy or negates it or something. But since the stupid, ridiculous Guild decided that it was all about the ring and not the person wearing the ring . . . You were also due to die, by the way, although that seems to have changed, thank goodness. Anyway, we need to get on with it. Where should we go?'

'Um . . .' said Effie.

'Perhaps this will help,' said Leander, getting his caduceus out of his rucksack. He seemed to have folded it down somehow, like a telescope. 'Hold it with me for a second. It might be like before.'

Effie and Leander held on to the caduceus together for a few seconds. The feeling was too strong to do so for any longer than that. It felt like a firework display was going off inside Effie's head. But it worked. Effie was able to put together all the clues that she had discovered until . . .

'I think we need to start by following them.' Effie pointed out of the door. There was a strange little convoy of vehicles – the Tusitala School bus containing the Superfans, Albion Freake's stretch limousine containing himself and his entourage, and, for some reason, a horse-drawn carriage in which Skylurian Midzhar was sitting next to . . . Raven Wilde! The convoy was just setting off in the direction of the moors.

'OK, let's go,' said Leander. 'I'll get my mum's car. It's just parked around the side. She won't mind.'

'I don't believe it,' said Effie as they set off. 'Skylurian Midzhar's got my friend too. It's worse than I thought. We have to stop her.'

'Do you know what she's doing?' asked Leander.

'I think so,' said Effie. 'I think I know exactly what she's got planned. We need to pick up my friends and then drive to Northlake village. You can drop me and my friend Maximilian off there. There are two horses . . . We can ride to the moor. If we do, we'll probably get there quicker than everyone else. They'll have to park and walk quite a way, I think. That way we can be prepared. We can hide, and . . .'

Effie and Leander found Maximilian, Lexy and Wolf in the foyer, waiting. They'd seen the convoy too and were anxious to follow it, especially now they realised the danger Raven was in.

'Oh, no, not again,' said Maximilian, sighing, when Effie told him her plan with the horses. But he was able to create a map for the others to follow and then he almost seemed like a professional as he helped Effie to tack up the ponies, according to Jet's calm and patient instructions.

'I see you've become wise,' said Jet, in his deep voice, when Effie mounted him.

'What do you mean?' Effie said back.

'You've lost yourself and found yourself again,' said Jet. 'That's what wisdom is. Now, shall we *vamos*? I believe that both dear Laurel and dear Raven are in danger.'

'The book,' breathed Skylurian Midzhar, grandly, from the top of the mound with the strange new set of metal doors that seemed to lead under the moor. In one hand she was holding aloft the limited-edition single-volume copy of *The Chosen Ones*. In the other she was holding – and occasionally swigging from – what looked like a champagne bottle full of bright gold liquid.

'The book, ladies and gentlemen, is a powerful thing indeed.

When we read a great book, we cannot help but give up part of our own soul to it. A book like *The Chosen Ones*, loved by generations of readers, bought by over ten million people, contains within its pages great power. So . . .' She paused here for effect.

To her left raged the great bonfire that she'd created, on which the Superfans had just tossed their copies of *The Chosen Ones*. Orwell Bookend was feeling rather bored, but several of the other Superfans were wailing in anguish and burning themselves as they tried to get some ashes from the fire to keep as a memento.

'So . . .' said Skylurian again. She drew out her ivory wonde and pointed it at Albion Freake. It wasn't a witch's wonde, despite usually looking like one. It was actually a trickster's stick, which Skylurian used mainly for smiting.

'So, quite why you think that I would produce a limited-edition single-volume version of such a powerful book to hand over to this vile, uncultured LOSER, to use one of his own favourite words . . .' Skylurian laughed. 'Of course, it could be argued that a book has even MORE power when its production has been bankrolled by one of the richest men in the world. To invest a billion pounds in the creation of the world's first magical super-weapon is just to give that super-weapon – which feeds on emotion, desire and passion – even more power. But to hand that power over to an idiot who does not even read? To give such magical riches to one who has not even epiphanised? Ha!'

'What on earth is she going on about?' Orwell Bookend asked the person nearest him, a maths teacher from the Mrs Joyful

School who was blubbing into a hanky over the loss of her favourite book. She didn't answer.

Overhead, the *Sterran Guandré* was developing into a great swirl of light and raw hue as ancient rocks flung themselves through the sky and exploded. There was every shade of every colour you can think of, plus some you undoubtedly can't. Some of the rarest colours had not been seen since the dawn of time, and there were others that didn't usually exist in that dimension. It was so impressive that the Northern Lights, still in exile from the Otherworld, shuffled over from the North Pole to have a better look. It clashed wildly with the *Sterran Guandré*, but it didn't care. The sky was soon a vast, wild, extravagant muddle of sights and sounds that no one had ever seen before.

So it said something for Skylurian's performance that all eyes were still on her. She took another swig from her bottle of golden liquid.

'So, Albion, darling, you poor, uncultured wretch, your billion pounds has gone to the local cats' home. Why? I don't need it. And anyway, once I've finished with this universe, there'll be no need for cats' homes anyway. Think of it as my little joke.'

No one laughed.

'So now I'm going to tell you all what I have got planned. Of course, I disapprove of those silly speeches made by villains that only give the so-called good guys the chance to ready their weapons and attack and so on. But I am quite confident that I can see all my enemies. I fear them not. And anyway, my plan gains more power the more it is spoken. So . . .'

'I wish she'd get on with it,' said Orwell, yawning. 'I haven't even started today's crossword yet.'

'I have created here a sealed vault,' said Skylurian, pointing at the metal doors in the mound. 'Here on the moors there are plenty of rips in the fabric between this world and the Otherworld. The material is always thin here, and never more so than on this night. Soon I intend to travel not just to the other side, but far, far beyond its nearest shores to a village called Dragon's Green, from where I intend to take control of the entire universe. To fuel my attack, I will require a few things. I already have this last edition of the most popular book to have been published in the last two centuries. When I close the doors of that vault – they can never be opened again, by the way, once they are closed, because the combination is a prime number that has not yet been discovered – I will be inside, with this book, whose power I shall consume, and this pure child, whose blood I shall drink, and . . .'

Hang on. Drinking the blood of a pure child? This was getting more interesting all of a sudden. Orwell Bookend had never been very gripped by long speeches on the power of books, but the sacrifice of a pure child? Now that was a lot more compelling.

Skylurian gave a sort of nod, and Terrence Deer-Hart brought Raven to her from where she had been hidden behind a drystone wall. Poor Raven looked as if she was trying to be brave, but everyone could see she was trembling. Her hands were tied together with rope, and her wrists were red from where she'd been trying to escape.

Wolf and Lexy were hiding in an old croft just behind the bonfire. Laurel Wilde, who Effie and Maximilian had already rescued, crouched with them behind a tree. All were waiting for their orders from Effie and Wolf. But the sight of her daughter bound and ready for sacrifice was more than Laurel Wilde could bear. She rushed towards Skylurian Midzhar, not sure what she was going to do.

'Don't take my daughter,' she said. 'Take me instead!'

'Ha!' said Skylurian. 'Well, well. Good. I wanted the author involved. Authors can always be relied on to turn up late to their own launch party and then say embarrassing things, but they are a strangely valuable asset when it comes to promoting a publication. Their death, I find, is what adds most value to a book. I'm surprised publishers don't use the technique more often.'

Skylurian raised her ivory wonde to smite Laurel Wilde. Terrence Deer-Hart looked on with some pleasure. If only Skylurian would smite every other author she published, then he would be the only one left, which would be—

'I disown the book,' said Laurel Wilde quickly. 'Ha! You didn't expect that, did you, you vile woman. You might think I don't understand magic, that I just make up silly stories about it. But I understand this much. If I disown that book, and tell you that I think it is pathetic, juvenile, badly plotted and horribly badly written, then it will halve, maybe even quarter, its power, and—'

'If that were true, do you think I'd have let you carry on talking?' said Skylurian. 'No, we at the Matchstick Press have always been subscribers to the theory of Death of the Author. Goodbye, Laurel, darling, you truly have been a great asset.' She raised her wonde further.

'And I thought we were friends,' said Laurel. She closed her eyes and waited to be smote.

28

The next few things happened very quickly. First of all, Albion Freake, who seemed to have taken a while to understand the situation he was in, and the information he was being given, ordered one of his men to grab Raven. This the man did, while Skylurian's attention was taken up with Laurel Wilde. So, in that sense, Laurel's bid to save her daughter had worked. When Skylurian turned to see who had grabbed Raven, Effie threw Wolf his sword in its benign form as a letter opener. Once it had grown to full size – which took less than a second once he had touched it – he leapt in front of Laurel and raised the Sword of Orphennyus to strike Skylurian.

'Oh, you silly – *ouch* – boy,' she said, as he brought the blade down through her body. 'I'm not going to pretend that that doesn't hurt. But you don't have the strength to overcome me. That blade only works on M-currency, and, frankly, you'd have to strike me billions of times to take away my immense power. The universe would – *ouch* – probably end first. So keep tickling me with your little blade if you like. Or perhaps I'll just do this instead . . .'

Skylurian raised her ivory wonde and smote Wolf. He fell to the ground, dazed. Lexy ran over immediately with a tonic. Meanwhile, Effie and Maximilian tried to save Raven. Effie couldn't use her Sword of Light on any of Albion Freake's men, none of whom were magical. But Maximilian was able to get in the mind of the man who had grabbed Raven and persuade him to let her go. Inside this man's mind he met a mage spy called Frankincense who was able to help him. 'We'll meet again,' she said, mysteriously.

While all of this was going on, the *Sterran Guandré* raged overhead. The two worlds were getting closer and closer. Many great things have been written about the *Sterran Guandré*, the one special night every six years when the un-ephinanised can drift into the Otherworld (sometimes never to return), and Otherworld monsters can find refuge in our world without hindrance from any officials and their silly paperwork. At this moment many such exchanges were taking place. Just at the moment when a psycho-geographer intent on discovering 'the wild' slipped from a mountain trail into the other realm, three vampires, a ghost ship and a moorhen possessed with the spirit of a poet all slipped into ours.

But there was also the Underworld to take into account. In the Otherworld, people live alongside their demons, facing them, fighting them and, in some cases, living peacefully with them. But in the Realworld our demons are pushed out of sight, deep down into the Underworld, where they live in their own dark and horrible zone. Sometimes these demons find their way into the Realworld, but never more powerfully than on the night of a *Sterran Guandré*.

And Albion Freake had a lot of demons.

The earth underneath him now started to move as all the battles raged around him. He knew he needed to kill this ridiculous woman who had stolen his money. He wanted his goddamn book! Why was his girlfriend looking at him like that? He'd have to do something about her. And he wanted to get away from this large, cold, damp, wild place full of strange hoots, wails, calls and all that goddamn hokery going on in the sky.

The earth moved under him again.

Most people have at least a couple of demons lodged in the Underworld. Something they are ashamed of. Someone they have hurt. But Albion Freake had personally ordered the deaths of at least a hundred people. He'd invested in weapons that had killed thousands more. When the ground opened up and his demons came pouring out, fangs bared, he didn't even try to run. Everyone looked away as they fell on him and tore his body apart. Everyone, that is, except the maths teacher from the Mrs Joyful School, who realised she rather liked watching evil people being eaten alive. The blood that spattered her sensible cheap skirt more than made up for the book she'd lost. She'd be able to tell her grandchildren about this.

Terrence Deer-Hart also rather enjoyed seeing the beginnings of Albion Freake's demise, although he was too squeamish to watch for very long. But he was happy that his main rivals – in love and in writing – were finally getting their comeuppance. He wasn't completely sure where he stood in relation to this vault idea, however. He assumed that Skylurian would simply come and get him when it was time for him to become the queen's consort of doom, or however it was she'd put it. But something was troubling him. And then when he tried to get Raven back from Albion Freake's men, one of them pulled a flipping gun on him! So he ran away and hid.

Meanwhile, the Cosmic Web chose this moment to launch its own attack. News that Raven Wilde, great friend to all living creatures, had been taken prisoner, had quickly spread from moor to town and back again. Slowly they came at first, headed by the brave and loyal robin from Raven's garden. Here came her three beloved tarantulas, carried safely on the back of a small barn owl. Here came the voles and shrews and mice and blackbirds and skylarks and hedgehogs. Here came rabbits and foxes and wildcats. Soon there was a great cloud of animals all attacking Albion Freake's men. The rabbits nibbled, the tarantulas bit, the owls used their talons. Soon the men were driven back to their limousine, never to return.

One of the rabbits gnawed easily through the ropes around Raven's wrists. The creatures couldn't get anywhere near Skylurian Midzhar, of course, but they had helped to release their witch friend, and that was the main thing. Later, when Skylurian's body decayed, as all bodies must, they would enjoy getting stuck into her remains.

For several minutes all was chaos. But when the chaos had started to calm down, one thing became horribly clear.

Skylurian had taken a hostage. Her wonde had shape-shifted into a sharp dagger, and this she now held to his throat.

'Help me,' he said weakly. 'Someone help me, please.'

Effie looked up. It was her father.

Skylurian had got Orwell.

Why would she have chosen Orwell Bookend of all people? By now, many members of the Guild had turned up on the moors, along with the mayor, the headmaster of the Tusitala School for the Gifted, Troubled and Strange, Mr Green, Mrs Beathag Hide, both Professors Quinn and various other local dignitaries and celebrities. Even Tabitha and Barnaby had appeared from somewhere in the darkness. Leander could not be seen by anyone, but he was there too, observing.

'Tabitha Quinn,' said Skylurian Midzhar. 'At last. Do fetch me the calling card, there's a good girl.'

'Of course,' said Tabitha, with a little smirk.

Tabitha went to Effie. 'Hand it over,' she said, holding out her thin, pale palm.

'Hand what over?' said Effie.

'Your calling card,' said Tabitha. 'The one that takes you to Dragon's Green. I saw it in your bag before. You'd better give it to me.'

'No,' said Effie.

'She won't give it to me,' said Tabitha.

'Well then, I'll have to kill her father,' said Skylurian. 'I think I'll do it slowly. Or maybe I'll take him into the vault with me, now that someone seems to have rescued my original human sacrifice.'

Skylurian Midzhar nicked Orwell Bookend's neck lightly with her sharp blade. A thin trickle of blood started making its way down towards his shirt collar. It was his best shirt, which he'd put on today because he thought he was going to win a big prize.

Effie looked at Skylurian. 'Let my father go,' she said. 'And then I'll give you my calling card.'

'Don't give it to her, Effie,' said Lexy. 'She's bluffing.'

'If I let your father go, do you swear you'll give me the card?' said Skylurian.

'Yes,' said Effie.

'And you know your word cannot be broken, since you are a true hero?'

'Yes. Now, let him go.'

Skylurian slowly removed the dagger from Orwell Bookend's throat. He staggered away, wiping sweat from his brow, and blood from his collar.

Effie took the card out of her bag and handed it to Tabitha.

'I told you I'd get you back,' hissed Tabitha.

'Yes, well, this wasn't the way to do it,' said Effie.

Skylurian took the card from Tabitha. Everything went quiet and still. She then pressed a button on a little remote control she was wearing around her neck. The metal doors opened and a platform emerged. Skylurian stepped onto the platform holding the last edition of *The Chosen Ones* in one hand and Effie's precious calling card in the other. The platform descended, and Skylurian Midzhar slowly disappeared into the earth.

The metal doors closed with a final clunk behind her. She would now be locked inside the vault for all eternity – except, of course, she was going to use the calling card and the power created by being the Last Reader of *The Chosen Ones* to launch herself on Dragon's Green, Truelove House and, presumably, the Great Library. From there she could go where she wanted, do what she wanted. That was the plan. And there'd be plenty of time for the last edition of *The Chosen Ones* to rot before anyone else could find it.

Effie still didn't understand exactly what the Diberi wanted with the Great Library, and how it would enable them to control the universe. But she'd felt the power it held when she'd been inside it.

'Oh my God,' said Lexy.

'You stupid, stupid girl,' said Mr Green, striding over to Effie, pointing his bony finger at her. 'Do you have *any* idea what you've done?'

Wolf glared at Mr Green. 'Leave her alone,' he said.

'I'm sorry,' said Maximilian to Effie. 'I tried to get in her head but she blocked me. She was too powerful. I tried to help save your dad without you having to give up the card.'

Wolf shook his head. 'We've failed you,' he said to Effie. 'I'm sorry. I should have tried a different strategy. I should have—'

'You haven't failed me,' said Effie, her voice shaking slightly. She looked at Mr Green. 'You want to know what I've done? Well, it wasn't just me, it was me and my friends. We've just saved the universe. Not that we expect any thanks, of course.'

'Don't be absurd,' said Mr Green.

'But how . . .?' said the mayor, coming over.

'Ignore these stupid children,' said Mr Green. 'We can punish them later. If there is a later, of course. This could be the end of everything. Skylurian Midzhar has locked herself in there with the last copy of *The Chosen Ones* in the world and—'

'They miscounted the books,' said Effie. 'That's not the last edition that Skylurian has taken into the vault with her. Oh, it looks very impressive and everything. But it won't work because it's not the last copy of the book in the universe. There's one more.'

'Oh!' said Raven. 'Of course. They would have counted one of the books twice – the one I gave you at home was the one your father handed in. That wasn't really one of the last ten books at all because it had already been counted.'

'What?' said Mr Green. 'Are you saying she's locked herself in there with a copy of the book that *isn't* a last edition?'

'That's right,' said Effie. 'It has no power at all.'

'But . . .' said Mr Green. 'But . . .'

Mrs Beathag Hide came over. She'd clearly heard everything. 'Are you not going to apologise to the girl?' she asked Mr Green. But he simply turned and walked away.

'So where is the last copy of *The Chosen Ones?*' asked Maximilian, once most of the adults had left. He was going to ride Echo back, and Laurel Wilde was going to ride Jet. Raven would go on her broomstick. Mrs Beathag Hide was taking Lexy and the Superfans home in the school bus. Cait was coming to pick up Orwell and Effie. Leander had driven his mother's car home, with his sister Tabitha sulking in the back. She knew she was due to be grounded for a very long time. No one could hear Terrence Deer-Hart sobbing for his lost love, unable to come out from his hiding place. No one was coming to pick him up. But he would get his revenge. He wasn't sure how, just yet. But this girl and her friends would suffer for what they'd done.

'It's in the Great Library in Truelove House,' said Effie. 'It's been there since the last *Sterran Guandré*. And I don't think I'm the one who saved the universe at all. I think it was my mother.'

'But your boon,' said Raven. 'Your calling card. It's lost forever.'

Effie shrugged. 'The universe is saved. That's the main thing.'

'I suppose I won't even get my thousand pounds now,' said Orwell Bookend, in the car home.

'No,' said Effie. 'Probably not.'

'Thank you,' said Orwell, after a long pause.

'Sorry?' said Effie. She wasn't sure her father had ever thanked her for anything.

'Thank you for saving my life,' he said, awkwardly. 'I know you had to give up something very important in order to do so. I won't forget.'

'That's all right, Dad,' said Effie. 'Thanks for saying.'

'Can it be replaced?' he asked, after another pause.

'Can what be replaced?'

'The little card thingy?'

Effie sighed and shook her head. 'No,' she said. 'No, it can't.'

Saturday was a strange, sullen, moody day, as if, after the excitement of the *Sterran Guandré*, the entire cosmos had a massive hangover. Effie tried to catch up with her homework and think herself back into being a normal girl who didn't visit the Otherworld. Of course, she wasn't normal at all. She'd epiphanised and was a true hero interpreter with a large amount of lifeforce and all the documentation she needed to travel to the Otherworld. So she could go whenever she liked.

Well, she could in theory, at least until the Guild came along and took her papers away and banned her from practising magic. But it didn't matter anyway, because she would never see her cousins again. She had saved them, and the Great Library, but in so doing she'd had to sacrifice ever going to Dragon's Green again. It had been worth it, but it had left Effie feeling sad and empty. Nothing as bad as the Yearning, of course. But it was still awful. Effie had all this lifeforce now, but nothing to do with it. She didn't even want to go to the Edgelands Market.

It was almost three o'clock when the doorbell went.

Then there was a knock at Effie's bedroom door.

'Someone to see you,' said Orwell Bookend.

Effie wondered which of her friends it was. She wasn't really in the mood for any visitors. She wondered how quickly she could send them away. But then a tall man strode into her room. Pelham Longfellow! But . . .

'We've been expecting you in the Otherworld,' he said. 'Everyone knows what you did.'

'I didn't do anything,' said Effie. 'Skylurian made a mistake. I didn't even have to be there.'

'That's not true,' said Pelham. 'You saved your friend. You saved your friend's mother. You saved the ten Superfans that Skylurian had planned to smite just before her descent.'

'I suppose so.'

'And you knew about the book. When did you work it all out?'

'A while ago. I guess when I realised what she was planning. I knew it wouldn't work because of the book I took at Raven's house. I could see all the sheets of paper with the figures all done in columns. It wasn't until later that I realised that the last copy of *The Chosen Ones* was in the Great Library, safe, where my mother had put it.'

'And so you saved your father, and let Skylurian lock herself in a vault to starve to death.'

'I feel a bit sorry for her,' said Effie.

'Yes, well. She brought it on herself. How did you know that it was her plan, and not Albion Freake's?'

'My friend found out that Albion Freake can't read. Pretty hard to be a Last Reader if you can't read a book. We worked out the rest of it from there.'

'Brilliant,' said Pelham. 'Well done.'

'Can she really not escape from the vault?' asked Effie.

Pelham shrugged. 'She'd have needed to make it completely secure so that the book could never be discovered and read again – at least not before it had decayed. She had to make completely sure she was its Last Reader, so I'd say she's stuck in there. She's not a mage, and so can't go to the Underworld. I don't think she has any direct way to the Otherworld. She's a galloglass anyway, so would have been expelled a long time ago.'

'Oh.'

'You did well out there last night, Effie. Another outcome had Laurel and Raven dead – and perhaps even you, too – with Skylurian on the loose ready to plan another nefarious scheme. That factory of hers . . .'

'I found out what it does, by the way,' said Effie. As quickly as she could she told Pelham what she'd found out about Miss Dora Wright and the tablets. 'But I think in the end it was all a scheme to fuel her attack on the Otherworld.'

'And that can't happen now, thanks to you.'

'How do you know so much about what happened last night?'

'Oh. People talk. I get around. It turns out there was no Diberi plot to get to the Otherworld this *Sterran Guandré* at all, apart from this one of Skylurian's. I think the European Diberi are planning something big, but I don't know what it is. So anyway, you were really the most useful of all of us last night. And we want to thank you. We're planning a big party for you in the Otherworld. But everyone wants to know when you're going to arrive.'

Effie sighed. 'Never,' she said sadly. 'But give everyone my love.'

'What do you mean, never?' said Pelham.

'I lost the card,' said Effie, tears coming to her eyes. 'I had to sacrifice it so that Skylurian would release my father and then lock herself in the vault. It's down there with her.'

'You do know she can't use it?'

Effie nodded. 'I suspected that. But it doesn't matter. I'll still never get it back.'

344

'I still don't see what the problem is,' said Pelham. 'You don't need the card to get to the Otherworld. Did you think you did? Oh, child, how quaint. You get the card merely as a symbol of your having the boon, but the real boon is inside you. Come on, do you think we care so little for you that we'd let our connection rest on a small piece of cardboard?' He shook his head. 'Look, it's three o'clock in the afternoon here. How about you come with me to Truelove House for a week of celebrations? You can be back here in time for supper.'

'But . . .?'

'Just follow me,' said Pelham. 'Where do you normally go through?'

'There's a hedge, five minutes' walk from here.'

'Good. Well, let's go.'

· 29

'So I never needed the card at all?' said Effie to Pelham as they walked down the street.

'You probably did the first couple of times. But the energy transfers to you. It's hard to explain.'

'So I can go to Truelove House whenever I want, from anywhere?' said Effie.

'It takes practice,' said Pelham. 'For now I'd stick to travelling through the impression you've already made between the dimensions. And we'll give you a new card when we get back. Just to be on the safe side. Travelling using a card is like riding a horse with a saddle. What we're about to do is more like riding bareback. But it should work. Now you say there was a hedge . . .?'

Effie and Pelham walked through the cold afternoon until they reached the old village green by the Black Pig pub.

'Right,' said Pelham. 'I want you to concentrate and do exactly what you would have done if you'd had the card.'

'I would have looked at it, and . . .'

'Well, look at the space where it would have been,' said Pelham. 'And go into a meditative state.'

'All right,' said Effie.

'Ready?'

'Yes.'

It was bright and warm in the Otherworld as usual. Effie walked through the gates of Truelove House and across the gardens with Pelham Longfellow by her side. Bees buzzed, birds sung, butterflies flapped about. Effie could smell flowers all around her.

'See,' Pelham said to Effie.

'Thank you,' she said back, grinning. 'I can't tell you how pleased I am to be back. I thought I'd never come here again.'

'Your sacrifice truly was a great one if you thought that,' said Pelham. 'Anyway, come on – I think everyone's waiting for us.'

Effie followed Pelham Longfellow in through the doors to the large glass conservatory. Inside the air was sweet and damp. Clothilde was there watering the plants, clearly waiting for them to arrive. When she saw Effie she immediately put down her watering can and smiled and clapped her hands.

Then, while Pelham went to get something from upstairs, Clothilde took Effie's hand and led her through the house to the large drawing room. The vast but delicate white curtains were billowing in the breeze coming from the open French doors. Effie could see on the table a pile of gifts, all wrapped in silver and gold paper and tied with turquoise ribbons. Was it someone's birthday?

'Cosmo wants to see you now,' said Clothilde. 'And then we're going to have a picnic tea on the lawn. Tomorrow Pelham's going to take you to Froghole to get your Keeper's mark, and your consultation, and any books and supplies you think you'll need while you're here. Then we'll have a big party.' She grinned, and pushed a lock of hair out of her eyes. 'Oh!' she said. 'We're going to have such fun together. And one day Rollo's going to cover for me in the library so I can take you clothes shopping. You can't imagine how perfect it's going to be!' She bit her lip. 'I'm so sorry you almost died because of us. And you had the Yearning.' Clothilde touched Effie's arm. 'I can't imagine what that must have been like. Anyway, we're here.'

While she had been talking, Clothilde had been leading Effie through the French doors and out across the lawn, where a picnic rug was ready for afternoon tea. Then they had walked down a thin pathway until they came to a summer house.

'He's in there,' said Clothilde. 'I'd better leave you to it and go and see how Bertie's getting on with the tea.'

Effie knocked on the door. When she heard Cosmo's gentle voice say 'Come in', she almost felt like crying, although she wasn't sure why. Not in a sad way, just with a kind of relief.

'Oh, child,' he said when he saw her. 'I'm so glad to see you in good health again. Last time you were here . . . Well.' He shook his head sadly. 'Sit. Tell me everything. But not if you're too tired. We can have tea first, if you like.'

But Effie wanted to tell him everything, so she did.

'You made a great sacrifice for us,' said Cosmo. 'Why?'

'Because you're my family,' said Effie. 'And because . . .'

'Go on.'

'Well, this is the nicest, most beautiful place I have ever seen. I just think it needs protecting. No one should be allowed to destroy it, or use it for evil. If I had to never come here again in order to protect it, then I would make that choice. I mean, I thought I *had* made that choice.'

'You can always come here, child,' said Cosmo. 'Whatever happens.'

'Unless I lose all my lifeforce again,' said Effie.

'Yes,' Cosmo nodded. He sighed. 'Yes, well, there is that. But now you are friends with a mage who will travel to the Underworld and bring back deepwater for you. That is something none of us has ever had before. It's a true blessing.'

'Yes,' said Effie. 'He's a very special friend.'

'And I'm sure you won't go into the library again until you've been taught how to do so safely.'

'No. I won't. I promise.'

'It wasn't your fault,' said Cosmo. 'The book led you in.'

'Cosmo,' said Effie. 'What is the Great Library? I know it's very important, but I still don't know what it does. And why does everyone see it differently?'

'Excellent question. You do know how to get to the heart of things, don't you? We experience the Great Library differently because it exists in another, higher dimension. We can't see in anything more than three dimensions, so anything more complicated than that has to be sort of folded down to fit our consciousness and made into shapes we can comprehend. Out of a many-dimensional library, your brain has to make something in three dimensions that it can understand.' Cosmo stroked his beard. 'Hmm. It is extremely hard to explain.'

'I think I understand, sort of,' said Effie. 'And what is the importance of the books? I mean, what does the library do?'

'What do you think it does?'

Effie shook her head. 'I don't know. Something to do with reality . . . But I don't know what.'

'Excellent,' said Cosmo. 'But what makes you say that?'

'Just a feeling,' said Effie. 'And I suppose if it's where everyone wants to invade . . .'

'Your instincts are good, child. So I shall tell you as simply as I can – although this is very, very difficult for ordinary people to understand. The Great Library holds the blueprint for the whole universe. People from your world sometimes refer to it as a "source code", although it is in no way digital. It is much more fundamental and ancient than that. Every book in the library controls some aspect of reality. Section 04F concerns the Big Bang, for example. Section 03B is music theory. The numbers 20–29G deal with quantum physics. And 18 and 19G are relativity. We have dictionaries for every language ever spoken. It's very important that the books are not disturbed. We look after them, read them, maintain them . . . It takes all our time. But looking after the Great Library is one of the most important jobs in the whole universe.'

'Why do you read the books?' asked Effie.

'Books need to be read. These ones especially. And they must never, ever be the subject of a Last Reading, at least not during the normal lifetime of the universe. They would confer too much power on the reader. One of the tasks of the Trueloves is to keep reading the books, century after century. We also shelve new books and—'

'Where do the new books come from?'

'Your world or our world. If something important is discovered – like Einstein's relativity, for example – and if enough people believe it's true, then the book goes in the library and becomes part of the source code of existence. Getting the book in is a very complex process, as it should be. But we are still making the universe, and the books reflect that. In our world, wizards like me are bound to go on a wizard quest every 10,000 moons or so. Roughly every thirty years. If we find new knowledge as a result of the wizard quest, then we can make an application for the knowledge to be bound and stored in the Great Library. But it happens very rarely.'

'Can a book end up in the library by accident?'

'Oh no, child. No.' Cosmo frowned, and shook his head.

'But *The Chosen Ones* is there. My mother put it there. Was it deliberate?'

There was a long pause, almost as if Cosmo hadn't properly heard Effie say that the book was there, or didn't want to hear it.

'Now that is a difficult question to answer,' said Cosmo, frowning. 'You must be tired, and we've talked enough for now.' He stood up. 'I think it's time for tea. And before that – presents!'

'Is it someone's birthday?'

Cosmo chuckled. 'In a manner of speaking, perhaps. We hear you are an interpreter as well as a true hero. That's a very valuable art indeed. So we've all been shopping and found you a few gifts. Come.'

Effie followed Cosmo back into the house. There, waiting by the table, were Clothilde, Pelham, Rollo and Bertie. They were all smiling at her. The pile of gifts looked huge – even larger than before.

'Well,' said Clothilde, 'are you going to open them?'

'They can't really all be for me,' said Effie.

'They are,' said Pelham. 'Come on. Get on with it. I want my tea and cakes. Bertie's made cream puffs.' He smiled and handed Effie the first package. 'This one's from me,' he said.

Effie took the small yellow box and carefully undid the pink ribbon. Inside was a beautiful silver watch with two rose quartz faces.

'Now you'll be able to tell the time in the Realworld and the Otherworld simultaneously,' said Pelham. 'I've got one too. It's invaluable.'

'Thank you,' said Effie, putting it on.

The next present was a brass key on a piece of light red ribbon.

'It's for the Great Library,' said Cosmo. 'Although we'll train you properly before you go in next time.'

Effie opened another parcel to find a large box of Otherworld Fourflower chocolates, which were her favourite thing to eat in the world. Another box contained a beautiful new silk jumpsuit from Clothilde, all wrapped up in turquoise tissue paper. It was a dark mauve colour, with gold stars on it. Then came fabric-bound notebooks, a pen and pencil set and a collection of inks in the most beautiful Otherworld colours: ivory gold, rose silver and the deepest turquoise.

'And I thought you'd make good use of this,' said Clothilde, passing Effie a book-shaped package.

Inside was a very old-looking book bound in thick cream cloth and edged with silver. It had a pure silk cloud-coloured ribbon with which you could mark what page you were on.

'It's a universal dictionary,' said Clothilde. 'You can use it to look up any word in any language. I think you'll like it.'

'Thank you,' said Effie. She hugged Clothilde and gave her a little kiss on each cheek. 'It's wonderful.'

Soon there was only one package left. It was a long thin shape with bulges near one end.

'Impossible to wrap,' said Rollo. 'But I did my best.'

Inside was a beautiful polished rosewood caduceus. The main shaft had two wise-looking snakes wrapped around it, and two carved wings at the top. It was beautiful, but also very big. Effie was just wondering how she would take it anywhere with her when Rollo took it from her and somehow shrunk it down to the size of a hairpin, which he held in the palm of his hand.

'I thought this would look nice in your hair,' he said. 'Although you could always just put it in your pocket, or wear it around your neck with your Sword of Light. It's up to you. You can also carry it around full size if you want to, if you were on a long journey or something and wanted to use it as a staff. But – and this is the really exciting bit – it also works when it's small. The craftsman who made it was very proud of it. He said it had been in his shop for years, but I knew when I saw it that it was the right one for you.'

'Thank you,' said Effie. She had always been a little frightened of Rollo, but now, as he drew her into a slightly stiff hug, she realised that he did mean well, even if he didn't always express it in the warmest way. He wanted what she wanted: what was good for Truelove House. And now she knew what they were looking after here – the source code for the entire universe – she also understood why he took it so seriously.

Effie took the small wooden hairpin in her hand. She was about to ask how to make it full-size again, but then she realised that she already knew. She thought about the technique that she used to travel through the calling card – when she'd had it – which had worked even without the card. The feeling she had when she concentrated on her Sword of Light. The feeling she'd experienced when she was trying to meditate her way out of the Yearning. She now looked at the small wooden caduceus and dropped her mind down into the deepest, calmest frequency she could reach. She willed the caduceus to grow again, and it did.

'I see you're learning magic, child,' said Cosmo.

'Yes, I suppose I am,' said Effie.

She shrunk the caduceus again and put it in her hair. She couldn't wait to begin using it to help her with her translations, and with working out what the Diberi might get up to next. One thing was for sure: she was always going to protect Truelove House, as long as there was blood in her veins. It was what it meant to be a Truelove.

'Well,' said Clothilde. 'Shall we all go and have tea?'

354

Effie followed Clothilde, Cosmo, Rollo and Pelham out into the warm afternoon, knowing that she was about to have the best week of her life. What would follow that, she didn't know. Probably more heartache, pain and difficulty as she continued with the fight against the Diberi. But she had her friends, and she had her family, and the sun was shining down on her from a perfect blue sky. For now, that was enough.

Acknowledgements

Thank you, as always, to my partner Rod Edmond, who read every draft of this book with love and care, and who has been the most wonderful companion on this adventure so far.

Thanks also to my family: Mum, Couze, Sam, Hari, Nia, Ivy and Gordian, for all the love, support and happiness you have given me. And many thanks as well to my extended *whānau*: Daisy, Ed, Molly, Eliza, Max, Jo, Claire, Murray, Joanna, Marion, Lyndy and Teuila.

Francis Bickmore deserves a special thank you, as always, not just for being my long-standing editor but for being such a lovely friend.

Thank you as well to all my other friends, students and colleagues, in particular Teri Johns, whose help and wisdom has changed my life for the better, David Flusfeder, Sue Swift, Alex Preston, Jennie Batchelor, Amy Sackville, Vybarr Cregan-Reid, Alice Bates, Steve Bates, Pat Lucas, Emma Lee, Charlotte Webb, David Herd, Caroline Greville and family, Martha Schulman,

Katie Szyszko, Amy Lilwall, Tom Ogier, Roger Baker, Suzi Feay, Stuart Kelly and Gonzalo Garcia.

I am very lucky to have a number of wonderful young first-readers. Thank you in particular to Molly Harman, Al Preston, Ray Preston, Leah Motton, Maddie Richardson, Isaac Richardson, Teuila Smith-Anderson and Matt McInally for your enthusiastic reading, and your insightful and encouraging comments on my writing.

I am also extremely grateful to all the lovely people I get to work with on these books. Thanks so much to everyone at Canongate, particularly Jenny Fry, Jamie Byng, Anna Frame, Alice Shortland, Neal Price, Megan Reid, Andrea Joyce, Jessica Neale, Caroline Clarke, Allegra Le Fanu, Becca Nice, Lorraine McCann, Alan Trotter and Sylvie the dog. Big thanks also to Debs Warner for doing a great job with the copy-edit.

My work has been very enthusiastically supported by so many wonderful booksellers, librarians and teachers. Thank you to all of them, and in particular to Simon Key at the Big Green Bookshop and Gudrun Bowers at the Steyning Bookshop.

Thank you to my brilliant agent, Georgia Garrett, for all her good advice. And lastly, a massive thank you to Dan Mumford for the amazing artwork for these books. My world is richer because of it.